FREMONT PUBLIC LIBRARY

3 3090 00569 6069

LESSON PLAN
FOR
MURDER

A MASTER CLASS MYSTERY

LORI ROBBINS

FREMONT PUBLIC LIBRARY DISTRICT
1170 N. Midlothian Road
Mundelein, IL 60060

WITHDRAWN

BARKING RAIN PRESS

This is a work of fiction. Names, characters, places, and events described herein are products of the author's imagination or are used fictitiously. Any resemblance to actual events, locations, organizations, or persons, living or dead, is entirely coincidental.

Lesson Plan for Murder: *Master Class Mysteries,* Book 1

Copyright © 2017 Lori Robbins (www.LoriRobbins.com)

All rights reserved. No part of this book may be used or reproduced in any manner whatsoever without written permission, except in the case of brief quotations embodied in critical articles and reviews.

Edited by: Cindy Koepp (www.ckoepp.com)

Proofread by: Rachel Roddy (www.facebook.com/rcwriter)

Cover artwork by Stephanie Flint (www.sbibb.wordpress.com)

Barking Rain Press
PO Box 822674
Vancouver, WA 98682 USA
www.BarkingRainPress.org

ISBN Trade Paperback: 1-941295-54-1
ISBN Hardcover: 1-941295-79-7
ISBN eBook: 1-941295-55-X
Library of Congress Control Number: 2017936181

First Edition: November 2017

Printed in the United States of America

DEDICATION

To Glenn

CHAPTER 1
THINGS FALL APART

If you wish to inflict the kind of pain that festers forever, consult an English teacher. They're easier to find than psychopaths, and they understand how to make people suffer. I speak from experience. Ten years of teaching English has taught me that emotional torture delivers slings and arrows that linger long after the initial attack.

I don't mean to imply that the skills required of psychopaths and English teachers intersect to any great degree, but success in either profession requires similar strength, as well as a similar ability to compartmentalize. Dr. Marcia Deaver was a case in point. Of course, all she did was call me a thief and a liar. A pinprick, really—hardly a case of outrageous fortune.

My feral colleague began her assault in the lobby of Valerian Hills High School. I was shocked to see her, but not because she was angry—there was nothing unusual about that. No, the surprise was that my fellow English teacher had executed a real life variation on the essay topic: *What I Did on My Summer Vacation After My Husband Left Me.* The overweight, elastic-pants-wearing Marcia had lost at least thirty pounds. My guess is that she invested all of the money she'd saved at the grocery store on a new wardrobe, a personal trainer, and an excellent facelift. Perhaps Botox.

Her expression was at odds with her appearance. While her smooth forehead seemed to advertise the latest in luxury bedding or Prozac, the look in her eye screamed Lady Macbeth on amphetamines.

I tried to compliment her, but Marcia cut me off, possibly to demonstrate that her physical makeover had not changed her personality. "Liz! Liz Hopewell! Stop blathering this minute!"

The two-word response nature intended died a silent death inside my head. Although I grew up in the Brooklyn projects, I never let those experiences influence the way I act now. I try not to, anyway. But there is a limit to politeness. I executed an about-face, and Marcia had to address the rest of her tirade to my back.

"Someone stole my desk chair! My $700 chair is gone. Disappeared. Have you seen it? Someone has to know."

"Not guilty, Marcia." Impressed by her passion, I stopped and held both hands wide to demonstrate my innocence. Unconvinced, Marcia continued to tail me. Her vehemence inspired me to take the stairs at a much quicker pace than usual. Thanks to her new level of fitness she didn't break a sweat, but I was more than a little winded. With Marcia still at my heels, I walked down the hall and entered my classroom. She examined the room, apparently to confirm I was not harboring her stolen property.

"Someone in this benighted excuse for a school is a petty criminal." Although she stomped her foot with enough force to smash an atom, the delicate shoe survived. "When I find out who it is, I will press charges."

Marcia was not at her best when dealing with human beings, but I'll admit right now she was a gifted English teacher. Her lectures on *Frankenstein* made every listener feel the utter pain and isolation of the characters. When she talked about *A Tale of Two Cities*, the horrors of the French Revolution came to life. But I'm not sure she was capable of discussing anything that didn't exist between the covers of a book.

I did not doubt Marcia's capacity for making people miserable. But she's like a heat-seeking missile—dangerous when headed in your direction, but capable of being diverted to a more appropriate target.

I logged onto my school email and stared at the spam in order to avoid facing Marcia. "Why are you bothering with me? Go find a custodian to harass. Or send out an email. I think all that weight loss has affected your brain."

"It's not my brain that's the problem." She narrowed her eyes and drew together artfully plucked brows. "I've already tracked down the custodians and cornered every possible suspect. Except for you. And don't give me that innocent expression. I know you're still angling to get my Advanced Placement classes. Like that's ever going to happen. You're not getting my classes or my Aeron chair."

Okay, maybe I was guilty of that minor misdemeanor.

Back in June, I answered an anonymous school-wide survey on what classes I wanted to teach. I knew it was a long shot, but I requested one of Marcia's Advanced Placement English classes and offered up my creative writing class to sweeten the deal.

Someone blabbed, the change never happened, and Marcia and I ended the school year on very chilly terms.

She eyed me, and with a nasty grin said, "As if you ever could take over my classes. How much about literature do you really know?"

I didn't bother to defend myself against her challenge to my intelligence. Instead, I sat in my standard-issue chair and swiveled from side to side, to achieve maximum irritation. Marcia circled the room with the intensity of a latter day Magellan in search of the Spice Islands. She was near the door when I stopped her.

I knew I would regret doing so, but I couldn't resist saying, "Before you go, I have to ask—what kind of diet are you on? And who did your hair?" I wasn't trying to flatter her or distract her. I really wanted to know.

Marcia put her hands on newly slim hips. "I'm not on a diet." She smoothed her hair, which a few months ago was the color and texture of Brillo, and now fell in soft brown waves. She pulled a few wisps in front of her ears and threaded her fingers through bangs that slanted across her forehead, which while now smooth, was still stern. "I did my hair myself."

"Yeah, right. And I'm the new swimsuit model for *Sports Illustrated*."

It takes a much cleverer response than that to slow Marcia's caustic wit. She pointed a scarlet-tipped finger at my chest and shot back, "What size suit?"

I couldn't let Marcia's nastiness go unpunished. It wouldn't be fair to her.

I strolled over to the window, did a double take, and gasped, "Oh my God! There's your chair! In the parking lot!"

She ran out of my classroom as fast as her four-inch stilettos allowed. In a war of wit no one conquers Marcia, but it's nice to occasionally score a point or two.

———

Marcia made me late for our first staff meeting, but since I'd sat through the same dreary exercises each September for the last ten years I wasn't worried. The only part about teaching I like is when I'm with the kids, and they would not arrive until the next day.

I hadn't seen most of my colleagues since June, and while I could not compete with Marcia's makeover, I didn't want to be her foil either. I brushed a streak of dust from black yoga sweats, which from many angles looked like zip-up pants. I tucked an errant bra strap under my tank top and checked the mirror to see if my half dozen strands of gray hair had recruited any new members. Lastly, I swiped my mouth with some Barcelona Red lipstick. Without artificial help my pale skin and dark hair and eyes tended to elicit queries about my health. Reasonably satisfied with the results, I locked the door to protect my belongings from the chair thief.

By the time I got to the auditorium, the first part of our opening day program had already started, and the only open seats were in the front row. A motivational speaker, Mr. Pescarelli, ("Call me Joe!") leaped onto the stage, eager to enlighten us about his Pescarelli Program.

After thirty minutes of imploring us to be the best we could be, Joe started a video of his Dickensian childhood and subsequent rise to success. The lights dimmed. I closed my eyes, positive that the presence of my colleagues and the loud voiceover would prevent me from falling asleep. Nevertheless, a short time later a cop, a cowboy, and a biker dude shimmied into my subconscious and beckoned me to join the rest of the Village People on the dance floor.

I opened my eyes. The bare-chested guy in a feathered headdress evaporated, and in his place Joe Pescarelli urged us all to share in a motivational team-building dance. What the hell. Only a dead person could resist the siren song of "YMCA." As the lights brightened and the opening beats began echoing through the auditorium I poked both arms in the air, clapped my hands, and began singing.

The auditorium seemed a bit quiet. I peered behind me. Not one other person was reliving sweaty evenings beneath a mirrored ball that shot multi-colored laser lights.

Joe Pescarelli said, "Let's give the dancing queen a big round of applause!"

Those who were not playing Candy Crush clapped. I avoided eye contact and took a bow. I wasn't sure if Joe had finished motivating us, but I barreled toward the exit anyway. There's no excuse so solid as one grounded in public humiliation.

The halls were deserted, except for Mrs. Donnatella, the school secretary. Red-faced and perspiring, she stood guard behind a table filled with our back-to-school folders. I was surprised to see her, for she rarely moves from her throne in the main office. I was in no mood to tangle with her, since she makes Marcia Deaver look like Glinda the Good Witch, but I couldn't ignore her. I initialed the checklist, grabbed my folder from the stack marked English Dept., and left.

Sunlight poured with brutal intensity into my classroom. I flipped through my folder, and to my horror, realized that in addition to grabbing the folder marked *Hopewell, Liz*, I also had taken the one marked *Deaver, Marcia*. I contemplated Marcia's probable response to this gaffe, and for both our sakes I was grateful burning at the stake was no longer in vogue. I longed to fortify myself with a furtive cigarette and a fresh cup of coffee before facing the shrew across the hall, but those restoratives were still hours away.

I peered into Marcia's classroom, hoping she had found her chair. Her room was on the shady side of the building, and the sudden relief from burning sunshine gave me goosebumps. There was no chair behind her desk. No Marcia, either. Relieved that I would not have to explain myself to my combative colleague, I decided to leave the folder on her desk, rather than admit my mistake to Mrs. Donnatella.

Marcia's room, like Marcia herself, had undergone a radical alteration. Never neat, it was weirdly—and wildly—untidy. On the floor Marcia's prized collection of vintage movie posters wound themselves into helpless spirals. Papers carpeted the area near her desk, and piles of textbooks were splayed on the windowsill, their bent spines protesting the rough treatment.

Was Marcia redecorating? I didn't remember her ever changing anything in her classroom, but perhaps her personal makeover inspired her to change her physical environment. But that didn't explain the mistreatment of the books. None of her students dared deface a book with so much as a single pencil mark or dog-eared page, and it was impossible that Marcia herself had treated those books so carelessly.

A breeze from the open window blew a few more papers across the room, and I retrieved them. Fearing that Marcia would walk in on me, I held the papers at arm's length in order to demonstrate my innocent helpful nature. I noticed that, in addition to piles of books and random boxes, Marcia had left her shiny red-soled shoes on the floor. They really were beautiful shoes. I put the papers down and walked around the boxes and behind the desk for a closer look.

I stared, but the synapses that are supposed to fire when visual information is conveyed to the brain refused to spark. I looked at Marcia's feet and at the undignified spread of her legs. Through a myopic haze I took in her gaping mouth and staring eyes. Underneath coral lipstick, the color of her mouth echoed the blue of her shirt. A thin stream of brown fluid trickled from an overturned coffee cup and landed, one drip at a time, on Marcia's face.

The walls dipped and swooped. I tried to keep myself from falling, but my hasty grip on the keyboard panel caused it to slip forward, and I nearly pitched onto the top of the desk. In slow motion, I moved the panel back to its original position. A large yellow envelope, the kind we use for substitute lesson plans, dislodged itself from the underside of the desk panel and spit into my middle. I caught it just before it landed on Marcia.

Behind me, the door creaked. Finally, screams broke the tension.

Mine, not Marcia's.

CHAPTER 2

HEART OF DARKNESS

I view with suspicion people who pride themselves on their accurate memory. Science has caught up with my prejudice, and it turns out eyewitnesses are not especially reliable, even those who swear under oath. But I could not burn from my mind's eye the image of Marcia's convulsed face and degrading posture. I needed a confidante, and my husband was the only available candidate.

"How do you think Marcia died?" I followed George into the bathroom.

"How do I think what?" He sniffed at the towel hanging next to the shower and tossed it on the floor. "And by the way, Liz, what do I have to do to get a little privacy here?"

It would take more than a moldy towel to distract me. "I repeat, how do you think Marcia Deaver died? I think—do you think—is it possible she was murdered? There are dozens, hell, by now there must be hundreds of people who hate her guts, but murder—"

"Was she the kind of person who bothered her husband when he was trying to get ready for work?"

George's sense of humor had never been more irritating. "Why are you so worried about being late? You got that promotion. I thought you'd be able to cut down your hours."

He took the last clean towel from the linen closet and turned to face me. "Think again. I'm a minor vice president of a real estate firm that's managed not to make mega-millions in New York City. More importantly, I have to get out of here. We're negotiating for a new office building in Brooklyn. I'm sorry about your dead friend, but I have a lot on my mind right now."

George paused to contemplate his navel, not as an aid to meditation, but to check the outline of his abdomen. He's proud of his abdomen. It is attractive, though not at all like the skinny torso of the guy I fell in love with twenty years ago. Of course, twenty years ago he'd have pulled me into the shower with him. Twenty years ago, the only real estate that interested him was the lumpy bed we shared in our first apartment.

I tried to keep his attention. "I have a lot on my mind too. Death trumps real estate. And to answer your question about Marcia, she didn't bother her husband when he was in the shower because she was divorced. And more to the point, I think she may have been poisoned."

My husband turned the faucets on full force. "Is there any evidence that the poor woman was murdered? She probably had a heart attack."

"I suppose that's possible. But Marcia looked so healthy. I saw her less than an hour before she died, and she looked better than she had in years. I hate to admit this, but there are plenty of suspects at Valerian Hills High School."

"That's ridiculous." George leaned over the edge of the tub to test the water, which resists any temperature not freezing or scalding. "I met Marcia and the rest of the bunch at that horrible fundraiser you dragged me to. If someone did kill her, he probably bored her to death. Anyway, we went over this ten times last night. Just put the whole thing out of your mind."

I wished I could put it out of my mind. "You didn't see her. She looked like she died—violently. Her face—it wasn't a peaceful death. She suffered."

George stroked my cheek, and the sudden tenderness reminded me of many tender moments. He said, more gently, "Finding her like that must have been awful, but that's no reason for you to start imagining some bizarre conspiracy theory. People don't die according to schedule. Your mother was only thirty-nine. And how old was your father? Do you even know?"

Of course, I knew when my father was supposed to have died.

I pulled away. "I don't want to talk about him. It's more important to me that you stick around. And this isn't about my father. This is about Marcia."

George went back to fiddling with the taps. "I know how you love to dramatize things, but this is real life. The only evidence that the woman was murdered exists in your head. Even those lunatics in the English department aren't that crazy. Look on the bright side. Maybe you'll get to teach those AP classes you're always talking about." Apparently feeling that this comment closed the conversation, George stepped into the shower.

I raised my voice to compete with the hissing water and clanking pipes. "I should be the one to teach AP, although I'll bet that horrible Caroline Cartwright has already sweet-talked both Gordon and Timmy. I think she has a bit of a crush on Timmy."

"Which one is Timmy?"

I knew the names of George's coworkers and it annoyed me that he couldn't remember mine. "Timmy is the assistant principal. Gordon is the principal."

George peered around the torn shower curtain and tapped his head, as if he'd come up with a brilliant idea. "Why don't you point out your superior qualifications? Offer to have sex with both of them. This way, if the Deaver woman was murdered, you can confirm your position as the prime suspect. You were the one to find the body."

If I'd started crying, George would have leapt out of the shower to comfort me. Subtler indications of emotion he tends to miss. Or ignore. Or make stupid jokes about.

I decided to play his game. "Tempting, but no. I don't find either Gordon or Timmy particularly appealing, though I guess I could try to fake it. I have been practicing."

George declined the bait. I wanted to assess my potential as a seductress, but the foggy bathroom mirror didn't reveal much. I combed my hair with my fingers and confirmed the fact that the time I'd spent taming each strand with a blow dryer, a flat iron, and two expensive hair products was wasted. A frizzy dark halo framed my face.

I swiped the mirror clear and used a second tissue to blot smudges of mascara that punctuated dark circles under my eyes. "For all I know, that creepy secretary decides these things, and I am definitely not having sex with her. If you ask me, there are plenty of suspects around besides the teachers."

Without comment, my husband handed me a chunk of plaster from where the rickety shower pole met the ceiling. The appeal of our modest Victorian home does not extend to the avocado green bathroom, which has not been renovated since the Kennedy administration. I lust over advertisements for Kohler and Moen, but George is betting that a new hot water heater is going to assert precedence over more aesthetically pleasing upgrades. When I complain, he reminds me this house was the one I chose. Although he works in midtown Manhattan, he wanted to move to a more distant suburb, similar to Valerian Hills, where new houses feature walk in closets, wall-to-wall carpeting, and central everything. I insisted we move to Oak Ridge, where turn of the century Tudor, Georgian, and Victorian homes exude the kind of charm and personality that is so expensive to maintain.

George muttered a few words to himself, and then, louder, said, "I'm asking you nicely: Get out of the bathroom. And don't waste your time playing Liz

Hopewell, girl detective. This is real life, not literature. And the reality of real life is that you get nervous just reading about crime."

I stood my ground. I didn't have to admit to something just because it was true. "I'm a lot tougher than you give me credit for. Plus, I could use the exercise."

"If you want to exercise you should start using the gym membership that gets deducted from the American Express card every month. I think you're averaging $100 per visit."

I let George have the last word. It was getting late, and I still wasn't dressed for work. I swapped plaid pajama bottoms for a long stretchy skirt that hid a multitude of ice cream sodas. I exchanged a faded tank top for a less-worn version and added three-inch high-wedged sandals. The extra height, plus the all-black ensemble, helped me pretend I wasn't short and didn't need to lose ten pounds. Maybe twelve. Fifteen, at the most.

I went down to the kitchen. The kids were already on their way to Oak Ridge High School. Ellie, fifteen years old and an aspiring dancer, had left her peanut butter and jelly sandwich on the counter. She also left a list of items she wanted from the grocery store. These included diet Jell-O, diet soda, and diet salad dressing. Sixteen-year-old Zach left four horribly smelling soccer socks next to Ellie's lunch. I threw the socks in with a load of other laundry, knowing that this would sap the remainder of the hot water. Energized by George's audible reaction to the suddenly chilly cascade, I scrubbed from the table bits of soggy cereal that were metamorphosing into concrete. Then I headed back to school.

Once again, I reported to the auditorium, where The Home and School Association provided us with a post-mortem bagel breakfast. I was surprised and grateful, since refreshments were eliminated from discretionary spending a few years ago. On the other hand, I was unprepared for this assault on my new diet, the one I had started two hours earlier. I decided if I ate a bagel but didn't eat lunch, that this would be the same as dieting.

Caroline Cartwright, the English department chairperson, looked at my plate. "Aren't you on the Atkins diet?" She believes that her British accent and her position as chairperson gives her license to express thoughts that most civilized people keep quiet. Even Marcia could barely keep up with her.

I flicked a few crumbs in her direction, trying to keep her far enough away that she wouldn't spy the cream cheese hiding in the bagel. "No, Caroline, now I'm on the Bagel Diet. All you have to do is eat as many bagels as you want and you lose a ton of weight."

Caroline stepped back, careful to preserve the ironed perfection of her pencil skirt. She did not deign to answer, but Bill Murphy, a former jock who is spreading into middle age, was impressed.

"Really? That's awesome!" Bill piled two bagels and a muffin onto a paper plate that struggled to bear the burden of the combined carbohydrates. He balanced the plate against the shelf of his belly. I hoped at some point Bill would realize the "Bagel Diet" was no substitute for Weight Watchers.

Here at Valerian Hills High School, we usually sit together by department, not because we like each other, but because we're lazy. I slipped in next to Emily Pearson, the least toxic teacher in the school. Emily, pale and serious, was as gentle as Caroline was aggressive. Every member of the staff, including the mild-mannered athletic director and the friendly custodians, terrifies her. All around us teachers spoke in subdued voices, as though we were already at the funeral.

The principal walked in, flanked by two police officers. Both wore bright gold badges on civilian clothes. Right Hand Cop was a cartoon character, with white hair and the kind of moustache that attracts crumbs. He shifted back and forth on his scuffed shoes, possibly to alleviate the pressure that his brown sports jacket inflicted on his middle. Left Hand Cop was tall and lean, with blue eyes and light brown hair. His linen blazer hung open to reveal a white shirt and a repp tie striped in red and gold. He looked like the kind of guy who didn't need privacy while taking a shower.

Neither was my type. I prefer short, skinny, eyeglass-wearing Upper West Side espresso-drinking and arugula-eating intellectuals. Someone in off-label jeans and a tee shirt, or a nerdy short-sleeved plaid number. If I ever were attracted to a cop, which is doubtful, he would have to be more like a Masterpiece Mystery detective than the hero of an action movie. Nevertheless, Left Hand Cop did have the kind of athletic allure that attracts some women.

Gordon and the cops stood together, at a distance too far away for us to hear what they were saying. While we waited for them to get started, Emily asked, "Do you think we'll all get interrogated? I'm so nervous! And what could I say? I barely knew Marcia."

"Excuse me?" Caroline looked down her nose. "You've been working with her almost as long as I have."

Emily turned pink.

Caroline often exempts Emily from the cattiness she dishes out to the rest of us, but we were all feeling a bit touchy. And I don't know why this is, but

Caroline's BBC accent makes nearly everything she says, even when it is not ill intended, sound like an especially nasty insult.

Emily stuttered through an unnecessary apology and an even more unnecessary explanation. "I meant, you know. I just, well, I didn't know her personally. I never saw her outside of school."

"None of us saw her outside of school," Caroline snapped. "Marcia Deaver thought she was too good for the rest of us." She paused and then added, "Not to speak ill of the dead."

"I wonder who's going to teach Marcia's Advanced Placement classes?" Perhaps it was a bit callous of me, but I really did want to know.

Emily, who has been teaching the same freshman curriculum for the last eighteen years, quavered, "I don't know anything about those books. They have to read *Moby Dick*!"

Caroline was equally disinclined, but being Caroline, she had to couch her answer combatively. "I'd bloody well love to see them try to make *me* learn a new curriculum."

Bill did not respond. I wondered if he, and not Caroline, would be angling for Marcia's schedule.

"Let's face it," I said, looking at each teacher in turn, trying to gauge which one was most likely to compete with me for the honor of being assigned the AP classes. "Marcia's students earned some of the best scores in New Jersey, and whoever takes over her classes is going to have tough time matching that."

Caroline threw me a pitying look. "Which is why you shouldn't get your hopes up, Liz. Marcia was teaching on the university level when they hired her. They'll probably look elsewhere for someone to take her place."

This information was news to me. "Why would she leave a college gig for a high school in suburban New Jersey?"

"Maybe her crazy Shakespeare conspiracy theories got her thrown out. If I had to guess, though, I'd say her charming personality ended her academic career. Unlike high schools, colleges don't hand out tenure like candy at Halloween." Caroline tilted her head and widened her eyes in Bill's direction. He was oblivious to her subtext and contentedly chomped on bagel number two.

I opened my mouth to further query Caroline, but she turned her attention to her pinging cell phone. I surveyed the rest of the staff. None of those mild-looking people seemed capable of committing a violent act.

In truth, the only person who seemed to possess the necessary fierceness was the victim herself. Marcia Deaver loathed every single member of the

English department. She thought Caroline a charlatan, Emily a dishrag, and Bill a dimwitted menace to the future of the English language. As for me, well, Marcia knew that I longed to teach at least one of her Advanced Placement classes. She frequently referred to me as a "full-time soccer mom," implying I could never devote the time and effort necessary to teach the exalted upper-level classes. Plenty of people at Valerian Hills High School feared and detested Marcia's acerbic wit. But I knew of no one who hated her enough to kill her.

Marcia was equally relentless, if less nasty, with her students, and yet—and yet—I had to admit they were devoted to her. Conspiracy theories aside, she was a damned good teacher.

I was pulled to attention when the principal and the two cops finally walked to the front of the room. Gordon released a series of disturbing guttural sounds—he is a most anxious public speaker, and the only way he can get himself started is by clearing his throat of the gremlins that plague him. Today, the throat clearing sounded a lot like an outboard motor in need of repair. We are so used to this disgusting habit we don't notice it anymore, but the noise did seem to startle the two cops. Gordon's public speaking skills are further eroded by his inability to look at anyone directly. He introduced the police officers to a friendly spot on the wall.

The unappealing detective spoke first. "I am Detective Brown, and I'll be doing the follow up interviews, along with Detective Harriman here. Dr. Deaver's death appears to be a tragic accident. I know you'll give us your fullest cooperation."

Tragic accident? That didn't sound like a heart attack to me. The room hummed with whispers. Caroline reached into her handbag, dabbed her dry eyes with a tissue, and checked her cell phone once again.

No one else pretended to weep. Marcia's death elicited shock and horror, but no real grief.

I looked up and saw that Hot Cop was watching me. I thought it unlikely that my mature charm was what distracted him from studying posters depicting famous athletes exhorting students to *Get in the Game and Read*, and I was right. Harriman approached, and said that he would interview me in the English office. Detective Brown stated that he would interview teachers in the conference room. Before Brown left he helped himself to the bagel buffet. He poured himself a large cup of coffee and spooned in four helpings of sugar.

Detective Harriman neither ate nor drank. I trashed the last two bites of my bagel and refilled my coffee cup before escorting him to the English office.

He looked around. "This office looks like a bookroom."

I followed the direction of his eyes. I'm used to the cramped workroom, but from an outsider's perspective, the office probably looked pathetic. "It is a bookroom. It doubles as our office. We are waiting for the athletic department to give up part of their thousand square feet of real estate so that we have more space."

Harriman did not respond to my editorializing. He pointed to an interior door wedged between two bookshelves. It bore a faded No Exit sign.

He examined the hand-lettered rectangle. "Why the sign?"

"That's a connecting door to Marcia Deaver's room." Marcia's many years of service to the district may not have earned her much money, but she did get the best classroom, in addition to the best schedule.

Harriman finished his perusal of the sign and turned his attention to the door itself. "Yes, I know what it is. But why the sign?"

"Marcia put up the sign. Even though she used the interior door to the English office all the time, she freaked out if anyone else did. If we needed to go into her classroom we had to use the door that opens to the hallway."

"Why?" Harriman's gaze was unwavering.

There was no way to explain the No Exit sign without speaking ill of Marcia. I shrugged and kept quiet. Let someone else explain the dead woman's dictates. Harriman didn't know Marcia, and I feared any accurate statement about her would sound snarky, or worse.

Harriman extracted a few pages from his bag. "I know you spoke with the police officers on the scene yesterday. I have their report, but for right now I want you to walk me through what happened."

I stretched my legs, happy to have an excuse to relieve the tension in my knees. "Fine. If you want me to literally walk you through it we have to start in my room." I offered Harriman my desk chair, which was the only comfortable perch in the room. He declined and folded his long frame into one of the metal one-piece desks we provide for the students.

Harriman took out a notebook and pen. "You were the last person to see Dr. Deaver alive. And the one who found her dead. I'd like you to review with me everything that happened yesterday."

I could contain myself no longer. "How did she die? What kind of 'tragic accident' did she have?"

Harriman didn't answer immediately. Finally, he said, "Looks like an overdose. Heart medication plus diet pills—not a good combination. Could have been an accident. Possible suicide. Ms. Hopewell, I need your cooperation. It's my job to ask the questions."

I took out a pen and some paper. I too wanted to take notes. "If that's how she died, I don't think I can answer any questions you have. Because that means I wasn't the last person to see her alive. Whoever killed her was the last person to see her."

Harriman jerked his head slightly, but did not react in any other way. Unlike George, he didn't debate the issue or my emotional health. "Why do you think she was murdered?" His voice and face remained expressionless. "What do you know about her personal life?"

"Well, we weren't exactly friends." That had to have been the understatement of the year. "But for heaven's sake, Marcia Deaver was an English teacher. So you can rule out suicide."

Harriman squelched a laugh. "Why? Are English teachers immune from depression?"

I smiled and shook my head. "God, no. But Marcia's entire life was ruled by the written word. She wouldn't have killed herself without leaving a suicide note." Or, in Marcia's case, a well-organized essay filled with appropriate literary references.

That thought—too frivolous to express—turned itself around and stabbed me. More than once I'd sat in the English office and eavesdropped as Marcia lectured her students. I didn't like her, but I'd learned a lot from her.

Harriman kept his pen on the paper but his eyes on me. "In other words, you only knew her professionally. You really don't know anything about her personal life."

If the reasons I gave Harriman were insufficiently convincing, I had others. "When I saw Marcia yesterday, she was totally transformed. She'd lost a ton of weight and was wearing a pair of fabulous shoes. I would kill for those shoes." Horrified, I clapped my hand to my mouth. Harriman didn't arrest me, so I continued my argument. "No one suffers the pain of dieting, not to mention an excellent face lift, in order to look good in a coffin."

The muscles around Harriman's mouth tightened, as if to check another smile. That wasn't the reaction I sought.

I didn't want to sound flip about Marcia's death. But talking about her was driving me crazy. All I wanted was to forget the coffee dripping on her face— and I was being forced to relive every nauseating minute. I pushed my own coffee aside. "I may not have been best friends with Marcia. But she deserves better than that. She was a proud woman, and she met a—a terrible end." I stared at the window in order to avoid looking at the detective.

Harriman placed tissues in front of me. "Ms. Hopewell, I'm sorry that you have to go through this."

I took a few tissues and blotted my face. I didn't want to talk until I was sure my voice wouldn't wobble.

Harriman tapped his notebook. "It's entirely possible that Dr. Deaver accidentally took an overdose of her heart medication. Did you know she had a heart condition?"

Once again, I had to admit that I actually knew very little about Marcia. I studied the dark streaks of mascara that had been on my eyes and now were on the tissue. "Marcia wasn't the type to discuss her health. She thought it was in bad taste...which, of course, it is. But I don't think it's any more likely that she accidentally overdosed than that she deliberately overdosed."

Harriman checked his watch and sighed. "Is this based on any evidence?"

That sigh annoyed me, and I forgot about everything except my certainty that Marcia had not committed suicide. "Yes. It's based on the evidence of her character. Details were important to Marcia, and she didn't make careless mistakes. I remember her lecturing us during a department meeting. She said we had to know every detail of every book and poem we taught, because details were like peepholes. One tiny opening in a door is all you need to see everything outside. Do you see what I mean?"

Harriman walked about the room. Maybe the tension was getting to him as well. "Yeah, I get it. What else can you tell me about her?"

I struggled to convey what Marcia was like. "Teaching was important to her, but she was also a scholar of Elizabethan literature. She didn't divulge many, if any details about her personal life, but she did speak often about her obsession with Shakespeare. She was an Anti-Stratfordian, which is a fancy way of saying that she was part of a group that believes someone else wrote the work we attribute to Shakespeare. There's a whole conspiracy theory connected with that. I think they're all crazy, but you can bet I never got into an argument with Marcia about it."

"That's very interesting." Despite his words, Harriman wasn't interested enough to record the specifics of Marcia's academic passion. Instead, he asked, "Tell me what you know about her friends, her marriage."

I looked at the empty page in front of me, and I scrawled a few words— marriage, Shakespeare, overdose—to relieve the blankness. "I can't. The little

I know I got from lunchroom gossip. All I can tell you is that Marcia was the first one here in the morning and the last to leave at night, even during the brief time she was married. She spent half her vacation time here."

I realized, finally, at least one of the things that had made me so uneasy in the moments before I saw Marcia. She, unlike the rest of us who use the first day of September to organize our classrooms, did not need time to prepare for the new school year, since she rarely spent more than a few days away from the school. So why was her room such a mess? I explained this to Harriman.

He hesitated, before relenting, "This would have been a matter of public record anyway, Ms. Hopewell, so there's no harm in telling you. There's a vacancy at the middle school, and there was talk about moving Dr. Deaver there."

I dropped my pen and didn't pick it up. I was waiting for some other impossible cosmic event to occur. Like, maybe a pride of lions would lie down with a flock of lambs. Perhaps hell was about to freeze over. Either of those events was more likely than Marcia being moved to the middle school.

Marcia was, if not the best, certainly the most devoted teacher in the entire Valerian Hills school district. Why would they reassign their highest performing teacher to the middle school? It didn't make sense. That was generally saved as a last humiliation for older high school teachers.

Gordon and Timmy love to burden expensive teachers, those who have reached the top of our modest salary guide, with a punishing schedule, an unending diet of cafeteria duty, and a constant sniping and griping that eventually grinds even the most granite hard employees into retirement. But Marcia could not possibly have been put in that category. She would have killed them, not the other way around. And, I had to assume that even Gordon and Timmy know that only a masochist, or someone in financial thrall to the mafia or a private college, would be willing to accept the pittance Marcia earned in her afterschool position as director of the school plays.

I stilled my foot from its nervous tapping. "That's not possible. She's too good at what she does. Plus, I found out—this morning, actually—that Marcia began her teaching career at a college. There is no way anyone would seriously consider moving her to the middle school, which in this town is an academic wasteland."

Harriman closed his notebook and put away his pen. "Maybe that's why they wanted to transfer her. It makes sense to put the best teacher where she'd have the biggest impact." Harriman pressed his momentary advantage at my hesitation and redirected the conversation to the events of the day before. We entered Marcia's classroom. Ducking the yellow tape, I pointed to the desk, the papers, the location of the body, the coffee stain. To my horror, I started shaking again. Tears slipped from my eyes, and I fished in my bag for more tissues. I couldn't stay in Marcia's room and also stay calm. Harriman followed me back across the hall.

"She didn't kill herself. I'm sure of that."

"You don't know that." Harriman's pulled the chair from behind my desk and I sat down. "Right now, no one knows." He put a hand on my shoulder.

I loathe being touched by strangers, even handsome, blue-eyed strangers, and I shrugged off his hand "I know. I saw her shortly before she died—was murdered—and she was stalking the custodians, trying to find her missing chair. That doesn't fit in with my idea of what someone about to commit suicide is likely to do."

Harriman looked confused. "Her chair? Why would someone take her chair?"

"Chairs are expensive. Hers cost a fortune."

Harriman sat a few inches from me and leaned forward. Generally, I don't like tall men. They make me feel short. But I didn't pull back. He smelled good. It wasn't cologne, or shampoo, or anything artificial that made his scent so appealing. His body gave off an aroma that was a little bitter and a little sharp. And faintly sweet.

The detective's eyes narrowed in concern. "Ms. Hopewell, are you sure you're okay?"

He probably thought I was crazy, so I elaborated upon the chair situation, "In an effort to cut the budget and improve education, the board of education decided to eliminate regular desk chairs, and to replace them with these flimsy plastic chairs. The rationale is that the district saves money on furniture, and the teachers won't sit down for fear of an unplanned lumbar puncture. So while the administration and the board of education park their rear ends on cushy seats, we have to buy our own. Marcia had a very pricey Aeron chair, and the fact that it was missing was kind of a big deal. I wish now I'd been more sympathetic."

As far as I could tell, the detective wrote down every detail. When he finished, he asked, "Is it usual for things go missing like that?"

I shook my head. "It's not that unusual for the furniture to end up in the wrong place, since over the summer the classrooms are emptied in order to clean them, but it is unusual for something to totally disappear. Even the new custodians know to take care of Marcia and her stuff. And none of the teachers would risk a run in with her. So it is weird. Have you found it yet?"

Harriman didn't answer. I tried to read what he'd written, but his tiny handwriting was impossible to decipher, especially upside down. Detective Brown joined us. The two detectives did not greet each other. I repeated everything one more time, trying to maintain my composure. I answered questions about possible enemies, grudges that people might have had, questions about Marcia's personal life. After a few minutes I realized the line of inquiry the detectives were pursuing made sense only if they thought Marcia was murdered. I couldn't wait to tell George.

Finally, I asked, "Didn't you say that you thought Marcia's death was an accident? Or a suicide?"

"We're covering all the bases," Brown said with patronizing smoothness.

That made me suspicious, as it would any insomniac who has seen as many reruns of *Law and Order* as I have. When the detectives trot out baseball metaphors, it's time for the interviewee to shut up. I tried to gain credibility by extending his baseball comparison. "In the process of 'covering all the bases' did you consider that you might be stranding a batter or two?"

Brown dismissed me. "Mrs. Hopewell, I believe we're done here."

His indifference stung. I could see that Brown had me filed me under the heading of middle-aged, boring English teacher and that he'd heard only what he'd primed himself to hear. In addition to being insulting, his attitude also seemed unprofessional.

I stood up and put both hands on my desk. "I am going to tell you what I told Detective Harriman: Marcia wasn't the type of person to do anything 'accidentally,' let alone overdose on her own medication. She was sharp and precise and careful."

Brown closed his eyes, and when he opened them he looked to the ceiling, and not to me, for guidance. "Mrs. Hopewell, Dr. Deaver was popping diet pills while taking heart medication. That's not the kind of thing a careful and rational person does. It is, in fact, what a mentally unbalanced person does."

"I won't deny you're right about that, Detective. There's a whole lot about her death that doesn't make sense to me. But you didn't know Marcia." I spoke with conviction, but it occurred to me that maybe I didn't know Marcia as well as I thought I did.

Brown pretended patience, but I think he was overdue for a nap. His eyes roamed to the computer, to the window, to every point in the room except my face. "Can you be more specific? You've already told us about the business with the posters on the wall and the empty bookshelf, all of which is easily explained by the fact that she was due to move to a different location. Do you have anything else?"

I couldn't think of one damned thing to say. The combined presence of the hot Harriman and the cold Brown was too distracting. If I had to describe them as they no doubt would have described themselves, I'd say they looked as if they had struck out on a called third strike. In the bottom of the ninth.

The two detectives waited. After a few silent moments Harriman said goodbye for both of them, and they left.

My back hurt, my neck was stiff, and my knees felt locked in a permanent vise of tension, but I forced myself back to my desk. That was when I remembered I still had Marcia's folder. I did pause for a moment. Really.

Marcia's folder held the same forms mine did. Nothing interesting there. That left the envelope, the one that had been hidden in the underside of her desk. It was marked *Substitute Lesson Plans*. The metal tab that kept the envelope closed was practically falling off. I fingered the closure and the flap opened, with almost no help from me. I thumbed through the papers, and for the third time in my life, I was unable to understand concrete and not terribly complex information.

CHAPTER 3
REMEMBRANCE OF THINGS PAST

I called George, but he didn't answer his cell phone. His work number went automatically to voicemail, and I already knew his irritating message, "I don't check my voicemail. Please email me."

I figured I should call the police, but I wasn't sure what to say. They had asked if I knew of anyone who had a motive for murder. The answer to that question was still no, but I knew now why Marcia's classroom was such a mess—and it wasn't because she was moving to the middle school. Someone had already searched it.

I cleared my desk and scrutinized each element of Marcia's "lesson plans." They looked legitimate, and to anyone who didn't teach English they would inspire no particular interest.

The lesson plan for Nabokov's *Lolita* got my attention first. Valerian Hills High School does not teach literature that, however brilliant, offers a sympathetic portrayal of a pedophile in love and lust with his twelve-year-old stepdaughter. More disturbing was the fact that letter-perfect Marcia made several errors concerning the plot. Among other anomalies, Marcia's notes referred to the protagonist's two children, who do not exist in the book. The lesson plan included a tag line: *To thine own self be true.*

The second lesson plan was for *The Talented Mr. Ripley*, Highsmith's tale of a charming young man who is a forger, swindler, and murderer. This too is not in our curriculum. And Marcia's notes referred to Mr. Ripley as female. The tag line for this plan was: *They did make love to this employment.*

The most baffling was Marcia's lesson plan on Oscar Wilde's play, *The Importance of Being Earnest*. In Marcia's notes, the protagonist is not Earnest, but the hilariously named Wilde Willing Billie. She added notes about Wilde's novel, *The Picture of Dorian Gray*, and referenced a 1985 movie of that name, but I was not familiar with it.

The quotation added to this lesson plan was: *Be thou as chaste as ice, as pure as snow, thou shalt not escape calumny.* The three italicized quotations were not from the books Marcia cited, but from *Hamlet*. And one of the quotations, *to thine own self be true*, was especially problematic. Marcia hated that line and scorned anyone who approvingly quoted it. She pointed out, quite rightly, that the character who says it is a scheming, pompous fool.

The last column on each page, which was supposed to provide evidence that the lessons correlated to the Common Core Curriculum Standards, instead listed a series of numbers, as if Marcia were auctioning off first editions.

For someone who's fairly ignorant of sports and pop culture, I'm pretty good at all kinds of word puzzles, but this literary enigma had me baffled. What was Marcia trying to tell me? I placed the papers back in the envelope and stashed it in my file cabinet for safekeeping.

Perhaps the answer key was in Marcia's other files. I tried the doorknob to her classroom, but it was locked. Stymied for the moment, I went to the English office, where Emily was ferrying crates of student folders into her room. She called over her shoulder that she had to leave to pick up her daughter. I followed her to the door and looked down the corridor. The hall was empty, except for Emily's retreating figure.

I waited for Emily to turn the corner, and then I returned to the office and tried to open the interior door that led from the English office into Marcia's room. The knob turned, but the door was blocked from the inside. I gently rocked the door on its hinges, and it opened a few inches. I pushed and strained to get through, but the door refused to budge any farther.

Those bagels didn't help my cause. But I remembered reading somewhere that if you can get your head through an aperture then you can maneuver your body through as well. I listened for the sound of footsteps, but was so nervous I could hear only a roaring sound in my ears. I poked my head into the narrow space. Then one shoulder, minus a small amount of skin. I paused as I contemplated the difficulty of getting my rear end to follow the rest of me.

The sharp sound of the English office telephone pierced the air, but I was stuck. I pulled my head back into the office, but my shoulder stayed wedged in the doorway. I stretched my fingers toward the telephone but couldn't manage the last few inches. Then Emily walked in. She stared at my sweaty, bisected body. She picked up the telephone, paused for one pregnant moment, and handed me the receiver. In my painful situation, a lesser person might cry. Not me, I laughed like a hyena, but sobered up when I heard Gordon's gargle on the other end. I heaved myself back into the English office, with only a wrenched shoulder and bruised ego to my credit.

As ridiculous as it sounds, even a teacher doesn't feel good about being summoned to the principal's office. Some atavistic response kicks in, and one can't help but feel a slight spill of anxiety. I don't think my abortive effort at espionage helped matters much. I couldn't figure out if I was having my first hot flash or was in the early stages of a heart attack. Then, there was more than a twinge of embarrassment at being caught by Emily. *Damn it.* Why couldn't she have left when she said she was leaving? Emily, with passive-aggressive determination, has never voluntarily worked one minute beyond what our contract requires, and she usually manages to get by with less.

I knew I owed the poor woman an explanation, but all I could come up with was, "I'll explain later!" I left her in the English office and barreled down the stairs. The main office is glass-walled, so I slowed to a decorous walk before I hit the hallway.

Gordon never bothers talking to teachers, except in response to parent complaints, and I couldn't imagine why he wanted to see me. I was, perhaps, a shade more sensitive than usual.

I stepped into the chilly main office and nodded to Mrs. Donnatella, the equally cool secretary (she scared everyone, the brave as well as the weak) and peeked around the corner into Gordon's office. Timmy, the assistant principal, was with him. They glanced in my direction, but did not acknowledge my presence. I averted my eyes, took a seat in the reception area, and waited to be invited to the inner sanctum.

The secretary regarded me with deliberate disinterest. Her lovely lilting name, Wilhelmina Donnatella, does not match either her personality or her physique. She is tall and heavy, like a football player past his prime. She hates, more than anything else, to move her fanny out of her chair. Her main source of amusement, other than terrorizing students and staff, is needlework. She has crocheted dozens, possibly hundreds, of little granny squares, and her computer, her files, and all the receptacles on her desk are adorned in polyester yarn. She favors baby colors: pinks and blues and pale yellows.

I waited, respectful of her position, until Mrs. Donnatella finished talking to her husband, in stomach-churning detail, about high blood pressure and kidney stones. Finally, she turned to me.

"Is there something you need?" She spoke in a two-pack-a-day New Jersey tough-gal growl.

I wondered how old she was. She always dressed in old lady clothes—big shapeless shirts over nondescript pants—and her pale blonde bob was glued into place, but as I studied her profile, I saw that her skin was virtually unlined. I realized she might not be fifty. It was her nasty expression that added the extra twenty years and more to her face. She's never mentioned having kids, and the only photograph on her desk is of a Persian cat. Too nervous to engage in chitchat I got to the point. "Gordon called me. He wants to talk to me."

Mrs. Donnatella waved me in, and in the spirit of goodwill I retrieved a ball of yarn that had rolled a few feet away. It was candy cane pink, and I assumed it would soon be wed to the potato-chip-yellow yarn on Mrs. Donnatella's desk, in a perfect marriage of junk food hues.

I walked into the principal's office. Gordon sat behind his desk, Timmy sat facing him, and the third chair was piled high with boxes of office supplies. There was no seat for me, and no move was made to procure one. What is it with this district and their miserly attitude about chairs for teachers? I moved Gordon's Class of 2011 Commemorative Flashlight and his dying begonia from the windowsill and made myself as comfortable as I could.

Assistant Principal Timmy began, perhaps as an oblique apology for his and Gordon's churlishness, "This won't take long, Liz."

My imaginary self had an eloquent response, but the real me said nothing. The real me doesn't want people to know what I'm thinking.

Gordon informed a stain on the carpet, "I know how much you've wanted to teach Advanced Placement English, and so we've decided to make you the new AP teacher. We'll hire someone to take over your schedule. It will be a lot easier to replace you than to replace Dr. Deaver."

My first thought was not annoyance that I was so easily replaceable, but anxiety that Bill would be upset. He does have seniority.

Gordon hazarded a quick look at me before returning his gaze to the floor. "You will, of course, give all of your lesson plans to the substitute teacher."

My heart beat faster. "So—does this mean that I'll get Marcia's lesson plans?"

Gordon considered this. "Yes, I suppose you can get them. But I'll have to get you access to the plans she filed online, since her room is still cordoned off. We hope to have a permanent replacement on board very soon."

Timmy's face flushed. "Actually, we already have someone in mind. Maybe you remember her? We're thinking we'll hire Ashlee Becker, the girl who did her student teaching here last spring. In fact, you might have had her as a student a few years ago. She was an awesome student teacher."

Ashlee Becker? *She* was taking my place? When she was in high school, Ashlee was a careless brainless twit of a student. Last year she returned to Valerian Hills as the laziest student teacher on record. Bill was her mentor, and besotted with her charm, he covered for her late entrances and early exits. Beautiful, yes. But smart? Hardly. And she redefined *Mean Girls* for a whole generation of her less well-endowed peers.

I told myself to shut up. I was starting to sound more and more like Marcia, and that was probably not a good thing. I hopped off the windowsill and thanked Gordon and Timmy. As I got to the door Gordon harrumphed. I know that noise, and it rarely presages anything good.

"Uh, hmm. You'll have to rewrite and resubmit the Advanced Placement curriculum," he told his desk.

I swallowed, before assuring him it would be my great pleasure to do this. But Gordon wasn't done.

"Well, there is one more thing! Isn't that funny? I almost forgot. You'll also get to take over Marcia's position as the Theater Club advisor."

I tried to gauge the two men's reaction if I refused. Was this some kind of test? Was this a requirement? Did I seem like the kind of idiot who would take on a whole new schedule the day before school started and also shoulder a full-scale musical production that involved fifty kids whose parents fervently believed that a future Ivy League acceptance was the only reason their little darlings would not be starring on Broadway? As if from a great distance, I heard myself say something that sounded a lot like yes.

I staggered back up the stairs. Desperate, I called George again. Unlike the question of what to do about Marcia's weird lesson plans, the issue involving the Theater Club was a true emergency. Miraculously, George answered, but not in a manner conducive to conversation. Without bothering with a greeting, he said, "Honey, I hate to put it this way, but unless someone else has kicked the bucket I can't take the time to chat. I've got wall-to-wall meetings all day today. And there's a good chance I won't be home until late."

Who was this person? Had some pod creature from outer space taken over the man who used to cancel meetings in order to have sex in the middle of the day?

"Look, George, this is important." I gave my husband a quick overview of my conversation with Gordon.

"Haven't you always wanted to teach these PA classes?" George asked impatiently.

"AP, not PA, you idiot. Yes, of course, but I can't take over an entirely new schedule and also run the Theater Club!"

I heard him clicking at his computer. It did not improve my mood or my reserves of patience to know that my problems were not sufficient to command his complete attention. After a few moments he said, "How much extra money will you make for running this theater thing?"

I don't multitask, and thus, unlike George, I did not type, check email, or listen to the latest on Bloomberg News. Instead, I poured my pent-up energy into jabbing a pencil into the mouse pad. "What difference does it make? Do you have any idea how much work it is? What about Zach's soccer? Or his science club meetings that take place all over the tri-state area? What about Ellie's ballet classes? Oh, and as a little side issue, I don't know what the hell I'm doing. I'll look like a moron!"

The sound of typing ceased, and I heard a female voice in the background. George muffled the phone while he spoke to her. When he resumed our conversation he sounded positively jovial. "Don't be so dramatic—ha hah—get it?"

I was not privy to whatever or whoever improved his mood. "I get it, and it's not funny."

There was a slight pause, and I heard him close the door to his office. "If you want to be serious, think about this. We're saving for two college tuitions, and we can use all the extra income we can get. The way you have Zach and Ellie signed up for SAT classes, and ballet classes, and God knows what else, we're bleeding money. Anyway, how hard could it be? They're kids, after all. It's not like you're going for an Oscar. All I'm saying is, we could use the extra cash, however much it turns out to be."

Money. It's all he thinks about these days. Money and the real estate market, which I guess for him is the same thing. "The extra cash is not without cost," I said. "And, to be clear, I'll be going for a Tony, not an Academy Award."

"Let's talk about this later. It's not exactly an emergency."

I tightened my grip on the phone, as if clenching it meant holding onto George. In recent weeks talking later meant not talking at all. "No! I haven't explained to you the most important part, which is about Marcia Deaver, because I was, completely accidentally you understand, reading about her, er, her lesson plans, and I found—"

"Really, honey, I gotta go." And with that, he went.

I calmed myself. George wasn't the only one who had work to do. I filled out an intrusive health form and hand-delivered it to the school nurse, instead of leaving it with Mrs. Donnatella, who collected such things. I doubted the secretary's commitment to privacy, and I wanted as few people as possible to know that I don't know my own blood type.

I checked the summer assignments for Marcia's students and realized I had to reread two novels in the next nineteen hours, as well as submit my lesson plans to Caroline, Timmy, and Gordon. I had no idea why all three needed to review them. My guess is that none of them actually do so. But I didn't want to screw up on my first task as the new AP teacher, so I completed them carefully.

I put Marcia's mysterious lesson plans into a folder marked Homework and tucked it into my briefcase. I drove home using the same route I always do, but I nearly missed the exit for Oak Ridge. Twice, I stared at a green light until vicious honking got me moving. What connecting thread linked the three books Marcia wrote about? When I told Harriman about Marcia's obsession with proving that someone else wrote Shakespeare's works the detective hadn't been interested. Would he treat her wacko lesson plans as equally irrelevant?

Well, maybe they were unimportant. But Marcia had put the envelope where it couldn't easily be found, and that meant she'd thought they were important. Although Marcia had believed in a lunatic conspiracy theory regarding Shakespeare, she hadn't been completely insane. I needed time to think.

At about five o'clock George texted that he wouldn't be home for several hours. I made the kids a soup and grilled cheese dinner. Afterwards, Zach went upstairs to his room, and Ellie commandeered the computer in the den.

I wanted to talk to someone—anyone—about those lesson plans. But who? I dialed Emily's number, but she didn't answer. I wanted to call Rebecca, my best friend since our childhood in the Brooklyn projects, but she was in London. Given the time difference and her brutal work schedule, she was either fast asleep or up late merging and acquiring with other financial geniuses.

With some reluctance, I called my sister. Susan is intelligent and generous, but she has a habit of turning every conversation toward herself. The Beautiful Woman Syndrome doesn't exempt sisters. I made up my mind that this conversation would be different. After all, this was an emergency.

Due to the miracle of caller ID she answered with, *"Bon soir, ma soeur*! I was thinking about you! You won't believe what happened to me today."

I hoped what happened to my sister did not involve a man. "Susan, I really need to talk to you about something."

"Mais oui! Hey! Guess what! You know that guy I was telling you about? The one who lives on the Upper West Side?"

I resigned myself to waiting. "Yeah, what about him?"

Her happiness bubbled through each word. "He asked me out! I ran into him at the Starbucks by Lincoln Center and we started talking, and we're seeing each other this Friday. He's from Montreal and speaks French. I can practice my French with him."

"You don't speak French," I observed.

Susan was offended. "No, my sarcastic sister, you don't *parlez français*. I've been taking classes for months, and I'm making real progress. But let's get to the important part."

I opened my mouth, thinking I was the important part, but Susan continued.

"What should I wear? I was thinking about that black, slightly off the shoulder shirt. Know the one I mean? For your information, I got it in Paris, in a store where they only spoke French."

"No stores like that exist in Paris. They'd go out of business." I popped open a can of Diet Coke—the champagne of suburban working mothers.

There was a brief pause, and for a moment I thought we'd lost the connection. In the background I heard the clatter of wooden hangers. When Susan spoke again, her voice sounded muffled. "If for once in your life you put aside all of your boring little suburban errands and came to Paris with me, we could shop together and I would show it to you."

I had to stop Susan before she gave me a complete inventory of her closet. "Susan, listen to me for a minute. A lot is happening right now, and I need your attention."

"Okay, what's going on?" she asked, in a lower, less emotional tone.

Now that I had the opportunity to speak, I hesitated. There was so much to tell. I began relating the lurid events as clearly as I could.

Susan's tone was sympathetic. "It must have been such a shock to find a dead body. I totally get that, but you're extremely emotional about the death of someone who wasn't a friend and who sounds like a real nut job."

I relaxed my grip on the phone. "You're right. We weren't friends. But that doesn't matter. I am certain that Marcia was murdered. The police said it was an accident, but they acted as if it was murder."

"If it was murder, I pick the ex-husband," Susan said, with some bitterness. "I was tempted to strangle at least two of mine, so my money is on him. What do you know about him?"

I closed my eyes, and with my free hand rubbed at my forehead, where a headache had taken root. "I don't know anything about him. I never met him.

The marriage didn't last long, and Marcia never talked about him, or anyone else. She didn't have any friends at the school, and never mentioned a human being who wasn't fictional or an author."

"Okay, so she was a very intellectual nut job," Susan groaned. "What did the detectives say when you gave them those papers you found?"

"Nothing, yet. I'm going to do that tomorrow. I didn't quite have time today." I tried to make my delay sound reasonable.

Susan let out her signature sign of exasperation. It sounded something like "puh." I could imagine her shaking her head at me through the phone. "You are also a nut job. Call the good-looking cop, give the papers to him, and let him decide if it's worth investigating. It's not your worry."

"I said I'd do it." *And I will do it. Right after I make a copy for myself.*

"Does any of this—do you think—?" She tried again. "Sweetie, have you considered the possibility that you're reacting this emotionally because of what happened to Mom? It's not like you to get so involved. You're the most risk-averse person I've ever met."

The headache spread to the back of my eyes. I got up and shook the last two Excedrin from the economy-sized bottle. "That's ridiculous. I'm not involved, I'm not risk-averse, and this has nothing to do with Mom. Those lesson plans fell in my lap." Susan is so tiresome. She harps on our past as if it holds the key to something important. But it doesn't. Faulkner, Fitzgerald—they both had it wrong. The past was dead. Dead and gone, and if it weren't for Susan, totally forgotten.

"If you don't want to talk about Mom's death—and you never do—let's talk about Alan Goldfarb's bar mitzvah," she said.

I swallowed the pills and some more soda. Excedrin and Diet Coke. Unlike the last six months of my marriage, it was a match made in heaven. "What the hell do the events from a bar mitzvah we attended thirty years ago have to do with Marcia's death? Have you heard a single word of what I've been telling you?"

"Are you sure it's been that long? Good God, we're getting old. Don't get yourself so worked up. Listen for a minute. I know it was like a hundred years ago, but I remember it as if it were yesterday."

Seduced by my sister's digression, I thought about that seminal event.

"I remember it pretty well," I admitted. "Grandpa was so angry that our family had such a terrible table. We were right behind the swinging doors to the kitchen, and every time a waiter came out Grandpa got smacked in the rear. How could I forget that?"

Susan laughed, and we began to reminisce. Mom and our father, aka The Lousy Bastard, drank whiskey sours. Really cool Uncle Bernie drank Harvey Wallbangers. Susan and I drank Shirley Temples, secure in the belief that this concoction was the height of sophistication.

Susan's tone sharpened. "After we left Alan's bar mitzvah, you said something felt weird. That's why, when you said you sensed something peculiar about Marcia's classroom, it reminded me of that night, and—"

Disbelief forced me to interrupt her. "I don't believe this. We were in junior high. You have trouble remembering a conversation we had last week."

"You don't give me enough credit," she snapped. "I didn't exactly have a great time at the bar mitzvah myself. After I fell off the bar stool following my fifth Shirley Temple, everyone laughed and asked if I was drunk. But to get back to the main topic—"

"The main topic is this murder at my school," I reminded her. "Do you think we could return the conversation to that issue?"

"For heaven's sake, be patient. It's all connected. After the party you defended me when The Lousy Bastard hit me in the head. Honestly, that's why I remember the bar mitzvah so well. You never did that before. God knows, Mom never stood up for us. But that night, you protected me." Susan's voice pitched a childish octave higher. "I love you."

"I love you, too, but I don't recall any of this, and I don't see any point in talking about our crappy childhood." As soon as the words were out of my mouth, the memory of Susan's bloodied hair rushed back. Her pretty hair, tied in a pink bow that was stained so badly it had to be thrown away.

Susan refused to let it go. "When I asked you why, you wouldn't explain. I always thought something happened that you wouldn't tell me. Mom died not too long after the bar mitzvah. I thought about it later, and I wondered if you'd found out the truth about The Lousy Bastard that night and never told anyone."

Typical Susan. I call her to talk about something important to me, and twenty minutes later we're on a forced trip down memory lane.

I swallowed the last of the soda. "I didn't find out anything that night, and there is no 'truth.' But I had this awful feeling that other people were talking about us behind our backs. I had the same feeling at Mom's funeral. I hated that feeling."

Susan was triumphant. "Exactly. You didn't know the details but you did know we had to figure things out. Well, same thing with this mess. Does something now make sense that, at the time, you might have dismissed? I mean, you're always telling me how great you are with reading books. Why can't you read people?"

Good question. Unfortunately, I didn't have a good answer. "I'm not good with people. They mystify me."

Susan laughed. "Yes! What do other people think about? Who knows? Who cares? Hey—try this, then. Think about what kind of fictional characters all of the potential suspects remind you of, and then maybe you'll be able to understand the real world. Then you can solve the murder!"

This wasn't the worst idea. Maybe that's what Marcia was doing with her lesson plans, connecting real people with fictional characters. I told Susan I'd think about it and call her back.

"Okay," I heard the triple click of the locks on her front door. "But don't call back tonight. I'm on my way out for a facial, manicure, and pedicure. Did I tell you I have a date for Friday?"

"Yeah, I think you mentioned it. I'll talk to you tomorrow."

I took Susan's advice. I thought about the murder of Marcia Deaver, and I thought about Alan Goldfarb's bar mitzvah. The buffet table was a marvel. Expensive fruit—cherries and grapes and glistening slices of kiwi—adorned every dish. Delighted by the excess, my sister and I denuded several platters of their garnishes. I also remember that conversations stopped whenever we walked by.

I lay down in bed and closed my eyes, the better to follow my young self through Le Parc Catering Hall in White Plains. Compared to us, Alan's parents were well off, and Le Parc, with its large vases of silk flowers, glossy parquet floors, and strings of twinkly lights seemed the very zenith of elegance.

Arlene and Ira Goldfarb greeted us in a subdued manner, quite without their usual warmth. Was that the first clue?

Heedless of Susan's spa treatments, I called her again. "Hey, whatever happened to Arlene and Ira? How come we stopped being friends with them and their kids?"

"Who the hell knows? Why do you care? I thought you were concerned with solving this murder at your school."

I sat up. "Well, you're the one who brought up Alan's bar mitzvah. I felt weird and embarrassed even before Grandpa started screaming at Arlene."

"I guess The Lousy Bastard borrowed money from them like he did from everyone else dumb enough to give it to him. People prefer to get paid back."

"I feel terrible about that." And so I did. Thirty years later, the humiliation still stung.

"Well, don't," answered my practical sister. "They had plenty of money and lived happily ever after."

Not like us.

In a tone that clearly telegraphed the end of Susan's interest in me, Marcia, and our shared past, she said, "I'm at the salon. I think I'll get highlights too. What do you think?"

"Brilliant. You'll look great."

Susan clicked a goodbye, and I returned to Le Parc. Something made me uneasy on the day Alan Goldfarb Became a Man, but my thirteen-year-old self didn't understand what it was. I was an adult before I realized most people at the bar mitzvah knew all about what The Lousy Bastard (aka Dear Old Dad) was up to. Everyone except Mom. My guess is she didn't know because she didn't want to know. Neither did I. I still don't.

If I were honest—and I feel honesty is vastly overrated—I knew plenty of secrets that night, so many years ago, while my parents and grandparents were fanned by the undignified breeze that the kitchen door flung their way every five minutes. I knew it when Susan fell off the barstool. I knew it when Ira and Arlene greeted my parents with less friendliness than they did the doorman.

About a year after the bar mitzvah, in the wake of my mother's death, I remained passive. I let the Lousy Bastard lie to me right up to the day he disappeared, and I never said a word to anyone, not even Susan. I should have been filled with rage, but I asked no questions and was careful not to give anyone any trouble. But now? I had enough fury in me to make up for millennia of silence. To hell with all of them.

CHAPTER 4
THEIR EYES WERE WATCHING GOD

The imaginary me had sex with a darkly brooding man with a complicated past. The real me nudged snoring George out of bed and got ready for work. I consoled myself for the loss of erotic excitement with the anticipation of teaching *Jane Eyre*, a book I've loved since I was twelve. Perhaps that is why the image of the young orphaned girl, cruelly banished to the Red Room, lives in my memory far more vividly than the adult Jane's pronouncement: "Reader, I married him."

Of course she married him, for God's sake. Charlotte Bronte takes her time—more than three hundred pages—before she permits Jane and Rochester to live happily ever after. George and I, on the other hand, were having a few problems. I waited for him to get out of the shower before I told him about Marcia's "lesson plans." George was as close to speechless as I'd ever seen him.

Finally, he said, "What on earth possessed you to read her files?" He went to the closet and yanked a clean shirt free of its plastic wrap.

"Why are you angry? Aren't you interested? Take a look."

George dropped his shirt and flipped through the papers. I knew he couldn't resist, any more than I could. He gave them back to me. "They don't make any sense. And they're private. What were you thinking?"

I tried not to get upset at George's unsympathetic tone. "Privacy has nothing to do with it. I wasn't looking to pry. As I've already explained to you, the envelope was stuck in between the keyboard panel and the top part of Marcia's desk. It launched itself into me five seconds after I found Marcia's dead body. I don't even remember taking it out of the room. Anyway, once I had it, as the new AP teacher it made sense to look at her lesson plans."

He gave the bedpost three quick taps to signal his impatience. "I thought you didn't find out you'd be teaching those classes until *after* you found the plans."

George's logic had never been less welcome.

I tapped the bedpost three times, mocking him. "You're missing the point. I did read them, so now what do I do?"

George doesn't yell, but he is a master of the enraged whisper. "You call the police and hand them over, which you should have done yesterday. Let them figure it out. I hope they don't end up arresting you."

I ignored him and studied the lesson plan for Oscar Wilde. I love Wilde's sense of humor, but Marcia's notes were menacing, not funny.

I realized George was waiting for me to answer. I shrugged. "Whose fault is that? You hung up on me."

George rooted around in his sock drawer, tossing socks that didn't make the cut into the trash. "I didn't hang up on you. You were complaining about that drama club."

I tried for a more conciliatory tone, but even I could tell my next words sounded sharp. "Let's not quibble."

George nearly snapped the buttons off his shirt. "Call the police, hand the papers over, and forget you ever saw them. Not that I think they mean much, of course."

"You can't have it both ways. Either they're irrelevant, in which case it doesn't matter when I give them to the police. Or, they're important, in which case we might be able to figure out what they mean." While George thought up a good answer, I reminded him, "The plans were hidden. Not locked away, but in a place obscure enough that they were unlikely to be easily found, other than by another English teacher."

"Whatever. But what that means, or doesn't mean, is not your problem. Hand them over and forget about them."

George was an English major, and although he ended up in the real estate business he is still a serious reader. He's also the smartest guy I know. I thought he'd at least want to discuss the literary references. But no. That office building in Brooklyn was more important to him.

I grabbed him by the lapels of his new sports jacket. "Unless the detectives majored in literature, I don't know what they're going to do with them. And I don't think they're gibberish. If you get rid of all the literary window dressing, what you have is a descriptive list of three people: someone who's preying on young girls, someone who's a forger or swindler or even a murderer, and some-one who probably made a gay porno movie. And that adds up to blackmail, which means there was nothing accidental about Marcia's death."

George, not without gentleness, pushed my hands away. "Let's not get ahead of ourselves." He studied the papers. "If Marcia were blackmailing people those numbers are probably her monthly payout. If you add it up it comes to $2,500. Pretty risky business for so little cash."

Since when was $2,500 a paltry amount of money? "That's after-tax dollars for a woman who's never going to get a raise of more than a fraction of a percent. It's not a million dollars, but it would make a nice cushion for her retirement. It would also explain her very expensive new outfit."

George finished dressing and said, "Be careful. Don't mention these papers to anyone at school. If they are evidence of blackmail, and that person knows you know it, you could be the next victim."

"No worries. It's not like I have a boatload of friends at work. I'll be careful."

"Careful won't cut it. Be smart, and don't blab." George leaned over but aborted his kiss when he caught sight of the clock. He ran to make the early train to New York.

I skipped breakfast and got to work an hour early. The parking lot was nearly empty, but the students had already blanketed the entrance to the school with bouquets of flowers and handwritten cards. I went inside and spent thirty minutes organizing my notes and commandeering the copy machine before I became conscious of a growing commotion outside.

I opened the window. Below, several girls loudly moaned their sorrow over the loss of their favorite teacher. I peered outside. Several news vans, dozens of cars, and hundreds of people crowded the parking lot.

Directly beneath the window, the captain of the cheerleading team wailed, "Dr. Deaver was, like, the most awesome teacher! We totally cannot imagine high school without her." With an air of great bravery and dedication she added, "All of us are going to wear a black armband in her memory to all of the football games."

I am certain if Marcia were alive she would have gored the kid for her assaults on the English language, but the reporter and camera crew who recorded the girl's sorrow did not seem at all put out. The trim, blonde, perfectly shod and coiffed newswoman offered the camera an expression of horrified sympathy. The rest of the cheerleading team wailed in unison. Parents were equally voluble, if a bit less emotional.

The cameraman moved closer to the building. The window of the copy room was directly behind the cheerleaders, and fearful I would appear on the nightly news, I walked outside for a better and less conspicuous vantage point.

The newswoman said, "The loss of a teacher is a tragedy, but the murder of a teacher, less than twenty-four hours before the students were set to arrive for the first day of school, makes the whole situation even more serious."

Murder? Twenty-four hours ago, Marcia's death was a tragic accident. I edged closer to the reporter.

She said, "I have here the principal of the school, Gordon McConnell. Sir, what can you tell us about what happened here? Is it safe to return?"

After a few honks and false starts, Gordon stated, "Dr. Deaver's death is a tragedy for the entire Valerian Hills community. Our sympathies go out to the Deaver family."

The reporter persisted. "But what about the children? And what about the other teachers? Can you guarantee their safety?"

Red patches broke out on Gordon's face. He said, "I want to make it clear that everything is being done to ensure the safety of our students and staff. We are working closely with the police department."

I was not confident that either Gordon or the police would understand how Marcia's love of literature, as well as her obsession with Shakespeare conspiracy theories, informed her life. I supposed plenty of people could analyze Marcia's lesson plans besides me, but would the police consult any of the English teachers?

I was uniquely qualified to assist in this investigation. After spending many of my formative years with The Lousy Bastard, I was an expert in deception, as well as literature. It's not every man who can harbor two wives and two sets of children in the same borough for fifteen years, but The Lousy Bastard had managed it.

Still, there was no reason to get involved. I could hand over the lesson plans and forget about them. I could, in fact, do what I did more than thirty years ago—let fear and indecision keep me quiet. George said Marcia's death was none of my business. But when does something become our business, whether or not we want it to? Substitute lesson plans are also known as emergency plans. I was Marcia's substitute. This was an emergency.

Marcia was talking to me.

CHAPTER 5

KING, QUEEN, KNAVE

I'll admit to a few weaknesses. I'm no hero. And I hate pain. Also, I don't like the outdoors and loathe being in the sun. I get nervous in closed rooms, and I'm not fond of high altitudes. You won't find me anywhere near a circus, especially the clowns. I figured my investigation would not put me in any of those situations, and that I ran no risk of encountering insects or rodents (including guinea pigs and hamsters.) Deciphering the coded messages in Marcia's lesson plans meant that my investigation would take place in the comfortable confines of my own head. No risk, no pain. A purely intellectual exercise. More exciting than the crossword puzzle and less risky than bungee jumping.

After the news crew left, Gordon stepped forward again. He did his usual harrumphing and humming. This time the tune bore a faint resemblance to the first few notes of Beethoven's Fifth Symphony, but without the passion and menace. Many of the questions were from parents made nearly incoherent over the possibility that Dr. Marcia Deaver would not be able to write college recommendations for their kids. Gordon was forced to admit that since Marcia was dead she would not be writing any more gems. There was a moment of stunned silence and a collective groan.

Eventually, we got the kids in the school and the parking lot cleared. The school psychologist and the nurse planned a series of grief counseling sessions, and the rest of us pretended this was a typical first day of school.

I've been teaching for more than ten years, and I know what to do and how to do it. Still, I was uncomfortable. It's not all that easy to take over from a dead person. I could tell from snippets I'd overheard in the hallway that the students had beatified Marcia.

I looked over the first group of the day and gauged them in the minutes before the class officially began. I started this class, as I do every year on the first day of school, by telling students that English is the most important subject and that my class is the most important class. I am perfectly serious when I say this, but it always gets a big laugh. I'm philosophical about that. I figure, by the end of the year I may convince a few kids I'm right. In high school, hope springs eternal in September.

I was midsentence when a six-foot tall boy with the neck of a bull and the scrunched up features of a spoiled baby chimp strolled in, took a seat in front of me, and effectively blocked the view of three tiny girls behind him. On his way he high-fived a few boys and appeared not to notice the fawning and forgiving giggles of the girls. Even without the roster I recognized him. He was a fearsome football player and a notorious jackass. Appropriately enough, his name is Jack. Jack Tumbleson, the only child of the president of the Valerian Hills Board of Education.

The students' interest in my class sharpened, as they waited to see my reaction. I ignored Jack until he snapped his fingers and waved his hand in front of my face, apparently confusing his desk at school with a seat at a ball game.

"What'd I miss?" he asked, without waiting for me to acknowledge him.

Obviously, what he missed was someone who would have taught him some manners, but I knew better than to let him dictate the dialogue. I handed out the syllabus and stayed dispassionate. "I'll let you know after school."

"Hey! I got football practice. I can't make it." He waited, but I didn't respond. He clarified the situation for me, "I'm captain of the team."

I didn't debate the issue, since I don't argue with kids. If the kid wins, the teacher loses the students' respect. If the teacher wins, she's one-upped a kid and loses her self-respect. Thwarted in his attempt to get a rise out of me, Jack settled into a quiet, possibly semi-comatose state, and I proceeded with the planned lesson.

The rest of the day went well. Jack failed to show up after school, but twin girls from my first period class paid me a visit. They were equally blonde and bubbly.

"Oh, hi, Ms. Hopewell!" Brittany (or possibly, Bethany) caroled. I greeted them and waited.

"We came here to check with you about the writing assignment," they said, in a charming sweet falsetto that high-achieving students are so good at.

I chatted with them for a few moments, and then the more talkative one mentioned, "You know, Ms. Hopewell, Dr. Deaver never would have let Jack into the class."

I thought about this. Was it because Jack was a jackass? That seemed reasonable. Unable to stop myself I asked, "Why not? Because he was late? It was a difficult first day of school."

Brittany and Bethany looked at each other and raised mirror-image eyebrows. "No, that's not why. He signed up for the class last spring, but Dr. Deaver said he was not Advanced Placement material. His mother called the principal and the superintendent and they got him in, but even so, anyone who shows up on the first day of school can't stay in the class if they don't complete the summer assignment. His mom is the president of the board of education, but it still doesn't seem fair."

They bleated the last few words nearly in unison.

Damn it. All the other students had arrived on time and had handed in ten-page essays. All except Jack. Who was the jackass now? I tried not to show my chagrin, but the B&B twins understood. After all, they weren't stupid.

I thanked the girls, and they smiled and left, but not before informing me that *their* mom had been elected president of the Home and School Association and would be calling me very soon about graduation plans. I told them I looked forward to talking to their mom, which was partly true. I anticipated that conversation with all the eagerness of a visit to the dentist, which, once over, is occasionally not as bad as the dread that precedes it. Their mission accomplished, the two girls left for a student council meeting.

I looked at my desk. One day. Over one hundred essays. Each essay ten pages. And it was still the first official day of school. I walked into the English office, determined to finally take possession of my students' writing folders.

All the other English teachers were squeezed into the narrow dusty space. I had forgotten that we had a meeting, but I was damned if I would admit it.

Caroline flicked a nod in my direction. "Awfully good of you to stop by." She gestured to the new face in the room. "As you can see, Ashlee Becker is back, this time as a member of our department."

I turned to Emily and tried to telegraph my annoyance with Caroline. Emily, however, was her usual quiet, inscrutable self. Bill, of course, was no help. He stared at Ashlee, looking even happier than he did in 2009, when the Yankees won the World Series.

Caroline pursed her mouth as if an especially sour fruit had invaded it. "Ashlee received her teaching degree from William Patterson University a few months ago, and she will be taking your place, Liz. So please be generous with your time." She turned to Ashlee and informed her, "We're all here for you if you need us, but really, Liz is the person who will help you out. You'll be teaching her classes. Not mine."

Ashlee was medium height, beautifully slender, and apparently would be competing with the high school students in the Inappropriate Wardrobe Department. Her skirt covered approximately twelve inches of real estate, beginning well below her navel and ending slightly south of her crotch. She looked like English Teacher Barbie, with the same perky nose, sweet smile, and blank expression as the eleven-inch doll. She stared at her phone as we walked across the hall to my classroom.

When I began working at Valerian Hills High School, my new colleagues guarded their lesson plans with more fervor than the Dementors did the prisoners at Azkaban. Although things have eased up a bit since then, we are still not terribly collegial. I was determined not to follow their pernicious example. I showed Ashlee my files and promised to email her all of my materials, including the lesson plans.

Moving her gum to a more convenient section of her mouth she informed me, "Actually, I got my own stuff."

Of course. What possible use could my files be to someone of her expertise?

"Great!" I worked hard to make my answer sound enthusiastic, rather than sarcastic.

Ashlee, unaware of any subtext, opened a closet door and inspected the contents. "Hey, thanks, no offense, right? In school the professors told us to, like, be on our guard against the old teachers, who are still doing things the old-fashioned way, y'know what I mean?"

Oh, I knew.

Ashlee circled the room as she spoke. "There is one teeny little thing you could do to help. Since I'm teaching your classes, don't you think it would be easier for me to take your room? And then, like, you could move into the other room? Timmy thought that would work best for me. You can leave everything here, and I'll use it if I got nothing else."

Ashlee was so annoying my first reaction was a stunned refusal, but I stopped myself in time. If I moved into Marcia's room I'd have complete access to her files, as well as to whatever else she might have hidden. If Marcia had left any other coded messages, I was probably the only one who would recognize them for what they were. Also, the setup of Marcia's classroom, with its interior door that led to the English office, would make it easy to eavesdrop. I agreed to make the change.

Her mission accomplished, she turned to leave, but paused as she got to the door. "Were you friends with the teacher who died? I didn't get to know her last year, when I was student teaching, and I never had her when I was a student." This wasn't exactly news. If Marcia had her way, she wouldn't have let Ashlee sign up for admittance to *Homo sapiens*, let alone her precious Advanced Placement class.

Ashlee shuddered and said, "But, I mean, like, everyone told me to watch out for her. They said she was a real, oh, you, know. An ugly old, uh 'witch.'" She put air quotes around the word witch, and left her perusal of her phone to train her pale green eyes at me. "You found her, didn't you?"

I swallowed the lump in my throat. "Yes, I did. And it was awful."

Ashlee nodded sagely. "My first year at college I had a roommate who tried to commit suicide."

I began to feel more sympathy for her. After all, she was still a kid. "I'm so sorry, Ashlee. How did she—how did it happen?"

"Pills." She clicked her tongue, in that universal signal of either pity or disdain. "It was seriously disturbing."

"Did you find her?"

She wrinkled her adorable little nose. "Yeah. Hello? It was, ugh, totally gruesome. My luck! I had to call 911 and then—" Ashlee's voice rose—"I had to ride in the ambulance with her! She didn't want to be alone."

I walked over to her. "That was very good of you."

Ashlee looked at her phone and laughed before turning back to me. "Yeah, but I mean, even though we were roommates I totally didn't know her. It's not like I told her to take the pills. Anyway, I had already told everyone in the dorm how crazy she was, and believe me, people felt really sorry for me, even before the whole suicide thing. The whole experience totally creeped me out. Plus, she was fat."

Once again, I reminded myself of Ashlee's youth. "Your roommate was deeply unhappy."

Ashlee shrugged. "Whatever. But some people need to get a life, y'know what I mean? Like, don't spend all day stuffing your face and then moan about how everything sucks. Like Dr. Deaver. She had no life either." Ashlee brightened. "But, her bad, my good! 'Cause now I've got this awesome job!"

I wanted to dent her indifference with a hatchet, and thus was not overly gentle in reminding her, "Feeling empathy for others is part of what makes us human."

"I have feelings." Ashlee wound a long strand of bright blonde hair around two fingers, twirled the ends, and got a faraway look in her eyes. "But it was still pretty fantastic to end up with a private room as a freshman. And it's pretty fantastic now to get this job. I've always been lucky that way, if you know what I mean."

Ten more minutes with Ashlee and Marcia wouldn't be the only murder victim. "If you don't mind, Ashlee, can you help me move some of these books and files into the other room? If we're going to switch rooms I'd like to get it done as soon as possible." I got the cart from the English office and started loading it with books.

Ashlee ignored the cart, the books, and my request. "I'd love to help, but I have a nail appointment. I was totally surprised by Timmy's phone call, and I need to get ready for teaching!" She examined her fingertips.

As much as I wanted to get rid of Ashlee, I couldn't help asking, "How did you happen to get the job so quickly? I didn't think it was even posted."

"I network." She laughed and tipped her head back, as if swigging a shot of whiskey. "Like, last year, when I was student teaching here, I organized these Friday afternoon pub crawls? They got, y'know, popular. So everybody started coming. Timmy, lots of teachers, even Gordon came to a few. So, they figured I'd really fit in well here."

Before I could further query my new colleague, Ashlee's cell phone jingled again. She signaled her goodbye with a flutter of soon-to-be-manicured fingertips.

I was in the middle of moving my files and books when I received help from an unexpected quarter. Jack Tumbleson, the Advanced Placement Jackass, showed up and without asking began loading a cart with my belongings.

"Ms. Hopewell! What'd I miss?" he laughed.

I chucked a few more files onto the cart. "I thought you had football practice?"

"Oh, that. I told Coach I'd be a few minutes late."

I sat down with him. Thanks to Brittany and Bethany, the B&B twins, I remembered to ask him for the summer homework.

"Oh, yeah, right, the summer homework," he repeated. He smiled in a way that I'm sure worked like magic on his mother. "You will not believe what happened. My computer crashed last night and I lost all my work. I'll make it up, I swear. Gimme a few days. Next Friday for sure. Or Monday at the latest. Honest."

Marcia would have tossed him out on his affable ass, but I lack her grit. I told him he could hand in the work and stay in the class, but that I would subtract points from his grade. He protested. I temporized. I am so spineless sometimes. It occurred to me that Jack, and his notoriously belligerent parents, benefited from Marcia's death, although it would be difficult to convince anyone outside our insanely competitive community that entry into an advanced level class is sufficient motive for murder.

Finally, I got rid of him, and I called Detective Harriman.

"Harriman here." His voice was flat, with a too-busy-to-talk sound in it.

"Hi, this is Liz. Liz Hopewell. From Valerian Hills High School." Despite an afternoon breeze that cooled off my un-air conditioned classroom, I started to sweat. My forehead, my arms, even my hands felt slippery and damp.

"I know who you are, Liz." He sounded amused.

"Oh. Well then, I wanted to let you know, that is, hmm, I found some evidence, some papers that belonged to Marcia, and I think that you should have them." Yes, I can be quite articulate when I rehearse.

"What kind of papers, Liz?" Harriman's next words made me sweat even more. "You know what? I'm headed in that direction. Why don't I meet you in your classroom?"

I was not nervous, because I didn't do anything wrong, other than hold onto what might or might not be important evidence for about twenty-four hours, which isn't that bad. It wasn't as if I planned to tell him about my procrastination. I smoothed my hair and looked in the mirror. My cheeks were flushed. I looked guilty, but good.

Ten minutes later Harriman walked in. "So, what do you have for me?" I handed him Marcia's "lesson plans." He flipped through the pages. "I don't get it. Why are you giving me Marcia's teacher files?"

"They're her substitute lesson plans. Her emergency plans. Except they're not what they seem to be. They're full of errors and weird notations."

The detective looked more closely at the cover page, and then shook his head. "How is that evidence? Do you think it points to her state of mind? People make mistakes."

I stood next to him and pointed to the title of the first lesson plan. "Marcia wouldn't make these kinds of mistakes. High schools don't teach *Lolita*, or any book in which adult men have sex with pre-pubescent girls. This is a very conservative town. A few years ago, two board of education members wanted to ban *Catcher in the Rye* and *Huck Finn*."

Harriman tilted his head and shifted his gaze from the lesson plans to me. "What made you decide to go through her papers?"

His tone was neutral, but his eyes were cold. I hurried to explain myself. "Well, it was a—an accident. The envelopes inside the folders were marked with the titles of books and I, well, I was interested in her—in her lesson plans. The English department is not what you might call a collegial group, and—don't get me wrong, I'm not complaining—I felt a professional interest, I would never..." Having lost both the subject and all possible objects of this sentence I stopped talking.

Harriman put the papers back in the envelope and the envelope back in the folder. "Liz, this is my job. If you're worried that you're responsible in some way, don't be. You're not."

I eyed the closed folder. "What are you going to do with this information?"

Harriman sat on the edge of my desk. "That remains to be seen. It might not be relevant to her death. And by the way, you can stop worrying about the condition of Dr. Deaver's classroom. If you think that was a mess, you should have seen her apartment. Every inch was covered in books and papers. There was only a narrow passage through all the junk, about a foot wide. There was barely enough room to walk from one room to the next."

I imagined stacks of the *New York Review of Books* and *The New Yorker*. Maybe Marcia collected avant-garde literary journals with titles like *The Clytemnestra Quarterly*. "What kind of books and papers did you find?"

Harriman shrugged. "So far, nothing that looks important. Just a lot of junk about Shakespeare."

Junk about Shakespeare? "I'm sure I told you that Marcia was obsessed with Shakespeare. Maybe there's a clue in all that junk."

Harriman didn't look convinced, but he didn't leave, so I kept going.

I held out my hand, and he gave me back the folder. "All of the citations in her lesson plans are from *Hamlet*. Two of them are definite threats." I pulled out the lesson plan on *The Talented Mr. Ripley* and recited, "They did make love to this employment."

I paused, but Harriman said nothing.

I prompted him, "Just so you know—the people Hamlet's talking about— they betray him. But he outsmarts them, and they die instead of Hamlet. That is, until the end when Hamlet dies, along with pretty much everyone else."

Harriman looked over my shoulder at the writing. "That would make more sense if Dr. Deaver were the killer."

"It would also make sense if Marcia knew that someone else committed murder," I argued. The next quotation provided the best evidence of blackmail, and I put as much expression as I could into the speech. "'Be thou as chaste as ice, as pure as snow, thou shalt not escape calumny.' Calumny—get it? Calumny is slander, the kind of thing that ruins your reputation. The kind of thing a blackmailer would use as leverage."

Harriman loosened his tie and sat back down. "I'm not ruling this stuff out, but it would take a team of experts to find anything useful in Dr. Deaver's house. And a team of ditch diggers. The piles of paper were as tall as you are. Dr. Deaver seems to have been one of those wacky pack rats, and that doesn't provide much in the way of motive."

I tried not to sound too eager. "Well, I'm not an expert, but I could take a look."

"No, Liz. Not possible. I appreciate the offer, but no."

That was fine with me. I didn't want to get too involved. That was the last thing I wanted. No sane person gets personally entangled in a murder investigation. Still, I did have that purely intellectual interest in the progress of the investigation, as any normal person would have. I was also worried. Tom didn't seem to understand that those worthless papers might be the key to Marcia's death. Marcia's killer.

There was no subtle way to ask what I wanted to know, so I just blurted it out. "How did you determine that she was murdered?"

"Her coffee. The meds were in the coffee. If she'd taken them herself, they would have been present only in the stomach contents."

So that was it. An easy deduction. And yet, I was unsatisfied. Harriman's description of Marcia's house made the woman I thought I knew for the last ten years recede even further.

Harriman broke into my thoughts. "Have you shown these to anyone else?"

I was happy to be able to tell the nearly unadulterated truth. George did not qualify as "anyone else." And my discussion with Susan was very general.

"No. I didn't tell anyone else about the papers."

Harriman nodded. He got up and walked towards the door, but he didn't leave. He examined the bookshelves that line one wall and picked up a copy of Jane Austen's *Persuasion*.

"Is this the kind of thing English teachers like?" he asked.

I wasn't sure what he was after. Was he preparing a monograph on the habits of English teachers?

I looked at the pale green cover and delicate black letters. "A lot of people like it. I know I do."

He opened the book and examined the frontispiece, which depicted a street in the city of Bath. "Do you mind if I borrow it?"

I agreed to let him borrow it, even though people never return books. But to deny someone a book is to consign oneself to the lowest rung of English Teacher Hell.

Harriman skimmed through a few pages while I packed my bag with student papers. He offered to walk me to my car.

Over my protests, he carried the heavy book bag for me. "Don't worry so much. And don't be stupid. Don't talk to anyone about anything. Anyone at all."

"Oh, no, I definitely will not do that, especially since I always thought she was murdered."

"That's what I mean." He stopped walking to look at me. "Don't talk like that around your fellow teachers."

I pulled at the book bag to get him moving again. "Do you have any other information that didn't make it to this morning's news report?"

"I can't discuss it with you."

This time I was the one who stopped. "Why not? I gave you evidence. You owe me."

Over his shoulder, he said, "No, I don't owe you. But I will give you my cell number. Call me if you need me, or if you find anything of relevance. And try to stay out of trouble." He gave me his card and closed his fingers around mine, dropping my hand a millisecond before I was going to pull it away. He looked at me sideways, out of dark blue eyes. I usually find blue eyes shallow and unappealing. His were deep and unreadable.

"You must be joking. I'm terrified of trouble, in fact I—" I stopped talking as a slight crackle emanated from the loudspeaker. I waited for the announcement, but all that followed was a soft click. I put my finger to my lips. Harriman stayed silent as he followed me into the parking lot and out of the range of electronically enabled eavesdroppers.

"Timmy and Gordon spy on us via the public address system. I don't want them or anyone else listening in," I whispered, even though there was no one to hear.

"Is that typical?"

I beckoned him to follow me farther away from the video camera that surveyed the area outside the exit door.

I took the book bag from him. "Shush. I don't know. I don't know why anyone would be listening after three o'clock. When Gordon and Timmy decide to go after a teacher they listen in during the toughest classes. They wait until an awkward moment, and then they do an unscheduled observation. Then they can put a bad report in the teacher's personnel record."

Harriman, forgetting he had said he would walk me to my car, ditched me and headed back into the school, presumably to the main office. It wasn't until I was driving home that I realized that not only was I in danger of being overheard by a disembodied eavesdropper, I also risked being overheard by anyone who stopped by the English office. The door that connected Marcia's classroom made it just as easy for someone in the office to listen to me as it did for me to listen to him or her. No wonder Marcia put up the No Exit sign. I was in a veritable hell of other people.

CHAPTER 6
THE ORIGIN OF THE SPECIES

Neither often-read novels nor reruns of the top ten most boring *Nature* programs were sufficient to overcome my insomnia. I tiptoed into the den, careful not to disturb George, and pulled out my laptop. The lesson plans contained evidence about a possible motivation for murder; the only problem was that I couldn't figure them out. Putting Marcia's obscure notes aside, I made a list of people who had the best opportunity to poison her coffee. This did not indicate a decision to more actively involve myself in the murder investigation. It was part of a purely rational interest in my fellow human beings.

I closed my eyes and tried not to worry about the irregular creaks, sighs, and groans of our very old house. When we moved from the city to the suburbs, I chose Victorian period details over comfort and convenience, but all this historic quirkiness came at a price. One minute you're joking about the funny noises coming from upstairs, and the next you're emptying buckets of water from your landmarked roof.

I mentally walked myself back into the auditorium. Marcia had been in hot pursuit of her missing chair, and she hadn't been at the meeting. Even under normal circumstances, Marcia didn't need a compelling reason to shrug off faculty meetings, and neither Timmy nor Gordon had the stomach to address her delinquency.

Had she been in attendance during the motivational speech we endured on the first day of school, I can guarantee she wouldn't have embarrassed herself by dancing to an old disco hit by The Village People. Last June, Marcia told the guest lecturer she wasn't going to let some "Gen Y kid with a phony degree from an online university" tell her how to teach English literature.

It occurred to me that Marcia's mordant wit concerning "phony degrees" might relate to the notes she'd written on *The Talented Mr. Ripley*. The title character was a forger and a cheat. I tried to figure out what other coded messages Marcia might have sent.

"What in God's name are you doing?" George's voice broke into my concentration with the startling force of a midnight text message alert.

I nearly fainted. "What am I doing? What are you doing, sneaking up on me like that?"

"I live here. And I was fast asleep when I had a nightmare that a herd of wild animals was charging through the house. Which, apparently, they are."

The television revealed two elephants furiously copulating. It didn't look like much fun for either of them.

Although George's tone was not inviting, I was happy to have some company. "I couldn't sleep. I can't stop thinking of poor Marcia Deaver and wondering who could have done such an awful thing. I hope it wasn't anyone I know."

George grabbed the remote control for the television and punched the off button. "This isn't a game, Liz. You'd better watch out. If you don't stop meddling in affairs that are none of your business, Marcia Deaver may not be the last victim."

"Is that supposed to be funny?"

George was grim. "Of course not. And don't be so defensive. I'm not threatening you, although the temptation is there. I'm reminding you that there is a cold killer loose in that school of yours, and for some reason you want to put yourself in the middle of a situation that may be extremely dangerous. I want you to stop this. It's not a game." He paused before delivering the sucker punch. "Do you want to put the kids and me in danger as well? I can't allow you to do that."

It takes a lot to wake my kids, but even they would have been roused by the volume I wished I could use. "You can't *allow* me? You're not my father."

George was calmer than he should have been. "No, but I'm Ellie and Zach's father. I have to protect them, even if the person threatening them is you."

The space that my lungs need to function got smaller. "That's not fair. I haven't done anything! All I've done is think about it. What are you, the thought police?"

George looked at me without affection. "You've been like a different person since you found Marcia. Why doesn't the thought of murder scare the crap out you? Because it sure as hell scares the crap out of me. I hate the thought that you're even inside the building where a murder took place. It could be some lunatic who's going after English teachers after having some bizarre experience with, I don't know, *Beowulf* or something. That would make you a natural target." He narrowed his lips and eyes into parallel lines, an expression I loathe. "You haven't discussed this with anyone, have you?"

"Of course not." I'm a good liar, which George knows perfectly well. George is not a good liar, because he doesn't practice and he lacks the necessary motivation. He didn't believe me, but he didn't argue.

He turned to leave. "If possible, I'm going back to sleep. If you're smart, you'll do the same. But whatever you do, don't talk to anyone at school. Don't talk to anyone in the neighborhood. Remember, the killer could be anyone. You may be good at analyzing literary characters, but your track record with actual humans isn't as impressive. So don't blab to anyone. You'll probably end up confiding in the murderer."

George's warning made me angry and anxious. That made me hungry, and I foraged in the kitchen for a while. There are few foods I don't like; even so, the pickings were slim. I settled for two Excedrin and one Diet Coke. After the double dose of caffeine the possibility of sleep receded even further. I was still angry with George, but I acknowledged to myself that his words had some element of truth to them. It would have been easier for me to admit it to him if he'd said them less angrily.

I did doze for a few hours and got through the next day without falling asleep in front of my students. Most of them returned the favor. At 2:55 I positioned myself at the door, so that I could waylay Emily on her way out. At 3:01 she exited her classroom, just ahead of the students.

"Hey, Emily! Got a minute?"

Emily slowed, but did not stop. "I'd love to, Liz, but my daughter has a doctor's appointment today."

Sometimes I wonder if Emily really spends every second of her time with Mavis, or if her daughter is just a convenient excuse. It will be interesting to see what happens when Mavis graduates from high school. I walked alongside her. "That's okay. My mistake—I thought you said Mavis's doctor's appointment was a few days ago."

Emily turned pink. "No, really! This is an eye doctor appointment."

Instead of heading to the parking lot, she beckoned me to follow her into the cafeteria, which was deserted at that time of day. "I didn't want to put you on the spot, and you don't have to tell me, of course, but I am curious about, well, what exactly were you doing the other day in the office...you know..."

Oh, I knew. Even the most incurious of humans had to wonder about my aborted attempt to break into Marcia's classroom. I had my answer ready. I figured Emily had no way of knowing I didn't find out about my change in schedule until after the telephone call.

"Since I'm teaching the AP classes I wanted to pick through Marcia's files. That was pretty embarrassing, though, when you came back to the office and found me stuck in the door!" I chuckled at the silliness of it all.

"Liz, the room was closed off. Were you really going to break in?" Emily would no sooner ignore a rule than she would her much indulged, highly demanding daughter. "You aren't concerned about the investigation into Marcia's death, are you?"

"Of course not! You sound like George. He gave me strict orders to stay as far away as possible." I was grateful for her interest and concern, and so I stayed very still. I was worried any move on my part would remind her she had to leave. If she had to leave.

"Are you going to listen to him?" Emily shivered, mimicking fright. "I don't want to get involved at all."

I searched for the right words, so Emily, or someone, could understand how I felt. And then I realized that I couldn't tell her anything without talking about Marcia's lesson plans. But if I couldn't confide in her, I could get information from her.

"Hey, that reminds me, do you remember seeing Marcia at the Back to School meeting? Or before that? Her chair was missing, and she was giving everyone the third degree. She even accused me. When was the last time you saw her?"

Emily's mouth opened, closed, and opened again. "I—I'm not sure. When Marcia goes to meetings she usually stands in the back. I'll think about it."

I pressed her, as gently as I could. "Where were you sitting? I looked for you, but I didn't see you. Did you blow it off?"

"Of course not!" Emily's face went from pink to red, and she became fascinated with a loose thread on her shirt. "I was a few minutes late. I sat off to the side, way in the back. I might have been in the bathroom when you looked for me."

I did not ask if she had stayed long enough to see my gyrations to "YMCA," and she was diplomatic enough not to mention it if she did.

"Let me know how the investigation proceeds," she said. "Maybe you should wait for me before you do any detecting. But don't start today, because I really do have to go." We exited the cafeteria, but before Emily could make her getaway Caroline swanned into the hallway and over to us.

"Why, if it isn't the dynamic duo!" she purred.

Emily responded with an authentic sounding sneeze and cough. She weakly waved her hand to indicate her inability to soldier on and abandoned me.

I turned to Caroline, and said with what I hoped was a tone of total disinterest, "Hi, Caroline, I was thinking of the presentation we had on the first day of school. Do you remember whether or not Marcia was at the meeting? I feel so awful about her death, and I was trying to remember the last time I saw her."

Caroline looked at me over reading glasses framed in tortoise shell and gold. "Well, look at you, Nancy Drew! No, dear, I don't remember whether or not Marcia was there, for the simple reason that I was not there myself. Department chairs got a pass out of the meeting, in order to prepare our own departmental agenda. Sorry to disappoint you. Ta-ta!" And with that upper class British brush-off, she left.

The school emptied, and the halls were quiet. Late afternoon was the best time to embark upon my own criminal endeavors, i.e., absconding with library books. I never officially check books out of the library, because after one week the librarian, now known as the media specialist, starts sending me nervously animated, emoticon-filled emails to remind me that the books are overdue. She sends them everyday. It's easier for both of us if I sneak the books out of the library. If I wait until after school, I have only the custodians to deal with, and they don't care how many books I take.

I roamed through the stacks of books and selected the half dozen on my list. On my way out I heard the back door of the library open.

I didn't hear any footsteps, which was odd. I called a greeting to my fellow book lover. Whoever entered from the parking lot didn't respond.

I tried again. "Is anyone there?" My voice sounded embarrassingly high pitched. On my next attempt, I made an effort to sound more authoritative. "May I help you?" Okay, so maybe that wasn't the most powerful approach, but it was all I had.

Still no response.

I ignored the sudden rapid beating of my heart. This was my chance to investigate. Who besides the cleaning staff or me would visit the library after hours? A guilty person, that's who.

I stepped back toward the bookshelves and held my breath. No noise. I walked with heavy tread to the hall door, opened it, and then loudly closed it. I remained inside the library, so the lurking criminal would think I had left. I listened again, but I was now too far away to hear anything. I silently backtracked. A faint rustling sound came from the stacks. Terrified it might be a mouse, I bolted.

On the other side of the double doors I reconsidered my retreat. Where was my sense of adventure? I realized, for about the thousandth time, that I hate adventure. People who embark upon adventures get hurt. But if Juliet could defy her parents and lie all night in a crypt, if Rosalind and Celia could run away to the Forest of Arden, if — well, if only I too could be brave.

I resolutely cast myself as a romantic heroine and took out my pen, in case I needed a weapon. I put my library books on the floor and steeled myself for combat, despite the fact that I was the least menacing kid in all of Brooklyn's Nostrand Avenue projects. The only two times I couldn't avoid a fistfight I got beat up pretty badly.

I banished my ten-year-old self and summoned Xena, the Warrior Princess.

Two steps later, that vision of my muscular alter ego receded, and instead I saw myself as a character in a horror movie, not the brave and beautiful one who survives, but the stupid and annoying one who is deaf to the menacing music and gets ambushed by the serial killer who then eviscerates her in an underground rat-infested bunker. (Full disclosure: I'm too afraid to watch scary movies, but I devour the reviews.)

Once again, I vacillated. I'm less afraid of human vermin than animal vermin. I had no idea this would prove to be such a liability.

The late afternoon sunlight mocked me. Breathing heavily, I braced myself to face whatever—or whoever—lurked within. I peered one last time down the hallway. Timmy, the assistant principal, stepped through the stairway door and headed in my direction. I rearranged my face, and replaced my plucky amateur investigator look with a bemused English teacher expression.

"Liz! Why are you still here?" Timmy asked.

In some school districts, working long hours is a virtue, but in Valerian Hills it is regarded with suspicion.

"Oh, I thought I left a book here, but I realize now that I didn't."

Timmy looked at the books on the floor.

I gave a laugh that even to me sounded fake. "Early senility, I guess. So sad when that happens."

Timmy didn't laugh. He looked puzzled. Then it occurred to me: What the hell was *he* doing there? His office and his parking spot were located at the opposite end of the building and two floors down. Timmy stepped around me, reversing our relative positions. Now he had his back to the library door. "If you'll excuse me, Liz, I have to check out something in the Media Center."

"Can I help?"

Timmy shook his head. "It's nothing. You look tired, Liz. You should go home and get some rest. This has been a difficult time for all of us. Go home to your family."

I nodded at Timmy's wisdom and turned as if I were headed back to my classroom. After a few steps I looked back. Timmy had not yet entered the library. He had his foot in the doorway, keeping the door ajar while he thumbed at his cell phone.

I walked through the doors of the same stairwell he'd used and waited. After a moment I stuck my head out. The hall was empty, and I figured Timmy was finally inside the library. The boys' bathroom was across the hall. I decided to stay there, with the door cracked open, until Timmy emerged.

Five agonizing minutes passed. Who knew how long Timmy would remain in the library? I worried he might exit through the library's back door. Perhaps it would be better to station myself in the parking lot. I checked my watch and my aching feet and decided to quit. I opened the bathroom door as quietly as I could and found myself staring at Alberto Silva, one of the custodians. It's hard to say who was more surprised. Alberto checked the sign on the door, to make sure it still read Boys Bathroom. I pretended to look at the sign with him.

"Oh my! I forgot my eyeglasses today!" I said, as if the lineup of six urinals failed to persuade me that I was in the wrong place. Alberto stared at me, smiled uncertainly, and asked if it was okay for him to start cleaning.

"Of course! I'll see you tomorrow! Have a nice day! I strolled down the hall, and before turning the corner, looked back. The custodian continued to gaze at me. I smoothed my hair and realized that my eyeglasses were perched on my head. I waved at him. He lifted two awkward fingers.

"*Hasta mañana!*" I called.

He smiled. "*Hasta mañana.*"

That's me. Ms. *Mañana*.

Chapter 7

The Secret Sharer

At the end of the following day I graded papers until the halls were clear of students and staff. As the daughter of a small-time crook and con man, I didn't have to worry about the logistics of breaking and entering. When I was a kid we were locked out of several apartments after nonpayment of rent, and I learned the finer points of picking a lock by the time I was nine. The Lousy Bastard figured no one would arrest a kid, so he used to send me in alone. I got pretty good at it, but I'm a little rusty now. It's been awhile since I've had to evade creditors, landlords, and the local bookies.

I tested my skills by breaking into my own classroom first, to see if a credit card would work. In a pinch I could use two bobby pins, but that usually takes longer, and I didn't relish the thought of any more embarrassing encounters with the custodians. One episode of being caught in the boys' bathroom was enough. A second proof of bizarre behavior might make me the poster girl for What's Wrong in Education.

I followed Susan's advice and tried to connect the fictional characters in Marcia's lesson plans with real people in the school. The notes on *Lolita* seemed like a good start, since they referenced a guy obsessed with a young girl and I knew two people who fit the profile: Timmy and Bill. By virtue of his name Bill was also a candidate as Wilde Willing Billie, so I started with him.

Bill took a lot of excitement out of my life by leaving his door unlocked. His classroom was a mess. It yielded no usable information, mostly because if there were something of interest in there it would have taken a team of archeological experts to unearth it. I poked in all of his desk drawers, but the only guilty secret Bill seemed to be hiding was a pile of unmarked papers, some of them dating to the previous year.

That left Timmy. While I'd had no idea what I might find in Bill's classrooms, I knew quite well what I wanted from Timmy's office. He had all the personnel files in his room. I'd never broken into a file cabinet, but I didn't think it would be any more challenging than picking a door lock.

High schools are not known for high-tech security. Nor are they overly concerned about privacy. Several board members had already expressed interest in installing video cameras in every classroom. Only the district's distaste for expenditure has kept the threat of constant surveillance from becoming a reality. That would have put a serious crimp in my investigation.

I tiptoed towards Timmy's office. The lights were out, the door was locked, and he was gone. I tried a one-snap with my Visa card, but it didn't work. Next I used my school ID card, which is bigger and more flexible, but even that was difficult, since my hands were sweaty with fear. As I jiggled the card I pondered giving up a life of crime and going home to cook dinner. Then, that gratifying snap clicked the bolt.

I had a tough time deciding whether or not I should close the door. If I kept it open and I got caught, at least I wouldn't look as if I were hiding anything. If I closed the door I was less likely to be observed, but I would seem to be guilty of breaking and entering, or at least of sneaking and snooping.

I closed the door. Then I opened it. Then I closed it halfway. I tiptoed over to the file cabinet, which was locked. I'd seen Timmy take keys out of the top drawer of his desk, but that was locked as well. I felt around under the desk and slid forward the keyboard panel, but if Timmy had any secret documents he hadn't imitated Marcia's hiding place. What I did find was a magnetic key case, wedged in the corner of the underside of the desk.

As I pulled the key case free, heavy footsteps sounded outside. I slammed the case back and turned my handbag upside down.

When Timmy walked into the office I was on my knees, collecting spilled coins. "What are you doing here?" he asked. I couldn't read his expression. His face was blank, whether from surprise or anger I couldn't tell.

I sat back on my heels. "I'm so glad to see you!"

Timmy, who delivers most words with the enthusiasm and subtlety of the cheerleading team, was uncharacteristically watchful. "What are you doing here?"

I chuckled and shook my head. "I was walking by your office and I thought I heard someone yelling. I looked outside and two girls from my class were having a, er, an emotional teenage moment. It didn't look serious, so I didn't pry."

He walked over to the window and checked to see it was locked. "How did you hear them from the hall? And what are you doing on the floor?"

I pretended not to hear the first question. "I was looking through my bag for my car keys, and I ended up spilling everything. If you find a load of change under your desk, it's mine."

Timmy sat behind his desk and pulled at the center drawer, which thankfully did not budge. "Sit down, Liz. As long as you're here, let's talk for awhile."

I finished shoving the detritus that lives in my handbag back inside, and I sat obediently.

"How are you?" He drummed the thick fingers of his left hand on the desk. With his right hand he felt for the key case. "I know this has been an especially tough time for you and all the other teachers in the department."

Solicitude for my well-being was not a sentiment I often heard from any administrator. I might have been grateful for the attention if I hadn't been trying so hard to avoid the tremors of what I was sure was an incipient panic attack.

With a smile and a nod, I tossed the conversational ball right back to him. "I'm fine. How are you holding up?"

Timmy took a deep breath and rolled his eyes toward heaven. "It's been a challenge, but all the teachers have been awesome, really, really, awesome. Anyway, if you need anything, let me know. Dr. Deaver's a tough act to follow."

Yes, indeed. Especially her final exit. "Speaking of Marcia, have the police gotten anywhere in their investigation?"

Timmy looked sad. "If they have gotten any new information they haven't told either Gordon or I about it. Let's hope this gets wrapped up soon, so we can put it all behind us."

I did not correct his pronoun usage, opting instead for a more flattering approach.

"Timmy, you're in a position to know so much more than the rest of us. Do you have any idea about who could have done such a thing?"

Timmy looked pleased. I'm sure it's a rare occasion when anyone thinks he has more intellectual wattage than the average traffic light. To be fair, I must add that he is quite attractive to many females. He is in his early forties and a bit beefy with eyes the color and depth of an inexpensive wading pool. Caroline loves sidling up next to him, but she is at least fifteen years in the wrong direction to interest him.

"I still think it was an accident." He slowly wagged his index finger at me. "Marcia Deaver may have had her differences with some people, but I can't imagine that anyone would want to kill her."

Trying to sound casual, I said, "I was wondering. I heard that Marcia was going to be reassigned to the middle school. Not that that has anything to do with this tragedy."

"Marcia? There were no plans that I know of to move Marcia. Whatever gave you that idea?" He sounded sincere and more than a little angry.

Many questions buzzed around Timmy's answer. Was he hiding the fact that he and Gordon had been planning to humiliate a veteran teacher who died in the line of duty? Or did he genuinely not know that someone, perhaps an especially pestilential member of the board of education, had it in for Marcia? Perhaps a group of parents, angry about Marcia's brutal grading policy, had been lobbying for her removal.

I decided to play dumb, which at that moment was not a big stretch. "Hmm, where did I hear that? Ah, well, you know how it is. This place is a rumor mill. But it's no secret that Marcia wasn't the most popular person in the district. Not to speak ill of the dead, she was rather outspoken in her opinions. Maybe she said the wrong thing to the wrong person."

Timmy didn't bite. He probably knew better than I did how "outspoken" Marcia could be, especially if he had been the target of Marcia's insinuations in her lesson plan on *Lolita*. Nevertheless, while I had no trouble picturing him as a predator of young women of legal age, I didn't see him as a pedophile. Like many administrators, under his bluster he is quite timid. He insisted, "Well, if we're dealing with a case of foul play, I'm sure whoever did it wasn't a member of our fine upstanding Valerian Hills community."

I did not tell Timmy that more than one member—present company included—of our Valerian Hills community had both the motive and the opportunity to commit murder. Timmy got up from his desk and leaned back against the window, his broad frame blocking bars of sunlight that angled through open blinds. He held me with a fixed stare from those shallow blue eyes. "You don't have to worry, Liz. I keep a close watch on everyone here. I know more—a lot more—than most people give me credit for. I'm watching everyone, all the time. You have to believe that."

The thought that Timmy was watching me did not make me feel safe. "I do believe that," I replied. And I did.

Timmy circled around his desk and faced me. Our knees were almost touching. "What do the other members of the staff think about all this?"

I hesitated before answering. I had trouble meeting his eyes, which gleamed with a calculation that I hadn't known he possessed. He leaned over me and put a heavy hand on my left arm. I tried, as inoffensively as possible, to squirm away, but he tightened his grip. I clutched my handbag with both hands. It was heavy, and a well-placed swing with my right arm could break a man's nose.

Timmy didn't look as if he had the swiftest of reflexes. Even mild expressions of violence scare me, but thanks to the Lousy Bastard's training, I was capable of kneeing him in the groin, smashing him in his face, and stabbing him in the eyeball with my car key if he tightened his fingers one more millimeter. I may have lost two fights to girl gangs, but one on one, against an unsuspecting target, I had a decent chance of at least getting away.

Diplomacy was my first line of defense. "I don't like talking about Marcia's death. And the people who have been talking all say the same thing, that murder is unthinkable."

"That's what I said!" Timmy released my arm. "Now, don't you worry yourself about this problem, Liz."

For a moment I was afraid he was going to pat me on the head.

Timmy leaned back. He ran his fingers through his quarter-inch buzz cut. "You have plenty on your plate, now that you're teaching the AP classes. You concentrate on that. We're all counting on you to hit it out of the park!"

Bleh. Baseball metaphors again. I love the game, but I am getting tired of always having to be on deck or swing for the fences. But heaven forbid anyone should suspect me of not being a team player.

In a move that embarrasses me to this day, I held my hand up in what had to have been the most awkward high five in the history of high fives. "I'll do my best for the home team!"

Timmy stared at my hand for a moment before responding with the appropriate gesture. "That's the ticket!" He bowed his head, and with a pious look he added, "It's what Marcia would have wanted."

We both knew that Marcia wouldn't have wanted me to succeed. She would have wanted me to fall on my own sword.

Timmy waited for my reply, and when none came he swelled with a deep sigh and said, "Well, she's with the Lord now."

I had my doubts about that as well.

CHAPTER 8

THE DEAD

Two days later I studied the contents of my closet in preparation for my visit to the funeral home. I've had plenty of time to lose the weight I gained when I was pregnant—more than fifteen years—but I've managed only to yoyo back and forth. Since at any given moment I could be one of several sizes, it's difficult to organize my clothes. And although my closet is stuffed with clothing, much of it has the scent of another era.

The unspoken law of dress codes often baffles me. That's part of the reason I wear black almost all the time. If I miss that perfect intersection of casual yet dressy, and sophisticated but comfortable, at least I'll be inconspicuous. I finally chose black pants and a black silk shirt. My feet hurt, so I wore the black sandals with modest two-inch heels. I pinned my rough brown hair into a reasonably smooth knot and surveyed the result. The mirror's verdict of the front view was fine, the side passable, but the back—clearly it was time to return to the gym, or start running, or at least diet with some measure of discipline.

I went downstairs and watched my husband demolish a stack of cookies while my son ate ice cream out of the container. I resisted getting a spoon for myself and immediately felt thinner.

"Where are you going?" George demanded.

Trying to make my mission sound inviting, I said, "I have one quick errand. Want to come? We can stop by Fitzgerald's for a drink right after." I really did want George's company. Perhaps if he came to the funeral, he'd understand how I felt about Marcia's murder.

George looked suspicious. "Right after what? What's the errand?"

"Right after we stop by the funeral home."

George groaned. "I'll pass. I barely knew the woman. I think I met her twice. Give me the highlights when you get back. On second thought, if I'm asleep, don't wake me up."

In an attempt to awaken his seemingly dead sense of adventure, I asked, "Aren't you curious? I wouldn't be surprised if her ex-husband showed up."

George looked at me out of narrowed eyes. "I thought we agreed that you would stay out of this."

I returned his stare and tilted my head in Zach's direction to remind him we don't argue in front of the kids. Ever.

I felt defensive, but in deference to Zach, kept my tone cheery. "I didn't agree to anything. It's not like I've even had the chance to do something. But if the opportunity comes up, I'll be ready."

Feeling brave and rather reckless I backed out of our narrow driveway, disdaining my usual cautious inching. My defiance was short-lived, for the car smacked the side of the enormous oak tree that stood guard at the edge of the driveway. I cursed and got out to inspect the damage. The tree was fine. The impact added a small and nearly imperceptible dent in the car.

I assessed my battle-weary vehicle. The dent was not visible at all from many angles. I sent a silent supplication to a pantheon of gods, praying for an absence of witnesses, other than divine ones. Taking a breath I looked left and smiled at my open-mouthed neighbors. Across the street, my daughter emerged from a car filled with hysterically giggling girls. I turned my back to the girls and saw my son and husband burst onto the front porch. Zach shook his head, and George looked even less amused. I attempted a breezy attitude and waved goodbye, hoping that my posture conveyed screwball charm and not mortified middle-aged anxiety.

Backing into the avenue, I finally got going amid a cacophony of honking horns. I wasn't quite ready for the funeral home, so I pulled into the 7-Eleven parking lot, where I sneaked a cigarette. I quit smoking many years ago, by which I mean that I never smoke where George, the kids, or anyone who knows me can see me. I felt fairly safe behind the dumpster at the strip mall. I followed the cigarette with a spritz of perfume and three pieces of gum. Finally, I was ready for Haberman's Funeral Home.

The building was an elaborate brick mini-mansion, squeezed between Frankie's Car Wash on the left and Glamor Gal's Nail Salon on the right. Sculptured beds of flowers and hedges trimmed into geometrically perfect shapes lined the narrow driveway, and the grass was a vivid, almost synthetic green. The exterior was so immaculate it felt unreal, like a stage set for a suburban comedy of manners. The parking lot was nearly full, and I counted myself lucky to nab an open spot just ahead of the car behind me.

Hoping to see Encouraging Emily I was instead waylaid by Catty Caroline. Caroline surveyed me from head to toe, as if examining a damaged sale item at Bloomingdale's. Her words were more welcoming than her look, which was probably the one she reserved for flawed discount clothing. "Liz, dahling, I'm delighted to see that you survived the trip."

Her voice was so damned irritating. The drawling vowels and too-precise consonants never sounded completely authentic. And the rest of Caroline was equally annoying. She was dressed in perfectly creased navy slacks, matching sleeveless shirt, and low-slung braided belt. Chunky gold jewelry marked her ears, throat, and wrists. It all looked great next to her perfect tan and streaked blonde hair. The most aggravating thing about Caroline was that she forced me to reevaluate my own sartorial choices. While I already knew no one would mistake me for a sexy, black-clad cat burglar, she made me feel positively frumpish.

I pulled at the back of my shirt, trying in vain to get it to cover my backside. I vowed anew to diet and exercise, so that, like Caroline, I would have no rear-view regrets.

I forced a smile and said, "I'm good. How are you doing, Caroline?"

"Oh, I am well." Caroline sneered as she stressed the adverb. "I happened to be driving by as you pulled out of your driveway. I'm so terribly pleased that you—and the people behind you—avoided a life-threatening crash."

Before I could respond, Caroline left me for a trio of middle-aged prom queens, who held court in the back of the room. They belonged to a group I've always found intimidating—ex-cheerleaders, still fit, still thin, and still wearing tiny skirts as their daytime outfit of choice—although now they dress to impress tennis pros, not insecure teenage boys. For the funeral home, they were decked out in elegant grays and blues. They avoided the obvious black, and I avoided them.

I sought refuge in the bathroom, but a group of teenage girls entered right behind me and enacted a bloodless but determined coup. They stared as I reapplied lipstick and checked my silent cell phone and burst into laughter before the door swung shut. I walked down a narrow hallway and into the main room, the one with the coffin.

I wandered about before joining the receiving line. The room was claustrophobically warm and thrummed with the low tones of many conversations. Quite a few current and former students were there, and I was struck by how emotional they were. A few kids were excitedly self-conscious, but others were genuinely sorrowed. Most of the adults acted as if they were at a subdued, but enjoyable social event. There was much air kissing and hushed laughter as old friends reunited at a safe distance from the corpse.

Emily stood alone, and I moved in her direction. I contemplated her fuzzy shirt and generous pants fondly. They were a welcome change from Caroline's ironed perfection and the prom queens' well-bred chic. But Emily is not quite what she seems. Although she dresses as if she is subsisting on a teacher's salary, her car and jewelry betray her true economic status. I forget what brand of Sherman tank she drives, but George has assured me that it costs more than several years of private college tuition.

Emily also possesses a large diamond engagement ring and a wedding band so brilliant the jewels announce their presence in even the dimmest surroundings. I've teased Emily about it, but it embarrasses her. Her husband makes enough money to allow her to lounge in suburban splendor without working, but she prefers to teach, as long as it doesn't interfere with her attendance on her daughter's every whim.

I looked around me before asking in a low voice, "Emily, who are those two guys in the front row?"

Emily squelched what might have been a smile. "The one on the right is Marcia's ex-husband, although it turns out they never actually got divorced." She dropped her voice to an excited whisper, "And the one on the left is—was—Marcia's boyfriend!"

I was impressed. Marcia, the stern and dedicated no-nonsense doyenne of the English department was having sex with one man (possibly two) and in her spare time she was deconstructing centuries of Shakespearean scholarship. No wonder she'd lost so much weight.

I prodded Emily for more information. "How well did you know Marcia? Did you already know about this boyfriend?"

Emily looked away. "I had no relationship at all with her, Liz. I hardly ever spoke to her, but I admired her as a teacher."

We joined the line that snaked past the coffin. I did not want to look, but at the last moment my eyes lifted of their own accord. My vision blurred as thirty years melted away. I knew that Marcia was in the coffin, but her face was not the one I saw. The floor lifted and fell beneath me. I do not voluntarily revisit memories of my mother.

Emily grabbed my elbow. "Are you okay?"

"Of course. I'm fine." I swallowed hard and kept moving. In a daze, I offered my condolences to people I didn't know.

After we walked past the receiving line Emily assured me, "You don't have to feel bad about feeling faint. Plenty of people get that way." I didn't answer, but squeezed her arm to thank her. I was glad it was Emily, and not Caroline, who witnessed my weakness.

The queasiness that had come upon me as I viewed the body didn't diminish. Anxious to leave, I turned too quickly, and as so often happens when my emotions are involved, my physical body failed to make the grade. My imaginary self—the one who looks like Audrey Hepburn—evaporated, and in her place Moe, Larry, and Curly took over. First, I bumped into an elderly woman with a walker. I apologized profusely and pulled into reverse, toppling into her equally frail companion. A group of very old people gathered around me. Perhaps they were hard of hearing and did not realize that their comments about how Some People need to watch where they're going were audible to all residents of the tri-state area. I smiled apologetically at each pursed lip and once again, this time successfully, managed to leave the reception area and escape into a smaller room off to the side.

Sometimes, in the aftermath of an embarrassing moment, a kind person will suggest that it all was not as bad as you remember it. This comfort would not be available to me, since as I turned the corner I heard a disembodied voice I could not identify comment, "She's in a hurry!"

I heard Caroline's distinctive tones answer. "Yes, dahling, but I can't imagine why. It's not as if she's spent much time getting what I call 'dressed' for the occasion. But I can tell you that I was right behind her when she backed out of her driveway and practically caused a three-car pileup."

There was a sound of laughter and shushing. My ears smoked with embarrassment. How long would it take to put the house on the market and move to some remote location where I didn't know anyone?

I couldn't get out, except through the room I'd just left. I unclenched my teeth and went back in. I circled around Caroline and made a beeline back to Emily. As always, Emily projected an unchanging image of marital, maternal, financial, and professional contentment. But what the hell did I know? Figuring this was not the time or place to attempt an assault on Emily's placid demeanor, I suggested we go out for a cup of coffee after a suitably respectful period of time elapsed. I suspected Emily would be more likely to talk freely in a café or diner than a bar.

Snake-like, Caroline slithered in behind me. Over my shoulder, she drawled, "Emily, my sweet, I agree with Liz, who for once has had a mahvelous idea!

Let's get the rest of the gang and we'll bond over this dreadful event. Actually, though, I think a drink is more in order."

Without waiting for an answer, Caroline swept through the room and summoned Bill and Ashlee. Bill quickly agreed to go, and then seemed to regret his answer when Ashlee revealed that she had a date. Emily had to wash her hair. Less than fifteen minutes later I found myself in a rowdy pub with Caroline and Bill. Bill received a boisterous greeting as we walked in. He installed Caroline and me at a tiny table in the back of the room and then went to the bar to "check on the game."

I looked at my watch. I could be home. I could be sleeping, reading, grading papers, or having a sinus headache. Under normal circumstances, those activities were preferable to an intimate discussion with the Vixen of Valerian Hills High School, but times were anything but normal.

Caroline inhaled her martini and signaled for a second drink. She looked at me with what I assumed was alcohol-inspired friendliness. "Did you notice the two guys in the front row?" she asked.

"Of course. Emily told me that the older guy was Marcia's husband and the younger one her boyfriend. What do you know about them?" I tried not to look too eager.

Caroline smirked. "The usual petty gossip. Nothing worth repeating."

Most of Caroline's conversation is gossip that isn't worth repeating, so her sudden discretion didn't deter me. Forgetting I wanted to play it cool, I coaxed, "Come on, Caroline. Throw me a bone. What do you know about them that I don't?"

With a candor I would never publicly permit myself she commented, "Well, obviously they both seemed out of Marcia's league. Especially the boyfriend."

"But what do you actually *know?*" I leaned forward. "What are the facts? To say that they seemed to be out of her league isn't all that informative. And Marcia looked pretty good the last time I saw her."

Caroline bared her chalk-white tombstone-sized teeth in what I supposed was a smile. "You should get out more. If you didn't keep yourself locked away in your classroom or the office you'd be a lot more interesting."

She breathed gin fumes into my face. "First, I'll tell you what I know about Marcia. She never divorced. She and her husband separated but never made it official. Marcia moved back in with her mother, but then, of course, her mother died. Then the boyfriend moved in with her. How long that lasted, or if it lasted, I don't know."

If Caroline knew how badly I wanted information she would clam up, if only for spite. I shrugged, as if I didn't quite believe her, and said, as if bored, "How do you know all this? Did Marcia talk to you about love life? I didn't think the two of you were that friendly."

Caroline looked skyward and scrunched her shoulders slightly towards each other. Although she directed her gaze at the ceiling, she made it clear that her disdain was for me and not the overhead light fixture. "Don't be ridiculous." She shifted her eyes to look at me directly. "Why would Marcia tell me about her personal life?"

Caroline was as slippery as an eel. Who knew if anything that came out of her mouth was true? I challenged her. "Then how do you know about Marcia's husband and her boyfriend and their various domestic arrangements if she never confided in you?" My head was swimming, and not from the dreadful glass of wine I'd been sipping.

She spoke as if I were being intentionally stupid. "How does anyone learn anything?" Caroline clicked her tongue against her teeth, as if to chastise me. "What's your bloody problem? Not jealous, are you?"

I restrained myself. "No, I'm not jealous. I'm merely interested. Apparently, you are, too."

Caroline took out a nail file and scraped at a hangnail. "I am both interested and jealous. How did Marcia end up screwing two guys so much younger and cuter than she was? I want to know her secret." She raised her eyebrows in a conspiratorial way and directed the freshly sharpened fingernail at me.

I couldn't help reminding her. "You're married."

Caroline gave me the full battery power of her teeth. "Married, not dead."

I was willing to cede the point, though as I stared at her, I couldn't help thinking that while Caroline may not be dead, certain facial features did show evidence of being embalmed.

I did not point out that Marcia was dead, and said, with as little expression as I could, "Tell me more."

"Aha, now that sex is involved you're interested. Why is that? Things okay at home?"

"Are you going to tell me or not?" I wanted to brain Caroline with a piece of her own rocky jewelry.

Not at all discomfited by my irritated tone, Caroline seemed to enjoy the opportunity to reveal the details. "Well, since you ask so politely. As you know, Marcia's marriage didn't last long. I ran into her husband shortly after they split, and he said they had remained friends. Not that I think we should put too much weight into that. He was probably cheating on her with someone half her age."

This didn't make sense to me. "He must have been attracted to Marcia, though. Why else would he have married her?"

She speared an olive from her martini glass, judged it edible, and popped it in her mouth. "Money, of course. You and that charming husband of yours are not rich. Marcia, however, actually had money. She inherited a nice chunk from her father and then got even more from her mother. I believe she put the money from her first inheritance into some tech stocks in the early nineties and got out before the market tanked. No fool, our Marcia."

I hadn't before considered the possibility that someone outside the school had a motive for murder. "So who inherits the money?"

Caroline examined the diamond sparkler on her left hand. "I wish I knew. Not I, unfortunately."

If Caroline was right, Marcia had been financially well off for a number of years. I wondered why it took so long for her to dip into the money. It wasn't until the day she died that she sported $625 shoes.

Caroline tends to stimulate the part of my brain that deals with unpleasant emotion. I rubbed the front of my head in an effort to engage a few more of the cells that govern rational thought. "If Marcia was so wealthy, why did she teach? Why didn't she retire and enjoy life? For that matter, why don't you? You told me last year you were thinking of taking an early retirement."

Carolyn tsked again. "Why Liz, how cynical of you. Like me, I'm sure that Marcia taught for the sheer love of teaching. Perhaps she wanted to make a difference in the world. Perhaps she thought, God help us, that the children are our future. Maybe she liked having a captive audience. No matter how crashingly boring she was, it's not like her students could walk out. Although maybe, just maybe, supporting two gigolos is a more expensive proposition than we know."

I itched to grab her shoulders and shake the information out of her, but settled for a polite, "What do you know about Marcia's boyfriend?"

"Ah, there I really do have a bit of information. He did some business with my husband."

"Her boyfriend is a used car dealer?"

Caroline bristled. "Neither my husband nor Grant would ever be involved in something so revoltingly déclassé. No, they both deal in vintage sports cars.

Did you notice that to-die-for MG roadster in the parking lot? No? Well, I guess anyone who is content to drive a ten-year-old minivan doesn't care much about fine cars. Of course, the way you drive, an expensive car would be a waste of money. They do say that the cars people drive reflect who they are."

Caroline drives a Jag, which must mean she stalks and eats her prey.

"Yeah, that's what car people say." I tapped one of her blood-red fingernails. "I'm sure that people who work in nail salons say the color of your nail polish reveals the real you."

Caroline is not used to being compared to minimum wage workers. She curled her fingers into a fist, and with a slightly less superior tone said, "Anyway, the MG belongs to Grant. Somehow I can't quite imagine Marcia, who was such a loser, with a sports car riding hunk."

Caroline's nastiness did not impair her perceptiveness. I too could not imagine Marcia speeding to her trysts in a red sports car. As many teachers do, Marcia drove a Toyota, and not one of the eco-friendly expensive Priuses, or road-and-gas-hogging SUVs. I think she drove an ancient Camry.

"Did you get to talk much with—what's his name? Grant?"

I was confident that Caroline would not have worried about transgressing any boundaries of taste or feeling while at the funeral home. Caroline believes, with some reason, that her birth and accent give her carte blanche in all social situations. She sounds so well bred most people don't even consider the possibility that her intrusive and unfeeling observations are indicative of a callousness that borders on the sociopathic. Caroline eyed her second empty martini glass. She raised her arm and waved her fingers to get the attention of the waitress before she answered me. Like so much that Caroline does, the gesture was both fascinating and irritating. Finally, she revealed, "I did talk to the ever-so-charming Grant at the funeral home, and he told me he's working on the next Great American Novel, presumably in between various entanglements with middle-aged women who support both his riding and writing habits."

I tried to ignore the fact that Caroline was better at sleuthing than I was. "Grant told you this?" I asked.

"He told me about the novel," Caroline snapped. She continued, in a softer tone, "And then he proposed that we meet."

I felt as if I were in the middle of a daytime television drama, kind of fascinated and repelled in equal measure. "What did you say?"

The waitress placed another drink in front of Caroline. She drained half the glass before telling me, "None of your business."

I drank some more of my vinegary wine and waited. When Caroline reached for the olive, I judged she was ready for more questions. Peering into the murky wine instead of at my colleague, I asked, "Well, then, did he say anything about Marcia?"

"What could he say, other than the usual? Let's face it, Marcia was pathologically antisocial." Caroline scratched at a splinter in the table as if she had a grudge against unvarnished wood. Her tone, which had been dismissive, became aggrieved. "She never showed up to my Croquet Luncheon. She never even deigned to RSVP. A real loser. Maybe Grant got tired of hanging out with such a depressive. Maybe the laddie is the beneficiary of Marcia's will. Maybe the not-so-ex-husband is going to get the goods. All I know is, there was plenty of money to provide a motive for murder, if that's what you're thinking. It's not like anyone is going to miss Marcia Deaver. God rest her soul." Caroline tossed back the rest of her drink. She placed her portion of the tab on the table and left.

I added my portion and left a generous tip. I'm a chronic over-tipper.

I looked for Bill, but he was deeply involved in a discussion about the Yankees' chances for a playoff spot and did not appear to see me. I dithered for a bit and finally caught his attention. Bill made a halfhearted attempt to get up from his barstool, but I waved him off. If he was disappointed that I wouldn't be joining him, he hid it well.

I suppose we all have something to hide.

CHAPTER 9
GREAT EXPECTATIONS

Over the years I have endured many poisonous parents. I prefer to correspond via email, but I admit the resulting dearth of personal interactions has drained a measure of humanity from the parent-teacher relationship. I offer the following Monday morning missive as evidence:

Dear Ms. Hopewell,

You did not return my phone call on Friday, and although I suppose you know that as a tenured teacher you can get away with all sorts of unprofessional behavior, I thought that my position as President of the Board of Education would at least make you think twice. Your disrespect for me—as well as for Jack—is typical of teachers today and is the cause of the current problems in education.

If I had my way you would suffer for your actions in the same way that you caused Jack to suffer when you gave him a C- on his essay, which he worked on ALL NIGHT. Other English teachers have given him top marks.

Suffice it to say that I am seriously disappointed in the decision to assign you to Dr. Deaver's classes. I can also tell you in complete confidence that I am not the only parent who is displeased with your performance.

I used to be a teacher before I became a top advertising executive working for a Fortune 500 company, and I think I know what I'm talking about. Bad teachers are not held accountable like they should be, but as the President of the Board of Education, I will change that.

Education is my top priority.

*I am setting up a conference to discuss how we can move
forward. I have taken the liberty of discussing these issues with
Timmy and Gordon, and I know they share my views.*
    Have a nice day,
Melinda Tumbleson (Jack's Mom)
President of the Board of Education,
Valerian Hills School District

I had lesson plans to finish, photocopying to complete, and grades to
enter, but Mrs. Tumbleson's email worked a sort of paralyzing venom on my
brain. I put everything aside, including my notes on possible murder suspects,
in order to frame an answer that would not come back to haunt me. Forty
wasted minutes later I was still scrutinizing each sentence of my third attempt
at a response. The first impulse was too angry (You loathsome moron...), the
second was too defensive (Let me explain my grading policy...), and the third
was just plain confused.

Emily stopped by to borrow five dollars for lunch, explaining—as if I
needed any explanation—that she hadn't had time to get to the ATM. The
school cafeteria doesn't extend credit. Before handing her the money I shoved
the envelope with Marcia's lesson plans into the top drawer of my desk. Then
I showed her Mrs. Tumbleson's email.

She blanched. Angry parents are her worst nightmare. "When was the last
time you talked to her?" Emily asked.

"Never! I haven't checked my voicemail since last year. I'm not even sure I
still know how. The parents usually email me. Although, now that you mention it, for all I know I've got fifty irate messages."

"Don't put anything in writing. Anything you write down can and will be
used against you in a court of law. Call her instead. If you're lucky, you'll get her
voicemail. Then you can leave her a message that you'll see her at the conference."

Emily's common sense cheered me. I needed all the emotional fortification
I could get, for the terrifying Mrs. Tumbleson did not ignore my telephone
call, but instead answered with unconvincing surprise, as if she were the last
person on earth without caller ID. Because my side of the conversation lacked
much in the way of wit, I offer here her side only:

*Hallo? This is She. Oh, yes, so very good of you to find a few minutes out of
your busy day to respond to my concerns. Hmm. Umhmm. I so look forward to
meeting you.*

We agreed on a mutually convenient time to have a conference.

Emily watched me, an anxious expression creasing her forehead. "How did it go?"

"Not bad. She sounded kind of like she was in the middle of an episode of *Masterpiece Theatre*, but other than that it was okay."

Emily laughed. "The Tumblesons spent one month in London during Jack's freshman year. Each year that passes she gets more British. That's why she loves Caroline so much."

"Then she should bond with Caroline and leave me alone."

Despite Mrs. Tumbleson's polite spoken words, the ones she'd written continued to haunt me. I tried to forget the insulting phrases, but it was difficult.

I did not want to visit upon Jack Tumbleson the sins of his mother, but his smug expression dared me to challenge him. Oh, if only. If ever I surrendered to that evil impulse I could slice and dice him like a piece of Swiss cheese.

I walked around the classroom to pick up the day's assignment. Jack's desk was bare. "Oh," he said, with perfect unconcern. "My mother told me not to hand in any more work until you guys have talked. She doesn't want me to waste my time."

"That was an unfortunate decision. You have earned a zero today. Don't make the same mistake tomorrow." Perhaps unwisely, I added, "Your mother does not make the rules in this classroom. I do."

Jack said, with a nasty little note of triumph in his voice, "We'll see, Ms. Hopewell. You don't make the rules in the school, either."

I really regretted the end of corporal punishment. Hell, I was beginning to rethink my views on both waterboarding and the death penalty. I reminded myself that he was a kid. And theoretically, I am an adult.

I turned to the class and said, "This is what is called a teachable moment. You are all smart enough to figure out what the lesson is."

As I looked around the room I couldn't decide if the class was with me or against me. The students were understandably confused. Even I didn't know what lesson was involved in the teachable moment. The energy that my anger sparked suddenly left. I needed a break, if only to splash some cold water on my face and breathe unobserved for a while.

Unfortunately, teachers don't have the luxury of unplanned visits to the bathroom. I thought about asking another teacher to watch my class while I made the hike across the school and down a flight of stairs to the lone teacher's bathroom, but I was reluctant to use up this favor so early in the year. I have trained myself to seven-hour stretches without a bathroom break (an achievement that gives me no little pride) and it takes a serious stomach ailment to force me into submission. I decided to be strong and continue with the lesson on *Hamlet.*

We followed Act III, in which Hamlet challenges Rosencrantz and Guildenstern. I asked the kids how they would feel if their friends were in league with their parents to spy on them, perhaps by providing access to a hidden Facebook account. The room buzzed with the woes of two dozen teenage Hamlets. We reached the scene when Hamlet challenges his false friends by brandishing a recorder or pipe. I used one euphemism after another to explain what Hamlet meant by "pipe" and "play."

I told the kids, "Think of a word that neither you nor I can say in school, a rude word that means, uh, well, it's a verb." No reaction from the class. I tried again. "Because in the last analysis, that's what Hamlet means when he says 'play.' He's pissed off. He tells his frenemies, Rosencrantz and Guildenstern, that they can't play a pipe, but they think they're smart enough to play him, if you know what I mean by 'play.'"

I grabbed a ruler from my desk drawer and stuck it in the face of a startled Jack Tumbleson, quoting, "Will you play upon this pipe?" The kids hooted and Jack drew back from his crazy teacher. I waved the ruler in front of the class, and said, "Do you think I am easier to be played on than a pipe? Call me what instrument you will, though you can fret me, yet you cannot play upon me."

I really had their attention now. They looked as wary as if I'd been holding a machete. I put the ruler down. "Now imagine how angry Hamlet is, and how much contempt he feels toward these two losers. He is warning Rosencrantz and Guildenstern not to, uh, not to…hmm. Hamlet threatens them by saying, 'Don't *blank* with me.'"

The kids seemed interested. Baffled, but interested. I searched for a G-rated word. "Hamlet says, don't *pipe* with me." I rolled my eyes meaningfully and stabbed my ruler into an imaginary Rosencrantz and Guildenstern, but still no luck. Finally, I said, "Think of a verb that rhymes with 'duck.' Hamlet tells them—no, he warns them—not to duck with him."

The kids laughed and then groaned as the bell rang. Even the best teachers don't often earn a groan at the sound of the bell. It was good to know I wasn't failing at everything.

The kids' interest in Hamlet makes sense. I mean, who wouldn't be fascinated by a guy who's good-looking, smart, witty, a snappy dresser, and—if we can judge by his dexterity at wielding a bare bodkin—probably an excellent dancer as well. I hate it when people disparage Hamlet for being indecisive. Hamlet could not bring himself to commit a cold-blooded murder until he was convinced that it was the moral thing to do. Nothing wrong with that. Even then, he kills only after he realizes that Claudius has poisoned his mother with a drink meant for him.

Hamlet was no killer.

But someone in Valerian Hills High School *was.* That someone probably lacked Hamlet's imagination as well as his moral sense. Perhaps I had been overestimating the Valerian Hills murderer. If so, this hardly narrows the field.

At three o'clock I checked my cell phone and saw that Tom Harriman had left a text confirming our meeting. I finally allowed myself a visit to the bathroom, where I refreshed my makeup and brushed my hair. I did one last email check, about thirty minutes after the end of the school. My inbox was bursting with messages from the parents, who managed to overtake ads imploring me to advance my career through the magic of an online degree. At the top, I saw that each member of the administration had also weighed in on my *Hamlet* lesson. How sharper than a serpent's tooth.

Harriman's text suggested that we meet at the police station, rather than at the school. As I read it, little knots of pressure in my forehead released. I hadn't realized how tense I'd been at the prospect of talking about the murder at the scene of the murder.

On my way out I met Caroline, who noted, in unconscious imitation of Marcia Deaver, "You're leaving early!"

"I do my grading at home, Caroline. I don't need people to see me working, since I don't have to prove anything to anybody." Except, of course, if I didn't have to prove anything to anyone I wouldn't have bothered justifying my exit. The woman would have made an excellent Claudius — duplicitous and deadly. I decided our department chairperson should go to the top of the list of murder suspects.

Caroline snickered. She may never set the academic world on fire, but she knows defensive guilt when she hears it. She put both hands on her hips—a definite power pose. "Marcia used to spend hours here. But Marcia was a one-of-a-kind teacher. I know the kids really miss her. Oh well, live and learn."

My cell phone buzzed again, which provided me with an excuse to end my eternally losing battle with Caroline. Harriman texted that he was running a few minutes late, which was all to the good, since I was as well. It wasn't until

I arrived at the parking lot of the police station that I realized that I'd left my case notes on my desk. I drove back to the school.

Although I'd locked up before I left, the classroom door was open. Papers carpeted the floor, and the bulletin boards were stripped bare. Either I was the victim of a prank, or someone besides me had decided to do some independent investigating. Memories of the day I found Marcia's dead body rushed back. Same room. Same situation. At least I was still alive. I ran to my desk, but the copies of Marcia's lesson plans, along with my notes, were gone.

I stormed into the English office. It was empty.

I raced to the window. No one outside.

For once, I was unconcerned with anything besides the hunt. I checked each classroom and bathroom. Still nothing. No one in the stairwell. No one in the hallway. Only the cries of the cheerleaders and the exhortations of the soccer and football coaches broke the silence inside the school. I got to the safety of my car. I was so focused on watching for possible assailants in my rearview mirror that I nearly missed the turn into the police station.

Tom Harriman started talking the minute I arrived, but I had trouble concentrating. My right eyelid twitched with a life of its own. My hands left damp prints on my handbag, and I learned first-hand what a cold sweat feels like. Those knots of tension in my forehead returned, and the resultant pain set a new personal worst in headaches.

Certainly, I was reluctant to explain that I had made copies of Marcia's lesson plans. I was made even more uneasy at the thought that whoever swiped the papers knew I was investigating the murder. My notes, while somewhat cryptic, clearly listed names and potential motives. And if what happened in my classroom was a student prank, that worried me too.

"Am I boring you?" Tom asked.

I rubbed my eyes in an effort to force the pain from my head. "Of course not. But part of my brain, I think it's the amygdala—no, maybe it's the hippocampus—thinks that someone is secretly spying on me. I guess that's redundant, if you're spying then of course you want it to be secret."

Tom squinted and frowned. "What are you talking about? Your brain? Someone spying?"

He broke off as Detective Brown walked in. Brown looked at me and then through me, as if we'd never met. Not that I want to be noticed, or admired, by a lumbering idiot like Brown, but his glance, so completely devoid of interest, was insulting.

"Detective Brown, you remember Ms. Hopewell?" Tom said.

Brown nodded in my direction, but still did not favor me with his complete attention. He spoke to me, but looked at Tom. "Yes, yes. Liz Hopewell, right?"

I pleaded guilty.

Brown kept his focus on Tom. "Mind if I sit in?"

Tom pointed to a cracked leather chair. "Of course not. We're just getting started."

Brown didn't ask me if I minded. For the record: Yes, I did mind. I didn't like Brown, and I suspected the feeling was mutual. The chair protested as he lowered himself into it. He and the chair wheezed a bit before settling in. The detective looked at me as if I were a veggie burger and he'd ordered a rib roast.

Before Tom could say anything more, Brown said, "What do you have for us, Liz?"

Hell will freeze over before I allow a putz like Brown to get away with that. "Not much, Henry." Had I but world enough and time, I would have called him Hank, in order to achieve maximum irritation.

I must have sounded more hostile than I planned, for Brown was momentarily silenced. So was I.

Tom eased open his tie. "Wait here, Liz—Ms. Hopewell. Help yourself to some coffee and we'll be back shortly." He signaled to Brown and they both left the room.

I love good coffee, but I'll drink industrial brews if that's all that's available. I poured myself a cup of inky fluid and fished two Excedrin out of my bag. I was a trifle embarrassed at my earlier incoherence, and I was relieved that I had the chance to regain my composure. The two detectives returned after a few minutes. Other than occasionally tapping his foot against the desk Tom was motionless. Brown leaned back in his chair and folded his hands across his belly.

Before I could make my confession, Tom said, "I asked you here because I want you to be straight with me. Did you get any drugs from Dr. Deaver?"

That was the last thing I expected him to say. "I don't know what you're talking about. I don't get drugs from anybody. Although now that pot is all but legal, I'm feeling pretty nostalgic about high school."

Harriman didn't laugh. "Okay, then. Did Dr. Deaver threaten you in any way?"

I felt as nervous as if Marcia really had been blackmailing me. I also didn't feel like answering any more questions until I knew what we were talking about.

"Why would you ask such a thing?"

Brown broke in. "Why don't you answer the question?" His tone was aggressive and his expression unfriendly.

My mouth went dry. "Marcia never threatened me in the way you mean. The last time I saw her she told me that she was going to press charges against whoever took her chair, but I don't think that counts. Now, would you please, please tell me why you asked?"

Brown put both hands on his knees and leaned forward. He was so close I could smell his stale sweat.

Tom looked at his computer and then tapped the printout on his desk. "Four months ago, Dr. Deaver began depositing money into her bank account, money we can't trace."

I itched to add this information to my notes. Then I remembered: someone else was now in possession of my notes.

I sat as far back in my chair as I could, but Brown's body odor reached me anyway. Over a rising tide of nausea, I told him, "It might help me answer if I knew what you were driving at."

Harriman spoke slowly, as if each word came to him from a distant place. "We found a large stash of pills in her apartment. The stuff used to be called fen-phen. It's a combination of diet drugs. Not easily available here, but you can get it in Germany and Italy, which is where she spent part of the summer."

So that's how she lost all that weight. "I'm not surprised to hear that Marcia was on fen-phen, but I doubt she was selling black market drugs. Otherwise, why wouldn't she have tried to sell me some? I asked her how she lost so much weight, and she didn't say a word about it."

Harriman didn't look surprised, angry, or upset. His handsome features remained calmly handsome. It didn't take a Sherlock Holmes to figure out that Harriman was keeping back more than he was telling me.

Brown could hardly contain his irritation. "Ms. Hopewell. You are here to answer questions. Please cooperate with this investigation."

Harriman, while not hostile, was no less intent. "We think she may have been blackmailing at least one person, and probably more than one person. So—just to be clear, are you sure you weren't one of her victims? Or one of her customers? It's okay if you were. This is a homicide investigation, not a drug bust."

I tried not to sound like the lady that doth protest too much, but I was, once again, feeling defensive. "I was not a victim. I didn't like Marcia, but not because she was blackmailing me, or because she was selling me diet drugs at inflated prices. She wasn't a likeable person. But now that you're thinking blackmail, I prepared some notes concerning Marcia's lesson plans. But I don't have them with me right now." I took a large sip of coffee to prepare myself. "There was—an, um, an episode at the school today."

Brown laced his fingers across his belly and leaned back. "What kind of 'episode?'"

"Last year several classrooms were vandalized, petty cash was taken, and we never found out who did it. I don't know if some kid decided to play a prank on me, or if some adult is still looking for Marcia's files. But anyway...someone trashed my classroom and took my notes. The notes that were attached to Marcia's fake lesson plans." Trying to make my transgression seem less toxic, I told them I would report the incident to Timmy.

Tom started to speak, but Brown overrode him. "What lesson plans?"

"The ones I gave Detective Harriman—gave both of you. The ones I found the day Marcia was murdered." The eye-twitching returned so violently I was sure both detectives could see it.

Brown smacked his head and then the table. "Are you telling me that you made copies of important evidence? And then wrote down who you thought murdered Dr. Deaver? And then left them at the school?" His tone rose higher with each question.

Harriman didn't waste time chastising me. He simply said, "First, we're going back to the school. Then you'll file a report with us."

On the way out, Brown asked, in a most unfriendly way, "How long were you going to wait before mentioning this?"

I wanted to take my own car, but Brown insisted that I ride in the back of one of the cop cars. I had to wait in the hallway while the two detectives searched the classroom. After they finished, Tom took one police officer with him and went through the first floor of the building. Brown searched the second floor classrooms with another officer, and a fifth cop babysat me.

Officer Ana Rivera looked sympathetic, but she wasn't the talkative type. Every time I opened my mouth she wrenched her gaze from her cell phone, but as soon as she delivered her monosyllabic reply she went back to her screen. I wanted to ask her for her cell phone number. Maybe if I texted her a question, I'd have a better chance of getting it answered.

The two detectives returned to my room and the rest of the cops, except for Rivera, left. Tom took out his notebook. He skimmed through a few pages and then said, "Let's start with the morning of the murder before we talk about today. Think, Liz. You've said more than once that something didn't feel right to you. What was it? Was anyone upset? Was anyone hanging around the school who didn't belong there?"

"As I told you before, the only one who was upset was Marcia. She was pissed off because her personal chair was not in her classroom. But Marcia being upset was not unusual, and I really don't see how the missing chair figures into this at all."

Tom wrote as he spoke. "I disagree. It was a good way to get her out of her classroom. The murderer needed to get to her coffee cup. She wouldn't take her handbag or her coffee if she thought she'd be dragging her chair through the school."

"Good point. What I think—"

Brown cleared his throat and said, "Before we go into what you think, maybe you can explain how you happen to be on the spot whenever anything happens. You got quite a streak going."

I jumped to my feet and faced him. The Lousy Bastard, curse his black heart, would have been proud of me. "Are you accusing me?"

"Ms. Hopewell, I am asking you about a series of coincidences." Brown started counting on his fingers, beginning with his pinky. "You were the last person to see Marcia alive. You grab her folder by mistake on the first day of school." Brown interrupted his recitation to put air quotes around the words "by mistake," nodding his head twice to emphasize the absurdity of my claim. "You find the dead body. You find her so-called lesson plans, which no one else knows anything about." He waggled four fingers in front of my face.

My fingers itched to slap his hand away. "No one knew about them because they were hidden. I found them by accident."

Brown kept talking, as if I hadn't said anything. "This classroom gets trashed again, exactly the way it was last time, and you just happen to forget something and are the first one on the scene. An awful lot connected with this case is traceable only to you."

I tried to breathe normally and still the occasional trembles that jerked my body. "The classroom isn't the same as last time. I'm not dead."

"Yes, Ms. Hopewell," Brown said in exasperation. "You're not dead. Are you sure there isn't something you can tell us that we don't know? Talk to me, Ms. Hopewell."

The guy had no idea who he was dealing with. Yes, I look like a dark-haired version of weak-willed Emily. But I spent a lifetime in the projects, where the cardinal rule is to tell the cops nothing. Through nearly clenched teeth, I said, "I have nothing to say."

Brown held his hands wide and kept his tone gentle. "We won't hold it against you, Ms. Hopewell, if you're straight with us now. Help yourself out here. Maybe you were upset. Maybe you were threatened. Perfectly understandable situation."

Bitter stomach fluid filled my mouth and made me gag. The room felt hot, and my forehead, my neck, and my back itched with perspiration. Harriman, Rivera, and Brown looked at me and waited for me to either stop coughing or pass out. No one offered to get me water.

"You're crazy. I've told you everything. I couldn't make this stuff up." Again, I felt myself protesting too much, too heatedly.

Brown looked smug. "I didn't say you lied. I'm giving you the chance to tell us what's really going on."

"The longer you concentrate on me, the longer it will be before you find the murderer." My response might have had more impact if I had been able to keep my voice and body from shaking.

Brown crossed his arms over his belly and stuck out his chin. "Yeah, well, there is one more thing. Do you usually lock your classroom door?"

I didn't hesitate. "Yes. Not during the day, but at the end of the day, yes."

"Who's got the keys besides you?" Harriman asked the question, but all three leaned forward to hear the response.

I wished I had a more helpful answer. "The principal and assistant principal. The custodians, of course. Actually, some teachers have the same key, so any of them could have done it. But I can't imagine a teacher committing this kind of vandalism."

Brown made a derisive noise. "Could you have imagined Ms. Deaver being murdered?"

Hah. I had him there. "Yes, Detective Brown. If you recall, I imagined it before you did."

Brown sputtered a bit, but recovered. "If you imagine anything else, you give us a call." He jerked his head toward Tom in lieu of saying goodbye. "Rivera can take her back so's she can pick up her car."

Once he was gone, Tom spoke. "Ana, you can go. I'll drive Ms. Hopewell." After Officer Rivera left, Tom said, "Stop worrying. It's all going to be okay."

Anger at Brown had given me energy, but with him gone I felt my muscles weaken. "Is it? How do you know that? And what's next? How can you ever figure out who murdered Marcia, if practically every single person at Valerian Hills had the opportunity to commit murder, and we have no idea who had the motive?"

"It's not going to be easy." Tom scratched a few notes onto his pad as he spoke. I tried to read them, but even right side up I struggle without my reading glasses. "Tell me, on the morning she was murdered, was Marcia carrying a bag of any kind?"

I closed my eyes to better visualize Marcia-in the hallway, in my room, and in the parking lot. "I'm not sure, so she probably wasn't."

Tom tapped his pen against the notebook. "If you're not sure then you're not sure."

I shook my head. I was certain now. "No. When I found Marcia her handbag was on her desk. It looked like a Chanel knockoff, but now that I know she was padding her retirement account, I think it may have been the real thing. Believe me, if Marcia had been carrying a Chanel handbag I would have noticed it even before I recognized the Christian Louboutin shoes. Why is her handbag important?"

Tom's tone was casual. "No reason. Just checking. So that's that. Now we need to coordinate the next round of interrogations in light of what happened today."

I looked out at the football field. "Maybe it was just a prank."

Tom joined me at the window and pulled the blinds shut. "Maybe. It might be someone who didn't finish searching Dr. Deaver's classroom on the day she died. Or it might be a warning. Is that a chance you want to take?"

"Of course not. I'm scared, and I wish that none of this had happened." I was also exhausted, but I couldn't leave without cleaning up some of the mess in my room. Tom stayed with me. We picked up papers, trashed the broken flower vase, and replaced the books on the shelves. Not for the first time, I was physically conscious of the way Tom looks and acts around me. He focuses so intently; it makes our conversations seem intimate, even though they're never personal. Maybe George was right, and Tom was using me, either to get information, or because he considered me a suspect.

If so, I could use him too.

I handed him a volume of *Moby Dick*. "All great detectives are creative. They break rules. That's what makes them great."

He weighed the book in one hand. "Oh yeah? What book did you read that from?"

For the first time in hours I felt happy. "No book. I made it up."

He smiled, but didn't take me up on my offer. "Doesn't matter. You're not a collaborator in this investigation."

"You need me. I'm the only one who can decipher Marcia's clues."

Tom didn't agree, but he didn't disagree. That's a sign of a good liar, and I appreciate that. I'm also a good liar. As any coward will tell you, it's an invaluable asset.

CHAPTER 10
THE TRIAL

It was after midnight when I gave up trying to get to sleep. Instead of engaging in a lofty study of Shakespearean tragedy, which was the homework I assigned to my students, I googled the comical—and baffling—name Marcia had appended to her lesson plan on *The Importance of Being Earnest*: Wilde Willing Billie. My search yielded a study guide for the novel *Into the Wild*, a LinkedIn profile for a money manager, and several articles on the actress Olivia Wilde. The only direct link to Wilde Willing Billie offered a few mildly pornographic images. None of them looked like anyone at Valerian Hills High School, but it was hard to tell. Wilde Willing Billie wore a huge blonde wig, cowboy hat, heart-shaped sequined sunglasses, and not much else. He had great legs, and I'm sure I could identify him if I saw him in a purple leather micro-mini skirt. I trolled various porno websites, but Wilde Willing Billie hadn't made it to the big time, so to speak.

It was a good night for movies, and I consoled myself by watching *Annie Hall*. I love that movie, although lately I worry that, like Woody Allen and Diane Keaton, George and I will end up with a dead shark instead of a happy marriage. We're starting to resemble Liz Taylor and Richard Burton in *Who's Afraid of Virginia Woolf?*

George stomped into the room during a very tender scene. "Come to bed. For Chrissakes, you're killing me. Every night you wake me up."

"I'm trying to be quiet and leave you alone. I can't read in bed, because you don't want me to turn on the light. I can't watch television, because you don't want me to spend the night in the den." Frustrated and furious, I threw the tissue box at him. "What the hell do you want?"

George caught the tissues and looked at me as if I'd lost my mind. "What do I want? I want a normal wife who sleeps in her normal bed and doesn't clump around the house all night long."

It wasn't the most romantic of openings, but it was good enough for me. I was willing to exchange throwing things at him to throwing myself at him.

"Is that a hint? I've been looking at porno sites, checking out Wilde Willing Billie. We're a little out of practice, but I think we can do him one better."

George was not amused. Or interested.

"Do you hear yourself? You're obsessed with this murder. Leave it alone, for God's sake. Just leave it alone."

I picked up the remote and muted the sound. I wanted to mute George.

"Why don't you say you want a different wife?"

"Because I don't. That's my point. I don't want a different wife. I want the wife I married. I don't want this new person who meets with strange men, talks all night on the phone, and doesn't want to sleep with her husband."

I crossed the room and put my arms around him. "It wasn't sleep that I was offering."

His face changed, softened. "Come on, then. But no threesomes. You and me. Leave Billie out of it." We tiptoed past the kids' rooms.

He pushed me onto my stomach and stroked my back and legs. "I love your skin."

I turned and faced him. "I love your smell."

In retrospect, that would have been a good time to shut up. A good time to use my mouth for more interesting things than daytime chitchat.

"I've missed you," I whispered.

"Mmm. Sssh."

"Why *are* you coming home so late?"

George flipped onto his back and looked at the ceiling. "Sometimes I have to go out with a client. Or one of my coworkers. It's not like I want to come home late."

And the moment, as they say, passed.

When I asked him whom he was meeting, I wasn't trying to put him on the defensive. I didn't think he was having an affair. I figured good old reliable George and I were simply going through a rough patch in our marriage. People do, don't they? And then they reconnect. But there was a little hesitation in his voice that made me nervous.

I propped myself up on one elbow and tried to read his expression. "If what you want is to get through to me you're going to have to spend time with me. I—I'm lonely. Don't complain that I keep you up at night when half the time I'm waiting for you to get home."

George sat up and grabbed me and hugged me so tightly I could hardly breathe. "I'm sorry. Talk to me now. What the hell is going on in that brain of yours?"

George didn't really want to know even one of the thousand things worrying me, so I told him what he wanted to hear. "Nothing. Nothing's going on."

George shifted his grip and held me at arms length. He stared into my eyes. "When we met, you told me you didn't have a past. You were so funny and pretty and smart, and I don't give a crap about that stuff anyway. But you lie to me. Don't think I don't know it. You've told me at least three different versions of your childhood. You lied to me then and you're lying to me now. Maybe you need to figure out the truth about yourself before you involve yourself in figuring out the truth about someone else."

All this emotion was exhausting me. "You're right. But not now. I'm too tired."

George released me. I put my arms around his neck, but he shook me off. That had never happened before. Not in twenty years.

One touch from him and I would have melted. He had to know that.

He snapped on his reading lamp and turned his back to me. Fifteen minutes later he was asleep. I stopped thinking about George, and instead thought about Tom and daydreamed of how we would unmask the murderer together.

Things don't always look better in the morning. George drank his coffee standing up and left without saying a single word to me. At one point in our relationship this silent treatment would have devastated me. Now I find it boring. I know that eventually he'll get over it, and there is no point in discussing the matter. In the past, I liked—no, needed—to talk things out and he didn't. Now we both don't talk things out. Too much trouble.

I drove to school down quiet tree-lined streets, and meditated, not for the first time, on the differences between Oak Ridge and Valerian Hills. People who don't know New Jersey might assume that all of its suburban towns are similar, but they're not. Upper middle class residents populate the town where I live and the town where I work, but the two are not interchangeable.

Some differences between them are concrete. In Oak Ridge, tastefully landscaped lawns surround century-old Tudor, Georgian, and Victorian homes on broad avenues and narrow side streets. In Valerian Hills, large houses with elaborate facades that do not match the other three sides are hidden from main roads on byzantine byways that realtors have romantically named cul de sacs but less invested observers refer to as dead ends.

The differences between Oak Ridge and Valerian Hills transcend the architectural. In the latter, the residents pride themselves on raising their children in an idyllic "Valerian Hills Bubble" of affluence and piety. Oak Ridgers prefer to dwell upon their proximity to Manhattan, and they consider themselves far more urbane and sophisticated than residents of more insular communities. As many New York City transplants do, I congratulated myself on choosing so desirable a location, but I also know I'll never really be at home here. It's too nice a place for me.

When I got to school, Harriman was in the parking lot. He was holding a copy of *Persuasion*—*my* copy of *Persuasion*—and talking to Ashlee. Well, good luck with that. Not that I cared, but I assumed when Harriman borrowed my book he would be discussing Jane Austen with me. I followed Harriman and Ashlee into the school. They disappeared into the classroom that used to be mine. I don't give a damn if Tom is interested in Ashlee. I do care if he's canoodling every female teacher in the school.

I felt like a fool. A very middle-aged fool.

But it's not as if I needed Tom or anyone else. I had given him far more information than he'd given me. The only thing he told me of any interest was the fact that at some point some idiot was interested in moving Marcia Deaver to the middle school. I realized, far more than Tom was able to, the outrageousness of that proposal. Time to move my investigation out of my imagination and into the real world.

I peeked into Emily's classroom and gave her the nod. She wormed her way to the hall. I waved away her polite greeting, "Emily! Do you know anything about Marcia Deaver being moved to the middle school?"

Emily looked shocked. "That's impossible! Why would they move her? That's stupid!"

"Of course, it's stupid. Did you know anything about it?"

"Absolutely not." Emily cupped one hand around her mouth, although there was no one around to hear her besides me. "I heard—in complete confidence, of course—that *Bill* was being moved to the middle school, which sort of makes sense."

"Why does it make sense?"

Emily looked behind her shoulder before she answered. "At the end of last year, I think—I mean I'm pretty sure—that Caroline may have mentioned to me—just in passing, of course—that Timmy wanted to hire a new teacher for the high school. In order to do that, someone here would have to take the open position at the middle school. Neither Gordon nor Timmy thinks that Bill is a strong teacher. Caroline said they want new blood."

"Why do they need new blood? What are they? Vampires?"

Emily didn't laugh. She whispered, "Caroline said that Timmy and Gordon were very impressed with Ashlee while she was student teaching."

I gave Emily my best you've-got-to-be-kidding-me look. "Yeah, that makes sense. The first thing I noticed about Ashley was her deep knowledge of the Western Canon. Come on, Emily, she's probably the only person on the planet who could make Bill look like Aristotle."

"Oh, Ashlee's not that bad. Not really. But no matter how much they wanted to hire Ashlee, there's no way that Marcia would have been transferred. I think you must have heard wrong." Emily chewed at her thumbnail. "I hope they don't transfer me. A few years after I got here they moved me to the middle school and then moved me back."

"Why did they do that?"

Emily had always seemed to be a fixture at the high school. It was as if she'd told me the flagpole and the school pride banners had temporarily moved.

She pulled again at her fingernail. "I still don't know. But it was very upsetting. Gordon was still the principal of the middle school. He was very nice about it. He said they needed a teacher who could bridge the gap between middle and high school. But I was miserable, and as soon as there was a vacancy here I was able to transfer back. I hope they're not thinking of doing it again. I've been here for a long time."

"I wouldn't worry about it, Em. Your job is safe."

Emily smiled in relief, although why she should think I have any credible information concerning the machinations of school politics I have no idea.

Then came the tough part. "You know, Emily, I was curious about one other thing. On the first day of school, Marcia was looking everywhere for her desk chair. Do you have any idea what happened to it? Did you talk to Marcia?"

Again, Emily had no clue. She shook her head, and then, with one panic-stricken look, bolted back into her classroom. She called over her shoulder, in a loud stagey voice that wouldn't fool a three-year-old, "No, Liz, I don't think I have any extra copies of that book!"

I looked behind me. Timmy was doing his rounds. I didn't bother to make any excuses, since Emily had already so eloquently telegraphed our truancy. I simply acknowledged his grimace with my own bared teeth and closed my door. I realized I would have to relinquish my habit of holing up by myself all day. The only way I was going to get the information I wanted was to engage with other people, and that meant having lunch at a more social setting than my desk.

There is an unmistakable whiff of seventh grade in the faculty room, where the boys and girls sit at opposite ends. The guys get the tables near the window and the girls get the tables near the door. The twain meet only at the centrally located copy machine, which spews noxious-smelling fumes into the DMZ. The men discuss sports and the ladies engage in genteel competitions to determine who has the most perfect child. When the conversation about children wanes, someone will mention the fabulous meal she cooked the night before. These meals are always very inexpensive and don't take any time at all to cook. I should take notes.

The school nurse and the student assistance counselor park themselves in the faculty room for all three half-hour lunch periods, and that by itself is enough incentive to drive me away. No other faculty member has the luxury of so long a lunch. The nurse is adamant about her need for nutrition. Kids have fainted, puked, and spiked fevers during lunch, but the nurse unconcernedly chomps on. Indifferent to their distress, the minimum requirement for getting her to move is someone going into anaphylactic shock.

At first, my entrance into the faculty room went unnoticed, and I saw that Emily was engaged in an intense conversation with Caroline. I didn't know Emily and Caroline were so friendly, and I hesitated before approaching them. They looked up and immediately fell into a stuttering silence. I told myself they could have been talking about someone other than me.

Emily loyally moved her chair to make room for me.

The nurse said, in imitation of friendliness, "Well, looky who's here!"

I slid a chair from the men's table into a sliver of space and took out a virtuous salad and bottle of water. I waited for the conversation to resume.

Caroline purred, "It's nice to see that someone around here takes my advice." Arching her brows at the other women at the table, Caroline explained, "I told Liz she should get out of her room once in a while."

Everyone laughed. I was the only one who didn't know what was funny.

Caroline stabbed at a few spears of asparagus and then turned her attention back to me. "How are your new classes coming along, Liz? A little birdie told me things are getting pretty hot for you."

"It's so nice of you to take an interest, Caroline." I tried to appear unaffected by what she said, but I didn't fool anyone, least of all Caroline, who, piranha-like, kills with a thousand tiny bites. I hoped Emily was not the one who told the others about Mrs. Tumbleson's vicious emails. At work, Emily was the closest thing to a friend I had. Was there anyone at the high school I could trust? My classroom and my privacy had been trashed. And anyone in the English department could have committed either—or both—transgressions.

There were plenty of people besides Emily who could have gossiped. Maybe Mrs. Donnatella told Caroline, or perhaps Caroline overheard a conversation between Gordon and Timmy. The kids themselves could have been talking about me.

I announced, with a minimum of quavering, "I'm fine. My classes are going really well. I'm not going for a hundred percent of the vote."

Caroline laughed. "Good heavens! The vote? My, my, from what I hear the polling numbers for Congress are better than yours."

For once, the male teachers were paying attention to the female tables. Bill laughed so hard he snorted milk up his nose, which derailed the brilliant reply that was about to occur to me. Emily avoided my gaze. I guess it's too much to expect support from a woman who is unable to utter the smallest word in her own defense.

Caroline thumped Bill on the back while the nurse watched him choke. The nurse was Off Duty for teachers as well as students. Bill's eyes streamed with tears of pain, but his hilarity was infectious. The entire room erupted in laughter, which I pretended to share. Who cares about these morons, anyway? I wouldn't voluntarily spend two minutes with any of them.

After Bill returned to his senses I checked out the rest of the faculty room. I was amazed to see that the formerly all-male bastion had been breached. Ashlee sat in queenly glory, delicately crunching on carrot sticks and cucumber slices. None of the men seemed at all put out at her intrusion.

I waited until an inane conversation about the other women's kids' eating habits petered out, and then asked, as if it were of no importance, "Did you guys hear that Marcia was supposed to be moved to the middle school?" Perhaps this approach lacked subtlety, but I was running out of time and patience. There was a general chorus of disbelief.

The nurse pursed her mouth and shook her head. "Do you think we should be talking about Marcia like that? It seems disrespectful."

I stared at my salad and moved a few leaves of lettuce around the container. "It's not disrespectful. I'm curious. It seems weird that the administration would do that."

Caroline looked bored. "I don't know where you got your information, Liz, but I think it's dead wrong. No pun intended, of course. Puns are so lame."

I refused to give up. "Then why was Marcia's room such a mess? Half of her posters were pulled down from the walls and a bunch of books were lying on the floor and on the windowsill."

Caroline patted her mouth over a fake yawn. "Don't go all conspiracy theory on us, Liz. I'm sure there's a good explanation for that. Anyway, the poor woman is dead. Let her rest in peace."

I gave up on my lunch and dumped the wilting greens into the garbage can. "I take that to mean you don't know anything about it?"

Caroline burned her eyes into my head, and said, "There is nothing to know. People start all kinds of rumors for all kinds of reasons. Look at what's happening to you."

Loneliness—real loneliness—bit me more deeply than at any time I could remember. I muttered goodbye and left. What was the point of trying to connect with other people? I had no one to talk to, no one to listen, no one to understand. Emily was fraternizing with the enemy. Tom Harriman was pursuing Ashlee with books from my library. My husband was angry and distant. My coworkers were in an ecstasy of *schadenfreude* over the problems I'd been having with the parents.

Emily followed me into the hallway. "Liz! You have to believe me! I didn't breathe a word about Jack or Mrs. Tumbleson's email or anything else."

"Don't worry about it. No big deal. But if you didn't talk, then you have to tell me who did."

Emily was silent.

"Please."

"I honestly don't remember how the subject came up, Liz. Really, you have to believe me."

Emily's face was the picture of remorse. What could I say? That I didn't believe her? I averted my eyes as Emily searched my face for forgiveness. We were both relieved when the bell rang.

I dragged myself through the rest of the day. The students seemed to sense my depression and were unnaturally cooperative and pleasant. This made me feel worse. Was I that pathetic? Taking a page from Emily Dickinson, every English teacher's favorite recluse, I decided that Because I Could Not Stop for Death, I could at least attempt success as a mother. After school I did two loads of laundry, put together a big salad, and cooked a pot of chili.

For once, everyone was home at the same time. Zach's soccer practice ended early, and Ellie's ballet class didn't start until seven. We all sat down to dinner together. Well, we didn't all sit and we didn't all eat, but at least we were in the same room at the same time. Ellie doesn't eat before she dances, but she joined us in the kitchen anyway. While we ate Ellie balanced one leg on the countertop and kept a running commentary on her upcoming audition for *The Nutcracker*. Insisting on equal time, Zach related the torments of AP chemistry.

If George had said one word to me it would have felt like a normal night. At least the kids didn't notice. After dinner George and the kids stacked the dishes in the dishwasher but left the pots, the pans, the countertops and the stove for the fairies to clean up. Miraculously, my cell phone rang. It was Susan.

I dropped the sponge and turned off the faucet. "I'm so glad you called! You won't believe what's going on in my life right now."

My sister is not easily distracted. "Your life? Wait until I tell you about my date with that schmuck from Starbucks!"

"Susan, I really need to talk to you."

"Hey, I'm here for you. You know that. But I only need you to listen for two minutes. I went out with that guy I told you about. Turns out he's a lawyer. He's a partner with some big firm of like-minded jerks. We had drinks at The Palm and then decided to stay there and order appetizers, which is fine with me since I'm dieting anyway and it's awkward to go out to dinner and not order food."

I put the phone on speaker and turned the faucet back on. I knew I'd have to hear every detail before it would be my turn to talk.

Susan continued, "Things were going fine. Things were going great, in fact. I wore the black, slightly off the shoulder shirt I told you about, and I looked really good. Then one person after another from his law firm showed up, and he, like, totally ignored me for...I don't know. Maybe it was twenty minutes, maybe a half hour. Whatever it was, I felt humiliated. He left me sitting there by myself. He didn't even introduce me to the people he talked to. Finally, he sort of apologized, but it's more like he was proud of himself for being so popular. Did I miss something? Cause I thought we were done with high school."

I scrubbed the counter and thought about the unintentional irony in Susan's words. "I'm beginning to think we're never done with high school."

"Liz, I haven't even told you the best part."

"Okay, I'm listening."

Susan emitted a strangled sound, something between a laugh and a growl. "The guy finally unglues his attention from his buddies when a totally gorgeous and really thin woman walks into the room. He mumbles something about coming back in a few minutes, and then he joins her at the bar and buys her a drink. I got up and left. For all I know he's still there, unconscious of the fact that I walked out. I'm still hoping the people at the next table who were laughing weren't doing so at my expense."

Not for the first time, I was startled at how my sister's life and mine ran on different, but weirdly parallel lines. "Oh, Susan! I'm so sorry. That sounds awful."

"Ugh. You have no idea how much time it takes to get ready for a date these days. Between the waxing, the tweezing, the blow drying, the manicures and pedicures...I lost hours of my life I'll never get back."

I dried off my water-wrinkled hands, thinking that a visit to a nail salon sounded rather pleasant. I have vivid daydreams of the day when I can leave work and head to the hairdresser.

Susan sighed into the phone. "Please. In addition to the humiliation of the whole experience and the time I wasted getting ready, I spent a ton of money at the hairdresser and nail salon and spa. You don't know how lucky you are to have George."

I tapped the speaker icon to turn it off. I've never spoken much to Susan about George, but I was bursting with unexpressed emotion. "I've been meaning to talk to you about that."

Susan interrupted, "Stop! I won't listen to one word against your husband. He adores you."

I locked myself in the bathroom and spoke in a low voice. "That's what you think. Things aren't going so well right now."

Susan adopted her most annoying didactic tone of voice. "Liz, you have no idea what it's like out in the dating world. It's not even a jungle. It's like an endless YouTube loop of humiliation and destruction. Did you know that I now have a better chance of being hit by an asteroid than finding a husband?"

"You've been married three times," I reminded her. "What makes you think you won't find someone else?"

Susan, who knows perfectly well how beautiful she is, said, "Oh, I don't know. Maybe it's my wrinkles and my gray hair."

"You don't have wrinkles, and you don't have gray hair. You're only three years younger than I am, but you look ten years younger, which is extremely annoying."

Sounding much happier, she said, "If you would come to my Botox parties you would look younger too."

I peeked into the bathroom mirror. "I won't deny I'm tempted. But I'm afraid I'll be the one in a thousand whose face freezes into a freakish mask." I stopped myself. "But Susan, I want to talk to you about my investigation. It's not—I'm not—well—let's just say I'm having a few problems."

Susan was probably also looking into the mirror, because she suddenly sounded far away, both physically and emotionally. "Listen, you want to hear problems? I'm going to have to find a new Starbucks to go to, because if I ever run into this guy again I'm going toss my skinny vanilla latte into his smug little rat face. Of course, on the plus side, I think I'll finally set up a meeting with that other guy from JDate. Or was it OKCupid?"

If I didn't get through to her I was going to go mad. "Susan, everything is going so badly right now. I don't know where to start."

"I'm so sorry about that, Liz. I wish I could talk right now, but I'm going out for drinks and some female friendship."

I didn't answer. What was the point? I said goodbye.

But perhaps Susan was feeling contrite, for she didn't immediately hang up in order to engage in a more interesting female bonding ritual. "Liz, remember what I said the last time we talked about this? Have you given it some thought?"

"Not really. I have no idea how our pathetic past, filled with lying bastards—"

"Lousy Bastard!" Susan corrected.

"Fine," I said. "Have it your way. But nothing in our past can help me now."

"Then you're kidding yourself. You never want to talk about what happened to us or to Mom, and that's really a drag for me."

I was firm. "There's nothing to talk about. The Lousy Bastard had another wife and another kid. And then another wife and for all we know, more kids. What is there to say about that? Other than the fact that it turned out he got the son he always wanted?"

Susan was silent for so long I thought she'd hung up. Finally, she said, "I'm not talking about his other family. I'm talking about the day Mom died. What really happened that day? They had that awful fight the night before."

I was having enough problems with my own marriage. The last thing I needed was to revisit the horrific example my parents had given us. "So what? The two of them fighting is not going to help me solve this murder."

"Do you remember Mom's funeral?"

Now I was the one who was ready to hang up.

"Susan, I've had enough of this conversation. Don't you have a date or something? We can talk tomorrow."

Susan insisted, "Nana and Grandpa accused the Lousy Bastard of killing Mom. And I don't think they were speaking metaphorically. Did he do it?"

"Everyone said she had a car accident. That's all I know. That's all I was told. As far as I know, the Lousy Bastard didn't put a gun to her head. She did that to herself when she married him."

"Yeah, right. Whatever. If you want to lie to me, that's fine. But you shouldn't lie to yourself."

Hearing Susan echo George so closely rattled me. They don't often read from the same playbook.

Thanks to my sister, memories of my mother's death disrupted my concentration on Marcia. There were blank chapters in both stories, and that bothered me. One of the many questions that remained unanswered was what my mother did in the hours before her car accident. She had left work early. No one admitted to knowing where she went.

The accident occurred at dusk. What transpired during those lost hours? None of my relatives ever told me what happened, and at the time I was reluctant to discuss something that caused them such grief. My younger self didn't have the wit to understand that their reticence created greater pain for me. And now it was too late. Everyone who could have filled in the missing pieces was out of my life. Or dead.

But there were plenty of people who had information about Marcia. Who felt real pain at Marcia's death? Her husband? Her boyfriend? I needed a socially appropriate excuse to contact them. Spending my childhood one step ahead of the law and an assortment of creditors has left me at a slight disadvantage when it comes to parsing the niceties of interpersonal relationships. As a kid, I learned how to deal with dunning phone calls, but as an adult I'm not at all sure about the protocol for condolence calls to people I don't know.

I texted Tom for information about both men. He did not respond. I searched the obituaries and found the name of Marcia's husband, but of course her boyfriend was not mentioned in the list of surviving family members. The boyfriend's website for his vintage car business was under construction and carried no information beyond that fact.

I called the only person I could think of, even though I wasn't sure Caroline would answer the phone. She picked up immediately.

"Hey, Caroline. It's me, Liz."

"Has the sky fallen?" She sounded amused, which I'm sure she knew was outstandingly annoying to me.

I pretended to laugh. "I wanted to send a sympathy card to Marcia's husband. Maybe to her boyfriend as well. Do you have their addresses, or any other contact information?"

"You little liar, you. What are you really up to? Are you interested in getting together with Grant? Because honestly, I don't think you're his type."

Thanks to the marvel of non-Skype communication my red face was not visible to her. "I don't know what you're talking about, Caroline. I thought it would be a nice gesture. So, do you have the freaking information or not?"

"No need to get so touchy, dear. I'll get it from my husband and give it to you on Monday."

I thought about asking Caroline to email me the boyfriend's name and address. It probably would make no difference, though. I expected that by lunchtime the next day every single person in the school would know that I was trying to get in touch with Marcia's boyfriend. I hoped the murderer wouldn't mind.

CHAPTER 11
CRIME AND PUNISHMENT

On Saturday morning I made lists, because as soon as something is written down I feel a sense of accomplishment, whether or not I actually get around to the task. Conspicuously absent from the list was anything connected to my husband.

At nine o'clock I drove Ellie and her friends to ballet class and then headed to the athletic field, where I watched all of Zach's soccer game. I sat in the bleachers with the mothers, and George stood at the fence with the fathers. Neither of us cares much about sports unless Zach is playing, but we try to fit in as best we can with our sports-mad peers. After the game I piled multiple loads into the washing machine, cooked enough food to sustain a small army, and dropped the equivalent of a ransom request at the dry cleaner's. George and I usually go out on Saturday night, but after the soccer game he closeted himself in his office. We still weren't talking.

I viewed with suspicion his meticulous disposal of his lunch dishes. He was either trying to make amends or demonstrating his unwillingness to put himself in the wrong. At five o'clock he still had not emerged from his lair. Any word on my part, no matter how distant, is usually enough to break down George's defenses, but I wasn't in the mood. I called Susan and arranged to meet her in the city. I informed George of my plans through his closed office door.

Susan and I spent a meandering and peaceful hour pacing through the Metropolitan Museum of Art. We finished the evening in the museum's balcony bar, where we consumed several expensive glasses of wine and two shockingly tiny plates of cheese and fruit. A chamber music quartet played in the background. The precise tones unwound the tension that knotted my muscles. The music and art suggested there is hope for the human race.

I no longer waste time mourning my move from the city to the suburbs, but I could not help briefly fantasizing about returning to a tiny apartment whose undemanding silence and clean kitchen greeted me at the end of each day. I still miss the anonymity of city life, which suits me far better than the loneliness of small-town scrutiny.

Susan broke our companionable silence. "I'm going to that resort at St. Bart's right after Christmas." She nudged me with her foot. "Why don't you join me?"

I tucked my feet under my chair, knowing my response would not please her. "You know I can't do that."

"Why the hell not? You have plenty of time off."

It is such a drag to have to explain to someone who has a flexible schedule and an unlimited budget why you don't have the same.

I did my best to be patient. "Time, yes, but not money. Plus, Ellie is performing all that week and Zach has an indoor soccer tournament. I don't want to miss either of those things."

Susan shuddered. "Good God. Can't that husband of yours do something for once? I like George, but honestly, Liz, I think you should make him take more responsibility for the kids. He certainly should do more around the house."

I agreed with her, but as so often happens, she missed the point. "It's not that. I *want* to see Ellie perform and Zach play. I enjoy it."

My sister gave an exaggerated sigh. "I understand some of what you're saying. But I don't understand why you have to see every performance. We'd have a great time together! The sun, the sea, the shopping. Hey, how do you like these shoes?" She held out one foot for me to admire.

No wonder she'd been nudging me with her feet. Shoes like that deserve to get noticed. "I love them, of course. Who wouldn't? Where did you get them?"

She swung one leg over the other, seriously discommoding two elderly ladies trying to navigate the narrow space between tables. "At a sample sale you were too busy to go to. You would not believe how cheap they were. I got them at seventy percent off!"

I looked down at my black wedge sandals that had taken me to school and to the funeral home and to the grocery store. "Maybe next time. After we pay off the house, the car, and the kids' tuitions, I promise to be a fixture at every sample sale in the city."

Susan signaled for another glass of wine. "You are really starting to bore me with all that domestic crap. By the time you indulge in yourself you'll be too old to enjoy it!" She ignored my protest and changed the subject to one that interested both of us. "How's your investigation going? That, at least, is exciting and interesting. I love my nephew, but I think I'll puke if I have to hear about one more soccer game."

I ate a cracker I had sworn would remain untouched. "I regret to inform you that Zach's soccer games are going a lot better than my investigation. I've had some ideas, but I'm too cowardly to carry them out. Confrontation is not my strong suit."

She squeezed my hand. "That's something we have in common. I'm also a big fan of procrastination and avoidance. So what ideas have you come up with?"

I took a scrap of paper from my handbag and started writing. As always, thinking was easier with pen in hand. "Marcia's lesson plans strongly suggest blackmail as the most likely motive for her murder. It also explains where she got all that disposable income. The other possibility in terms of her extra income is through the sale of fen-phen, of which she had an ample supply."

Susan's jaw dropped. "You're kidding me! Why didn't you mention this earlier? Can you get me some?"

"Not funny."

"Fine. Be that way." She grabbed the pen and paper and doodled a few pictures next to my list. "Okay then, you already have several suspects. What have you done to follow through on those leads?"

"I went into Bill's classroom when he wasn't there—"

Oblivious to the fact that the chamber music players were in the middle of a very soft passage, Susan screeched. People on both sides of us stared in disapproval, but she was unrepentant. Or, more likely, unaware. "Oh, my God! I wish I had been there to see that! Did you break in?"

I tossed an apologetic look at the art-and-music-loving people sitting next to us, and very softly told her, "I didn't have to. But I did have to break into Timmy's office." I wasn't proud of doing so, but I wasn't ashamed of it either.

Susan was all business. "Bobby pins or credit card?"

I snapped my fingers to demonstrate my expertise. "Credit card, thank God. It's been a long time since I've had to fiddle with the inside of a lock."

She looked regretful. "Yeah, but you always had a nice touch. I was never half so good as you. Okay—I'm happy you're getting more involved. And it's good to know that the Lousy Bastard bequeathed to us something other than years of therapy. What did you find in Timmy's office?"

After impressing Susan with my daring I hated disappointing her, but there was no getting around the fact that I had still not garnered much information.

"I didn't find anything in Timmy's office because he walked in on me."

She choked with laughter. "What did you say to him? I wish I had seen that."

My face grew warm and my stomach went a little jittery. I hadn't exactly covered myself in glory. "Something dumb. He didn't really question me much—he thinks I'm eccentric, in an English-teacherish way. I may try again on Friday. He's got the high school personnel files in his office. I'm curious to see if there's any indication why, or if, the administration was planning on moving Marcia to the middle school."

She placed both beautifully shod feet under the table and sat straight. "You think it's a clue? What difference does it make?"

I took back the paper and pen. I drew lines from Marcia's name to every other person on the list. It was a long list. "I admit her teaching assignment doesn't seem to have any bearing on the murder, but it bothers me. Something's not right about that. So yeah, maybe a clue."

She frowned and angled the paper so we could view it together. "I see the problem here. Everyone at Valerian Hills theoretically had the opportunity to commit murder. No matter how early Marcia got to school, someone could easily have planned to get there before her and absconded with the chair. Her coffee could have been poisoned at any time after she arrived."

"I agree. But it had to happen while Marcia was out of the room. So whoever did it had to be on site to see Marcia leave."

Susan lifted one finger and the waiter reappeared. "More of everything," she told him and turned back to me. "Have they traced the source of the poison?"

The two ladies who sat next to us leaned closer. I lowered my voice. "It wasn't poison, exactly. It was an overdose of Marcia's own medication, plus a few diet pills."

Susan drank from her wine and nodded her approval to the waiter. "Wouldn't she taste the pills in her coffee?"

"I guess not. Marcia took her coffee black, with about five packets of Sweet'N Low, so she probably wouldn't taste any difference even if the killer added gasoline. That indicates that the killer was someone who knew her well—really well. I've known her for years, and I didn't know she had a heart condition."

She shot me an accusing look. "You don't exactly invite those kinds of confidences."

Susan's observation was not wrong. I haven't avoided friendship at Valerian Hills High School, but I haven't sought it out, either. Up until Marcia's murder, that worked well for me.

There was no point in revisiting territory we'd covered multiple times in the last twenty years. "I vaguely remember something she said once about high blood pressure, but I can't imagine that anyone at school knew her well enough to know what meds she took."

Harriman's remark about Marcia's handbag suddenly made sense. The killer must have known Marcia carried her medication with her. Or maybe he planted the pills when she was out of her room. Marcia was looking for her chair, and she wouldn't want to be burdened with her handbag if she had to haul her furniture across the school.

I wasn't averse to having the killer be someone outside the school. "Even though I think it's most likely that someone at the high school poisoned her, I'm guessing both the boyfriend and the husband knew she had a heart condition and the medication she was on."

With a coy smile, Susan tapped my arm. "You should find out from your boyfriend if Marcia had any guests the night before."

I ignored the reference to my "boyfriend," because I have never given Susan cause to think that I found Tom interesting, or that I enjoy his company, or that I find him at all attractive. Also, I needed to keep her from veering into talk of boyfriends before she began reminiscing about either her ex-husbands or her latest dating disaster.

"Come to think of it, Marcia always brought a cup of coffee from home. We all do. If the boyfriend spent the night with her, he could have poisoned her cup before she got to school."

Susan agreed, "He could have slipped it into her mug. Not difficult, *ma chère.*"

"Poor Marcia provided the means herself. If we consider the motive, though, I'd say Timmy—or some other guy with a penchant for young girls—had the best reason for offing her."

Susan laughed, "Maybe. But I'd love to meet Wilde Billie."

"I googled him. No Wikipedia entries and so far, no luck on YouTube. I did find a few pictures. Don't get excited, though. They aren't that good, but they're enough to convince me he was one hell of a drag queen. It's tough to tell what the person under the huge blonde wig and cowboy hat looks like, but he did have great legs. I'd recognize those legs anywhere. Marcia's notes said the video was from 1984, and I'm still looking. I'm a little worried Homeland Security or the NSA is going to start wondering why I'm visiting porno sites for pedophiles and drag queens."

Susan swiped at her phone, looking for pictures of Wilde Willing Billie. "If even the Internet can't help then what we need is another murder."

I couldn't help flinching. "God forbid. I don't think I can take the shock of another death. I've barely slept since the day I found Marcia."

She put her phone down and patted my hand. "Forget I said that. But if the murderer won't provide new clues we'll have to work with what we have. Don't worry. I'm on the case!"

"That's very encouraging. But you're in New York and I'm in New Jersey. How exactly are 'we' going to investigate together?"

Susan ignored these practical impediments. "Tell me about that detective, Tom Harriman."

This was not good. Once my sister starts thinking about potential mates, all other subjects lose their gloss. "There's nothing to tell. I give him information, and he gives me garbage."

"That's not how you described the detective the last time we spoke. What's changed?" she asked, with no little interest.

I thought about the last time I saw Tom. "I don't know. He's been mooning after that young teacher I told you about, Ashlee."

She was amused. "You're jealous!"

In my eagerness to deny any interest in Tom Harriman, I knocked over the bud vase on our table. "Don't be ridiculous," I said as I mopped the table with my napkin. "I am not jealous of some dull cop and a brainless twenty-something. But I don't want to be taken advantage of. If Tom wants to schmooze with every female teacher in the school he can, but I am immune to his smarmy charm."

"You think he's charming," she said, in a singsong voice that still irritates me.

"No! I don't find him charming."

She took out a compact and inspected her face. "Well, I want to meet him. I'd like to see what all the fuss is about."

Nothing good could come of Susan's desire to meet with Tom. "He's too young for you."

"If he's not too young for you, how can he be too young for me?"

"He *is* too young for me." I checked my watch and calculated how long it would take to get to Penn Station. Miss one train and it's a sixty-minute wait in chairs only slightly more comfortable than the ones my school district provides.

She read my mind, as only sisters can. "Quit worrying about your train schedule and pay attention to me. I recently decided I want a very young lover for a change. What do you think? I think it would be fun."

"As the mother of one teenage boy and the teacher of many others I might not be the right person to share that with."

Susan stuck one finger in her mouth and pretended to gag. "Don't be absurd. I don't mean that young. My God, even as a teenage girl, teenage boys turned me off. No. I'm thinking someone about ten years younger than I am. Hot, but not boring or embarrassing. Let's face it; unless I want to pay for the privilege I have only a small window of opportunity to make it with a guy who has all his original hair and teeth. So introduce me, Sis. You're already married to George."

"Even if I weren't married, and Tom wasn't ten years younger, he's still not my type. Not your type either," I amended.

She flicked back her hair. "How do you know what my type is? I think my next boyfriend, or lover, or husband should be someone more...hmm...more down to earth, more a man of the people, *n'est-ce pas*?"

Man of the people? My sister had married, in order: a penniless indie filmmaker, a successful writer of pop psychology books, and a high-powered lawyer. There was probably no way to slow her down.

"Maybe you want to wait a few days before planning the wedding."

Susan is not easily put off. "You always complain that I never visit you. Well, I'm coming to visit next Saturday...no, make that Friday. I'll meet you at the school. What train should I take?"

The town of Valerian Hills has no train station. "You'll have to take a very slow bus. If you want to take a train you have to meet me at my house."

"Don't try to talk me out of it. It'll be fun." She resumed her perusal of her phone, this time to check on busses.

Still hoping I could dissuade her from visiting me at work, I said, "I'm not sure the high school is where I should be focusing my investigation. I asked Caroline how I could contact Marcia's husband and boyfriend."

"And?"

"And she hasn't gotten back to me yet."

"Don't take this the wrong way but—"

"Don't!" I implored. But there's no stopping anyone, even your sister, who has made up her mind to say something hurtful that you shouldn't take the wrong way because it is intended for your own good. "Whenever anyone says that, it means they're about to tell you something you really don't want to hear."

She said, more gently, "I get the feeling that most of your investigating is going on in your mind. If you're really serious about finding Marcia's murderer you'll have to be more direct. That's where I come in. I can help get things moving."

Susan has a knack of saying things that make theoretical sense. I know from experience that acting on her suggestions often yields results decidedly different from what she's promised, but I felt cornered. She drank the last of my wine and signaled for the bill.

As we got up to leave, the old lady facing me winked and said, "Good luck, girls! Sounds like fun."

Susan was delighted, and on the way out paid for the ladies' tea and cookies.

I got to Penn Station in enough time to see my train leave. I was starving, but thanks to former Mayor Bloomberg and his intrusive insistence that restaurants list the number of calories for each food item I can no longer console myself with Nathan's French fries. I wish I didn't know one serving packs enough calories to feed a family of four for a week.

I returned to a house blazing with lights. When I was growing up leaving a lone bulb burning in an uninhabited room was a capital offense, but I have been unable to persuade a single Hopewell to my way of thinking. Television sets remain playing long after the watcher has left the room, computers are never turned off, and if I died the toaster would never again experience an unplugged moment. Only George was home. He was sitting in bed, reading a biography of John Adams.

He said hello. I suppose that denotes a thaw in our cold war.

"How was dinner with your sister?"

"Fine. We had fun."

George's next move was unwise. "How come you always meet her in the city? Why can't she make an effort to come visit you once in a while?"

"She's coming next Friday and is staying for the weekend."

George knows when he's lost, but he doesn't go down without a fight. "Too bad I have a big meeting next week. I'll have to leave you two to amuse yourselves."

I yanked the covers over to my side. "I want a divorce. I want the house, the car, the kids, and all the money."

"Can I have that in writing?"

I'm not sure either of us knew if the other was kidding.

CHAPTER 12

CAN YOU FORGIVE HER?

The next morning I returned to my classroom and contemplated the vitriolic emails that cluttered my inbox. Quite a few parents were still perturbed about my interpretation of *Hamlet,* in which I implied (but never openly stated) that Hamlet told Rosencrantz and Guildenstern not to, uh, screw with him.

No one likes homework, so I ignored the personal attacks and provided each parent with a link to various articles of literary criticism. I sent the emails individually; I did not want to facilitate the formation of an anti-Liz Hopewell chat room. I kept to my desk during lunch, where I wrote my lesson plans and graded papers.

After lunch, my students weighed in on a series of carpe diem poems. I love them, and there's nothing high school students like better than discussing the merits of having sex at a young age. Brittany offered to read Marvell's poem "To His Coy Mistress" aloud. She read well, and stumbled only a bit when she got to the part about his mistress's breasts. Although the word "poetry" is an instant soporific to many kids, the slightest mention of female body parts has the opposite effect.

After Marvell explains how he'd love to spend all of eternity admiring his mistress's body, the tone and pace of the poem changes: "The grave's a fine and private place/But none I think do there embrace." Yeah, Marvell is still talking about having sex immediately—a sentiment my students never fail to appreciate—but it was the part about dying that got me. Which meant two things. One: My sex life is less interesting than death. And two: What the hell was I waiting for? I took Marvell's and Susan's advice to heart and decided to get to work. As in, time to seize the freaking day.

On my way to our faculty meeting I stopped by Emily's classroom, pleased to find her still there. Emily usually dashes to our meetings immediately after the bell rings. Perhaps she feels this atones for her stealthy early exits. As I stepped inside, she gave me her startled rabbit look. Caroline was lounging in the corner of the room.

It was one thing for Emily to converse with Caroline in public forums, like the faculty room, but it unnerved me to find Caroline so comfortably, and privately, ensconced with Emily. Hadn't Emily always been as disdainful of our department chairperson as I was? I thought back to Emily's meaningful glances and pitying looks and wondered if I'd misread her. Emily said so little. I assumed that we felt the same way about the other staff members, but it's possible that her silence is not agreement. I've never been able to understand nice, shy, modest people, so it's difficult for me to analyze Emily.

Caroline nodded at me, and said, "Greetings, Liz. Ready for another meeting?"

Emily looked a bit shamefaced. "Caroline and I were talking about our lesson plans. Are you ready for the meeting today?"

"Did I miss something?" I asked with as little expression as possible. "Why would I have to get ready for a meeting that's sure to be a rerun of every other meeting?"

Caroline widened her eyes, as if surprised at my ignorance. "Gordon wants us to bring samples of our lesson plans." She swallowed and pressed her lying lips together. "I'm sure I told you about it."

The woman has no shame.

The three of us walked to the Media Center, which used to be known as the library. Abandoning whatever she and Emily had been discussing before I arrived, Caroline described her most recent Mediterranean cruise. Employing a tone that was a bit too loud and a bit too kind, she let me know that she was covering up a private exchange with Emily that concerned me. I'm not very good when it comes to subtext that isn't literary, but Caroline tossed enough faux innocence into her narrative for even clueless me to understand. She hadn't yet responded to my request for the contact information for the men in Marcia's life, but I wasn't ready to remind her. Caroline had already had enough satisfaction at my expense.

There were no refreshments to cushion the pain. Austerity was back. With *Hamlet* and murder still on my mind I darkly paraphrased to my fellow English teachers that I supposed even in Elsinore the funeral bak'd meats eventually ran out. The others either thought the comment was in bad taste or they missed the reference and didn't want to admit it.

Gordon warmed up his vocal cords with a few guttural honks and then reviewed the agenda. The principal spoke first about the ongoing investigation into Marcia Deaver's death, and then, in what I hoped was an unconscious connection, segued into threatening the English department with dire consequences if the students did not perform well on the upcoming standardized tests. His face turned an unpleasant shade of purple as he sputtered about last year's SAT scores, state assessment scores, and AP scores. Gordon projected a slide onto the smart board. I squinted at the tiny numbers. From where I sat, it looked as though the kids had improved from the previous year. They hadn't done better than last year's class, but they had improved in comparison to their own performance.

Emily's face was a perfect blank. She looked one tick away from drooling, so I leaned forward and whispered to Caroline, "Look at the scores. Doesn't it look as if the kids did better last year than they did the year before?"

Caroline peeled her gaze from the papers she was grading. "Hmm. Maybe. Hard to tell."

I persisted, "Well, isn't it a little strange that Gordon would yell at us for *improving* test scores? I don't think it's fair to analyze the numbers the way he's doing it."

"Honestly, Liz," she answered, brandishing her papers at me. "I really don't give a damn. Now, if you'll excuse me, I'm busy." Caroline resumed grading the paper of the next unfortunate student. I hoped I was not the cause of the resultant spurt of red ink on the page.

After another quarter hour Gordon ran out of steam. He introduced the faculty members who would be presenting the professional development lesson for the staff. The district used to pay professional consultants to provide the required hours, but the grim economic climate and a general distaste for all things educational motivated the board of education to force teachers to do it for free. It makes sense. After all, if they have to waste our time, there's no advantage to doing it with their money.

Ashlee swiveled her way to the podium in spiked heels. Mackenzie, who began teaching history a year ago, met her midway. I felt a collective intake of breath.

They were teaching *us*.

For the first time I missed Marcia with gut-wrenching pain. I could almost hear her voice, dripping with sarcasm, asking what pearls of wisdom these two, with their vast experience, would be able to offer her.

I tried to keep an open mind, but I couldn't overlook the fact that Mackenzie was as oblivious to current events as she was to American history. Ashlee had been teaching for less than a month. I told my mind to shut up and assumed what I hoped was a neutral expression.

There was a low murmur of appreciation from the men. I risked a look around me. Bill's face was scarlet, and his eyes were glued in the most fatuous fashion on Mackenzie. I worried he would have a heart attack. Caroline's face was as expressionless as I hoped mine was. She slashed her red pen across the essays of hapless students and did not look up at all. Emily was eyeing the exit doors. I did not trust myself to look at anyone else. When the best lack all conviction, the worst...well, the worst end up talking about you behind your back.

Mackenzie and Ashlee distributed handouts with perky illustrations and several amusing cartoons.

Ashlee spoke first, "Oh. My. God. I am, like, sooooo nervous!" Everyone laughed along with Ashlee's giggles.

Mackenzie fiddled with the controls for the smart board. "Ashlee and me have been working on this for the English department and the social studies department, but, like, any of you guys could use it? Right, Ash?"

Ash nodded.

The screen sprang to life. Mackenzie pointed to the picture of her and Ashlee at the beach. "Okay, so, what do people do when they get home? Hello-o! They log onto Facebook. Or Instagram. Or whatever. Trust me, it's not homework they're looking at. And who can blame them? Let's face it, schoolwork is bor-ing."

Mackenzie and Ashlee proceeded to explain how to utilize Facebook to engage the kids in literature, history, and science. They showed a humorous YouTube video about Facebook. They invited us to friend them. The mood was light, quite unlike the usual dour atmosphere that infects most faculty meetings, and I saw Timmy and Gordon exchange self-congratulatory smiles. I thought with increasing sadness about Marcia. I was so repelled by Marcia's threats to my colleagues I'd forgotten about her brilliance as a teacher.

Mackenzie and Ashlee gave an excellent performance, and they received a warm round of applause. Ashlee provided the coda. "Don't forget you guys, the next pub crawl is Friday! Right after school! Be there!"

A chorus of woo-hoos ended the meeting. Emily was still sitting by my side. Her eyes were shining.

"Don't you think having the kids post to Facebook is a good idea?" she asked.

"Absolutely," I replied, patting my backpack full of student papers. "It's going to be way easier to go online and check a few postings than to grade a pile of essays and papers."

Emily, who is impervious to sarcasm, smiled and headed for the exit. I shelved further attempts at wit and searched for Timmy. He was talking to Ashlee. He pried his gaze away from her, clearly annoyed at my interruption.

"What can I do for you, Liz?"

"I was just wondering if you had Marcia's husband's address. I want to send him a condolence card."

"That's nice of you. Ask Mrs. Donnatella in the morning."

"Okay, I will. You know, I'm not sure I even remember his name."

This was true. I'm not good with the names of living people. But ask me the author of any book, and I'm all over it.

Timmy hesitated. "Uh, I don't know. I'll have to check."

Gordon, who was busy congratulating Mackenzie on her fine performance and academic rigor, turned our way. "Bellinger. Something Bellinger. I'm pretty sure he's in Floral Park."

I checked the white pages. There were only two listings for people named Bellinger in Floral Park, and one of them was a deli. The other was for William Bellinger. I punched the address into my phone, and despite the threatening skies, headed out to...well, I wasn't quite sure. But I was doing something. Seizing the day. Or what was left of it.

CHAPTER 13
THE IDIOT

Willliam Bellinger lived in a modest apartment building not far from Ellie's ballet studio. I needed a plausible excuse to barge in on a man I'd never met, and I tried to think of what a normal person, someone like Emily, would do. I purchased a platter of cookies and returned. If Bellinger lived in a private house, my assault on his privacy would have been easier, but I had to explain myself over the crackle of the intercom. In the movies people push their way through when residents buzz other people in, but the dwellers of this apartment building weren't popular. They also weren't all that trusting; the one person who entered using his key closed the door in my face. After two more tries, Marcia's husband buzzed the door open. I rode the creaking elevator to the sixth floor. The unshaved greasy-haired man didn't bear much resemblance to the cleaner version I'd seen at the funeral.

"Who are you?" He stood in the doorway and didn't let me pass.

"Liz Hopewell." I had to speak loudly, in order to compete with the sound of ESPN television anchors blaring their predictions from the living room. I opted for the cheery tone of a Food Network cook. "I was a friend of Marcia's. I wanted to give you my condolences and to bring you this." I offered my sops, but unlike Cerberus this creature seemed disinclined to move aside from the gates of hell.

He stepped into the hallway, forcing me to retreat. "Marcia said she didn't have any friends at school."

Truer words were never spoken.

"We were more acquaintances than friends," I confessed. I peeked around him into his apartment. "But I really miss her and I feel terrible about what happened."

I don't know what excess of emotion prompted the quavering in my voice, whether of nervousness or genuine grief, but it did the trick. Bellinger let me in.

Once I was in I couldn't remember why I thought visiting him was a good idea. The apartment smelled of stale food and unwashed clothing. Bellinger pointed to the sofa, pale beige with irregular dark blotches. A dirty trench coat that closely matched the upholstery was in a crumpled heap in one corner. I sat on the edge of the cleanest looking section, a few feet from the coat and two grimy socks and behind a glass-topped coffee table, which was stained with a dozen different rings. Two beer bottles, both empty, stood in the middle. I used the edge of the cookie platter to move them to one side.

My host was barefoot, with long curving toenails that gave his feet a wild bird-like menace. He watched me out of half-closed eyes, as if the sight of me was putting him to sleep. That crocodile gaze didn't fool me. Bellinger reminded me of the bookies who used to hang out at Junior's Restaurant on Flatbush Ave., many years before irony moved to Brooklyn. To look at those small time crooks you'd think they had nothing more pressing on their minds than cheesecake, when really, they were planning to whack The Lousy Bastard's knees if he didn't fork over the money he owed them.

Bellinger reached over the arm of the sofa to grab the remote and turn off the television. The sudden silence was unnerving. He stopped in between the door and a short hallway that led to the kitchen, and I had to turn to look at him. Worst of all, I didn't know what to say. Well, perhaps that wasn't worst of all. Worst of all would have been if this guy were the murderer. He bolted the door, which was unnecessary. I tensed the muscles in my legs. If he got within two feet of me, I'd knee him in the groin and then make a run for it.

"Thanks for inviting me in." I edged toward the end of the sofa, and he walked back toward the door. "But I can't stay long. My husband is downstairs waiting for me."

He turned to look through the peephole. "Why didn't he come up?"

"Oh, he didn't really know Marcia."

Satisfied that no one was outside the apartment door, he turned back to me. "Neither did you."

It figures that Marcia, whatever else was wrong about her, had married a man not pleasant, but not stupid. It's a wonder they separated; they seemed like a perfect match.

We appeared to be at a bit of an impasse. He seemed more interested in my handbag than in me, flicking glances at it as if he were a purse snatcher on the subway, timing his grab to coincide with the opening of the doors. He offered tea, which I declined.

I loathe tea. Also, I was not about to imbibe any liquids from a prime suspect in a poisoning case.

"Did you know Marcia was going to be reassigned to the middle school?" I unwrapped the cookies, to give myself something to do. "That really surprised me."

Whatever the guy was expecting, it wasn't this. "I don't know what you're talking about, or why you're here. So let's start with that. What the hell are you doing here?"

"Marcia told me all about the Shakespeare conspiracy. I'm—I'm a member of the, uh, the DeVere Society, and I want to know if you have any of the research she did. Maybe you have some papers that belonged to her, papers that you don't need?"

His sleepy look evaporated. "Cut the crap. I know exactly what you're looking for. I don't have it. But if you know something, I want in. Marcia was doing real well. New shoes, new clothes. New everything. Including a new boyfriend. Get me the list. We can be partners."

Bellinger looked again at my handbag, which I held on my lap. I removed my key ring and held it in my right hand. You can poke a guy's eye out with a well-placed stab. But it's not an easy move from a sitting position.

I stood up. "What list?"

"If you want to play games go somewhere else. So if all you got is cookies—" He glanced at the coffee table. "—you can save both of us some time and get the hell out of here."

Something Bellinger said didn't ring true, but anxious that he would either kill me or toss me out on my rear, my brain refused to come through with the answer.

"No. I have more than cookies. Look, I know Marcia was blackmailing at least three people. I'm not sure who they are."

He crossed his arms and leaned back against the door. "Tell me something I don't know. Or like I say, get the hell out."

I looked straight at him. "I told you everything I know."

He scratched his head and a shower of white flakes rained into his eyebrows. "You're a lousy liar."

That hurt. I'm a good liar. The problem was, we were reading from two different scripts. I tried to pry him from his scenario, so that he could begin reading and responding from my point of view.

"This is about murder."

Bellinger snapped his fingers in a series of rapid-fire cracks that he pointed at my head. Then he dropped his arm and rubbed his thumb against his other fingers, in the universal sign for money. "For you, not for me. For me, this is about cash. And you're wasting my time."

He crossed the room and slipped a pair of ancient loafers over his bare feet. As soon as he moved I circled around the sofa toward the door. He walked a few steps toward me and smiled. "Tell me what you do know. Maybe I can help. Get me the list. We can go in together, fifty-fifty."

"Do you know who killed her?"

I didn't think this was funny, but he laughed and shook his head. He got so close I could feel his breath, which smelled as if a small animal were decomposing in his mouth.

"What's your rush?"

I pulled back. The room began to feel very small. Now it was my back that was against the door.

"Just relax." He gestured toward the sofa. "Sit down. No one's gonna hurt you. How did you find out about the blackmail?"

I did an about-face, snapped the lock and swung the door open.

He slammed it shut. "You're not going anywhere until I get the list. I think you have it—or you know where to get it."

I looked around the room. The windows were shut tight and had an undisturbed film of greasy dirt over them. The only way out was through the door, which Bellinger now blocked. Perhaps instead of trying to escape I should explain to him that I was a middle-aged English teacher whose interest in murder and blackmail was purely theoretical. No threat to anyone, not even her own students. That was one option. The danger, though, was that telegraphing weakness might not be the safest bet.

I let my Brooklyn accent out of its suburban prison. "If I'd'a had the list, then what am I doin' here? All I got are her lesson plans. The names you're looking for were coded into the plans, but I couldn't figure 'em out."

"Give them to me." He reached one hand to me and kept the other pressed against the door.

"I gave 'em to the police. They're working on it."

"You are either giving me the list right here, right now, or you're taking me to it."

This wasn't the first time I'd been threatened, even after discounting various escapades with irate landlords and dear old Dad. Just last year, after making an illegal U-turn on a deserted street, two cops who were waiting for a law-abiding middle-aged woman to commit a minor traffic violation stopped me. Their lights flashed, they pulled me over, and they demanded to see my license and registration. But for the first time in my life I didn't have my license. I had dashed out of the house to rescue Ellie from a party that was getting out of control. I also didn't have my most recent insurance card.

The police ordered back up. It took forty minutes and four cops to determine that what they had on their hands was a slightly overweight—but still attractive—mother and her terrified daughter menacing the leafy streets of suburban New Jersey.

This situation was much like that one. I was being mistaken for someone interesting, when the last eighteen years of my life have been devoted to the opposite. I couldn't push the cops aside and race to safety. But Bellinger didn't exactly have the criminal justice system behind him.

I took two rapid steps back towards the sofa. He anticipated my move and followed me, but I was faster. As soon as he lunged away from the door I grabbed one of the empty beer bottles and threw it at his head. He ducked. I made as if to grab the other bottle and as soon as he dove for it I flung the door open and raced down the stairs.

"Tell your husband I said hello," he yelled.

I think I heard him laugh. I ran down all six flights of stairs, hoping the footsteps behind weren't Bellinger's.

When I parked, I'd left myself plenty of room front and back, but in the short period of time I'd been away two monster SUV's had wedged me into a parking spot I could never have wrangled into on my own. I seesawed back and forth, desperate to get out, but fearful of punching a dent into the expensive cars that boxed me in. Crunching the steering wheel beyond what either nature or Chrysler minivan engineers intended I broke free and drove to the end of the block towards a large intersection. I was certain, even without GPS, that I needed to make a left turn. The turn signal flipped to red just as I got there, and I had to wait until each lane of traffic moved before I could put the sight of Bellinger's apartment building out of my rear view mirror. I fidgeted with the steering wheel as two cars lined up behind me.

A sudden wind brought a heavy sheet of rain, and the skies darkened. I could barely make out the street signs. When the GPS finally emerged from her coma, she told me to turn around. I ignored her, because a most welcome sign invited me to spend some time at the mall. The safest of safe havens.

CHAPTER 14

THE LONELINESS OF
THE LONG DISTANCE RUNNER

W hen I first moved to New Jersey, enclosed shopping centers made me short of breath. The canned air and imitation daylight unnerved and tired me, but eventually I made my peace with that ultimate suburban shopping destination, the Long Hills Mall. My only lingering anxiety was the fear of losing my car in the parking lot, and so I usually mark the latitude and longitude of my location with the care of an Arctic explorer. As I made my way from the car to the mall I checked again and again to see if Bellinger had followed me. I'd remained in sight of his house for what had felt like eternity.

I headed for the always-soothing shoe department. Shoes don't require a visit to the dressing room. Shoes don't shame you with tight zippers. Most important of all, shoes don't ask you to buy them now, for when you lose weight later, and then stubbornly refuse to fit until they are definitively out of style.

I found a lovely pair of comfortable suede clogs. They were not on sale. As I debated spending twice as much money as was reasonable for such a purchase, I had the feeling I was being watched. The saleswoman who had brought me eight pairs of unsuitable discounted shoes and one pair of perfect expensive ones was indeed eyeing me. Was anyone else interested in my shoe purchase?

The men's shoe department was separated from the women's by a narrow stone barrier filled with silk flowers. There weren't many men shopping. The lone salesman bent over a chair to talk to an invisible customer. Across the aisle the cosmetics department, with its maze of curving counters and mirrored columns, made casing the joint impossible. I paid for the shoes, and, feeling an unaccountable anxiety, did not stop at the Estee Lauder counter, despite the tempting giveaway they were offering. It pained me to forego the free wrinkle cream, but at the rate I was going I wouldn't live long enough to use it.

I did stop to buy a small coffee, which I purchased for its calming, not its stimulating effects. I was already jazzed with nervous energy. Coffee, clunky handbag, and large shopping bag in tow, I headed back to the car. I was in the section of the parking lot that fed directly into Bloomingdale's when I entered the mall, and when I finished shopping I exited from Bloomingdale's. Nevertheless, my car was persistently not where I left it. The air in the underground parking lot was heavy, and my heart started racing. I tried the next level up.

Don't panic. Don't panic. Don't—I traversed one aisle after another in despair, randomly clicking on the remote button on the key fob, hoping to see a response from the car.

The cavernous space was quiet, except for the sound of footsteps. I turned but saw no one. I felt like the protagonist of a spy movie, and I launched into a simulation of the most cinematically approved moves I could think of. Yes, I was scared, but I also felt like combination of *Harriet the Spy* and Harrison Ford. I don't think either Harriet or Harrison would have allowed a bulky shopping bag and a sloshing coffee cup to slow them down, no matter how thirsty they were for either a great pair of shoes or a jolt of caffeine, but I was unwilling to abandon my burdens simply to ensure verisimilitude. I did feel slightly ridiculous. I was either acting like an idiot, peering around corners and lurching from behind pillars and cars, or I was allowing trivial belongings—like new shoes and coffee—to delay a safe departure.

I quieted my breathing and searched for a suitable resting place. No sense avoiding a killer only to die of a heart attack. I paused behind a Lincoln Navigator large enough to house a family of four. A minute later I heard footsteps pass the front of the car.

This felt less and less like a game. I waited ten long breaths before peeking around the huge bumper. All I could see was the sweep of a trench coat. Was it Bellinger? I dashed back behind the car. A voice, made spooky by echoes, called out a name that sounded a lot like mine. I didn't answer. I doubled back and took the stairs to the next level up, pausing every few minutes to flatten myself against the wall in case bullets should fly. When I reached the top I peered around the corner. A car that looked a lot like mine beckoned. I was not seduced by the apparent ease of escape, and I took a circuitous route, stopping every few yards to hide.

The parking lot on the upper level was nearly empty, and there were few sanctuaries left. I made the final dash in a flurry of spilled coffee. I got in the car, locked the doors, and put my key in the ignition. I looked left to gauge my distance from an ill-placed pole. A face filled the window.

Terrified, I started screaming at the top of my lungs. The car lurched backward and hit the pole.

George was so startled he jumped back and nearly screamed in response. We stared at each other.

"What were you doing?" He had a most peculiar expression on his face. "I saw you leave the mall, and when I called out to you, you ran away. Have you completely lost your mind?"

Before I could answer a police car zoomed behind us, lights flashing.

"Step away from the car."

George's face, which had paled in response to my screams, turned red.

"Officer," he said, without stepping aside, "this is my wife."

The police ignored his statement. "Step away from the car. Now."

They weren't playing, and they weren't kidding. George reluctantly moved away from me.

"It's okay, officers," I said, trying not to laugh. "He really is my husband. It's fine." The police officers looked unconvinced, but at least they didn't have their hands ready to seize their guns. I briefly considered pretending that George was an abusive husband, but I was concerned the police officers might lack a sense of humor. Also, George did not look in the mood for a joke.

I was loath to get out of the car and reveal my coffee-stained clothes, but I sacrificed my pride in order to convince them George was not likely to be violent. The four of us inspected the pole and the rear of the car. The pole was fine—barely a scrape in its neon green paint. I was afraid the police would give me a ticket, but all they wanted was my license and registration and insurance. For once, I had all three.

The police pretended to leave, but I saw them standing beside one of the pillars that I had used a few minutes earlier as a hiding place. It was reassuring to know my moves had a certain street cred.

I turned back to George, so we could continue our argument. "Why were you spying on me?"

"Don't be ridiculous. I wasn't spying on you. I want to know why you screamed *after* you saw my face. Are you hiding something from me?" He peered into the car.

"What could I possibly be hiding from you? I didn't even know that you were the creep who was following me. I thought it was some creep I didn't know."

With George and the police watching me, I felt safe enough to do a brief reconnaissance of the parking lot. Of course, no one was there, other than a weary-looking mother, accompanied by four sulky teenaged girls. "So...did you see anyone following me? Someone in a trench coat?"

George followed me. "All I saw was my wife stumbling around the parking lot as though she'd lost her marbles. That was before you hit another innocent piece of concrete. I guess I should be happy that so far you've only smashed into inanimate objects."

I clenched my hands to keep myself from belting him. "I wasn't 'stumbling about.' I hate it when you say things like that. It's very demeaning. But just to clarify: you saw no one—no one who looked, uh, suspicious?"

He grabbed my shoulders "Liz, what is this about? What are you up to?"

I didn't answer. What could I say? He'd never understand.

He let go of me and reached into the car. "Please don't tell me you've bought another pair of shoes. You're like the Imelda Marcos of New Jersey."

I took the bag from him and tossed it back in the car. "Don't change the subject. I want to know why you're here and why you're spying on me. And what's in *your* shopping bag?"

George put the bag behind his back. "If you won't tell me why you think someone was following you I won't tell you what's in the bag. As for why I'm at the mall, you told me to take Ellie to her ballet class. She wasn't sure she had a ride back, so I figured I'd kill some time here. I was on my way out when I saw you."

I reached behind him. "What's in the bag? What are you hiding from me?"

He stepped away. "Nothing."

"Then let me see it."

He waved a blue collared shirt at me. "For heaven's sake! It's a golf shirt. I returned the plaid shirt my mother bought me that you hate so much, and I got myself a golf shirt."

It wasn't until later that I wondered if there was anything else in the bag.

He replaced the shirt and asked, "Happy? And by the way, now that you're here, you can drive Ellie home. But I still want to know what the hell you were up to in this parking lot."

I looked at his feet. "You're wearing sneakers."

"Excellent observation, Sherlock. The point being?"

I didn't tell him that someone who wasn't wearing rubber-soled shoes was in the parking lot with him and with me. I did tell him I would take Ellie home.

I collected my daughter and continued to inadvertently spread good cheer. She spotted the shopping bag, opened the shoebox, and shrieked, "Mom! Mommy! I love you! How did you know I wanted the new Uggs clogs?" I craned my neck around Ellie's arms as I made a left-hand turn that met with honking disapproval from oncoming traffic.

"Huh? What do you mean?"

Ellie laughed and exclaimed, "I can't believe you didn't realize that these were Uggs! Mom, you're from a different planet."

"Yeah, that's me. The Mom from Mars."

Ellie consoled me. "Don't worry about it, Mom, cause I love, love, love you! Thank you so much! You're the best!"

The loss of a pair of shoes was a small price to pay for so much affection. Later, Ellie forbore complaining about the green noodle and spinach dinner. She ate all the spinach, and Zach and George ate all the pasta. I consumed what has become my go-to meal, Excedrin and Diet Coke, with a black coffee chaser.

Had my visit with Marcia's husband paid off at all, other than to alert her possible murderer that I was suspicious of him? I did find out that he knew about Marcia's blackmailing activities. Could he have followed me to the shopping mall? Or maybe he was the one who trashed my classroom. I strained to remember everything he'd said, sure that he'd let fall a clue, but nothing clicked.

My efforts had yielded more questions than answers. The one thing I did feel sure of was that Mr. William Bellinger seemed quite capable of murder.

CHAPTER 15
EAST OF EDEN

T he secretary, not the principal, runs the school. Without Wilhelmina Donnatella the copy machine would stay jammed with paper, the supplies would remain locked in the vault, and the tech support team would never return from their endless coffee breaks and lengthy lunchtime expeditions.

I doubted Mrs. Donnatella's influence extended to the level of making personnel decisions, but she was probably a mine of information about how those decisions were made. The secretary was centrally located, geographically, in the main office, and strategically, at the nexus of the teachers and administrators. She was also at the top of my list of people I needed to interview.

Mrs. Donnatella was not a likely candidate as the target of Marcia's lesson plan on *Lolita,* since the book featured a pedophile, and she loathed children even more than she loathed adults. And I shuddered to imagine her as the porn star, Wild Willing Billie. But she was cold enough to fit the profile of the lying, cheating, swindling, killer Marcia had targeted in her lesson plan on *The Talented Mr. Ripley.*

After signing in, I mentioned, as if in passing, that I had purchased a large number of delicious cupcakes. She admitted to a fondness for cake, and I gambled that her affection for cake might spill over into affection for me.

A few hours later, I brought a dozen Magnolia Bakery cupcakes to the main office. I got there as she was finishing the last crumb of her sandwich.

"I was thinking about you," I said, holding up a white beribboned box, "and I want you to try these cupcakes. They are absolutely to die for!"

She wasn't suspicious at all. Everyone treats her with saccharine tenderness, and she accepts this homage as her due.

Mrs. Donnatella unbent a bit. She peered into the box and extracted a chocolate cupcake. Without being prompted, I pulled up a chair to join her.

From across the desk I saw her weigh her choices. On one side of the balance the cupcakes beckoned. On the other side was an unencumbered lunch hour. With a grimace, she chose the cake. I waited while she poured a raspberry cream concoction and five packets of Splenda into her coffee.

While she mixed and stirred I scanned her desk, but as usual, the surface was clear of papers. A wicked-looking pair of scissors, roll of tape, and large black stapler were the only visible items, other than her bag of yarn.

Gordon and Timmy were manning the cafeteria, and the office was quiet. I would never get a better opportunity to question her. I opened with, "Things must have been so difficult for you in the aftermath of Marcia's death."

The secretary nodded, her mouth full.

I crossed my legs and leaned back. "You know something weird? I heard that Marcia was going to be moved to the middle school. I wonder what *that* was all about."

"That's none of your business. None of mine, neither." Mrs. Donnatella bit into the creamy center of the cupcake. Through a mass of crumbs and dark fudge she said, "Who you talking to, anyway?"

I averted my eyes from her slowly moving mouth. "No one. I'm not talking to anyone. I just heard. Maybe at a faculty meeting."

"I don't make these decisions. I may have heard something about that, but I can't confirm it. I am a confidential secretary." She made it sound like Secretary of State.

"Then you know everything." I pursed my lips and nodded, to indicate my understanding of her exalted position. She didn't disagree.

I picked up a caramel cupcake, but used my peripheral vision to watch her. "I didn't hear about the decision to transfer Marcia until after she died, so I didn't think much of it. But why would anyone want to transfer her?"

Mrs. Donnatella shrugged one massive shoulder. "You know what the parents are like in this district. Maybe someone complained."

I immediately thought of Mrs. Tumbleson, whose nasty emails poked holes at me at least three mornings a week. In every message she reminded me she was Jack's Mom and The President of the Board of Education. As if I could forget.

I knew Mrs. Donnatella was talking about Marcia, but what if she were also talking about me? Distracted from my main mission I asked, "Who? Who complained? About what?"

She put her glasses on to better gauge my guilt. "Maybe Ms. Deaver—Dr. Deaver—wasn't as great a teacher as she thought she was. I heard the test scores were pretty bad last year." She looked angry, as if the students' bad grades were my responsibility. Which, I guess, in some part they were. Her scrutiny made me so nervous I offered her the rest of the cupcakes.

The change in emotion was immediate. Never before had she been so close to smiling at me.

Pressing my advantage I asked, "What was going on in Marcia's classroom before she died? Her chair was missing; the room was a mess..."

Ignoring my query, the secretary removed several skeins of yarn from her workbag and held out her latest creation. "Have you seen my baby booties? I got green, pink, blue, and yellow. I think one white."

I examined the green booties but didn't pick them up, since the color matched the mold on my bathroom tiles. "I don't need baby booties. Right now I'm more interested in finding out what happened to Marcia."

Mrs. Donnatella picked up her crochet hook and pointed it at me. "Who knows what happened to that poor woman? I felt so sorry for her." She stabbed the hook in and out of the weave. "This job was her whole life. She didn't have kids like you do. You got two kids, right?"

Typically, any mention of my children sidetracks me, and I start thinking about the adorable pictures of Ellie and Zach I could show, if I weren't determined to avoid mimicking people I find annoying. "Yes, but to get back to Marcia, who wanted to transfer her? It doesn't make sense to me or to anyone else I've talked to."

The needlework stopped. "Who'd you talk to?"

If she could be cagey, so could I. "A few people. I'm going to talk to Gordon and Timmy next, but everyone knows you're the one in charge here. Spill!"

Mrs. Donnatella likes to tell people the school would fall apart without her, but my guess is she doesn't often receive independent confirmation. She relaxed slightly, but not enough to respond with anything more than an elliptical answer. She wet her index finger and thumb and drew out a length of yarn. "Liz, you have nothing to worry about. I happen to know that as of now no one is planning to transfer you."

"I am not worried about being transferred. Unlike Marcia, I wouldn't lose five seconds of sleep over it!" I tossed the remainder of my cupcake in the trash.

Mrs. Donnatella looked disapprovingly at the waste of a cupcake. "Cool down. You're pretty excited for someone who doesn't care."

I moved my chair so the desk no longer divided us. "Listen, I don't care, but Marcia did and you know it. So what gives?" Time was running out, and I was losing patience. I had sacrificed my pride, my free time, and my cupcakes; and I wanted recompense.

Mrs. Donnatella slid closer to her desk, avoiding my gaze. She moved the box of cupcakes out of reach, perhaps concerned I would change my mind if she didn't fork over some information. Sweeping her desk clean, she looked pointedly at my coffee cup, still parked in her territory.

Finally, she said, "These decisions are made at the highest levels. They are made based on performance, evaluations, and standardized tests." She sounded as if she was reading from a manual.

I gripped my coffee cup, keeping it planted on her desk. "But you know about the backroom stuff, don't you?"

Mrs. Donnatella glanced at the principal's open door. "Don't be so dramatic. There is no backroom. Marcia had a big mouth and she got on the wrong side of plenty of people. Make sure you don't do the same."

I am no more paranoid than the next person, if you assume most people are one twitch away from mania.

"Why?" I asked, with more force. "What have you heard? Is Mrs. Tumbleson still gunning for me? No wonder Marcia wouldn't let her wretched son into the class!"

"Mrs. Tumbleson is leaving the Board of Education in June, right after Jack graduates. I suggest you keep a low profile until then." She changed her tone and became extremely businesslike. "I can give you one piece of advice. Don't ask either Timmy or Gordon about it. They won't say a word. I should know."

"Why wouldn't they say anything? What difference does it make now?"

She clicked garishly decorated nails against the desk. "Personnel decisions are privileged information."

I ignored the bell summoning me back to class, trusting that in my absence those well-behaved AP students would not inflict permanent damage on the room or each other. "What's so privileged about decisions that are published online in the minutes of the board meeting?"

Mrs. Donnatella wiped her mouth and put the chocolate and red-streaked napkin in the garbage. "By law, the discussion that the board members and administrators have about personnel is confidential. You know that. If you want my opinion, and it seems you do, there will be no record of that discussion. If it ever happened. If it's even true. Which I don't have no idea about at all. So no point in talking about it to me or anyone else." She tapped her computer and the screen lit up with flickering closed caption videos of the interior of the school. "And, uh, yeah, not to be rude, but I have work to do. And don't you need to be somewhere?"

I thanked Mrs. Donnatella and left. She should have thanked me. She got cake. I got crumbs. I rushed to my classroom. The kids proved my faith in them was not misplaced, but my department chairperson was less trustworthy. Caroline used my brief absence as an excuse to rummage in my closet. A Nieman Marcus shopping bag filled with paper, markers, and Post-it notes was at her feet.

Not at all disturbed at my interruption, she said, "The kids told me where you keep your supplies. I'm running low on a few items. I'll take these, plus some poster paper. You don't mind, do you?"

I looked into the denuded closet. "Actually, I do mind. I only have a few sheets of poster paper left until the supplies come in. You can take the rest of the stuff."

Caroline made no move to return the paper. "Oh. Well then, I'll only take some."

"Sorry, I can't spare any." I pulled a sheaf of paper out of her bag and held onto it.

Caroline's medically enhanced forehead did not crease, but a few strands of hair escaped the discipline of her chignon, as if to register their own silent argument. I looked pointedly at the door. Caroline is not often thwarted. I turned back to the kids, who interrupted their covert texting in order to watch the spectacle of two teachers sniping over fifty cents worth of paper.

"Show's over," I told them. I walked deliberately to the back of the room and closed the connecting door, and then stood in front of it, forcing her to use the door that opened into the hallway.

Indirectly, Caroline did get the last word. Shortly after she left I received a high importance email from Timmy, reminding me that teachers should NEVER be late to class, ESPECIALLY after lunch. The email was sent to the entire staff, but the timing was more than a little suspicious.

At the end of the day I called my sister to report on my conversation with Mrs. Donnatella. Susan was not impressed.

"Why didn't you ask her what all the secrecy was about?" she demanded.

"I tried! I assume they don't want to let anyone know that they were planning to humiliate a woman who was murdered." I heard a noise that sounded as if it were coming from the hallway, but no one was there. I closed my door and locked it. In a softer voice, I continued, "I asked Mrs. Donnatella three times about the decision to reassign Marcia, and I got nowhere." In the brief silence that followed, I heard another rustle, this time from the English office.

As quietly as I could, I crossed the room. I put my hand over the phone to mute Susan, who said, with unfortunate clarity, "I think you should focus on Timmy. He is the only suspect who might be in on the decision to move Marcia. He also had the best motive for murder."

I swung open the connecting door. On the other side pink-faced Emily hugged a ream of paper. "Oh, Liz, I was just leaving to do some printing. I need to print a few things."

For a completely normal person, Emily certainly has her weird moments. I closed the door before returning to my sister.

"Timmy is too wimpy. He can't even face down Caroline. I don't see him taking on Marcia. And anyway, if we think Marcia was murdered because she was blackmailing him, it doesn't make sense that Timmy would dare to reassign her."

Susan asked, "How well do you know Timmy?"

I walked over to the window and watched a line of cars snake towards the exit. Timmy's car was still in his parking spot. "Other than his penchant for leaving early and cornering nubile teenage girls while he's here, I don't know all that much about him."

Susan didn't let up. "Compare him to sleaze balls from our past. Is he a con man like the Lousy Bastard? A charming card shark like Nana? Or a moron like Grandpa? We have to go with what we know."

I thought about Timmy's cowardly habit of yelling at meek honor roll students for their petty infractions and ignoring tough kids' felonious behavior. "He's got a few characteristics of each. He can be as charming as Dad—"

"Don't call him that!" implored Susan.

"Sorry. He can be as charming as The Lousy Bastard, and he is undoubtedly as adulterous. On the other hand, he's probably about as dumb as Grandpa. He's not nearly as smart as Nana. He couldn't bluff a game of Old Maid, let alone canasta, poker or bridge." I scribbled notes as I considered each possibility. "I like the idea of profiling our subject. I'm stymied by the fact that I can't rule out anyone on the basis of either opportunity or means, and we have plenty of motives for not only Timmy, Caroline, and Bill, but a host of other people. So maybe we can solve the mystery through psychology."

"*Très bien*!" said Susan, excited about this new game. "So what does our guy, or woman, look like? Psychologically speaking, of course."

I thought again about Marcia's lesson plans. If there was a connecting thread between the three works she listed, it was that all three protagonists were gifted liars. "If the killer is someone in the school, he is a damned good actor. No one I've spoken to has evinced even the slightest nervousness or guilt except for Emily, and she feels guilty for things she hasn't even done."

"No wonder you're such good friends with her," Susan commented.

"Yeah, that's funny." I checked the parking lot again. Most of the cars were gone. Emily's was still there. It was one of the few times she hadn't left early to wait upon Mavis. "Actually, we're not such good friends. I mean, I like her, and I've known her for as long as I've been working here, but it's not like we socialize outside of school or anything. She's more an acquaintance than a friend."

"Did anything happen to make you change your mind about her? I thought you two were close."

"No. Nothing happened. We're friendly enough while we're at school, but we don't ever get together after three o'clock. I realized that even though I like her and get along with her I don't really know her." Even though I was talking to Susan, I felt lonely. And stupid. How could I have not known Emily wasn't really my friend?

"I know what you mean." Susan sounded anxious, which was not typical. She was always so confident. "Sometimes I assume that I'm friends with someone I think I know well, and I end up spilling my guts to a completely unsympathetic person. Right now I'm dealing with an incredibly vicious young intern, an *All About Eve* impersonator whom my boss recently hired. I absolutely cannot stand her, and—can you believe this? I think she's after my job.

"The little bimbo is about twenty-two-years-old; she's the best friend of the boss's daughter, and she acts like the most privileged person in the world. I was explaining the situation to one of my coworkers, and instead of tea and sympathy all I got out of the miserable traitor was a scolding about not welcoming new talent. Talent? Hah! Whatever public relations talent the little slut has, it's not between her ears."

All of a sudden, I felt less lonely. "Don't be bitter. Even though I know what you mean. There are two women here, Ashlee, who started teaching in September, and Mackenzie, who's been here all of one year, and despite near-perfect ignorance they've become the standard for the rest of us. Yesterday Ashlee asked me if she really had to read *Romeo and Juliet* with the kids. She wanted to watch *West Side Story* and be done with it."

"That's not funny," Susan said with a laugh.

"Who's trying to be funny? Susan, I am not kidding. I feel like the last bastion of Western civilization here. I can't help speculating about what would happen if I died. Everyone would heave a huge sigh of relief right before they race to download Spark Notes and shelve Shakespeare in favor of something they think is more 'relatable'—ugh—such a horrible word."

In a more cheerful tone Susan said, "I'll see it all for myself this Friday."

I began straightening the mess on my desk in preparation for Susan's visit. "Why not meet me at my house? That way, you can take the train to the Oak Ridge station and walk to my place. If you come to Valerian Hills I'll have to pick you up from the bus stop, which I can't do until after school. By the time we get back everyone but the custodians will be long gone."

Susan ignored this suggestion. "Can't you pick me up any earlier? I want to see the scene of the crime." When I didn't respond, she was undeterred. "If you can't pick me up I suppose I could get a cab. Do you have cabs in the suburbs? What about Uber?"

"Valerian Hills has a car service," I admitted. I didn't relish having my separate worlds collide. "I suppose I could sneak out during lunch. Can you get here that early?"

"Absolutely. I'm owed at least ten more vacation days. Use it or lose it. Hey, while you're at it, get the sexy detective to meet with us."

I felt a little breathless. The last thing I wanted was to introduce Susan to Tom. I tried to remember what Susan didn't like about the various men in her life. "Trust me, he's not sexy. He looks a like a Boy Scout."

Susan must have gotten over her previous aversion to wholesome types. "Whatever. We'll talk more about it when the time comes. Let's concentrate on the here and now."

I was about to hang up when she emphasized, "Make sure Tom is at the school on Friday. Don't forget. Or pretend to forget."

I didn't trust Susan's motives. "Why do you want to meet him?"

She laughed as if I'd made a very clever joke. "Don't be so paranoid. I want to meet him because I'm bored."

If she were with me, I could have shaken sense into her. Phone conversations are more challenging. "Susan, this is an investigation into a murder, not a setup for a date."

She didn't answer me.

"Susan, if you change your mind, go straight to my house. You know the door is never locked."

She blew a Bronx cheer into the phone. "Yes, I do know that, which I find mildly disturbing. You'd never guess that you grew up in Brooklyn. Don't you worry about burglars? Serial killers? Lost pizza delivery guys?"

I've come a long way since those days in the projects. "A little bit. But we've all locked ourselves out of the house so often we've decided not to bother trying to keep other people out."

Another Bronx cheer. "Oh, yeah, that makes a ton of sense. Especially when you're tracking a killer."

CHAPTER 16

BLEAK HOUSE

eorge woke me up in the middle of the night It was just after four. My tee shirt was damp, and my heart was racing. I nearly belted him.

"I know I'm going to be sorry I asked this, but what were you dreaming about? You were moaning and turning like a cement mixer." Not the most sympathetic opening, but I took it anyway.

"Weirdly, I dreamt I was sleeping and that I was woken up by the sound of voices. I got up and started going from one room to the other, looking for these disembodied sounds. It was like it was, and wasn't, our house, if you know what I mean."

George nodded, but he seemed to be going back to sleep. As Conrad pointed out with gloomy perspicacity, we live as we dream, alone. I poked George, and he struggled to pay attention.

"The next thing that happened is I followed the voices into the bathroom. All of a sudden, it was like all the dreams where you feel as though you're falling, except this time I was falling down our laundry chute."

This got his attention. "At least you couldn't get hurt. There would have been ten tons of laundry cushioning your fall."

I pulled the blankets away from him. "If you're going to wake me up, you can't make jokes. You have to at least pretend to be sympathetic."

"Sorry. Is what happened next going to take a long time?" He punched a few pillows and settled into a position more conducive to sleep than conversation.

"No. You woke me up as I was headed toward the basement. I wonder what this dream means."

George patted me on the back, turned to face the other side of the bed and mumbled something about clean socks. I skinned out of my flannel pajama bottoms and tee shirt and pressed against him.

"Why don't you distract me from my misery?" I whispered in his ear.

But he was already snoring. I stared at his unresponsive back and listened to the rumble he made with every exhalation of breath. It was as if we were living in two different time zones. The old George was always, as he used to say, ready. Lately, though, he seemed to be on a schedule. And if we missed that window of opportunity—as we did every time we argued—there was no makeup sex left in him.

The house was cold, with a pre-autumn, pre-dawn chill. I dressed in sweats and went downstairs, suppressing a shudder as the dream returned in its inexplicable horror.

I sought solace in the kitchen. I loved my kitchen. After many years of scrimping, we'd finally gotten enough money to replace the cracked Formica, peeling linoleum, and broken cabinets. Post-renovation, every surface glowed with warmth. But the soothing kitchen did not calm me down. Was guilt keeping me up? I realized with a start that it was my turn to provide snacks for the soccer team, and I had forgotten to bake.

What was so awful about going to a bakery? Would some council revoke my Good Mother License? Would it really humiliate Zach all that much if I let the bakeshop have a go at it for once? Or, if I wanted to be really radical, couldn't these high school kids bring a snack for themselves?

I lost the argument with myself. Unwilling to traumatize my son with the humiliation of store-bought pastries I pulled flour, sugar, eggs, and chocolate chips from the shelves, and while I waited for each batch of cookies to bake I sliced oranges and apples. Impressed with my own motherly dedication I forced myself to descend into the damp and creepy basement, and I tossed the laundry into the dryer. Then I returned to bed and watched the sky grow light.

As usual, Ellie was the first to wake up. Her pre-school primping ritual is so rigorous it takes her at least an hour to make herself what she calls presentable. She walked into the kitchen and sniffed suspiciously.

"What's that smell?"

"Cookies for the soccer team. Do you want me to pack a few of them in your lunch?"

Ellie could barely contain her disgust.

"Mother? I think you know I'm on a diet? In case you haven't noticed, I no longer eat sandwiches, and if I can't eat sandwiches I certainly can't eat cookies. I need a salad, low fat dressing on the side and a bottle of water. And please remove those repulsive little piles of lard from my sight."

I looked at Ellie's narrow waist and matchstick arms. "Why are you on a diet? You're not fat. Actually, you're so skinny Dad's starting to worry about you. I'm starting to worry about you."

"I'm not skinny for a dancer. I might be skinny for a normal person, but I'm not trying to be normal. I'll never get into a professional ballet company if I can't get down to the bone. Not to mention the fact that auditions for *The Nutcracker* are this weekend!"

I watched as Ellie completed her transformation into Mr. Hyde. Her voice leaped up another octave.

"You do know that this is the most important weekend of my life? If I get stuck in one of those roles where you're part of the scenery, I will die! One of the girls in my ballet class told me that last year the director kept calling one of the company members Sugar Plump instead of Sugar Plum. Two weeks before the first performance he gave her role to the understudy." Ellie shuddered violently. "Can you imagine anything more humiliating?"

I could, but this didn't seem like a good time to discuss personal details from my youth.

"Listen to me, Ellie. If that director, or choreographer, or whoever, ever says such a thing to you, or to any other kid for that matter, I want you to tell me. I am not paying that school a small fortune in order to have them turn you into a neurotic, anorexic mess."

Ellie could barely contain her horror. "Mother—Mom—if you ever do such a thing I will honestly die of embarrassment. Don't you think I can handle things myself? I'm not a baby," she wailed. "You're my mother. You're supposed to help me, not destroy my career before it even gets started."

I opened my mouth, but Ellie did not wait for an answer.

"The competition this year is fierce. Do you understand how important this is for me? Do you?"

George and Zach entered as Ellie wrapped up her tirade. George leaned over, and although he spoke to Ellie his gaze was directed toward me.

"Gee, honey, I have no idea where you inherited this obsession with your weight."

"Hey, don't blame this on me. I need to lose weight. Ellie is getting so tiny I'm afraid she won't have the energy to dance."

Before Ellie could continue her conniption I told her, by way of consolation, "Aunt Susan is coming this weekend. We'll all go out together after your audition." Ellie brightened at this information, but George and Zach groaned.

Zach was impatient. "I love Aunt Susan, Mom, but I will be busy on Saturday."

"Me, too," George added.

Only Zach laughed at that. "Uh, Ma, I hate to change this fascinating subject about who's nuttier, you or Ellie, or for that matter, Aunt Susan, but some people care about getting to school on time." He gave me a wary but hopeful look. "So, any chance that my uniform is dry? I have an early lab today and I need to get out of here."

I gave Zach his exquisitely clean and dry uniform, Ellie her tights and leotard, and George a pair of socks. I left them to their own devices and drove to work in an excess of anxiety. Was Ellie anorexic? Was Zach getting enough attention? Would George and I ever be really close again? Worries about my family alternated with haunting memories of my nightmare. The creepiest part of the experience was hearing the disembodied voices. My dream self had recognized the voices, but my waking self was clueless. Big surprise.

Despite my troubled reflections, the hours at school passed quickly. Before leaving to attend Zach's soccer game I checked my actual mailbox. I waited until 3:01 to go to the main office in order to avoid meeting either the secretary or the principal.

On the bottom of a pile of consumerist detritus, I found a white envelope with no return address. I extracted the single sheet of paper and read the following: *Listen Bitch You better shut up or YOULL BE NEXT.* There were no identifying marks on the paper or the envelope, other than the postmark, which indicated it had been mailed from Clairmont, a town approximately equidistant from Oak Ridge and Valerian Hills.

I peered into the hallway. I don't know why I was afraid of someone finding me, or finding out about the anonymous letter, but I was. I bypassed the recycling bin in order to crush the filthy thing into the garbage. The paper stuck briefly to my damp fingers, long enough to remind me that the letter, as vile as it was, was evidence. I resisted the impulse to destroy it.

I got a yellow interoffice envelope and put the letter in that. The extra insulation made me feel better about polluting my handbag. I sent a neutral text to Tom Harriman and went to Zach's soccer game.

Driving to the field was difficult. Instead of training my eyes on the road ahead, I concentrated on the cars behind me. When one of them made the same two turns I did I panicked, did a quick U-turn, and drove in the opposite direction.

Several paranoid moves later, I made it to the field without causing any serious traffic accidents. Although the previous night had been cool, the morning had brought a September heat wave that enveloped all of northern New Jersey in a sticky haze. My sinuses and the overcast sky indicated rain was coming, and I half hoped a sudden downpour would postpone Zach's game.

My appearance at athletic events is not often met with much excitement, but in the aftermath of the murder I experienced a level of popularity unmatched since I arrived in the third grade with a bag of Pixie Stix. Two Supermoms graciously made room for me and pressed me for details about Marcia. I managed to update them on the murder investigation without divulging any information beyond what was available in the newspapers. But even murder could not compete with another, weightier topic: the High School Boys' Soccer Team Pot Luck Kick Off Dinner.

Mitzi Brewer, soccer mom extraordinaire, stated, "Liz, I know we can count on you for a main dish."

The only way I could refuse this request would be if I were immediately moving to a different hemisphere, so I told myself it doesn't take too much more time to fix pasta for twenty than it does to make pasta for four.

I reached into my handbag to make a note of this new obligation. Instead of grabbing my smarter-than-I-am electronic device, my fingers found the envelope that held the letter. The gritty paper felt unclean. From far away, I heard someone call my name.

Mitzi, who was sitting a few feet away, looked expectantly at me.

"Yes or no? Can you do it?"

"Yeah, of course, absolutely. Love to." It was several minutes before I found out I had agreed to make the Decorating Committee my life's work.

Mitzi studied her iPad. "Liz, I think we may put you down for Ribbons and Bows, which of course is a subcommittee of the Decorating Committee. How does that sound?"

Ribbons and Bows. How hard could that be?

Thankfully, the game was close, and the mothers put aside their potluck plans to watch their kids. Anxiety about unconsciously signing up for more volunteer work waned and was replaced with anxiety about surviving long enough to attend the actual event.

I saw Tom Harriman standing on the opposite side of the field, scanning the bleachers. Leaving the other parents to support the home team without me, I made my way around the fence. "What are you doing here?"

He held up his phone. "I got your text. And this is where you said you were going to be. What's happening?"

I handed him the threatening letter, which he placed in a plastic sleeve.

He whistled softly as he read. "Who have you been talking to lately?"

I trembled as I mentally tallied the number of people I'd questioned. "I think it might be easier to list the people with whom I haven't yet spoken."

"This is not a game, Liz. You've managed to threaten someone, and we need to know who. I told you not to talk to anyone about the murder."

Although it wasn't cold, I rubbed my arms to erase goosebumps. "It's a waste of time trying to scare me. I'm already terrified. Anyway, how was I supposed to investigate without talking to people?"

Tom stepped around a muddy patch of grass. "You weren't supposed to investigate. Answer the question."

I held onto the wire fence and watched the game, so I didn't have to look at him. "Fine. I talked to a few people in the English department, like Emily and Caroline. I may have brought up a few sensitive topics in the lunchroom, in which case another ten people know. Caroline tells everything she knows to Timmy, Timmy tells Gordon, and Gordon blabs to Mrs. Donnatella. Or the other way around. Oh, and I paid a condolence call to Marcia's husband. No big deal."

Tom smacked an adjacent tree. "Jesus Christ. Why not run a public service ad during the World Series?"

"Too expensive." I let go of the fence to ease the pain in my hands. Red stripes crisscrossed each palm.

He pulled gently at my shoulder, forcing me to face him and not the field. "What exactly did you try to investigate? I need to know what you said, so I can figure out what set this guy off."

"Guy? You think it was a man?"

His lips tightened. "Sorry. Person, not guy."

"I've talked to Timmy and to Marcia's husband about the murder. Timmy said exactly nothing. Bellinger knows about the blackmail and wants in on it. I don't know if that makes him more or less likely a suspect. He seemed pissed off that Marcia left him, but not like he was so upset about it that he'd kill her." I rubbed my eyes, trying to remember exactly what Bellinger had said. "Maybe he'd kill to get his hands on whatever information Marcia was using to extort money. But then wouldn't he make sure he had that before he killed her? 'Cause right now he's screwed. Unless he inherits."

Tom tensed and stood straight. "When did you talk to Bellinger? After the funeral?"

I tried to make my visit sound innocuous, as normal and routine as a sympathy card. "No. I paid a perfectly respectable condolence call. I might try Marcia's boyfriend next. At least he was more attractive."

He reached to me, held his arm rigid, and then dropped it. "Liz—stop. Just stop. You think this is cute, but it's dangerous."

"You think I don't know that? I spent a half hour trying to lose a car that wasn't following me. My classroom has been trashed, and I'm pretty sure that even though no one seemed to be tailing me today someone was stalking me at the mall. And now this letter." I felt the burn of tears. "But as long as whoever wrote it is still out there, I'm not going be safe doing nothing, either. I'm—I'm caught."

An errant soccer ball sailed over the fence. Tom used both hands to throw it back onto the field. Clearly, an ex-soccer player. After he acknowledged the hoots from the kids, he said, "Wrong on all counts. The closer you get, the higher the stakes. The murderer will kill you. Is that how you want him found? By providing the clue yourself?"

Tom was wrong. I was scared—I didn't feel clever or cute. I was as scared as I could be.

"I've given you the letter and everything I know. You've told me nothing."

His voice was cold. "I'm an officer of the law. You have to talk to me. Anything else is obstruction of justice."

It was too late for him to get all official with me, and I ignored his change in tone. "I've thrown myself into harm's way to help solve this case. Show some appreciation. Tell me what you've learned."

His tone, but not his position, softened. "I can't do that. You wouldn't want me to reveal details about this letter or about your personal life. You would be in even greater danger if anyone knew that you were the one who found Marcia's files. Of course, Bellinger already knows."

I didn't give up. "If we take Marcia's lesson plans as a starting point, the killer is probably a charming psychopath, like the guy in the lesson plan for *The Talented Mr. Ripley*. But I don't know many charming people at Valerian Hills High School. Or in Oak Ridge, for that matter. So maybe it is the boyfriend."

Tom crossed his arms. "No comment."

"Or maybe the killer is involved with an underage girl. Bellinger lacks charm, but I could imagine him a slimy pedophile. But if the killer is a 1980's-era drag queen Bellinger is off the hook. No style at all. Speaking of which, surely your police department can find what Wilde Willing Billie is up to these days."

Tom walked down the side of the field, following the boys' play. "I am going to remind you once again that if the killer's motive was to get out from under Marcia's fist then you are not safe. I'm not going to let you sucker me into telling you anything that will put you in any more danger than you've already put yourself in. This is not a theoretical puzzle, and you are not Sherlock Holmes."

I followed him. "I'm tired of being told who I'm not. I'm not Sherlock Holmes. I'm not Martha Stewart. I'm not Marcia Deaver. What makes this so infuriating is that I don't even want to be like those people. Well, maybe Sherlock, but without the needles and cocaine."

He stopped and laughed. "Take it easy, English Teacher. I actually read that book, *Persuasion*, which you gave me. It wasn't bad for a girl book."

Although I hate it when people classify Jane Austen's work as exclusively feminine, I cut him some slack. "It's not a girl book. People call everything Jane Austen wrote chick lit to try and sell more copies or make her work seem cool."

Tom was unconvinced. "Trust me, only a girl could read about the main character and not want to hurt her. She was a little too much on the weak side. She let other people talk down to her and treat her bad. Guys hate that crap. No wonder it took so long for her to get married."

I may sometimes be at a loss for words when it comes to defending myself, but I'm always up to the challenge of defending Jane. "Anne Elliot was stronger than anyone! Let the other characters underestimate her. Jane Austen doesn't, and you shouldn't either."

Tom turned his palms upward and shrugged, as if to say he'd enough literary criticism for one day. "You shouldn't take these things so personally. I told you I liked the book."

"It's important to me that you understand that Anne is complex, and intelligent and passionate, too."

Tom didn't look happy. I wondered if he'd tried to discuss *Persuasion* with Ashlee. He did have the book with him that morning.

Unexpectedly, he put both hands on my shoulders. "Could you be quiet for two seconds, please, and listen to someone else for once? In fact, it would be better if you stopped talking altogether. If anyone mentions the murder, I want you to say something along the lines that you've been really busy and you haven't been giving it much thought. Tell them you're leaving it to the police, which I wish was true."

I stared past him and didn't answer. Tom took my chin and turned my face towards his. My skin was so starved for attention the warmth in his hand traveled like an electric current through my body. His gesture forced me to look directly at him.

I swallowed my nervousness. "That is a brilliant plan. The only problem is you're here right now, and dozens of avidly gossiping soccer moms—and quite possibly my husband and son as well—are wondering why we're talking."

He dropped his hand from my face.

"Tell them that I'm... Damn. What should you tell them?"

"Maybe I'll say you're a soccer trainer. Most of these kids have personal trainers."

Tom shifted his weight from one foot to the other, as if unsure whether to stay or go. I turned back to the game and watched the boys kick the ball and each other in a mash-up of bobbing heads and twisting bodies. A skinny leg emerged from the pileup and tipped the ball into the goal. The Oak Ridge parents erupted in deliriously happy huzzahs and the cheerleading team did a victory dance. Ten Oak Ridge soccer players piled ecstatically on top of the kid.

As if to douse the hopes of the opposing team, heavy raindrops began to fall. The well-prepared parents of Oak Ridge took out their umbrellas emblazoned with the team logo and they continued to cheer Our Boys.

Go Team.

CHAPTER 17

LUCKY JIM

had copied the poison letter so I could study it for clues, but I found the words were burned into my mind, and I needed no concrete reminder of the terse message:

Listen Bitch You better shut up or YOULL BE NEXT.

On the face of it, the letter exonerated Bill, Caroline, and Emily. None of them would commit such egregious grammatical errors. I wasn't as sure of Ashlee, not that I ever considered her a possible suspect. She might blithely murder the English language, but her youth and beauty queen serenity made it unlikely she would have to kill someone to get what she wanted. I had to consider, though, that an error in grammar might be a ploy on the part of an English teacher to divert attention away from the English department. Further complicating matters was the possibility that the killer might have calculated that someone would come to that last conclusion, and he or she might have engaged in a kind of double fake. I needed George's analytical mind, but I was so afraid of his probable response that I didn't tell him about it. I called Susan, but my sister's cell phone went directly to her voicemail.

Having expended my weekly culinary energy making cookies, I ordered pizza. In the time it took to prepare a salad, Zach and George selfishly wolfed down the whole pie. I didn't bother protesting, since George would have pointed out that I'm "watching my weight" and pizza is not on any known diet, unless I decide to create one based on carbohydrates and fat. If only.

As usual, the kids went their separate ways immediately after dinner. George parked himself in front of the television, and I sat at the kitchen table. I had done something to threaten someone. Who was it? And what had I done, or said, to provoke the response?

I had no nightmares that night, probably because I didn't sleep long enough to get into the REM cycle. By morning, I felt sick with fatigue. I conserved energy by pulling the closest skirt and shirt from my closet, skipping the intermediate step of checking to see how I looked. As usual, Ellie was already awake, having selected and discarded multiple outfits until she found the perfect match.

After I emerged from my two-minute toilette, Ellie shook her head at me. "Mom! What are you wearing?"

I looked down at my skirt. "Is this a trick question? It looks a lot like a skirt."

Ellie walked over to me for a closer inspection. She lifted a section of fabric with two disdainful fingers. "Mom, please don't take this the wrong way, but you look terrible. That skirt is sagging all over the place. You can't appear in public like that."

"I don't have your exacting standards, Ellie. I'm fine with being clean and relatively unwrinkled."

Ellie laughed. "Believe me, I know. But, please, Ma, go back upstairs and look at yourself."

I took her advice and examined myself in a full-length mirror. Ellie was right. The skirt hung in unattractive folds. I thought about the implications of this unexpected development. I pulled a pair of pants from the Siberia section of my closet and put one cautious leg in. Then the other leg. With a slight intake of breath I zipped them on. A Miracle Had Occurred, next to which the whole episode with the loaves and fishes paled.

I modeled the pants for Ellie. She was highly complimentary, and noted, without apparent bitterness, that while she was the one who had to lose weight by Saturday, I was the one to visibly drop the pounds. We sort of bonded over the pants, and I left the house feeling considerably happier than when I woke up.

I was also cheered by the prospect of having Susan visit me. I calibrated the time I needed to drive my sister from the bus stop to the high school. It would take only five minutes to drive there, but Susan wasn't due to arrive until midway through my twenty-nine-minute lunch break. The urge to smoke a cigarette was nearly unbearable, but I didn't want to chance running into any of the Valerian Hills parents, who would undoubtedly email the principal if they saw me leisurely puffing away during school hours.

Ten tense minutes passed. No Susan. I frantically texted her. She assured me that she would be there in three minutes. Eleven minutes later the bus lumbered up to the stop. I tossed her bag into the back seat and narrowly missed slamming her foot in the passenger door.

"For God's sake," she cried, checking her shoes and jacket for damage, "What the hell is wrong with you? What's the big deal about arriving five minutes late? What can they do? Give you detention? Send you to the principal's office?"

I didn't bother answering. I swerved into my parking spot and barreled toward the school while she followed at a more leisurely pace. It was as I feared. I was late, and not by two minutes. This was a problem. The only way for anyone to get into the building during regular school hours is to get buzzed in. By Mrs. Donnatella.

I waited impatiently for the secretary to move her large, lazy finger to the intercom. I knew if I pressed the buzzer more than once she would take her revenge by leaving the office to go to the bathroom. Although she could see me over the closed camera, she demanded to know my name and my business. After a minute or two of deliberation, she risked letting me into the building.

"What the hell is going on here?" Susan clicked down the hallway at a pace far too leisurely for me. "Are you telling me you're not allowed to leave the school during the day? Is that even legal?"

"We're allowed to leave, but the administration frowns on it."

Susan's outrage did make me think, though. All of a sudden, something I had always taken for granted did seem a bit...Burdensome? Ridiculous? Disrespectful? No. *Demeaning.* It felt demeaning that a middle-aged professional woman had to worry that someone might find out she'd left the building during her lunch break. Susan was not shy about expressing her opinions.

"Well, that's crazy. Once again, I must point out that you *teach* high school. You're not actually *in* high school."

I installed Susan in the faculty room and suggested that she keep her opinions private for the next two and a half hours. With any luck, my colleagues would assume Susan was a new substitute teacher and would ignore her.

My classroom door was closed. Inside, the kids were talking to each other in low voices. I made my way to the front of the room and canvassed the rows of faces.

Brittany and Bethany looked up from the poster they were coloring together. "Where were you, Ms. Hopewell?"

The kids looked suspiciously pleased with themselves. "Uh, I got held up. What's going on in here? What's so funny?"

Brittany and Bethany laughed, "Oh, Ms. Hopewell! Three people were looking for you. But we told them that you weren't feeling well and would be right back. They never suspected a thing! We've all promised not to tell."

I looked around the class. They had covered for me and they were proud of themselves. Even Jack the Jackass had a pleasant look on his face. I suppose there are worse jobs in the world.

Caroline sauntered into my next class, using the connecting door from the English office. No wonder Marcia used to barricade herself from unexpected intrusions; I nearly fainted when she threw open the door and entered with the drama of the Wicked Witch of the West.

"I was rather concerned about you, Ms. Hopewell," she said, with saccharine sweetness that belied her evil expression. "You weren't here, so I emailed Timmy to let him know that I would find someone to cover your class for you. Luckily, I ran into your sister in the faculty room. She told me you had finally made it back from lunch. How are you feeling now?"

Homicidal. That's how I'm feeling. Through gritted teeth I said, "It's nice to know that there's always someone watching."

Susan was my next unscheduled visitor. I should have known she would refuse to be warehoused in the teacher's room. She meandered in, waved at me and the class to indicate her non-presence, and sat down to listen. After a few minutes of sonnets she lost interest and left. I followed her down the hall and explained that she had to go back to the teacher's room or go to the main office to officially sign in. We have strict rules about visitors. They need a Visitor's Pass, which is electronically printed out, complete with driver's license photo. Which Susan doesn't have, since she doesn't know how to drive. Visitors aren't allowed to wander about under any circumstances. They have to have official business in the school.

ISIS doesn't stand a chance in Valerian Hills.

My sister did not reappear until nearly three o'clock. Looking very pleased with herself, she asked, "What's on the agenda?"

I sorted through the weekend pile of papers that had to be graded. "Nothing. We go back to my house and we work on the psychology of the case."

"Hmm. Let me say goodbye to Timmy first." Without bothering with a mirror, Susan swiped her lips with gloss. "If he's not there we can break into his office."

"Timmy? When did you talk to him? What did you say to him?" I demanded.

"I saw him about an hour ago. Don't worry. I was extremely discreet. But it took ten minutes of arguing with that filthy dragon of a secretary before I could get into his office."

This was bad.

There is no way to predict what Susan will do or say. I worried Mrs. Donnatella would deny me office supplies until five minutes after hell freezes over. And even that might be an optimistic time frame.

On most Fridays, Timmy leaves at least fifteen minutes before the students, so he can exit the parking lot quickly. Today he was in his office.

He nodded at me and greeted Susan with a big smile. "You didn't tell me you had such a charming sister, Liz."

I remained tongue-tied as Susan replied, "And Liz didn't tell me that she had such a charming boss."

I looked for a garbage can to puke in.

"Timmy," said Susan, settling into a chair and crossing her legs, "I was just telling Liz how impressed I was that things are running so smoothly after all that dreadful tragedy. That had to have been so difficult—to keep the school running *and* deal with the murder."

My sister has no shame.

"It's a big job, but I have an awesome staff." Timmy swung at an imaginary baseball. "As an administrator there are times when it helps to be a switch hitter."

"I'm sure you're equally impressive from both the right and the left," Susan said, and they both laughed as if this were the wittiest statement since Dorothy Parker cast her pearls across the Round Table.

Susan dangled one leg back and forth. "Have you come up with any ideas about who could have committed murder?"

Timmy looked mesmerized by her foot. "It could not have been anyone in Our Fine Valerian Hills Community," he responded, repeating nearly word for word what he had already opined to me.

"I really respect your loyalty," said Susan, with a knowing tilt to her head, "but you know everyone so well—don't you have any suspects?"

Timmy moved his gaze to Susan's skirt, which was artfully hiked up across tanned thighs. He wrenched his stare from her lap and did his best to look at her face. "Dr. Deaver did make a number of enemies. She was very opinionated, and she wasn't very tactful. Even the custodians didn't like her."

"Really? That's so interesting. Tell me more about it," breathed Susan.

Timmy looked as pleased as I've ever seen him. "Marcia complained that the custodians didn't do a good job cleaning her room. During the contract negotiations with the custodial staff she went to the Board of Education meeting and spoke strongly about that. She suggested outsourcing the custodial work and brought documentation that seemed to indicate that the board could save a considerable amount of money if they fired all of our current workers. The custodians didn't take it very well."

Susan said, "I'm sure not, those poor guys. I guess it all worked out, though?"

"Well, that depends on what side you're on. The contracts were renewed, but the workers took a big pay cut. Of course, I'm not suggesting any of the custodians would commit murder. I'm only using that as an example of how Dr. Deaver made enemies."

I suggested, as if it had just occurred to me, "If she made enemies among the custodial staff, then she might have done so with the teaching staff as well." *Or the administrative staff.*

Timmy stiffened. "I don't think so. Only the custodians had a reason to hold a real grudge against her. Anyway, the cleaning staff has had some changes lately. We don't have that same turnover in the teaching staff."

Until now.

After a brief silence, Susan asked where the principal was.

"Gordon's already left," said Timmy.

She smiled as if just the two of them were in on the same joke. "It's the same deal at my office. It isn't the boss who runs the place, is it?"

Timmy started to answer, looked at me, and stopped talking.

I hated to break up this love fest, but I wanted to head off another High Importance email about Teacher Tardiness. "Timmy, I'm afraid that I was a few minutes late today—"

Susan broke in on my explanation, and to my horror told Timmy the details of the kids' cover-up. I considered the pros and cons of leaving New Jersey under the Federal Witness Protection Program.

Susan said, "The kids really love Liz. They were so adorable. I guess when you're a great teacher the kids know it."

Timmy wrinkled his brow and looked at me as if we'd never met. I don't think I ever figured in his mind as a candidate for Teacher of the Year.

I hoped Timmy would leave so we could investigate. Sneaking around a deserted school was more appealing with a partner. But he looked as if he were cemented to his chair. Maybe he was trying to prove to Susan how indispensible he was, even in a rapidly emptying building. Before we left he took her hand and held it in both his hands. He walked us—Susan—to the door and invited, "Come back soon. I'll give you the Grand Tour."

Susan looked into Timmy's flat blue eyes, extricated her hand with delicate efficiency, and promised to return. We walked down the hall together.

Susan wiped her hand on a tissue. "I hate sweaty men. And sweaty married men are the worst."

This was too much. "You are unbelievable!"

Susan was impatient. "What's so unbelievable? Do you think that people are going to confide in you if you aren't sympathetic to them? You have to hide your feelings better. I can see that you think he's an idiot. And he may be dumb, but he can see it too. Get off your high English teacher horse for once."

"You can see what I'm thinking because you know me. But he really is a moron; and therefore, he doesn't see it."

Susan stopped short and put her hands on her hips. "Don't be too sure about that. I understand how you feel, but you can't let other people understand how you feel. Trust me; I've already got a pretty good idea what kind of place this is. I wonder if the teachers in our high school were this clueless."

"I'm sure some of them were. Just not all of them. Education has taken a big hit lately. Susan, it's like an intellectual desert here. I'm all alone, with one camel and no oasis."

Susan threw her arm around my shoulders. "I'll buy you a drink, Lawrence of Arabia. You can tell me all about it."

I took a quick detour to the mailroom, scooped up my mail, and plopped it in my school bag. I turned toward the parking lot when Susan grabbed my arm.

"When are you going to call Tom? Are we meeting him here or at the police station?"

I shook her off. "Sorry. He's busy."

"He's not busy. You didn't call him," Susan accused.

"What do you want me to say to him? That my sister wants to have an affair with a younger guy?"

Susan considered this. "Not in so many words. Tell him I want to meet him to talk about the murder. I'll take it from there."

"It would be too embarrassing to call him. He'll think I'm stalking him."

Susan planted her feet and refused to move. I relented, and agreed to text him.

"Make sure you tell him that you need to meet with him!" Susan clamored.

I sent the message. Tom immediately responded, texting that he would be at the school in five minutes. Susan grabbed me and headed to the bathroom to primp.

CHAPTER 18

THE THREE MUSKETEERS

Tom immediately offended Susan by asking which of us was older. My sister is only a few years younger than I am, but she looks much younger than I do, and she did not take kindly to the idea that the time and money she spent on her beauty treatments was not clearly visible.

Since Susan seemed incapable of a response, I said, "I'm older."

He looked from my face to Susan's and back again to me. "You'd never know it. Not like in my family. My brother's ten years older than me. But you didn't text me to talk about that. What's going on?"

I had forgotten to prepare a reason for interrupting his work, but Susan recovered her resourcefulness. "I'm worried about Liz. What do you think she should do about this murder investigation?"

Tom spoke slowly and emphasized almost every other word. "She should make it clear to every person she's spoken to that she is no longer interested in the murder, in Marcia Deaver, or in anything else that the killer might find threatening. Poison pen letters don't necessarily mean the writer is a killer, but in this case it's a good bet. If you want to help your sister, tell her that."

Susan pouted. "That's no fun. Liz and I could do the kind of spying that you can't. She's here all the time. And I'm here now." Susan walked over to Tom and put a hand on his arm.

Perhaps another woman might have felt slighted or jealous, but I was happily married and thus didn't care at all that Tom Harriman was looking deeply into Susan's eyes and that they both appeared to have forgotten I was even in the room. I coughed.

Tom slipped his arm from Susan's grasp and turned an anxious look in my direction. "I can't do my job if I'm constantly worried about what you're up to."

I assured him, "There's nothing to worry about. I'm fine. Susan and I are going back to my place, so you can go back to work."

Susan amended my suggestion. "Why don't you join us? We can talk murder. Or other things. Your call."

"I'm tempted, ladies, but I can't make it. Maybe next time." Then he left.

Susan was thoughtful. "I think he likes you," she said, with an emphasis on the last word. "Can't you see that? Why didn't you tell me?"

Because I'm a married woman, that's why. Rather than explain the concept of marital fidelity, I told her, "The only person in this building he's really interested in is the killer. And I mean that in a good way."

Susan grabbed my nose, in a childhood reference to Pinocchio. "You little liar, you. I know men. He is attracted to you, and like the clueless ninny you are, you don't see it. Or maybe there's something you're not telling me."

I blushed, for maybe the first time in fifteen years. It wasn't just my face that was warm. The rest of me was too. We headed home. Zach and Ellie went to the movies with friends, and Susan and I had the house to ourselves. George had already told me he was going to be late—again—and then texted me that he missed the train. It was nearly 11:00 before he got home, and after a quick greeting he barricaded himself in his office.

We went out to the front porch. Susan took her shoes off and rubbed her toes. "Isn't it kind of late for your husband to be getting home on a Friday night?"

I poured some wine. "Yeah. He's working on some big deal right now, and I hardly get to see him."

She picked at a few loose twigs on the wicker table. "How do you know he's not working on someone and not something?"

Our relaxing evening turned sour. George was not, could not, be cheating on me. I felt my forehead get tight. "Don't insult him or me, Susan."

Still pruning the table, she said, "I'm not insulting anyone. I'm pointing out, from extensive experience, that when one spouse is interested in a third party, the other spouse usually is as well."

I slammed the wine glass on the table. "What are you talking about? I'm not interested in anyone but George. And vice versa."

Susan tossed a grape at me. "You looked about sixteen years old when Tom walked in. No wonder he didn't know which of us was younger. If I'd known the score, I wouldn't have bothered having you ask him to meet us. I've been married enough times to know what I'm talking about."

That gave me an easy out. Susan's love life is a source of unending interest, and we spent the next hour viewing potential dates. Lots of men looked appealing to me, but Susan was far more savvy about the unwritten rules of online dating.

The next day began with a flurry of activity. First on the list was getting Ellie to the ballet studio. Two hours before we had to leave, I heard her banging her dresser drawers open and shut and sighing with gale force drama. I made coffee and sat down with the newspaper, waiting for the storm to pass. Ellie finally appeared in her leotard and tights.

She darted back and forth, from the bathroom to the kitchen. "Ma! Mom! Mother! Look at me! Do I look okay? Do you think I should wear this leotard or the one with skinny straps? What about my hair? Wear the ribbon or take it off? How do I look? Tell me the truth."

I felt a tiny catch in my throat. "You look beautiful. Don't change a thing."

"You always say that," she accused.

I set my coffee down. "I'm telling you what I see, Ellie. I see a beautiful, talented girl."

Ellie's voice went up a notch and she pleaded, "I don't want to know what you see! I want to know what normal people see!"

I kissed her cheek and then pinched it. "I'm normal. Most of the time, anyway."

Her eyes crinkled, and I wasn't sure if she was going to laugh or cry. She said, her mouth curving down and then up, "You're not normal. You're my mother. You're prejudiced."

Susan entered and took in the situation. She showily examined Ellie from every possible angle.

"Ellie, you look great. I would lose the ribbon, though. Too Alice in Wonderland, if you know what I mean."

Ellie looked as if she'd received the Ten Commandments from God himself.

"Yes! You are so right about that. But I feel like my hair needs something." Ellie nervously poked at her bun.

Susan rummaged in her handbag and handed Ellie two jeweled hairpins. "Try these. They're my lucky barrettes. A little bit of glitz never hurt any ballerina."

Ellie hugged Susan and ran back to the bathroom. Susan made a face at me.

I poured Susan some coffee and explained, "She's feeling a little nervous, which is ridiculous. I mean, these people see her everyday in dance class. I'm sure they cast the stupid ballet weeks ago and they're just making the kids go through the motions."

She yawned. "I don't envy you. Don't get me wrong, Ellie is great, but I remember what a total brat I was at her age. I'm surprised no one brained me."

"I was tempted on more than one occasion. With you and with Ellie. Meanwhile, not to change the subject—" I removed the copy I'd made of the poison letter and gave it to Susan. "Speaking of problem people, we still have to figure out who sent me my little love letter."

Susan studied the paper. "Do you have any ideas at all?"

I still wasn't sure whether the errors in grammar were inadvertent or deliberate. "I think it was a woman. I'm not sure why. Maybe the 'bitch' part?"

"Yeah. When men want to intimidate as well as belittle women they use the 'c' word. Also, I don't see a guy writing a letter and then posting it, but I could be way off base with that. On the other hand, if you're going to go around murdering people you do need some semblance of organization."

Thinking of Gordon, Timmy, and Bill, I warned Susan, "Don't think of the guys who work at Valerian Hills as grown men. Most of them suffer from a serious case of arrested development. They still laugh at bathroom jokes."

"Your high school doesn't have a monopoly on babies with beards. Wait till I tell you about my latest dating fiasco."

"The lawyer? You told me already."

"No, this is someone different. Another online dating site."

I told Susan to put off the more lurid details until we had enough time to do them justice. Ellie reappeared, and she consented to eat three paper-thin slices of apple. Susan and I feasted on coffee before I drove us to the ballet studio.

Ellie said goodbye in the car. "You don't have to come with me, Ma. I'm not two years old."

"Maybe you'll need moral support."

She dug in her dance bag to check, for the thousandth time, that she'd remembered her pointe shoes. "Why? Do you think I won't do well?"

"Don't be ridiculous! I'm being supportive. You know, mother-type stuff." I reached around to hug her and offered a fist bump, which she found hilarious.

Ellie mouth relaxed into a smile. "Be supportive by buying me something fabulous at the mall. Not by embarrassing me at the studio. I'll text you when I'm done."

I pressed two protein bars and a juice box on her and hoped for the best. Susan and I waved good-bye and headed to the mall. Ellie's nervousness was infectious. Even the shoe department failed to hold my interest. I didn't know how long the audition would take, and I couldn't help checking my cell phone every other minute. I provided the requested moral support by buying Ellie an overpriced scarf and reasonably priced sweater at J. Crew. Susan was fully engaged in the mall experience and unwilling to exit, so I left her in the capable hands of a Nordstrom's professional shopper and drove back to the studio.

Ballet Mothers lined the benches, and I took my place beside them. I didn't know many of them since Ellie had only recently begun taking classes at this studio. I tried to read, but it was difficult to concentrate. Ellie's nervousness had me jiggling my foot and staring at my book as if it were written in a different language. I knew how disappointed she would be if she didn't get a good role in the ballet. Forty more minutes passed before the door to the studio opened. No sign of Ellie. The mothers of the children who were released pressed their lips into encouraging smiles. They exhorted their kids to hurry up so that they could accomplish the next task of the day, acting as if after the audition each of them were due to star in an evening performance at Lincoln Center in front of an adoring crowd.

The mothers of the children who were asked to stay for the remainder of the audition did their best to iron out triumphant and relieved smiles. They sighed and said they didn't know how their kids would be able to handle a major commitment to the ballet company, what with all the hours of school-work those future Nobel Prize winners had to do for Academic Decathlon.

I couldn't pretend to be anything other than very purely happy for Ellie. I had been worried that because she joined the school so recently the teachers would overlook her talent in favor of kids they knew better. Ellie had been terrified she would be asked to exit early. The only problem now was an issue of time. When would they be done? Even Susan could not shop for too much longer. I asked the receptionist when she thought the audition would be over.

She had one pencil behind her ear and one stuck in her hair. The phone was lit up with multiple calls. She punched the hold button, and clearly overcome by the harassing questions of the other mothers she answered helpfully, "They'll be done when they're done."

In search of an absorbing pastime that didn't require too much concentration, I decided to tackle the mess in my handbag. I exhumed shredded receipts, bits of candy wrappers and expired coupons, along with a pile of junk mail. Then I got to a suspiciously thin unmarked envelope. No postmark—someone had simply left it in my school mailbox. How had I missed this? I nervously extracted the single sheet of paper. The typed message was terse and clear:

I warned you once all ready. I am watching you. And your kids.

CHAPTER 19
INHERIT THE WIND

If the valiant die but once, I'm destined to experience a thousand deaths. I'm not brave to begin with, and the letter terrified me. My body reacted to the threats with sudden shuddering shakes, as if I were going into shock or suffering from random drops in temperature.

As soon as I left the studio to pick up Susan I inhaled two cigarettes in rapid succession. I was so nervous I practically drove the car into a ditch. The unaccustomed amount of nicotine made me even shakier. I silently handed Susan the letter.

"Oh my God! This is amazing!" Susan sounded as delighted as if we'd both been invited to a party at the White House. "You must be getting really close. This is so exciting!"

"How can I be getting close if I have no idea who killed Marcia? What if this insane person really does decide to go after the kids?" I choked on the last two words, overcome with guilt. "What if this lunatic is watching us right now and decides to threaten you? How 'amazing' would that be?"

Susan read the letter again. "Calm yourself. I'm sure that I, at least, am safe. And if the murderer wanted to come after you, I don't think he or she would have warned you off. I think the killer would have, well, you know."

I tried to still my unsteady hands as we made an illegal U-turn, having missed the entrance to the ballet studio. "Believe me, I know. And if the murderer doesn't get me first I wouldn't be surprised if George poisoned me. He's going to freak out. As well he might. Susan, I'm freaked out."

Unmoved by either my distress or the distress of the drivers around me, she held out a leather case. "Have another cigarette. It'll calm you down."

"No thanks. I'm still queasy from the last one." I pulled into the parking lot of the ballet studio and got out of the car. "And don't you smoke anymore. Here comes Ellie."

Ellie strolled out of the school.

I spritzed myself with perfume to hide the evidence. "How did it go?" I searched her face for signs of elation or despair. Ellie doesn't do things by halves.

Ellie shrugged. She looked bored. But as soon as the door closed she nearly strangled me in a hug. "I'm in! I'm in!" she cried.

Susan turned to look at Ellie. "So! My lucky hairpins helped!"

Ellie then threw her arms around Susan. "Aunt Susie! You're the best! We won't find out until Monday how they're casting the ballet, but I will definitely get a good role. In the end, they kept only about seven of us, and I was picked to stay."

I was so relieved I almost forgot about the threatening letters. Yeah, I know disappointment and sorrow are part of life and part of growing up, but it's so much worse to see your kids in pain than to be in pain yourself.

Although my stomach had configured itself into a tight pretzel of nerves, I figured Ellie must be starving. "I'm so proud of you! Let's go celebrate."

We went to the Indiana Diner, where Ellie regaled us with a step-by-step description of the grueling audition process. My daughter seemed to be able to maintain her poise under even the most unnerving conditions, a character trait she did not get from me.

Ellie celebrated with a chocolate egg cream and croutons on her salad. "This means I'll get to really dance and wear pointe shoes and not prance around in a dorky party dress. I'm going to wear a tutu! I'd rather be in the back of the corps de ballet in a tutu than the front of the party scene with a pukey hair bow. Plus, they let the kids be the understudies to the understudies, which is really awesome, since we get to rehearse with the professionals. I'm like, so happy I could die!"

Susan said, in a teasing tone, "Stop talking about dying. Your mother is a bit sensitive about the subject."

I felt my chest get tight. "Susan, please! Let's not talk about that right now."

There are few things I could have said that would have fanned Ellie's interest more. If we hadn't been in public I would have gagged my sister with the nearest napkin.

"Ouch! Ellie, I think you should know that your mother just kicked me." Susan threw me a wicked smile. "Don't look at me like that, Liz, your daughter should know what you're capable of doing under pressure." With that, Susan gave Ellie an abbreviated version of my pathetic attempts at investigating Marcia's murder.

Ellie looked at me as if she'd never seen me before. "Mom, this is totally awesome. I want in on this. You and me and Aunt Susie can be a team. All for one and one for all! We'll be famous."

I didn't relish refusing my daughter anything, but I was seriously scared. "Ellie, this is the end of the line. I am beside myself with remorse right now, thinking that I've put you and Zach and Dad in danger. I'm quitting. Not that I ever really did anything."

Ellie put her arm around me and gave my shoulders a shake. "No way. You can't quit. You're always telling us not to quit. Remember when I wanted to drop honors math? You wouldn't let me, even though I suffered horribly. How can you live with yourself if you quit? I'll lose all respect."

I shook my head. "Forget 'respect.' I think 'live' is the operative word here. I don't want to end up like Marcia, and I don't want some crazed killer holding my family hostage." I appealed to my sister. "Susan, back me up here."

Susan looked out the window. She seemed fascinated by the rear view of Four Marzinetti Brothers Barber Shop. In a most reluctant tone Susan admitted, "Your mother is right, Ellie. How would you feel if something happened to her?"

Ellie looked contrite for a moment and then brightened up. "It's probably too late to quit." Her voice rose dramatically, "If you don't find the murderer, you can never feel safe again."

She did have a point. The same point that made sense to me until the killer targeted my children. I was firm. "Maybe you should give up dancing and take up law. Or hostage negotiations. But no matter how good your argument is, it's not going to work. So let's drop the subject. And don't say anything to Dad yet. I, uh, I want to tell him myself." Susan winked at Ellie, who winked back.

Ellie was disappointed not to be the bearer of such exciting news, but since she had the prospect of recapping her entire audition for George and every single one of her friends, and then updating her Facebook page in order to inform the rest of the planet, she was able to maintain silence.

Susan left early on Sunday, which immediately lightened George's mood. He likes Susan well enough, but gets cranky when she hangs out for too long. He has never understood our relationship.

I planned our Sunday dinner with an eye to making him happy. I roasted a chicken and added a pile of potatoes and vegetables. It's one of George's favorite meals. Mine too, since after fifteen minutes of prep time the food is on its own. We opened a bottle of wine. After dinner, and George's third glass of wine, I pulled out the letter. I wouldn't have shown it to him at all, but I felt guilty that Ellie was in possession of information George did not have. I didn't want to ask Ellie to keep anything secret from her father, especially since she had started sending me meaningful looks, replete with raised eyebrows and rolling eyeballs. George thought she was coming down with the flu, which Ellie found hysterically funny.

I handed George the second letter.

"When did you get this?" he hissed, in a remarkable imitation of his own daughter.

"I picked it up before I left school, but I didn't read it until this morning. Or, maybe it was yesterday."

George looked from the letter to me and back again to the letter, as if expecting one of us to go up in flames. "You're insane. Certifiably nuts. When were you planning to respond to this threat? I want you to call the police. Immediately."

My heart beat a bit faster. "Actually, I've already called them."

George tapped the letter against his palm. "So you haven't totally taken leave of your senses. Did you call them yesterday?"

This was awkward. "Hmm. Well. Yes. I mean no. Not exactly. I called them after the first letter."

"This is the second letter?"

George gets annoyed, gets irritable, and gets testy. He is rarely really angry. But my news about the threatening letters had him as enraged as I'd ever seen him. Not a pretty sight. I tried to smooth things over. "What can the police do now? What can anyone do now? I'll call them tomorrow."

George sent me that narrow-eyed, thin-lipped look that makes me want to kick him. Under normal circumstances it's the expression he saves for corrupt dictators and mass murderers. "What are you talking about? Do you think the police station is closed? It's not like the bank, Liz; I believe these guys work on the weekend."

I tried to stay calm so that he would stay calm. "I know that. But we probably need to talk to a detective, or something."

"The more important question is what we're going to do now. Why am I the only one freaking out? How are you going to get out of this? How are you going to get the kids out of this?" He slammed his open hand on the table over and over again.

As much as I wanted to, I couldn't look away from that pounding. "I don't know! What should I do? Send out a district-wide email saying I don't know anything about the murder and don't want to know anything about the murder? And what if the killer doesn't believe me? Susan said if the killer wanted to murder me he or she would have done so without warning me ahead of time. Do you think that's true?"

He snorted. "I hope it is true. But don't leave your coffee cup unattended for even a second. Call me after you talk to the Valerian Hills police. I think we need to contact the Oak Ridge police department as well. I want Ellie and Zach to be on their guard, and I want the police to be aware of the fact that the kids have been threatened. While you're at it, call that idiot principal, too."

"What about you?" I asked.

"I'm a big boy. I can take care of myself."

When I asked George "what about you" I meant that I wanted to know what he would be doing to help take charge of the situation, and I was distracted by his selfish answer.

Anger gave way to fear, as one horrible scenario after another charged in front of my mind's eye. "Don't stand too close to the train tracks. Be careful crossing the street. Don't *you* leave any coffee cups unattended. We have no idea who is threatening me."

His lip curled. "It's got to be someone at your school. Susan is probably right about something for the first time in her life. We won't be safe until they find the killer."

I repeated my theories to George about the identity of the author of the letters. He suggested a third and more chilling possibility.

"You're letting yourself get distracted by a side issue. You keep talking about the killer's need to obscure his identity. But I think the killer felt genuinely threatened, and had to at least try to warn you off. If there is a red herring in the letter, it's probably an afterthought. We have to hope the police find who it is. And fast."

I was so blinded by tears I could hardly see. "But what if they don't find him? Am I supposed to live in fear for however long the rest of my life is?"

He made no move to console me. "I don't know. I guess we'll just have to wait to find out." For a moment he looked sorry for his harsh words, but he didn't apologize.

With that encouragement I went to bed, but as usual, not to sleep. I watched one hour after the other change on our ugly digital clock, on whose face the numbers glowed hellishly red. Maybe I would sleep better if I had a more soothing clock.

By morning I had a blasting headache. Despite my empty stomach, I took two more Excedrin. I'd rather have a stomachache than a headache. Ellie came bounding down the stairs and gave me a conspiratorial smile.

"What's the plan, Mom?" She twirled around the counter and ended in a dramatic curtsey.

I handed her a salad with a separate packet of dressing. "Hmm. I think we're both going to school. Then you'll go off to ballet class, and I'll pick you up at the usual time."

Ellie peered into the plastic container and nodded her approval. "Don't be such a dork, Mom. You know what I mean."

I poured coffee with a hand that trembled so badly half the liquid sloshed over the side of the cup. "Ellie, be careful. Report anything suspicious to the principal. Don't hesitate to call the police, or a teacher, or anyone if you feel threatened. I'm going to call your principal right now. Daddy's going to talk to the police. We spoke to Zach last night. Be aware of who's around you. Don't tell anyone anything."

She stopped pirouetting and said, a bit uncertainly, "Uh, right. Yeah, of course. I know that."

"Ellie, have you told anyone about this?" I burned my lips on the coffee and dropped the cup. It shattered into a thousand dangerous shards.

Ellie jumped away from the glass. "No one, Ma. Anyway, don't worry about me. I can handle myself." I looked at my daughter's open and expressive face and at her narrow frame.

I stared into her eyes, trying to impress upon her the seriousness of the situation. "If you feel threatened, Ellie, run. Don't wait to figure out whether or not your fear makes sense. Run first and ask questions later."

She followed me to the broom closet. "Mom, I'm not a baby. I know what to do. It's the modern era. We've been getting this message since nursery school, not to talk to strangers."

I swept up the glass pieces, uncomfortably aware of the truth of George's words. I had put my children in danger.

Testing her, I asked, "Really? What would you do if a car pulled over and someone asked you for directions? What would you do?"

Ellie's upper lip quivered.

Again, I looked intently into her eyes. "You would run, Ellie. You would run like crazy. It's better to be dorky than dead. And if a guy grabs you, knee him in the crotch."

Ellie almost laughed at that last bit of advice. I know my daughter. She was too proud to admit she felt vulnerable, and too smart not to understand what I was telling her.

Not much relieved, I called the principal of Oak Ridge High School, who didn't seem as if he had too many more IQ points than Gordon.

When I asked him if he had any questions, he said, "Just to be perfectly clear about all this, Mrs. Hopewell, neither I nor anyone in the school has any responsibility here at all."

"Not exactly. Just to be perfectly clear about this, Mr. Cuthbert, I'm holding you personally responsible for the safety of my children. I regret I do not have time to explain this to you a third time, but I will be happy to make an appointment for my husband to see you this afternoon."

Principals hate talking to fathers even more than they hate talking to mothers. Even mild men seem to worry and intimidate them, and George can get vehement where his children are concerned. Mr. Cuthbert declined the pleasure of an in-person conference.

Zach came downstairs, winked at me, and said, "Give 'em hell, Ma."

I did my best to give him instructions about how to stay safe, but he seemed to consider the entire situation in light of a huge joke. I sternly tried to impress upon him, as I had with Ellie, the need for extreme caution. Zach responded by promising to get me a deerstalker hat and a magnifying glass. His attitude rubbed off on his sister, and ten minutes later the two of them left for school as if they hadn't a care in the world.

My first task when I got to school was not likely to soothe my nerves. Immediately after texting Tom about the latest threat I made my way downstairs to the main office. I could no longer put off getting my new supplies. Mrs. Donnatella has the key to the supply room, also known as The Vault.

The Vault actually is a vault. It is a windowless interior room with a thick steel door and a heavy lock. We warehouse priceless items inside, such as Post-its, construction paper, and Scotch tape. We also put our midterm and final exams there. Timmy and Gordon treat those tests with the same security, solemnity, and ceremony as the guards at Buckingham Palace do the crown jewels. Less amusingly, the vault is located three long feet past the mailroom and persuading Mrs. Donnatella to make the trek is no easy task.

Since she was not crocheting, she was on the telephone. I waited while she talked to her husband about glucose, gastritis, and bypass surgery. I stood at a respectful distance and tried not to telegraph my impatience. Finally, the secretary hung up the phone. She regarded me with her hard, slightly bulging eyes. I looked at her hair, which was shellacked into its usual pale bob.

"What have you done with your hair? It looks great!"

Mrs. Donnatella put her hand, as large and heavy as a man's, up to pat the top of her head. "Do you like it? I thought it was a little too short," she said, in her deep Jersey-inflected growl. "I'm always tellin' them not to cut it too short."

I sighed, "I know what you mean. But I like it short. It's definitely a younger look."

Mrs. Donnatella is no fool, but she is nonetheless prey to the same weaknesses other women share. I couldn't tell her with any degree of conviction that she looked thinner, because I had no idea what was going on under the tent-like shirt that covered her stretch pants, and for the same reason I couldn't realistically compliment her outfit. Besides, the woman is not comatose. Even she must realize that she never looks thinner and never wears nice clothes. Complimenting her hair was my only option, since I find it difficult to even look at Mrs. Donnatella's flamboyantly painted and decorated fingernails.

It was time for the kill. "Oh, Mrs. Donnatella, would you mind opening the vault for me? I have to pick up my supplies."

The temperature in the office immediately dropped to below freezing.

"Where are your supply forms?"

I was ready. "Filled out, approved, and filed online," I answered, with as close an approximation to relaxed goodwill as I could manage. I handed her the printout, so she could verify that I was not going to abscond with an unapproved number of pencils.

Mrs. Donnatella resentfully heaved herself out of her chair, knocking over her crochet bag. She reached down to untangle the yarn, which had wound itself partway around the double wheels of a chair leg, but I leapt into action and did it for her. I followed her rear end to the vault. She's so tall, it isn't far below my eye level.

I went inside the vault while she stood guard by the heavy door. I piled paper, markers, tape, scissors, Post-its, and pencils into an untidy bundle and unsteadily walked down the hall. I can't claim total victory in our exchange, as she literally made me pay for my request.

"Have you seen my newest toaster oven covers?" She laid an assortment of items on her desk.

I put down my burden to admire the blue and pink *schmatte*, and then gutlessly agreed to buy it. I don't even have a toaster oven. Then I bought a pillow crocheted in bilious yellow. Mrs. Donnatella assured me all the money she makes goes to a children's charity. I told her I would pay her later, but she preferred to get the cash immediately.

I returned to my classroom, dropped the supplies, grabbed my purse, and returned to the main office. The secretary seemed pleased, probably because she finally found someone spineless enough to buy her crappy crocheted wares. She resumed her interrupted telephone call, cradling a ball of Pepto-Bismol pink yarn and a lethal-looking crochet hook. Before I left, I heard her say she had purchased the list of baby supplies. I felt guilty about doubting her charitable intentions.

I returned to my classroom, where I realized, to my horror, I had left my coffee cup unattended in the unlocked room. I sniffed the cup. I stared at it. I took a sip, and although it tasted fine I spit it out. Emily walked in as I wiped my mouth. She seemed to have a knack for walking in on me while I'm making an idiot out of myself. As usual, though, she considerately did not comment upon my predicament, and she looked away as I tissued off the remaining drool.

"How was your weekend?"

Every Monday Emily asks me about my weekend so she can update me on the athletic and academic prowess of Mavis, her athletically and academically gifted daughter.

"Good. I'll catch up with you later, Emily; I want to put this stuff away before the kids show up."

"I'll help you," she offered.

We shelved supplies while she gave me a play-by-play description of Mavis's field hockey exploits, and then described the brilliant essay Mavis had written on *The Crucible*. Caroline walked in as Emily recited Mavis's insightful analysis.

"So fascinating to hear about your daughter's life, Emily. But as your department chair I'm here to remind you we have a faculty meeting today. We were supposed to have an English department meeting, but Timmy and Gordon have co-opted our time in order to go over the test scores. Apparently the little buggers took a nap during the last state assessments. Not that I care. Nor should you." She opened the closet door and examined the neatly piled supplies, sniffing as if they gave off a noxious odor.

I couldn't help myself. "Maybe one of our new teachers could give a workshop for us. You know, tell us how to do our job."

Caroline closed the door and smirked. "Don't be bitter, Liz. You won't get anywhere in this district with that attitude."

I blinked at her. "What do you mean, 'get anywhere?' Where would I be going? I don't want to be an administrator. I only want to teach. What can they do to me?"

Caroline brushed her hands as if wiping me, and any responsibility she might have for my future, off her palms. "You could be looking at cafeteria duty for the rest of your professional life. As the English department chair I don't have a duty period, but I seem to remember it wasn't all that much fun. Of course, you do get the chance to bond with the students."

Caroline had a point. Cafeteria duty is not onerous, but it isn't fun. All it requires is a strong stomach, the fortitude to stand for sixty minutes in a cacophonous din, and a taste for administering the third degree to students unlucky enough to have to use the bathroom.

After many miserable years of cafeteria duty and one study hall from hell, I finally scored hall duty. This is the summit of every teacher's ambition: to sit undisturbed and grade papers in the middle of the day. It is such a prize, Timmy has attempted to beef up the requirements so the allocation of duty periods is less blatantly unequal. Now, instead of staying seated for the entire period, hall duty teachers are required to periodically walk through the school and check the appropriate bathrooms. But Timmy's noble endeavor backfired. Being required to roam the halls made an already sweet deal even better, since there is no way for the administrators to know if the teacher in charge is checking the hallways, making telephone calls, or chatting with friends. I have taken many an illegal bathroom break as well.

In yet another innovation, hall duty teachers now have to carry walkie-talkies, the sight of which I find hilariously phallic. I don't know how to use them, but I find the crackling and honking that the handset emits a source of entertainment when my enthusiasm for grading papers wanes.

I spent my next hall duty period texting Zach and Ellie to make sure they were okay. They managed to text me back without getting their cell phones confiscated by their teachers. I left George a message and let him know that I was still alive. Finally, I started my mandatory walk through the school.

In a partially screened alcove outside the library, I saw Ashlee and Timmy. They were standing very close to each other. Ashlee's back was to me, but Timmy frowned as he saw me coming.

"What can I do for you, Liz?" Timmy took the walkie-talkie from my hand.

Although they were in a somewhat compromising position, I was the one who felt awkward. "Nothing. I'm checking the hallways. I have hall duty."

"These work better when you turn them on," he said, and he turned the dials so that the sound of static filled the hall.

I shrugged. "If there's an emergency I'll brain the guy with it." No one laughed.

Ashlee turned to Timmy. "I'll see you later," she said meaningfully.

Timmy's face was as blank as one of our expensive smart boards. He stood there admiring his football-themed tie and smiling to himself.

With every appearance of diligence, I walked down the hall. Then I scooted down the stairs and into the bathroom, where I finally called Tom Harriman to tell him about the latest poison pen letter. We agreed to meet after school. He instructed me not to tell anyone at school about the letters. Just as I was about to ask if anyone else had been threatened, the nurse walked in on me.

There is no place in a school to have a private conversation. Sometimes I go outside, but then I'm locked out and have to get buzzed back in. I do understand Mrs. Donnatella's pain; she has to put down her crochet hook and wheel her chair six inches to the left of her desk. Last winter she kept me waiting so long I flirted with frostbite.

At the end of the day Emily came by my room on her way to the faculty meeting, which I had inconveniently forgotten about. I was stuck. I didn't want to make excuses to Gordon and Timmy, so I texted Tom I would be late. He didn't bother texting me back, and ten minutes later I saw him enter the room.

Gordon invited Timmy to open the meeting, but Timmy declined. He didn't look well, and he announced that he would email us the information he had been planning to present. Of course, both Gordon and Timmy could email us the information they tell us every goddamned week, and we could forever skip this useless exercise, but that is a complaint for another day.

Gordon warmed up his vocal cords with an imitation of several small animals fighting over a carcass. He turned his back to us and spoke directly to the smart board, which was set up in the front of the room. And then he began his tirade. Unaware, or indifferent, to either Harriman's presence or Timmy's discomfort, Gordon harangued us once again for the students' performance on last year's tests. He finished his inspiring speech with a direct hit at the English department. "I am particularly disappointed in the Language Arts grades. I don't want to point fingers, but we expect our students to do much better on the reading and writing sections of the test."

I felt guilty and humiliated. Why couldn't Gordon have come to an English department meeting if he were so upset with us? Why did this have to be a public flogging? I spent the rest of the meeting poring over the student test scores. Eventually, Gordon's voice broke, and that ended the first part of the meeting. He introduced Tom and then left for more salubrious climes.

Tom looked handsome and serious. His low voice carried farther than either Gordon's grumble or Timmy's whine.

"I want to update the staff on the status of our investigation. We are making significant headway. But we also need your help. This is to remind you that if you have any information at all, about Dr. Deaver, about the day of the murder, or about anything else that seems suspicious, please let me know immediately. I also would like to know if any of you have received unusual communications of any kind. You all have my contact information. Are there any questions?"

There was a moment of silence. Very few teachers ask questions during staff meetings, because it simply prolongs the agony for everyone else. The nurse, however, hates to let pass an opportunity to show off. She waved her hand at Tom.

"What exactly do you mean by 'significant headway' detective? And what kind of 'communications' are you talking about?"

Tom smiled with beguiling charm. "You know I can't divulge that information. I am not here to give particulars, but to get them."

The nurse frowned. "Those instructions are pretty vague."

"Not if you know something. In that case, the instructions are very direct. I'll give you some examples: On the day of the murder, Marcia Deaver did not go to the meeting that all of you were required to attend. Did any of you notice, either on your way to the auditorium, or on your way back, anything suspicious, anything that didn't fit? Have you become aware of any animus that anyone might have felt toward Dr. Deaver?" He paused to look around the room. "I don't need anyone to speak up publicly; in fact, I counsel you not to do so. But I also counsel you to contact me privately. Not doing so could prove dangerous for you. Especially if you have been contacted or threatened in any way since then."

Timmy got to his feet and feebly tried to get us to quiet down, but the buzzing of conversation overpowered him. He looked confused and a bit upset, and his shaky tenor got higher and weaker. He lifted his drink as if to toast his own defeat and took one quick gulp and then another. He swallowed hard.

His face turned the color of the blue sports drink he held in his hand. He gasped for air. In stunned silence we watched him fall. He seemed to do so in slow motion, his bulky frame dropping to one knee before resting face down.

Ashlee screamed loudly, and fifty cell phones called 911. The nurse, with obvious reluctance, began mouth-to-mouth resuscitation, pausing in between breaths to thump on Timmy's chest. Moments later the ambulance pulled up to the school, followed by four police cars with flashing lights. Detective Brown got into the ambulance with Timmy. Tom left four police officers with us and instructed us not to leave. He went with the crime scene unit to investigate the rest of the building.

The meeting came to a decidedly informal end. We huddled in small groups as we waited to give our statements to the police. Emily called Mavis, to see if her daughter could survive an hour on her own. Caroline continued to grade papers. Ashlee made and received dozens of texts. I called Ellie to tell her that she might need to get a ride with one of the other dancers. Then we waited.

Ten minutes later a second ambulance blared into the main driveway. I could not see much from the oblique view that the Media Center offered, but it looked as though the paramedics were tending to another victim.

We did not find out until the next day that the occupant of the second ambulance did not follow Timmy to the hospital. He went directly to the morgue.

CHAPTER 20

GONE WITH THE WIND

I waited impatiently at the drive-through of the closest Dunkin' Donuts. An iced latte seemed too festive for this tense and tragic moment, so I ordered a black coffee instead. The coffee and a cigarette got me through my drive to the Jersey State Ballet studio. I didn't go inside. The last thing I felt like doing was engaging in Ballet Mother talk. If I had to hear even one parent confide how talented her daughter was I might poison someone myself.

I tried listening to NPR, but the hosts of "All Things Considered" were considering yet another volatile day on Wall Street, so I turned it off. My personal life was providing enough of a roller coaster ride. I didn't have to hear about the gyrations on the stock market as well. I checked the time again and again.

Where was Ellie? Where the hell was Ellie? Suddenly frightened, I rushed into the studio. Ellie emerged from the dressing room, pink-cheeked and relaxed. She let me hug her before demanding, "What's for dinner? I'm starving."

That, at least, was one question I was prepared to answer. "Lasagna. If you don't mind stopping, I can pick up some bread to go with it."

She made a gagging sound. "Are you joking? Please tell me you're kidding."

"Why would I be kidding? Everyone likes lasagna. I made it over the weekend, so it's all ready to be heated up."

Ellie turned up her nose. "Well, you can heat it all you want," she said, with as much disgust as if I'd suggested eating stewed garbage, "but I am not eating it. I think you know that I'm rehearsing right now? What role do you think I'll be playing? A dancing elephant?"

Tears slipped out of my eyes. I clasped my hands to prevent them from shaking. Ellie took one look at my face and quickly shepherded me to the car.

"For God's sake, Mom, get a grip. I was kidding about the lasagna." She thought for a moment. "Even though I'm not kidding about not eating the lasagna. I'll make myself a protein shake."

I shook my head at her. "It's not dinner, Ellie. It's something else that's upset me."

Eager, but far more wary than she'd been a few days earlier, she asked, "The murder? Something about the murder?"

Under normal circumstances, I seek to shield my children from the harsh realities of life. But now? Now my kids needed the truth.

"Our assistant principal is sick. He's in the hospital. I don't know what happened, but he got sick after drinking something. I suppose it's possible that what he drank didn't make him sick. But that's not all. After Timmy left for the hospital, the ambulance returned and took someone else."

Ellie looked at the Dunkin' Donuts coffee in the cup holder next to me and the coffee mug in the holder next to her. The cup optimistically proclaimed its owner the World's Best Mom.

"Don't drink from that," she advised.

"I didn't. I'm not going to, either."

Ellie tossed the remaining coffee out the window. "Just in case you forget," she explained. "Also, what if there's a time-release capsule inside and it releases a poisonous gas once you accelerate past 50 miles an hour?"

I laughed at her dire imaginings, but I also didn't go above the 45 mile per hour speed limit. My cell phone tinkled, chimed, and buzzed, but I didn't let Ellie look at it.

I pulled into the driveway and took out the phone. One text message after another and one phone call after another announced the same news. Gordon was dead. Gordon was dead. Gordon was—

The kids and I were in the middle of dinner when I heard George's peculiar foot-stomping routine announce his presence at the front door. I ran to him, but he held me at arm's distance.

"Have you seen the news? Your high school is the lead story."

"Seen the news? No. I don't have to see news about the high school on television, George. I was there." I searched my husband's face for signs of sympathy and concern.

He latched the door. "Call the locksmith tomorrow. I want this place secured tighter than Fort Knox. Thanks to your nutcase disorganization, we're sitting ducks."

"You've never complained that we don't lock the doors."

George stroked his chin and pretended to be pensively patient. I gave him The Look, the one that says I will kill him if he argues with me in front of the kids. He dropped the subject until Zach finished his forty pounds of lasagna and Ellie drank her evil-smelling protein shake.

As soon as they were out of the room, George said, "Hmm. Let me see. Have things changed at all around here? Oh yeah, right. There's a psychopathic killer in your school. And then there's that little matter concerning not one, but two threatening letters." He started tapping on the top of the counter, each rap a little louder than the one before. "No need to worry; let's continue to leave our doors wide open and unlocked, since my wife can't manage to avoid locking herself out of the house. Yeah, that makes much more sense."

I tried to say something, but George was unstoppable.

"No, you know what? Let's go on television. In case there are a few people in the Western hemisphere who don't know we keep our doors unlocked. Don't bother worrying about me or the kids."

For once in my life, I rejected guilt. "You want the locksmith called? If you're that worried, you can call him yourself. I'm in a classroom all day. I can barely get to the bathroom. You sit next to a telephone in a private office."

George's face turned red and he pressed his lips together. "Can't you do anything without an argument? This is your fault and your problem. Take care of it." He helped himself to a square foot of lasagna and took it up to his office.

I stared at the crusty pan, the sink full of dishes, and the sticky countertops. There was no sense wasting all of my furious energy, and so I scrubbed every inch of the kitchen. It certainly needed it. Suburban Clean Machine Cleaning Service had been slacking off. I'd call them after I called the locksmith.

I crawled into bed and turned on the television. I hadn't wanted a television in the bedroom, but George insisted. Was that the first sign our marriage was going south? He paid more attention to the inert screen than he did to me.

I tuned into the local news show. The governor's bulk filled the screen, against a backdrop of Valerian Hills High School.

"This is an outrage! The good taxpayers of New Jersey deserve better. That is why I am proposing that we cut the ineffective local police forces that do more harm than good, and replace them with more efficient metro centers. The taxpayers of this great state are strapped economically and we can't afford this kind of waste." The governor paused and clasped his hands. "In the meantime, our thoughts and prayers go out to all the community and family members."

There was a flurry of questions, but the governor simply raised his meaty hand and made a strategic exit. The scene changed to the street outside the hospital. A perfectly plucked young man spoke seriously into his microphone.

"I have here a teacher from Valerian Hills High School. Can you tell us in your own words exactly what happened?"

I sighed. Whose words did the reporter think she would use, other than her own?

Ashlee had had time to repair her makeup and brush her hair.

"Oh, it was just awful, y'know? I was like right next to him, and one second he was fine, and the next second he was on the ground? I am completely and totally freaked out." Ashlee's mouth turned down in sorrow, but eyes sparkled with excitement.

The newscaster looked straight at the camera. "There you have it. A Tragedy in Suburbia." The young man shook his head, and then in a cheery voice said, "And now, a look at the weather! Bright skies and plenty of sunshine are in the forecast for those of you hoping for one more weekend at the Jersey Shore. Am I right, Bob?"

Before Bob could offer his confidential opinions, I turned off the television. I sat on the edge of my bed and stared at the yellow legal pad that bore evidence to my obsession with finding the identity of the murderer. I put it under the mattress.

The incongruous strains of a happy Chopin waltz floated from my cell phone and broke my concentration. Ellie set the music for me in place of a jarring ring tone, but the lilting melody, which she claimed would stop me from starting in alarm every time the phone rang, had never seemed less apt.

Susan yelped, "Liz! Are you okay? I saw the news. What the hell is going on out there?"

"Exactly what you saw on television," I answered. The emotional toll of dealing with Timmy's collapse and Gordon's death and George's unreasonableness was exhausting. "I've just about had it. Sue, I'll call you tomorrow."

"Don't be ridiculous. We have to talk now, or I will die of curiosity. I won't keep you long; I got back early from a very boring first date. I didn't even order coffee. I'm telling you, I don't know why I bother with all these dating sites." She spoke with some regret. "I suppose this means we cross Timmy off our list of suspects. I had him in the Number One spot. So what do we do next?"

The pressure of everything that had to be done weighed me down. "I have no plans other than to get locks for my doors and windows. And George wants an alarm system."

"You can hardly blame him." She broke off to click the three locks on her door. "On the topic of security, let me tell you about the ex-CIA agent I went out with last Friday. I won't waste your time talking about tonight's miserable encounter."

"I'd love to hear about it, but I'm pretty tired. Maybe tomorrow?" I didn't have the energy to share my worries, and I wasn't up to listening to stories about Susan's dating woes.

"It can't be tomorrow. You can't talk during the day and I have plans for the evening. It has to be now."

I took off my shoes, propped my feet up, and waited for the latest bulletin from the dating front.

"So, this guy I met at a conference in Boston, who I thought was really cute, calls me up. He's in town and staying at the Dream Hotel, so I figure he's at least got money. We met there for drinks, and then—"

George stomped down the stairs.

"Susan, I'm hanging up."

"Wait—" she protested. I clicked the off button on the phone.

George glared at me. "I suppose that was your sister? Why doesn't she get herself a life and leave us alone?"

I put the blankets over my head. Sometimes avoidance is the only way out.

Two hours later, everyone was asleep. I retrieved my yellow pad and pen, tiptoed into the den, and started thinking. Did Timmy get a threatening letter? I needed to know if he had been warned before he had been attacked. Timmy has as much subtlety as the average five-year-old, and he easily could have aroused the killer's suspicions without realizing it. Whom could he have scared?

I went back to the psychological profile Susan and I had started. The assaults on Timmy and Gordon changed all previous assumptions. Whoever the murderer was, he or she was not as intelligent as I'd assumed. It would obviously take a much larger quantity of drug to kill a healthy man of forty than it would a fifty-something woman with a pre-existing heart condition. Even if all the other factors had been equal, any idiot could figure out that a man weighing 250 pounds is going to be harder to poison than a woman weighing 125 pounds.

I diagrammed the position of each person at the meeting relative to Timmy and Gordon. Ashlee had been sitting next to Timmy, and Caroline had been close by. It would have taken an enormous amount of luck and a very cool head to have poisoned two drinks during the meeting. Even one would have been difficult. It occurred to me that the drugs that poisoned Timmy might not have been in the sports drink. The coffee pot is in an alcove that also houses the copy machine. As with Marcia's murder, nearly anyone in the building could have poisoned the pot. I wondered if there was some tactful way for me to discover who had used the copy machine.

If the killer poisoned the coffee pot, and not individual drinks, there were two possibilities. One was that the attacker had been willing to harm all three people who had coffeepot privileges, i.e., Gordon, Timmy, and Mrs. Donnatella, even if only one person was the intended target. To me, that indicated a psychopath at work, and although Valerian Hills High School is peopled by the strange, the resentful, and the abnormal, I couldn't immediately come up with anyone who had that level of insane hatred.

The other possibility was that the killer intended to poison all three, or, given the outcome, at least two out of three. Obviously, Mrs. Donnatella had the best opportunity. If she had done the poisoning, then only Timmy and Gordon would have been affected. I added Caroline to the list of suspects, and not simply because I dislike her. Caroline's habit of lounging about the main office made her a likely suspect. Her presence would not have excited any interest or suspicion, since that is her de facto headquarters.

Over and over again, I ran through each possibility, seeking patterns and looking for clues. For once, my lunatic family members, with the possible exception of the man whom I reluctantly admit is my father, offered no plausible model of criminal behavior. I hail from a very low-budget group of crooks.

Grandpa was a bagman, that is, he held money and other stolen goods in exchange for a small piece of the action. I remember visiting him and my grandmother and being walled in by stacks of televisions, stereos, and air conditioners. Like me, Grandpa avoided really risky situations, but I later learned he'd come close to prison on more than one occasion.

Nana was a very genteel and kindly card shark. She sweetened her opponents' losses with gifts of Barton's chocolates and homemade poppy seed cookies. In all, my paternal grandparents were charming and highly idiosyncratic shysters, but violence was not their strong suit, unless you count the loud arguments they had over such vitally important topics as the relative merits of cherry versus strawberry cheesecake. I prefer not to think too hard about what my father was capable of doing. There's a reason Susan and I refer to him only as The Lousy Bastard.

Literature should have provided at least a few leads, but no parallels came to mind. I doubted the Valerian Hills killer was an evil genius, and fictional villains have a tendency toward creative evil.

The next day the school was mobbed once again by reporters and parents. Lights flashed and cameras whizzed. Mrs. Tumbleson's too-familiar voice echoed through the building,

"All staff members: this is the President of the Board of Education speaking. Report immediately to the main lobby, where you will receive your morning assignments."

With Gordon dead and Timmy in the hospital we were leaderless. I feared Mrs. Tumbleson would take up residence in the high school, and thus be able to harass the teachers in person instead of by email. I had enough on my hands with her constant pressure regarding her son Jack, my annoying Advanced Placement student.

I peered into the main office. I was relieved to see that Mrs. Donnatella was safe, until she opened her mouth.

"What are you doin' here?" the secretary asked. "Your assignment is outside."

Emily was the only other occupant of the office. She has a warm relationship with Mrs. Donnatella, which I attribute to her frequent purchases of crocheted goods.

Before I could say anything Emily explained, "You know how I feel about crowds. I thought I'd hide out here until things simmer down."

"I'm sure they don't need every single teacher." Caroline popped her head out of the mailroom. "Even though, I don't know, maybe it's me, but I think we're supposed to go outside."

I refused to allow her to intimidate me. "Then why aren't you there?"

"Mrs. Tumbleson told me to keep an eye on things in here," she said triumphantly.

"Same here," I lied. Caroline, Emily, and Mrs. Donnatella looked at each other and did not comment.

"I'm going to get a walkie-talkie from Timmy's office," I said, and boldly turned the handle on the door.

"The door is locked," said the secretary. "No one is allowed inside. You can have my walkie-talkie." I took the walkie-talkie but did not leave.

"What are you guys going to do?" I asked.

Mrs. Donnatella examined her nails. Just as certain male teachers have seasonally adjusted ties, their female counterparts adorn themselves with similarly themed manicures. The secretary's nails were painted a violent orange, and the tip of each finger bore a tiny decal depicting pumpkins and other fall vegetables. She flicked an invisible speck of dust from her thumb and began to scrape foreign objects from underneath each nail with a lethal-looking nail file. It was mildly disgusting to watch. We seemed to be at an impasse.

Emily hesitated and then said, "I'll keep you company, Liz."

I left the office with Emily in tow. We walked through the two large gyms, where several teachers had been assigned to babysit students who had missed the textcaster message about the delayed opening. We walked up to the library, but the door was locked, and the media specialist, aka librarian, waved us away. Emily turned to leave, but I knocked. The librarian cracked open the door so I pushed my way in.

"The Media Center is closed until further notice."

"Why?" I searched her face for signs of illness. "Have you been poisoned, too?"

"That's not funny."

"I'm not trying to be funny. I'm trying to find out why the library is closed."

The misnamed Joy looked frustrated. "It's closed because I closed it. And I closed it because someone has been sneaking into the library."

This was interesting. Timmy had evinced an attraction to the library this year that I'd not noticed before. A few weeks ago he'd claimed to be getting a book, which even at the time I found highly suspicious. And a few hours before he was poisoned he was outside the library. What kinds of multimedia events were going on there?

Emily coaxed, "Joy, I am so interested in finding out how you knew someone was here. Were there books missing? Any kind of vandalism? Problems with the computers?"

I was grateful for Emily's help. I wanted to strangle the librarian, but Emily stared at Joy as if the other woman were about to divulge the definitive answer to Einstein's Unified Field Theory.

"Marcia was the last person who complained about the custodians. And she's dead," the media specialist said.

Emily asked the question I was thinking. "Do you think one of the custodians had something to do with that? I can't imagine any of them as a murderer."

"That's not the whole story." Joy pursed her mouth, as if afraid that unintended words would fly out of her.

We waited a bit, and after a pregnant moment, Joy unburdened herself. A slight flush darkened her skin. "I found a condom," she admitted.

I could hardly suppress a horselaugh. Yes, it was disgusting, but it was also hilarious.

I asked, as delicately as I could, "Was it used?"

Joy looked at me with as much disgust as if I'd been the one having sex in the stacks. "I will not answer that. The point is, someone is sneaking in here and doing God Knows What. And now, if you'll excuse me."

We took the hint and left. Joy locked the door behind us with an audible snap. Emily and I made our way down the nearest staircase, breathless with suppressed laughter.

Emily pressed her hand to her mouth. "Shush! Hush! We shouldn't be laughing. Think of poor Gordon. And poor Timmy."

That did sober me up. I left Emily in her room and went to retrieve my coffee from my car. I returned to the office and tossed the walkie-talkie onto Mrs. Donnatella's desk. The excitement of the morning began to wind down.

The kids arrived and went to their classrooms. They were in an awkward position. Most of them despised Timmy, and now that he had been attacked I sensed they felt uncomfortable. I had planned on giving them a test, but half the students were absent. The police had once again taken over the building and the halls were anything but quiet.

My head started throbbing. I grabbed the Excedrin bottle from the back of the drawer and palmed two pills without looking at them. As soon as I swallowed, Jack the Jackass whooped.

"Hey, how do you know the pills aren't poisoned?"

The rest of the class laughed and shushed him. Horrified, I realized he had a point. Should I embarrass myself by running out of the room? Or risk dying in order to save face? It wasn't an easy call. I sprinted to the bathroom. There I gagged myself until I regurgitated the pills, which left a burning sensation in my throat all day. I had never been able to throw up on demand before. Normally, I will writhe in agony for hours in order to avoid it, but I found it surprisingly easy to barf when motivated by the desire to not die.

After class I went to the English office, where Bill was aimlessly shelving books. Bill was such a nice guy; I hated to think he might be the murderer.

"Have you heard any news about Timmy?" I asked him. I put a few books in the bookcase to keep him company.

Bill rubbed his chin. "Not directly. My wife talked to his wife yesterday. Timmy's going to be okay."

"Does Timmy have any idea who put the drugs in his drink?" I looked closely at him. He looked uncomfortable, but I wasn't sure if his discomfort was guilt or indigestion.

He looked off into the distance and scratched his head. "No idea. I can't imagine who would want to harm Timmy. Nicest guy in the world."

I knew it was impolitic, but I couldn't resist. "Not like Marcia?"

Bill shrugged. "Nah. That's not what I meant." He turned away and addressed me over his shoulder. "Well, good talking to you. Gotta go." He walked back into his classroom, sat down at his desk, and added another layer of paper to the sediment that had been accumulating since disco died.

I got back to my classroom in time to hear that we were having a lockdown drill. I felt sorry for Timmy. He loved lockdown drills.

We have various levels of security during lockdown drills. Today the code was Orange, which meant we had to keep our doors locked and were not allowed to leave the room. Under Code Red conditions we also have to turn off the lights and sit where we can't be seen from the windows or the door.

I did my best to continue to teach as the police led their trained dogs through the otherwise deserted hallway. Under normal circumstances, the police bring their dogs in no more than once or twice a year, and the focus is illegal drugs, not prescription medications. I wondered if the dogs were going to check the classrooms.

Judging by the conversation in the faculty room half the teachers in the school were on Lipitor, beta-blockers, and diuretics. I wished I'd been more attentive during the lunchroom talk about high blood pressure, cancer, and diabetes. Conversations about medical matters make me feel sick, and I usually leave the room when anyone begins describing symptoms, procedures, or medications.

Between Marcia's death, Gordon's death, Timmy's near miss, and the dogs sniffing outside the door, it wasn't easy to get the students to concentrate. The only thing on their minds was murder, and I was pleased to be able to satisfy this craving with *Macbeth*.

I couldn't decide if it was a serendipitous or unhappy coincidence that we were studying a character renowned for his degeneration from wartime hero to reviled mass murderer. The kids were unusually animated.

Brittany and Bethany insisted that Macbeth had always been a cold-blooded murderer, and that he was responsible for each evil act.

For some reason this riled Jack Tumbleson, whose contributions to class discussions usually were limited to requests for extended deadlines. Jack protested, "Macbeth wouldn't have killed anyone if it hadn't been for Lady Macbeth. He didn't want to do it. She ruined his life with all that nagging."

I listened to Jack's opinion respectfully. It can't be easy to have someone like Melinda Tumbleson as a mother, and Jack is probably an expert on the topic of nagging.

"If Macbeth was too dumb to think for himself, that doesn't mean he's innocent." Brittany showed no signs of backing down, even against the popular Jack Tumbleson. "And anyway, Lady Macbeth doesn't tell Macbeth to keep killing people. He does that by himself."

I felt chills run down my back. Freaking Shakespeare. He nails it every time. Someone had felt pressured to kill Marcia. Then, like Macbeth, the killer couldn't stop. The killer's moral sense died when King Duncan/Marcia did. The Valerian Hills killer got caught in his own ambition, his overactive imagination, or, perhaps, his lack of imagination. He—or she—was becoming increasingly dangerous. Like Macbeth, the killer would stop at nothing.

At the end of the day, I handed out sealed envelopes to the students. Inside, a letter addressed to the parents, and signed by Board of Education President Mrs. Tumbleson, explained that Gordon was dead, Timmy was on medical leave, and she was seeking a replacement. But the kids already knew.

CHAPTER 21
DESPERATE REMEDIES

I received an emailed invitation to view Gordon's remains at the newly popular Haberman's Funeral Home. I felt tired and ill but went nonetheless. I hadn't especially liked either of the murder victims, but I felt a painful sympathy for those who did. An even less welcome email came from Mrs. Tumbleson. The text of her message was as follows:

> *Dear Teachers,*
> *I applaud the professionalism of our fine staff. As you no doubt know, tonight is Back to School Night for the parents. Do not discuss anything relatable to the recent unfortunate events. Parents can direct their inquiries to me, although I will NOT be available for questioning tonight.*
> *You are required to incorporate new technology into your presentations. The taxpayers of this town did not pay for all this equipment to have it sitting in a corner.*
> *In the meantime, I will unofficially assist in keeping things running. The middle school principal, Kathie Dorp, will also be here. I want all of us to be team players. There is no I in Team. Thank you in advance for your cooperation.*
> *Sincerely,*
> *Melinda Tumbleson (Jack's Mom)*
> *President, Valerian Hills Board of Education*

I was mildly surprised that the parents' Back to School Night had not been postponed in deference to Timmy's hospitalization and Gordon's death, but the high school schedule is so tightly packed with important events there was probably not another open date for the next three months.

In honor of the occasion I hung student work on the walls, cleaned the shelves and windowsills, and coaxed dust balls out of the corners of the classroom. The cut in the custodial workforce is being visited upon the teachers and students in all sorts of unpleasant ways, and the school had never been dirtier.

As soon as the school day ended I raced home, showered, and dressed in a skirt and jacket more elegant than any of my usual daytime outfits. I wriggled into a pair of tummy control pantyhose, which did nothing positive for my tummy but blew a huge hole in my comfort level. Lastly, I pushed my feet into high-heeled pumps that somehow no longer fit. Do shoes shrink? Had the weight I'd lost in my thighs moved to my feet? I got back in my car before traffic from the city kicked in. I smoked one restorative cigarette and spritzed myself with enough perfume to hide the evidence. Lastly, I chewed three pieces of peppermint gum. Sure that I had erased all signs of smoke I pulled into the parking lot and limped to my room. The shoes already hurt like hell.

I was early, so I took off my jacket and wiped my perspiring face. My hair, which less than one hour ago had hung in obedient shiny strands, rebelled in the humid air and began frizzing around my face in an unattractive halo. I gave up on glamour and pinned my hair into a severe bun. Not especially attractive, but very English Teacher.

The most important part of my preparation was my speech. If I timed it well the speech would leave no time for questions from the parents. I readied my PowerPoint presentation for the smart board, which would indicate that I, like the board, was intelligent. It's important that the parents not have to listen for ten minutes without being visually entertained as well.

The Home and School Association had laid out cookies and coffee in preparation for this event, but I was never sure how welcome the teachers were at the refreshment table. Some parents offer cookies; other look put upon when we help ourselves. I couldn't remember if I'd ingested anything except for coffee, and I was starved. I walked into the cafeteria, and under the censorious eyes of several parents made off with two cookies and an apple.

I hid in the English office. Bill and Ashlee were already there. Emily had not yet arrived, and probably would not do so until one minute before the night's festivities began.

Caroline blew in on a cloud of Opium perfume. "I come bearing gifts, my children." She laid two pounds of cookies on the desk. "I saw Mrs. Tumbleson and she insisted I take this platter. I, of course, won't eat any, which is why I still wear the same size now as I did in my twenties."

That statement was accurate. Although Caroline is more than ten years older than I am, her daily exercise regimen and starvation diet keep her in a heavenly size two. Various facial fillers smoothed out any aggressive inroads on her face, and the only hint to her true age was her obsession with how much longer she has to teach before she can retire.

Caroline said, as if as an afterthought, "By the way, Liz, I think Mr. and Mrs. Tumbleson are looking for you."

I left the English office and did not provide a forwarding address. Caroline knew perfectly well that if Mrs. Tumbleson was looking for me she was gunning for me. I fled to the teachers' bathroom, and in the company of a few other refugees I rechecked my frizzy hair and melting makeup. I reminded myself that Back to School Night is a limited engagement.

The night passed in a blur of speeches, parents, and cookies. I saw Emily briefly; she sidled into her classroom as the parents made their way down the hallway and left without saying goodbye. Most of the parents seemed pleasant and pleased. Then, the Parents from Another Planet arrived.

Mrs. Tumbleson led the charge. Before I could begin my speech she called out, "*Mrs.* Hopewell!" as if to challenge my married status. When I looked in her direction she asked, "What are you doing to see that Our AP Kids are getting the same fine education from you that they did from Dr. Deaver?"

If the parents scented blood, I would be eaten down to the bone. "Read the handout on the curriculum," I answered with neither rancor nor any deference.

Mrs. Tumbleson's nasal whine cut through my speech again. "Mrs. Hopewell, I understand from my son Jack that you've only covered two major works so far. How are you going to make up for lost time?"

Some parents looked uncomfortable at this frontal attack, but others nudged each other in amusement. Why overt nastiness moves some people to admiration is something I've never understood.

"Mrs. Tumbleson, we are on the same schedule as last year. Once again, I suggest that you check the syllabus. I think it will answer your concerns."

Three more minutes elapsed. I tapped efficiently at the smart board screen, but after several obedient turns the damned thing wouldn't move. I tapped with more force, but the slide of Shakespeare regarding our audience with sober interest remained stubbornly stuck. There was a moment of suspense, and I finally went over to the computer to manage the fiasco from my desk. I surreptitiously checked the clock, as did most of the parents. I stopped worrying. The whole damned exercise was only ten minutes long and I was in the home stretch. The smart board cooperated at the last second, treating the parents to a movie screen-sized view of the information on the handouts that I had given them, which echoed exactly the speech they'd just heard.

I am so Multimedia.

The bell rang, signaling the parents to leave, but Mrs. Tumbleson had one more question. "Mrs. Hopewell, I understand you've never taught AP before. What exactly qualifies you to teach this class?"

I had prepared myself for that very question. "Intelligence, education, and experience." I turned a fierce eye at the rest of the parents. I dared them to email me with their questions, and I made my way toward the door.

Mrs. Tumbleson stood in the way. *Screw this.* It was after eight o'clock. If I wanted to go to the bathroom, by golly, no one was going to stop me. Incredibly, Mrs. Tumbleson followed me down the stairs. This didn't bother me, since the teachers' bathroom is not open to the public. I inserted my key into the lock and politely closed the door in her face. By the time I emerged, she, along with all the other parents, was gone. I got my handbag and headed for the door when the silence suggested to me the relative safety of the building. I realized I had the perfect chance to investigate. I walked downstairs. If anyone interrupted me there were a million reasons I could give for poking around the main office.

The entire building had emptied out in record time, rendering unnecessary the excuses I'd prepared. I checked the teachers' sign-out sheet. Not every name was initialed, but since many teachers don't bother to sign out until the next morning when they sign in, I wasn't worried about stragglers. Every section of the main office was open so the custodians could clean up. The rooms were illuminated only by muted night-lights. I grabbed a walkie-talkie, figuring I could claim to be returning it.

Timmy's office was dark, but unlocked. I got Gordon's Commemorative Flashlight (Valerian Hills High School Lights Up the Future of Education). Unlike every single flashlight in my house, it worked. I felt around under Timmy's desk and found the magnetic key case. There were two small keys inside. One of them unlocked the large file cabinet that held personnel records.

I flipped through the folders twice. Marcia's file was missing. This didn't make sense. If the police needed Marcia's file they would have made copies. Teacher files are their Permanent Record Cards. They follow you into the afterlife.

I sat back on my heels to think. My feet throbbed and my pantyhose was engaged in digging a deep trench into my abdomen, but I heroically withstood the pain. I doubted I would get another chance like this one, and I was damned if I was going to waste it.

Then I heard a creak and a wheeze, as the outer door to the office opened. I felt my pulse quicken as the door closed with a soft click. I turned off the flashlight. Should I speak out or no? An innocent person lurking outside would think I'd lost my mind if I sat silently in Timmy's dark office. Or worse, I might look guilty. On the other hand, if it was the murderer I didn't want to advertise my presence.

I have had many times in my life when I couldn't make up my mind about something, but this one took top honors. *Think!* I implored my sluggish brain.

No. Thinking was not enough. I am capable of doing nothing and thinking until well into the next century without making a move.

Decide.

I crawled under Timmy's desk. That made it harder to hear what was going on in the interior office, but it kept me relatively safe from discovery. The sound of footsteps grew fainter and disappeared. My pulse slowed sufficiently to allow blood to flow to my frozen brain. It was then that I realized Marcia's information was probably in an inactive personnel file and perhaps was in a different drawer. I waited a few more minutes. I heard a door click.

As quietly as possible, I crawled back over to the file cabinet. I kept the flashlight pointed down and away from the door. I opened the file drawer another few inches. The files I wanted were in the back of the bottom drawer. I cautiously pulled at the folder, but as I grabbed the Inactive File the drawer gave a slight squeak.

The sound of footsteps resumed, got closer to me, and then stopped once again. Either there were two intruders in the office, or the original stalker had pulled the same trick I had executed when I was spying in the library.

I figured if the intruder were innocent he or she would speak out. If not, I could start saying my prayers to an appropriate deity. I held my breath. I saw the shadow of an arm, and then the night-light in the office went out with a menacing *click*. Other than the faint glow from the parking lot I was in complete darkness, and whoever was in the office was undoubtedly looking for me. I heard heavy footsteps walk into the mailroom and saw the uneven sweep of a flashlight. The footsteps went past the vault. My stalker stopped outside Timmy's door.

The time to think was over. I ran across the room, jerked the window open, and jumped. My exit was not as impressive as it sounds. Timmy's office is on the first floor and a tangle of bushes line the wall outside the window. At worst I was risking a sprained ankle. I landed on the sharp needles of thick evergreens. I swam my way out of the tangle, tossed my painful shoes away, and sprinted to my car, blessing the invention of automatic locks.

I gunned the motor and screeched out of the parking lot. I turned off the automatic headlights, and as I got to the turn I coasted down the hill. At the intersection I checked for oncoming traffic, which in Valerian Hills on a week-night is practically nonexistent. I ran the red light and zoomed onto Route 23.

I could not control my breathing, try as I might. I swerved into a nearby strip mall and punched at my cell phone.

"Tom! It's me! Go to the school! The killer is at the school, in the office. Go!"

Against the sound of music and loud voices, Tom said, "Huh? Who is this?"

Words started, stopped, and jammed up in my throat, kind of like twelve lanes of traffic funneling into the two-lane Holland Tunnel. "Tom! It's me! It's Liz! Go to-to the high school. Bring backup. I'm in the parking lot of the Dunkin' Donuts. Come get me."

"*Where* are you?" Loud male laughter—not Tom's—blurred his voice.

I banged my hand on the dashboard. "Oh my God! Am I not speaking English? Listen carefully. I'm in the Dunkin' Donuts on Route 23. The killer is in the school right now. Come get me. No! Forget that! Go to the school first! No flashing lights. You can get in through the open window in Timmy's office. Bring backup."

I heard a door slam and the background noise got softer. Tom's voice was low and clear. "I'll send someone to get you."

Before I could insist on returning to the school with him, he hung up. I waited inside my locked car, slumped down in the seat so no one could see me. After several geologic ages passed, a police car with flashing lights pulled in behind me. A cop who looked to be about fifteen years old approached. I rolled down my window. He said respectfully, "Ma'am, I'm supposed to bring you in. Please get in the car."

"No. I'm not going in your car. I'll follow you."

The poor kid looked baffled. "Uh, ma'am, I'm supposed to drive you. I'll make sure you're safe," he said hopefully.

I felt sorry for him and sorrier for me. I didn't want to sound impatient; after all, the guy came to rescue me. I ran my fingers through my hair and smoothed out the places on my face where fear was undoubtedly digging wrinkles as deep as the San Andreas Fault. "Listen, it will be a lot quicker and a lot easier if I follow you or you follow me. I'm tired, and I'm kind of stressed. What's it gonna be?"

The kid shrugged his shoulders and I followed him to the police station. Once there, I hobbled in my stocking feet around to the back of the car. I rooted around for my gym bag, which I keep in the trunk in case I ever have enough willpower to exercise. Although I've committed many a fashion faux pas I've never before descended to the level of wearing a skirt with sneakers, but we all have our limits. Given half the chance I would have chucked my completely no-comfort pantyhose and finished the night bare legged.

I followed the cop inside. Things were buzzing. Officer Rivera pointed to a plastic chair and indicated I was to sit there without bothering her. I called George, gave him an expurgated version of the events of the evening, and instructed him not to wait up for me. Twenty minutes later he showed up at the police station, pale and tense. He didn't say anything. He wrapped me in his arms and we stood there. As we waited, George picked bits of twigs and leaves out of my hair.

Finally, Tom returned, along with four other officers. I found my voice. "Did you get him? What did you find?"

"Just these." He held out a pair of black high-heeled shoes. "Do you know whose they are?"

"Uh, they're mine. I'll explain later." That "later" was going to be never. In the glare of neon lights, in the safety of the police station, I started to feel defensive, as if maybe I'd overreacted. Tom relinquished the shoes without comment.

Detective Brown inserted a fresh sheet of paper onto a clipboard. "I'll hold off for now asking what you were doing in the building after the staff left." He tossed me a most unpleasant sneer. "Instead, let's get to the actual episode, which of course wouldn't have happened if you hadn't been sneaking around. What exactly did you see, Mrs. Hopewell?"

I recounted the entire episode. The detectives looked at each other and said nothing. All that reticence started to get on my nerves.

Brown observed, "Then you didn't actually see anything. You heard a creak and assumed it was the murderer."

"No, no. The person who was walking around was very obviously trying not to make any noise. He stopped every few feet and waited. It was terrifying. My life passed before my eyes." I hoped I didn't sound as defensive as I felt.

Brown interrupted, "Did it ever occur to you that the person who scared you was perfectly innocent and that you scared him?"

"Why would an innocent person turn the night-light *off*? An innocent person would have turned the light on. The person walking around that office was hiding something. Or, he was looking for something."

George said grimly, "Or someone."

I shivered as the two detectives looked at each other.

"Why do you say 'he?'" asked Tom. "Did you manage to see who it was?"

"All I saw was the shadow of an arm. The office was so dark the arm could have been either sex. But the footsteps were very heavy and sort of flat-footed. It didn't sound like a woman. Oh, I don't know," I said, frustrated with myself. "I could be wrong. I'm not sure."

"It doesn't sound as if you're sure of anything," commented Brown.

George threw his narrow-eyed, thin-lipped look at the detective, an expression I found much less objectionable when it was directed toward Brown and not me. "Look here, detective, if my wife says the person was threatening, then the person was threatening."

With exaggerated patience Brown said, "We found two very nervous custodians, who were locking up for the night. We'll interview them again to see if one of them turned off the night light."

"No." I wasn't going to let Brown bully me. Or interpret the night's events in the way that suited him. "It wasn't the custodian. If it were, he would have called out to see who was there."

"Not if you scared him. Both custodians said they finished cleaning the office right about the time you say you were there. They didn't hear anyone or anything." Brown sank his chin into his neck and looked at me from under his brows. "If we accomplished anything tonight, I think it should be that you, Mrs. Hopewell, stop playing detective. Leave the detecting to us."

I ignored him and spoke to Tom. "Hold on. I think we're missing something."

"Again?" asked Brown, with exaggerated patience.

"Don't take that tone with my wife." George's face was red. His grip on my arm tightened. "Come on, Liz. We're going home."

"Please, George. Wait a minute. We really are missing something. The parking lot. What cars were left in the parking lot?"

Tom looked regretful. "We checked that out, Mrs. Hopewell. Two cars were there. Both belonged to the custodians on duty. That's it."

I tried to keep the note of triumph out of my voice. "But when I left, there were three cars there."

CHAPTER 22

THE STRANGER

I woke up with heart-pounding anxiety several times during the night but did not get out of bed. I was too filled with dread. I listened as rain pelted the metal gutters outside my bedroom window, a sound I used to find soothing, but now felt like a dangerous intrusion.

Morning arrived with brutal force. I felt as if I had sand in my eyes and sandbags on my back. I could hardly drag myself out of bed. George suggested I take the day off, but I wanted to check up on my colleagues. Also, our absences are strictly monitored and censured.

I showered and dressed and drove to school as if in a dream. Two daytime custodians joined me outside Timmy's office as I surveyed the damage to the bushes. Despite my weight loss I'd made an embarrassing dent in the greenery. I walked around the parking lot, trying to remember where I had seen the three cars. Things looked so different during the day I had a hard time pinning down the exact location. I decided it didn't matter; the driver of the third car might not have used his or her assigned space.

On my way to my classroom, I passed by the open faculty room. Inside, I saw the remains of last night's refreshments. Bill was busy scooping up enough food to survive a seven-year famine. "Hey," Bill said, honking cheerily, "I'm not being a pig. I'm going to bring some of this stuff to the English office before it's all gone. Help yourself. There's plenty for all."

I shook my head. The terror of the night before, the terror of what might come, and the sight of Bill shoveling neon-colored cookies into his mouth at seven o'clock in the morning undid any appetite I might have been able to muster.

Bill seemed unaware of my mood. "Home and School also left lemonade." I walked over to the refrigerator, took out the lemonade, and without comment poured it down the sink.

"Hey! Hey! Whaddaya think you're doing?"

I didn't answer. I walked out.

Bill followed me down the hall. "What? You think it might be poisoned?" he asked. He tried to keep his voice down, which caused tiny globules of cookie to spew out of his mouth. "Is that what you think?" he repeated, unselfconsciously wiping his mouth with the back of his hand and his hand on the back of his pants.

I forced myself to look him in the eye. "I don't want to take any chances. Do you?" He looked back at me with wide eyes. He forgot to close his mouth; from my vantage point, I could see the glint of dental work in the upper hemisphere of his mouth. He protected the cookies from me by taking them into his room instead of leaving them in the English office.

One by one, bleary-eyed teachers entered the building, picked up a plateful of sweets, and dropped, exhausted, into their chairs. Most teachers give tests on the day after Back to School Night so they can rest, but that nearly unilateral decision results in all-day exam marathons for the kids. I took pity on my nervous students, and instructed them to exchange their essays and critique each other's work. Very cooperative. Very multiple-intelligence oriented.

It's a good compromise. The kids have one more chance to improve their grades, and we all get a relatively easy day. When it comes to grading papers the students are far more rigorous than I am, and most kids take delight in criticizing their fellow students' work. After they get done goring each other, my grades look like gifts from heaven.

My cell phone buzzed all day. George, Zach, Ellie, and Susan left messages. I usually text with the same attention to grammar and usage I use when I write, but I had neither the time nor the energy for such niceties, and I answered them all with a brief and *au courant* "Kk" and "xoxo." For once, I didn't want to concentrate on the murder. I wanted to think about something else. As the kids murmured over their work I turned to the standardized test scores, which were posted online. In truth, I was afraid I would fall asleep during class, and I needed something to engage my brain that had nothing to do with murder.

Gordon's tortured analysis of the kids' test grades seemed skewed, and I was curious to see what the actual numbers were. Although I'm no math genius, I also do not have the sort of math phobias so many English teacher harbor, and I welcomed the diversion. First, I checked the overall test scores of last year's graduating class. They were indeed lower than the scores of the previous year's graduating class. But when I compared the scores with the ones that the same kids had earned in previous years, the result was quite different. Intrigued, I started scrolling through each student's scores, comparing the grades that each had gotten several years before with the ones they'd gotten this year. Excited, I tallied the percentages, typed the whole thing up, and emailed it to my colleagues and to Timmy.

I was ready to blow this thing wide open, and I envisioned myself in the role of an investigative reporter. In this daydream I was beautifully dressed, ten pounds thinner, and featured in a segment on *60 Minutes* as a brunette version of Lesley Stahl. My colleagues were not impressed. Not one responded to the email. I stopped Caroline in the hallway to discuss the test scores.

Caroline drawled, "And we care about this because...?"

"Because the analysis is wrong and unfair. Teachers are getting a bad enough rap as it is. I don't want my evaluations to depend on bad data."

"I repeat: And we care about this because...?" Caroline repeated.

I felt deflated. "I guess we don't care, then."

Bill stopped to listen in. "Caroline's right. But if it makes you feel better..." He shrugged and held his hands wide.

I searched for reasons why we should care, other than to salvage my pride. "Our contract is up this year. This could be part of our negotiations. I thought we should put this information out there."

Caroline reverted to her exaggerated, super-sweet, kindergarten-teacher voice. "Listen, my innocent child, teachers are not getting a bad rap because they're bad teachers. And our failure to get a raise was not a function of the test scores. But by all means, follow through on your brilliant little crusade. Don't go potty over it, though. You're getting more and more like Marcia Deaver everyday. I mean that in a good way, of course."

That shut me up more effectively than anything else could have done. Caroline was right. Marcia was forever arguing, debating, and pointing out flaws in how the school was run. I most emphatically did not want to position myself to take over her much-despised role, and I regretted my hasty email. As it turned out though, the information I sent had all the effect of a tree falling in an uninhabited forest. I tried not to be bitter.

All over the country school districts were being investigated (or not) for falsely reporting positive test results while we at Valerian Hills labored under falsely negative reports. But there were worse things...like putting oneself and one's family in danger. I was done with all that as well. Goodbye, Charlie Rose and Terry Gross. It was fun while it lasted.

At lunchtime I received a charming email from Timmy. There was no greeting—no dear, no hi, no hey.

> *I appreciate all of your hard work on the test scores, since Do Your Best is part of our Honor Code. I see that you have not updated your online grade book in over a week. Even at this difficult time, I expect a high level of professionalism from our staff.*
>
> *Mr. and Mrs. Tumbleson called me and emailed me about your performance. They expect to see Jack's grades updated in a timely fashion, as per our last conference. We can't ask the kids and the parents to uphold the Valerian Hills High Standard of Excellence if the teachers don't do their job.*
>
> *I will be back in the office on Monday. Have a nice day,*
> *Timmy*

Having a nice day didn't seem likely, but I tried to improve the odds by avoiding the main office. At three o'clock, Tom Harriman came to my classroom. He and Brown had spent the day interviewing staff. We waited for the students to leave. It didn't take long. The entire building felt poisoned.

I beckoned Tom to the open window, where noise from the athletic field would make it difficult for any electronic lurkers to hear our conversation. Even with that precaution, I was nervous enough to keep my voice to a whisper.

"How did Gordon die? Was he poisoned in the same way that Marcia was?" Tom didn't answer.

I slammed the window shut. "If you don't answer me I'm not going through with this reenactment. I'm going to go home."

Tom was unimpressed. "You can't go home. I'll subpoena you."

"You can subpoena me all you want, but if I don't get some information from you I'm not playing." I wasn't kidding. I saw no reason to relive the nightmare of Back to School Night if the only role I had was that of a pawn.

With obvious unwillingness, Tom said that both men had been poisoned.

"Was it in their individual cups, or was it in the coffeepot?"

Tom stared through the window at the line of departing cars. "We think it was in the coffeepot, but we're not sure, since the secretary cleaned it before she left for the day. Since the coffeepot is in the main copy room, the entire staff had the opportunity to kill either man, or both. Half the school admits to being in the copy room at one point or other—not that they have the choice.

It's like Grand Central Station in there. We've got plenty of suspects, but we're a little short of clues."

"I disagree," I countered.

Tom checked his cell phone. "Is this another Liz Hopewell psychological profile? We happen to have one or two experts working on the case already."

"Don't be nasty. I was simply going to point out that our killer is giving away one clue after another. Mr. X is even more ruthless than I imagined. Anyone could have drunk from that pot. I occasionally steal an inch or two of coffee when I run low. Do you even know who the intended victim was?"

Tom pulled out several sheets of paper and fanned them across two desks. "It seems as though Timmy was the primary target. Mrs. Donnatella was gone by the time Timmy left for the meeting, and anyway she drinks tea. Gordon's wife told us that Gordon doesn't drink caffeinated coffee after lunch. If the murderer knows the habits of all three, Timmy was the only intended victim. If the killer didn't know about what they usually drink, then any of the three could have been the target. Or, all of them could have been targeted. It could simply be a matter of chance that Gordon did drink regular coffee that day."

I scribbled a few lines on a Post-it and affixed it to the last sheet of paper. "Is it possible that Timmy poisoned himself? That's a good way to deflect suspicion."

Tom tapped his pen against the desk. "Many things are possible."

"You told me he didn't receive anything near a fatal dose. So how could Timmy have not received a fatal dose and Gordon did? Timmy's not all that much larger than Gordon. Of course, Gordon is much older than Timmy. Did Gordon have a heart condition?"

With an impatient gesture, Tom gathered the papers into a single pile. "Yes, damn it, he did. Is there anyone in this school who isn't dying of heart disease?"

Once again, I regretted my solitary lunchtime habits. "I'm not sure. Right now they're dying of murder. But it is a stressful job. Bill had a heart attack a few years ago, shortly after his fiftieth birthday. Emily's husband has some health problems and so does Mrs. Donnatella's husband, but I'm not sure what they are."

"Yeah, we got all that already." He looked expectantly at me.

I was at a loss. "Right. So what do you want? What can I tell you?"

"What are people saying in the faculty room, or in the hallway about all this? What's the buzz?"

I picked up a pen and started writing, hoping to jumpstart my unresponsive brain. I listed Emily, Caroline, and Bill. "It's surprisingly quiet. People are scared. The teachers are staying with the usual topics: annoying students and obnoxious parents. Of course, there's still plenty of bragging about their own kids and really gross discussions about personal health issues that I think should remain between the patient and the doctor." I added the librarian and the secretary to the list. "Between chats about kidney stones, blood pressure, and gastritis, I'm ready to throw up. So, to get back to my original question: Could Timmy have taken just enough medication to make him sick, in an effort to prove his innocence?"

"Sorry, Liz, but no comment."

Whether or not Tom wanted to comment, I knew I did. "Gordon drank all of his coffee. Timmy didn't. How could the killer know that Gordon would drink more coffee than Timmy? Or that Timmy would keel over that way?"

Without answering me, Tom got up and walked into the hallway.

I stayed at my desk and looked into my coffee. Black. No sugar. I called out, "Hey, Tom—what exactly was in their coffee?"

Having ascertained that Ashlee was no longer in her room, he returned to me. "The lab reports aren't complete yet. I should have an answer later today."

"I don't mean the chemical analysis. I mean, what did each one put in his coffee? Milk? Sugar? Fake sugar? That might make a difference. Maybe Timmy drank less because his coffee tasted bitter. I happen to know that Mrs. Donnatella drinks her coffee with flavored cream and five packets of Splenda. The killer could have put a pound of insecticide in it and I don't think she'd notice the difference in taste."

Tom rubbed his face. His eyes looked tired and bloodshot. "I wasn't tempted to take a sip. I'll find out later. Right now, I don't know."

I had an uneasy feeling that I had missed something important during my conversation with Tom, but I couldn't figure out what it was. He agreeably repeated most of his end of the exchange, but I had no epiphanies. The nagging discomfort receded.

Tom and I went down to the main office, which looked as innocent as it always did. Crocheted squares covered nearly every surface of Mrs. Donnatella's desk. A needlepoint pillow on her chair posited *Babies Are the Bridge to Heaven*. In spite of her charity work, I had no idea Mrs. Donnatella was so sentimental about babies. It seemed out of character for a woman with so tough a façade.

Timmy's room was once again locked. The custodian unlocked it for us and we walked in. Tom checked the room, which looked exactly as it always had. "What were you looking for? I don't get what you were thinking."

I tugged at the locked file cabinet. "I wasn't thinking. I was going with my instincts. I had this stupid idea that maybe the personnel files held a clue about Marcia. I still have problems wrapping my brain around the decision to reassign her. It still doesn't make sense to me."

"We have all of Marcia's files. You could have asked me."

This was annoying. "I did ask you. You didn't answer me. But since you have the information I risked my life to get, you might as well tell me what I want to know."

Harriman said, "Her file had nothing in it about either her move to the middle school or her test scores, which apparently were not great."

Once again, I felt called upon to defend the Valerian Hills English Department in general, and Dr. Marcia Deaver in particular. "But that's not true! Her AP scores were the same as the year before. And as for the state test scores, Gordon said something very similar at our last meeting, but he's wrong. If you track the kids' scores from one year to the next, they've actually improved, and not by a little bit. They've improved a lot."

"That's not what I heard," Tom replied, still not terribly interested.

"Who told you that?" I swallowed hard and made a conscious effort to speak more like James Earl Jones and less like Tweety Bird. I read somewhere that people pay less attention when the person speaking has a high-pitched voice. "Whoever said it is a liar, and maybe a murderer as well."

Tom made himself comfortable in Timmy's chair. "Detective Brown was the one who found out about it. I think he got his information from Mrs. Tumbleson."

I had assumed Mrs. Tumbleson's unofficial presence in the school was a way for her to manipulate and intimidate Jack's teachers and hadn't assigned any more sinister intention. I admitted, "Mrs. Tumbleson is my favorite suspect, but only because I don't like her."

Tom rolled the chair back and forth, between the window and the desk. "Mrs. Tumbleson and Marcia had some sort of meeting before school on the morning Marcia died. Mrs. Tumbleson said Marcia had agreed to allow Jack into the class, but of course, that was impossible to confirm after the fact."

I knew Tom was being generous in telling me this, but I wished he'd done so earlier. "In light of that information, it doesn't make sense that Mrs. Tumbleson murdered Marcia. In fact, quite the opposite. We're looking for someone whom Marcia was intimidating, not the other way around. Last year, Mrs. Tumbleson's son had the lead role in the musical, which Marcia directed. I couldn't believe that anyone, even Mrs. Tumbleson, would be able to bully Marcia, and yet there was no other explanation for why Jack got the lead role. Jack can't carry a tune to save his life. He sounded like a sick moose."

Tom looked thoughtful. It wasn't until later that I realized he'd told me what Mrs. Tumbleson had told him. That didn't make it true. I remembered Mrs. Donnatella telling me that Mrs. Tumbleson was leaving the board at the end of the year. Madam President clearly loved the power of her position, and with Gordon dead, her presence in the high school was stronger than ever. She had taken to strolling the hallways like a latter day member of the East German Stasi. I examined the pictures on Timmy's desk. He had a pretty wife and two adorable kids. I wondered how Ashlee felt about that. And I wondered what Tom thought of Ashlee.

In the outer office, the sound of unanswered telephone calls reminded me of all the unanswered questions that revolved around the case. "I can't get what you've told me to make sense. Marcia wasn't the type to allow anyone, even Mrs. Tumbleson, to pressure her—so what happened? I mean, that information doesn't help at all. It's like a reverse motive. Do you have any evidence that the tables were turned? And that Marcia was able to dig up some dirt on Mrs. Tumbleson?"

Tom got to his feet. "No. So let's drop it for now, and talk about last night's fiasco. Then I have to go."

"Really? What's the rush?"

He checked his phone. Whatever it was he saw there, it didn't make him happy. "No rush. But we both had a long day yesterday."

I showed Tom how I had hidden behind the desk, and how I had been able to see the shadow of someone's arm. Tom turned off all the lights, so I could judge the height of the person to whom the arm belonged, but even with all the lights off and the shades drawn we couldn't get the room and hallway dark enough. Between the ringing telephone and the distant hum of a vacuum cleaner, the school was still too noisy for him to mimic footsteps. In short, we got nothing done.

I reluctantly agreed to meet Tom after sundown. I debated telling George what I was up to, and without too much internal deliberation decided it was unfair to unnecessarily worry one's spouse. I called George at a calculatedly early hour and left a message saying I had to return to school for a meeting.

I scooped up Ellie and her friends, deposited them at the ballet studio, and bought a pile of cold cuts and bread from the local deli. Everyone likes sandwiches, and those they could make themselves. In deference to Ellie's new refusal to eat practically anything that wasn't a salad I bought her an overpriced platter of veggies and added some grilled chicken I hoped was worth its weight in gold, since that was approximately what it cost.

I was beginning to feel as though I lived at Valerian Hills High School and was an occasional visitor at my own house. I thought about Tom as I wove my way through the back roads. I wondered if he were seeing Ashlee. I should tell him that I think he can do better.

My cell phone buzzed several times. I checked the telephone numbers of the incoming calls while I waited for a red light to change. I know this will not relieve me of a serious ticket and fine if I'm caught, but under the circumstances I decided it was worth the risk. Ellie texted that she had secured a ride back home but would be late. Zach texted to tell me he would be studying at a friend's house until late. George texted that he had a meeting and would be late. The locksmith left a voicemail message saying he was sorry to have missed me again.

This was mostly good news. At least no one, other than the locksmith, would miss me.

A fierce honking from the car behind me galvanized me into action. I put my phone back in my handbag but the sudden acceleration sent it into the far reaches of the passenger side of the car. I resisted the dictates of my Brooklyn childhood and New Jersey adulthood and did not give the finger to the person behind me, who could not wait the three nanoseconds it took me to respond to the green light.

I pulled into the parking lot and brazenly left the car in the principal's spot, right in front of the school. Let them sue me; there was no way I was parking any farther away. Tom was already there, but I didn't see his car at first. He had pulled into the narrow corridor that separates the gym area from the rest of the school. Under normal circumstances the only vehicle that uses that space is the lawnmower. Tom's car not only fit in, it was mostly obscured by a curved driveway and greenery.

We walked in together. Tom's face was grim and set and he held me, rather uncomfortably, by my elbow. Did he think I was going to run away? The shadows were already gathering, a harbinger of the winter to come. The school was lit only by night-lights.

We silently entered the main office. I don't know why we were both so quiet; perhaps the drama of the last days and weeks were draining both of us. I realized I had left my cell phone in the car. I wanted to go back to retrieve it, but Tom told me not to bother, saying we wouldn't be at the school for very long.

I went into Timmy's room, and Tom turned out the light. All of a sudden, the terror of the night before consumed me. I may have mentioned that I'm not brave. At this critical juncture I started hyperventilating and felt faint. I know it was stupid to feel so scared with a police officer right outside the room, but I could not suppress an overwhelming sense of danger. I opened the window, partly because without some fresh air I was afraid I would faint, and partly because if anything went wrong I wanted to be able to fly out of there. I hid behind Timmy's desk and looked toward the wall where twenty-four hours ago I'd seen the shadowed arm. The silence was complete. I felt the individual beats of my pulse. I heard footsteps.

Something felt wrong. Tom was supposed to be on my left, but the foot-steps sounded as if they were coming from the right. I saw the dark reflection of Tom's arm as he reached to turn off the light. Without warning, the crash of metal shattered the silence. I screamed as if my life depended on it.

CHAPTER 23

HE KNEW HE WAS RIGHT

I leaped from behind the desk and then froze with fear and indecision. The window or the door? I didn't know where safety lay. A disembodied hand flicked the light switch. Outside the office, Tom had both hands wrapped around his gun, and the gun was pointed at Alberto Silva's heart.

A large metal dustpan dropped from the man's trembling fingers. "Don't shoot!" Alberto implored. His arms, lifted high over his head, trembled.

"What the hell are you doing in here?" Tom kept the gun pointed at the custodian.

"I heard voices. Mr. Timmy told me to keep an eye on the office. I didn't do nothing!" Alberto stayed frozen in position, his eyes fixed on Tom.

I too was afraid to move. "Tom, I think you should put the gun away. This is a mistake."

Tom drew down his gun. He did not apologize, but told Alberto, "You can go about your duties. Stay out of here for the next thirty minutes."

The custodian slowly lowered his hands. With his forearm, he wiped his brow. "Hey, man, no problem. I'll get started cleaning in the hallway. Is that okay?" Alberto bent down to retrieve the dustpan, but kept his gaze on Tom. He backed off down the hallway and didn't turn around until he got to the door.

Tom nodded and turned to me. "Ready for take two?" he asked with a grim smile.

"Take two? I'm ready to be committed. That poor man." I peered through the glass doors and into the hallway. "You nearly frightened him to death."

Tom's face was set, and he didn't seem to hear me. He waved me back into Timmy's office.

Before I complied, I checked the hallway again. The custodian lurked at the edge of the hall, pretending to be very busy with garbage bags. I was worried about Alberto. He's a hardworking guy and didn't deserve to be dragged into this mess. "I think he's afraid to let you out of his sight. You should apologize to him."

Tom looked outside the office and shrugged. "I'll tell him to go clean another floor of the building."

"That's ridiculous. You told him we'd be done in thirty minutes, but it's only going to take about two minutes. Leave the guy alone."

"What the hell. Whatever."

This was a side of Tom I hadn't seen. "Why are you so angry? I'm the one who's lost ten years off the end of my life. As you've pointed out more than once, this is your area of expertise. The closest I've ever gotten to this much excitement is the last time I let myself be persuaded to go on a roller coaster."

"We'll be done soon," Tom promised.

We repeated the whole little exercise without incident. Since I had already heard the footsteps, we didn't maintain silence, and paradoxically, that made it much easier to concentrate.

After a few more tries I got up from my crouched position. "I am certain that whoever was here last night is a little shorter than you are, but not by much. I think the angle of the arm was sharper last night. Your arm was nearly parallel to the floor. I'm pretty sure the guy who was here last night had to reach up a few inches more."

Tom walked back and forth, from the interior of the office into the hallway. "Let's try it again. I'll buy you a drink afterwards."

"In my next life you can buy me many drinks, but I'm done here tonight. If I don't get home I'm going to collapse in my car and have to sleep in the parking lot."

He reluctantly agreed to let me go. The custodian waited at the far end of the hallway. We were nearly at the front door before he headed back to the office. I waved goodbye to Alberto. I felt guilty about scaring him, even though technically it was Tom who pointed the gun at his heart. I stopped at the alcove where Tom was parked. "You should do a better job of apologizing to Alberto. He looked ready to faint. I don't blame him. I was ready to faint."

Tom kept walking. He followed me to my car. After I unlocked the doors he checked the interior. Satisfied no one was there, he said, "The guy is fine. Not everyone is as sensitive as you are."

"Sensitive? Are you kidding me? I'm a basket case! I'm ready for a nice long stay in an asylum. I won't even have to sign the papers myself. My husband will be more than happy to do it for me."

Tom finally smiled. "Tell him to hold off for a few more days."

He drove behind me for about a half-mile before he turned his way and I turned mine.

The house was empty when I got home. I was still a wreck. Gambling that neither George nor the kids would show up for at least another half-hour, I parked myself on the back porch with a medicinal glass of wine and a cigarette. I normally don't smoke at home, but this was an emergency. I called Susan and related the whole episode to her. I had anticipated her customary amusement at my cowardice, but for once my sister was deadly earnest.

"Liz, I think you're in danger," she warned.

"You've only now come up with this idea? I've gotten two threatening letters, so you're going to have to do better than that."

Susan's sounded more serious than usual. "Don't be flip. I think you're in immediate danger. Why do you think you were so scared tonight?"

I yawned, tired out from a sleepless night and nerve-wracking day. "Because I'm a neurotic lunatic. I was sitting not three yards from a police detective, and I still couldn't control my nerves. Honestly, Susan, I'm ready to move. George has threatened over and over again to sell the house and move to a town with lower taxes. Well, I'm ready to go tomorrow. I'm actually not joking. My own house has started to scare me."

Susan snorted. "You might want to think about getting some locks on the doors. The last time I was at your house, the kids' friends treated your kitchen like it was their personal fiefdom. I was afraid to appear downstairs in my pajamas, thinking some teenager might burst in while I was having coffee, so he could help himself to a sandwich and some cookies."

"It's not that bad. Some kids knock."

"You can be sure that anyone threatening you will not knock first. Please, get an alarm system and some security. You're asking for trouble."

I felt a slight vibration in the wooden slats of the back porch. "Hey, speaking of knocking, I think I hear someone at the front door. I have to ditch the cigarette. Be right back."

"Do you think George and the kids don't know you smoke?"

I got to my feet a bit stiffly. The last twenty-four hours had given my knees an unaccustomed workout. "Of course they know. But since we pretend I don't smoke, I end up not smoking ninety-five percent of the time. Well, lately it's probably closer to eighty percent of the time. But I have an excuse. I'm losing my mind. Anyway, they think it's your fault, and you're a bad influence on me."

"Well, thanks for that. I'll hold the line. Check the door." I snubbed my cigarette and hid the butt in the recycling bucket. I waved away any lingering telltale smoke and went back in the house. From the kitchen, I heard the front door click and close.

"Hello? Is that you, George?" There was no answer. I walked into the living room. No one was there. "Hey, Susan, are you still there?"

"Yeah. What's going on?"

"Nothing. I thought I heard the front door close, but no one's here." I called upstairs but all was still silent.

"Get out, Liz. Get the hell out of the house right now!"

I hesitated. "There's no one here, Sue."

I thought I heard a faint sigh, but my house often makes human noises. I said as much to Susan.

Susan's voice was frantic. "Get out! Get out!"

Once again, I made my getaway, but this time I felt ridiculous.

"Where should I go? What about George and the kids?"

"Get in the car. Stay on the line."

I got in the car and started driving around the block. "This is ridiculous. What should I do about George and the kids?"

"Let's see…if only there were some wireless device that you could use to alert them…"

I braked at a stop sign and hit the speaker button on the phone. "Very funny. Okay, I'm hanging up and calling the rest of the family. I have no idea what I'm going to tell them."

I drove about a half mile from my house and pulled over to the side of the road. I called George and explained the situation to him. He told me to call the police and to tell the kids to meet us at the Indiana Diner. I called the kids, but of course got no answer. I then texted them, telling them we had an emergency and they should not go home. I used all capital letters and didn't abbreviate a single word. At the Indiana Diner I ordered four meals to go. One by one, the rest of my family showed up.

While I was waiting I called the Oak Ridge police department, although I was slightly embarrassed at the thought of the cops inspecting the house. The cleaning ladies were due to come the following morning, which meant that from a housekeeping perspective, the house was at its worst. I usually clean the night before the cleaning service comes, and I wished I would have at least stacked the dirty dishes in the dishwasher and wiped down the bathroom before I left.

Looking at things from a positive point of view, it was lucky the doors weren't locked, since I didn't have to wait at the house in order to let the police inside.

We returned to a blaze of flashing lights and police cars. The chief of police said he wanted to talk to us, but he limited himself to addressing George.

George said, "Elizabeth, perhaps you'd like to tell the nice man what you've been up to."

I kept my temper and told the cop a highly abridged version of my recent activities.

The policeman said, "After you contacted us about the threatening letters we kept an eye on the house. We don't have a lot of violent crime. Where were you, Mrs. Hopewell, when you heard the intruder?"

The embarrassment I felt at the unsanitary state of the house was nothing to the embarrassment I would feel if I had to admit that my middle-aged self was sneaking a cigarette in the backyard like a delinquent teenager. The two men looked at me expectantly. It wasn't a difficult question.

"I was cleaning up the backyard. I mean, the back porch. I was cleaning the back porch. I was on the phone with my sister, and I thought I heard someone either on the front porch or at the front door."

George smacked his head. "Your sister again! When are you not talking to your sister?"

The policeman turned the doorknob and inspected the unused locks. "We'll continue to keep an eye on the place, Mr. Hopewell. But you might not be so lucky next time. If you see anything suspicious, call immediately. And get those locks installed. An alarm system isn't a bad idea. We'll get an immediate call if anyone tries to enter."

"Yes, my wife is taking care of that now," George said.

The cop considerately looked away. "I'll talk to the neighbors now."

I hoped the neighbors wouldn't mention my smoking, but wasn't too sanguine about my chances. They're a nosy and somewhat censorious bunch.

Finally, the cops left and the excitement ended. I parceled out the food I'd bought at the Indiana Diner, but was too wired to sit down. Perhaps a hot bath would calm me. As I got to the top of the stairs, I heard the refrigerator door open. I screamed bloody murder.

"Stop! Don't drink anything! Stop, stop, stop!" I almost broke a leg going down the stairs. Ellie started crying.

"I'm sorry, Mom. I took one of your diet sodas. I didn't think you really minded all that much."

I hugged her tightly. "It's not that! Even though diet soda is bad for you." When Ellie squirmed, I loosened my grip. "It occurred to me that if we did have an intruder here that he could have poisoned something in the house." This did little to calm Ellie down. George and Zach came bounding into the kitchen.

"What the hell is going on now?" asked George, looking from Ellie to me.

I told him as quickly as possible what had scared me.

George sucked in a mouthful of air. "I should have thought of that myself. Or the police should have thought of that."

"I'm going to throw out everything in the house." I opened the refrigerator door and took out milk and juice. And soda.

Zach stopped me. "No! That's evidence."

We stared at the containers as if each one had started spewing nuclear waste. For the first time Zach and Ellie looked scared. I was bitterly sorry that I had done this to them, but relieved that now they would be more cautious.

George clapped Zach on the back. "Good thinking. Don't touch anything. Don't eat anything. We'll call the police tomorrow. In the meantime, you kids can buy breakfast and lunch at school. We'll eat out tomorrow. Then we'll throw every goddamned thing in this house out in the garbage."

Ellie was pale. Her back was pressed against the wall, as if she needed extra help standing up.

George sent a meaningful look in Zach's direction. "Why don't you help your sister get to level nine in *Mystique Magique?* I know she's really close."

Ellie peeled herself off the wall, and she and Zach went upstairs to play the arcane video game they both love. George and I propped a kitchen chair under the back door and placed a bookcase in front of the front door. It wouldn't keep anyone out, but it would at least alert us if anyone tried to get in. When we got upstairs, Zach and Ellie were stretched out on the sofa in the den.

"I'm not sleeping by myself," said Ellie.

"Of course not. Your mother has scared the hell out of all of us. I'm starting to feel sorry for her students."

The kids laughed and seemed to relax. I pulled out two sleeping bags and we camped out with the kids for the night. Just one big happily neurotic family.

CHAPTER 24

THE ALTAR OF THE DEAD

My body hurt with that bruised feeling you get when you're sick. In the morning, George kissed me goodbye with more than usual feeling. Ellie was a bit weepy, and Zach waited for her so they could walk to school together, something they hadn't often done during their high school years. I waited for them to leave, so I could figure out why the house looked different.

When we moved to Oak Ridge the real estate agent assured us that this "Queen Anne Victorian just needed a woman's touch," and at the time I felt confident that at least I was the right gender. It turned out that the "touch" the house needed included a new boiler, hot water heater, roof, plumbing, and electrical wiring. The driveway had to be repaved and the fence replaced. The charming curved exterior of the house encased bedrooms whose eight-sided perimeters grudgingly gave way to tiny closets and to drafty windows that let cold air in from three directions.

The one room that gave us unalloyed pleasure was the kitchen. Even the stainless steel appliances that we bought after much anxious consultation gave off a muted glow. The refrigerator (interior water and ice maker, large capacity, extra everything), which had welcomed my late-night rambling and foraging, looked the same, but it had been defiled, even if the food inside had not. Our worn furniture and bargain basement curtains, which fell far short of being dignified as "window treatments," would never make it into a magazine shoot as anything but a "before" picture, but I felt a sudden fierce possessiveness of *my* house.

I'd always vaguely thought of the place as a way station, a stopover in between the cramped but romantic apartment of our early life together and the dimly imagined hipness of the apartment of our future. The invasion of the night before had the effect on me that is roughly analogous to a man who looks on as a seemingly unattractive female removes the cold cream and the glasses, lets down her hair, and disrobes in order to reveal a beautiful woman. I was reluctant to leave my ugly duckling darling, and I drove to school very cautiously, to the obvious displeasure of the car that tailgated me.

After ten years of bringing lunch to school I was empty-handed. This was not a matter of economy or diet. The food at school is tasteless at best and downright nauseating at worst. I still harbor queasy memories of the day I ate the metallic-tasting macaroni and cheese, or the time I tried the Thanksgiving Special. I bought a salad from the cafeteria, but it didn't taste very healthy. There was a slimy edge to some of the lettuce and the dressing tasted slightly sour. If I managed to elude the mad murderer of Valerian Hills I didn't want to fall victim to *E. coli*. I tried the soup next, but it was so salty I had to toss it out as well. I ended up with a rubber bagel. The cafeteria lady was somewhat surprised that after ten years of avoidance I had bought three lunches in one day, but she made no comment.

I took the frozen and reconstituted bagel back to my desk and ate it in a catatonic haze. The bell rang, and the kids came into the classroom, buzzing loudly about the test I was about to give. I had scheduled tests for all but my last class of the day. It gave me time to think. As my students wrote and sighed, I set down the events of each day and analyzed what occurred. I felt, with what was probably unjustified optimism, that I already possessed all the pieces I needed to solve this puzzle, and that if I thought long enough about it, I could put it all together.

I don't often indulge in memories any further back than the day I met George, but the mystery of my childhood seemed inextricably mingled with the events of the last few weeks. Faulkner notwithstanding, I liked to think that the past really was past. But even if the past was still hanging around, waiting for another go at my life, what help was that? If The Lousy Bastard had taught me anything, it was that criminals do not feel guilty. That's what makes them such good liars. They believe their own constructed stories.

I remembered how, with fairy-tale timing, one year and one day after my mother died The Lousy Bastard sat me down and told me his miserable self-serving narrative. I felt sorry for him, which shames me now. I loathe my trusting younger self, and I won't allow myself to be gulled ever again. Whoever killed Marcia was no more likely to feel remorse than The Lousy Bastard. The killer was someone so coldly certain of his or her own superior standing that regret was beside the point.

The last class of the day trooped in. I had no test for them. Instead, we discussed *Romeo and Juliet*. We reached Juliet's beautiful musing—*What's in a name? That which we call a rose—*

Damn it. Shakespeare again. The guy had all the answers to all the important questions. What's in a name? The identity of the murderer. That's what's in a name. Shakespeare, the man who so often punned with his own name—*Will*—gave me the name I needed, the one I'd been looking for since the day Marcia died.

I waited impatiently for the last bell of the day. After school, we were summoned to a staff meeting. I ignored the command and concentrated on putting together what I already knew. Marcia, her missing chair, the mysterious details concerning her proposed move to the middle school. Marcia, lying on the floor behind the desk where I now sat. Marcia, her coffee cup. Marcia, the test scores. Marcia, and the dossier that threatened shame to anyone who didn't pay up.

Identification of the killer was not enough. I needed proof, but I couldn't find any custodians. In the days after Marcia's death, neither I nor the police got any relevant information from the cleaning staff, because the right answers are embedded in the right questions, and we were too quick to dismiss the custodians' disclaimers. Even the wrong questions could have given me the clue I needed, but I hadn't listened carefully enough.

I got up from behind my desk. Once again I followed in Marcia's footsteps and walked the length of the school in search of what was lost.

Unusually, I found all of the custodians in the library. I asked them once again about the first day of school. They agreed they had spent the morning moving furniture. One young man stated that he had removed a chair, but the chair was not Marcia's. He was positive. And with that, I had all the information I needed.

Whom had Marcia threatened?

I had suspected Timmy, Caroline, and Bill. Except Marcia never threatened anyone named Bill. She threatened Billie—*Willing* Billie. Marcia's command of the English language was impeccable, and I'd never known her to make an error in grammar or spelling. If I had her skill, not to mention her wit, I would have realized long ago that the two letters that end the name Billie indicated the person was female. That meant that Bill, my easygoing, cookie-eating, middle-aged colleague, was not the target of Marcia's extortion. Unlike Juliet, Marcia knew perfectly well how important a name was, and Marcia's last literary allusion finally made sense.

Marcia labeled the blackmailing letter she wrote to Billie *The Importance of Being Earnest.* I assumed the homosexual allusions were a reference to Oscar Wilde, the author of the play. But the title of the threatening letter addressed to "Billie" was not merely a reference to the author; it was a reference to the play itself. Much of the farce in Wilde's comedy depends on a name. Earnest. Just as this farce depended on a name. Not Bill. Not Billy. *Billie.*

I walked down the stairs and toward the main office. The halls were silent. Everyone was at the staff meeting. Rain pelted the windows, and the athletic fields were empty and dark. It wasn't cold, but the landscape held autumn shadows, and the fluorescent lights seemed unnaturally bright.

The custodians had not yet cleaned the halls or the classrooms, and the floors were littered with bits of paper, a few pencils, and some candy wrappers. This was atypical; the cleaning staff usually did the hallways immediately after school. It was lucky that for once they had been congregated in the library, instead of being scattered across the building, since I didn't have to hunt down each person individually to ask about Marcia's chair. I didn't want the custodians or anyone else to interrupt me. I didn't want to have to make excuses.

I crossed the lobby. I did not rush. I was afraid. For once, physical pain was not what I dreaded. The thought of facing evil was what made me shake. I hadn't seen my father in many years, and I did not imagine that I would see him again. I didn't even know if he were still alive. I certainly did not imagine I would ever again have to confront someone who equaled him in his contempt for human life.

I walked into the main office. The interior reception area was very nearly silent. The only sound was the muffled crack of hailstones, which attacked the windows of the exterior offices so fiercely they sounded as if they would pierce the glass. Those offices ringed the perimeter of one small wing of the school. I checked each one. Some doors were locked; some were open. None were inhabited.

I returned to the central area. I stared at the secretary's desk and at the personalized Post-it notes. Wilhelmina Donnatella. Willie. *Billie.* I walked around the desk and leaned over her chair. I examined the crocheted seat cover, with its horribly personal smell and human imprint. The yarn was a filthy yellow and was tied with faded blue ribbons to the frame of the chair. The chair was wedged between the wall and the desk, and there wasn't much room to maneuver. I had to crouch under the desktop, and in doing so I knocked over a metal file holder. Its crash terrified me, but the sound brought no response.

Everyone was still at the meeting. I slowed my breathing, turned the chair over and bent down to read the faded writing. The bottom of the chair was stenciled, in permanent marker, with Marcia's initials and Marcia's room number.

Finally, the right question. The custodians had not been asked if they had moved Mrs. Donnatella's chair. They'd been asked about Marcia's chair. In the first day rush of moving desks and chairs and file cabinets from the hallways and into the freshly painted rooms, it was doubtful that the custodian remembered the identity of the furniture. Even if anything did strike someone as odd, it was unlikely any of the custodians would mention the coincidence. They are a hardworking and underpaid group of men, and in the current era of big budget cuts none would admit to an action that might put him on the next chopping block. They've already lost half their staff and most of their benefits.

I started shaking. I grabbed the dusty legs of the base of the heavy chair to turn it right side up. I stopped as I heard the door open. There was no use hiding behind the desk, since the overturned chair was clearly visible. I was jammed between the wall, the chair, and the desk.

Heavy, familiar footsteps walked toward me. I tried to back out, but a sharp point dug into my neck and stopped me.

Mrs. Donnatella said softly, "You're supposed to be at the meeting." She pressed harder into the hollow above my collarbone. "And here you are. I didn't even have to go looking for you."

I crouched awkwardly. The secretary breathed into my hair, emitting a nauseating stench of decaying peppermint and stale coffee.

Her tone was conversational. "I never liked you. And I won't miss you." She gave a sudden jab to the side of my neck. "You think you're so much better than everyone else. Like Marcia. You think you're so smart."

She grabbed my hair with vicious force. My head jerked back and I heard the snap of scissors as she sliced off a hank of my hair. She sprayed them over me. "See how easy that was? I could cut your neck just as easily."

I stared at the severed strands of my hair. They looked so helpless, trembling slightly from the shaking of my body. The horror of Mrs. Donnatella's voice paralyzed me. She spoke calmly, but the tips of the scissors moved with reflexive jolts. I moved my hand to my neck.

She cracked the blades against my head and advised, "Don't do it. I don't want to finish you off here, but I will if I have to."

I knew, from many detective novels, that you're supposed to get the killer talking. "Why did you kill Marcia?" I asked.

Mrs. Donnatella seemed uninterested in bragging about how clever she'd been. She pressed the scissors against the back of my neck and grabbed the rest of my hair to jerk me to my feet. I didn't know where the major arteries in my neck were, and I hoped the secretary was similarly unsure.

"Shut up."

"Okay, then, why did you kill Gordon? Did he suspect you?"

"Gordon was a moron. If he'd done what I told him to do, he'd be alive now. So it's his own fault."

"You'll get caught," I whispered around the lump in my throat. "I'll scream. The whole building is full of people."

"I don't think so. Everyone is at the meeting. I told the custodians they have to report to the library to give it a good cleaning. There is no one here for you."

"Wait! You said yourself that I'm supposed to be at the meeting. Someone will come looking for me!"

"I told Caroline you had to go home early. No one will be looking for you."

She pushed me toward the vault. The door, halfway open, blocked the narrow passage in front of me, and Mrs. Donnatella blocked the way behind.

I wasn't sure how crazed a homicidal maniac Mrs. Donnatella was. I've heard that crazy people are extremely strong. I decided that if I lived to tell this story I would hit the gym every freaking day for the rest of my life.

Then I told myself that Mrs. Donnatella was in worse shape than I was. She may be taller and outweigh me by a good forty pounds (maybe more, now that I've lost so much weight) but she's not what I would call agile.

I didn't think I could wrest the scissors from her without risking a severed artery, and I was afraid if she fell on me she would sink the blades six inches into my body. I should have been able to outmaneuver her. But she had an iron grip on my hair, and the scissors were pressed tightly against my neck.

My whole life did not pass before my eyes.

Just one day.

The day my mother did not come home. The day she disappeared. The day the woman who hesitated to take a single aspirin loaded up on Valium, took off in her car, and didn't come back.

I could not let this happen to Ellie and Zach. I couldn't let them wait for me, the way I waited for my mother all those years ago.

I stomped my heel into Mrs. Donnatella's squishy shoe. She cried out, and although she didn't fully let go of me, her grip loosened. I tried to get behind her. She slashed downward at my neck. The blades slit the skin on my shoulder without digging in too deeply, but her clenched fist slammed me so violently I stumbled onto my knees. I grabbed at Mrs. Donnatella's leg and pulled as hard as I could. As she fell, she knocked me flat, and I bit my tongue. Blood dripped from my mouth and neck.

I reached up, but I was too late. Mrs. Donnatella wildly stabbed at my head and arms. I swung away from the scissors. My head cracked against the heavy steel door. After that, Mrs. Donnatella needed only one shove. I fell backward into the vault. She slammed the door shut. I heard the lock snap.

It was completely dark in the vault. Not even a sliver of light penetrated the heavy metal door.

Blood pooled in my mouth and the salty sweet liquid made me gag. I spit it out over and over, and then gave up. I touched my neck and shoulder. Blood dripped through the fabric of my shirt, but I didn't feel it spurting, so I figured it was still possible I would not bleed to death. My head ached from the impact of the door. I felt very cold. I concentrated on not going into shock.

I could not tell if the impenetrable blackness I experienced was a result of the physical loss of light, or the waning of conscious thought. I banged on the door and yelled, but I could sense the futility of my efforts. How long would it be before someone opened the vault? Unless someone noticed my absence fairly soon I would suffocate amid the pathetic piles of school supplies. I felt along the perimeter of the door, hoping to feel a breath of air along the joints.

A slight vibration gave me hope. I took off my shoe and started pounding. A faint sound, and then, beautifully, the door opened, and I fell into the arms of Caroline, our faithful, faithful, leader.

Chapter 25

Sense and Sensibility

George met me at the hospital. A few hours and many stitches later we went home. I had to rely on pills for the pain, when what I really wanted was a stiff shot of something heavily alcoholic.

"How did Caroline know I was in the vault?" My mouth had a hard time framing the words, since my forehead, my jaw, and most of the rest of my face felt as if it had been put through a fine-mesh meat grinder. My lips and tongue were swollen and painful.

George looked grim. "She didn't. She explained to me that as the department chair, she knew the combination of the lock. While everyone was at the faculty meeting she decided to 'refresh her supplies.' If she weren't a thief as well as a liar, you'd be dead."

I didn't care what brought Caroline to my rescue. I still felt grateful. "So I guess that's the good news. But I still don't get the sequence of events."

George smoothed a few strands of hair back from my forehead. "Me either, since I was more interested in getting to the hospital than I was in interrogating that police detective. He came to the hospital, by the way, but you were busy getting Frankenstein stitches."

I felt at the bandages. "I'm old enough to be in a permanent turtleneck sweater anyway. Too bad I didn't think to tell the surgeon to lift my neck while he was closing me up. I'm more worried about my hair. Bring me a mirror."

George scrunched up his face. "Maybe you should wait until tomorrow. You've had a pretty bad day already."

More determined than ever, I pointed to the dresser. "Give me a mirror."

George went over to the dresser and handed me a small hand mirror. My face was bruised and my skin had an odd greenish cast to it. My mouth was puffy and red. The welt at my jaw line made it seem as if I had a double chin. I had a heavy pad of bandages about my neck. But it was my hair that made me cry. I looked as if I had backed into a wood chipper. As much as I complain about my frizzy mane, I still like having long hair. A part of me was gone. I said as much to George, who unhelpfully pointed out that it would grow back. Before I could record a new request for a divorce, Zach and Ellie piled into the bedroom.

I figured we could stay married for at least one more day.

Once again, I had to give a statement to the police, but this time they had to come see me. Thanks to the pain medication I slept through the night, but I still couldn't move my head off the pillow. Even a short walk to the bathroom left me weak and nauseated. Luckily, the cleaning ladies had worked their magic while a homicidal maniac was threatening me, so I didn't have to worry about the state of the house when the detectives arrived.

Slowly, and with some assistance from George, I struggled into a clean tee shirt and sweat pants. I'm not the negligee type.

Tom was solicitous and Detective Brown grudgingly polite.

"How did you fix upon Mrs. Donnatella?" asked Tom.

I was confused. "How did you? What happened while I was in the vault?"

Tom made himself comfortable. "If you weren't wounded I wouldn't give in, but okay, I'll go first. I came back to the school with Brown. There were some inconsistencies in several of the statements we got on the day Gordon and Timmy were attacked. We went to the faculty meeting, looked over the attendance sheet and saw that you and Caroline weren't there. The last time that happened we ended up with one person in the hospital and one in the morgue."

He paused, and Brown took over. "I checked the parking lot against the chart that marked where each person's car is supposed to be. Both your car and Caroline's were there. So you had to be somewhere in the school. I flagged Mrs. Donnatella in the parking lot. She said you told her you had to leave early. Unless you'd somehow managed to get home without your car, she was lying. Harriman got to the office at the point that Caroline found you."

Tom said, "I'm surprised Donnatella left you alive. The only thing I can think of is that when you fought back she panicked. She really wasn't the type to stab someone. She probably would have preferred to poison you, but she had to work with what she had. I guess she was going to go back to the school later that evening to finish you off."

Cold chills snaked up my back, and I felt sick all over again. To my usual fears about rodents, high places, and the effect of the sun on one's general health and complexion, I could now add being locked in a small, dark, airless room.

Tom distracted me from my newest obsessive fear. "Okay, now it's your turn. What made you believe Mrs. Donnatella was the killer? Or as I like to think of her, Willing Billie."

I wanted to say it was a burst of inspiration, but that wasn't quite accurate. "I think it was more like an accumulation of events that didn't make sense. On the first day of school, Mrs. Donnatella was stationed outside the auditorium. What was she doing there? She never leaves the office. It's not like we need her to hand us our folders. I think she waited outside the auditorium in order to give herself an alibi. On a hot day you couldn't blast her out of her air-conditioned lair with a nuclear bomb. She never moves quickly, but that morning she was out of breath and flushed."

Tom asked, "Isn't that when you picked up your folder and Marcia's?"

The fog in my head started to clear. "Yes! Of course—she needed more than an alibi—she needed Marcia's dossiers. And she didn't find them in Marcia's classroom. That's why Marcia's room was such a mess. She probably went nuts trying to find the evidence. Even though I'm not sure that she would even recognize the lesson plans as evidence."

Tom said, "I don't think she counted on anyone leaving the meeting as early as you did. And the mess in the room made it seem logical that Marcia was packing up her classroom in order to go to the middle school. Don't forget—quite a few people thought that Marcia was so distraught she committed suicide."

I started to shake my head, but the movement set off terrible clanging pains. "No sane person would believe that a woman who'd lost a ton of weight and was wearing beautiful clothes was going to commit suicide. Even Mrs. Donnatella knew that—it's probably the reason she made up the story about Marcia moving to the middle school. For most people, that would not be sufficient motivation to commit suicide, but if your job is all you have, the loss of your position would be devastating. Total humiliation for a very proud woman.

"The rumor she started about Marcia's reassignment was what really got me going. If Gordon and Timmy exiled Marcia to the middle school, and then the high school kids' test scores went down, the parents would go ballistic. Also, we know Marcia was blackmailing people—and here I'm thinking Timmy—so she could have used that information as leverage to keep her position at the high school if it were threatened. The biggest problem with that whole story was no one knew anything about reassigning Marcia. Not Gordon, not Timmy, not Caroline. Only Mrs. Donnatella, who is probably the person who told Mrs. Tumbleson. Not the other way around."

George asked, "Why didn't anyone suspect Mrs. Tumbleson? What made you eliminate her?"

I still regretted having to exonerate Mrs. Tumbleson.

"Yeah. That was more a wish than a real suspicion. Watching her ghoulish pleasure in taking charge after Gordon died remains one of the more disturbing episodes in my professional life. Anyway, it was Mrs. Donnatella who lied about a couple of things."

"Was it about the test scores?" asked George.

All of the seemingly random inconsistencies began to make sense. "Well, that, too. But on the day I went to see Bellinger, he was very bitter over the fact that Marcia had left him. But Donnatella told me that he'd left Marcia, and that Marcia was extremely depressed. All that was a lie. Marcia had a boyfriend, an ex-husband, a career, an active membership in the DeVere Society, and two thriving side businesses, one in smuggling fen-phen, and one in blackmail. So much for everyone who thought she had no life. The woman had enough lives for two people. Idiot that I am, I suspected Bellinger and not Donnatella."

Tom said, "There was also that business about her drinking tea. There was no reason for her to deny being a coffee drinker, unless you need to explain why you didn't drink any coffee on the day it was poisoned."

I felt at my hair and shivered. "Mrs. Donnatella is resourceful. I'll give her that. But even if I didn't see a clear motive for her murdering Gordon and trying to murder Timmy, the timing of those attacks should have tipped me off much sooner. I'm to blame for that—and I don't think I can ever forgive myself for being so terribly, horribly stupid."

George, who had been leaning back in his chair, abruptly planted his feet on the floor and sat up straight. "That's crazy. Don't talk like that. Donnatella's the guilty one—not you."

"I'm going to tell myself that for the rest of my life. But I'm not without blame. You warned me—told me not to talk to anyone in case I started confiding in the murderer. Well—and it pains me to say this—right after I told Donnatella I was going to ask Gordon and Timmy about the decision to move Marcia to the middle school she attacked them. Maybe they were already asking her some uncomfortable questions. But maybe if I hadn't brought it up, she would have been in the clear. No one else really cared about Marcia, her teaching assignment, or her test scores."

Tom paced about the room. "The big problem all along was that there were so many people who had a compelling reason to kill Marcia. She was blackmailing Timmy and Donnatella. She had a very bitter ex-husband. Even the custodians hated her."

As the English teacher in the room, I felt responsible for taking so long to deconstruct Marcia's clues. "I know. It wasn't until I put together that hideous joke concerning *The Importance of Being Earnest* that I realized that our Wilhelmina Donnatella was Marcia's Willing Billie. What was important wasn't the issue of sexual preference. It was literally about the importance of a name."

George said, "She looked so good in the pictures you showed me. And nothing like how she looks now. But I thought Wilde Billie was a drag queen, not a woman."

Tom hesitated. "There's a good reason for that. Wilde Willing Billie was William before she was Wilhelmina. She got married after the sex change, and she and her husband were trying to adopt a kid. They'd been on a waiting list for years, and had saved every dime they had. Marcia was bleeding her for money, and I don't blame Donnatella for worrying that a transsexual former porn star with an ailing husband might not make the cut."

I thought of all of the baby clothes Mrs. Donnatella had so carefully crocheted. I would kill anyone who got between me and my kids. I would kill to keep them safe.

George said, "You always complained that the secretary was the one who ran the school. I thought you were kidding."

"I know. Honestly, I also thought I was kidding. So much so, that I complained about the analysis of test scores. I thought Gordon was off his rocker, telling us that the scores were terrible when they really weren't. That was Donnatella again. She volunteered to number crunch the test scores, and she told Gordon the language arts grades were really bad, especially the scores for Marcia's kids—again, in an effort to discredit Marcia. Gordon, of course, never checked the numbers himself."

"What about Timmy?" asked George.

"I don't know—what do you think, Tom? Was Timmy the same kind of threat as Gordon?"

Tom looked grim. "Not sure yet. It's entirely possible Donnatella poisoned the pot, and was perfectly unconcerned at the possibility that someone else might die."

"I'm guessing something tipped Gordon off to the fact that Mrs. Donnatella was the source of the rumors about Marcia. Hopefully that someone wasn't me. He either confronted her with it, or she simply worried he would find out."

George leaned back again and studied the ceiling. "I still don't get the whole business with ditching, or switching, the chairs. What did that accomplish? All it did was draw attention to Dr. Deaver."

I tried to sit up, but a flash of pain convinced me to stay still. "Tom figured it out awhile ago. Mrs. Donnatella had to get Marcia out of her classroom, and she had to be reasonably certain Marcia would leave both her handbag and her coffee mug behind. If Marcia thought she would be hauling her chair around the school she probably would want to have her hands free. The question, of course, is how Mrs. Donnatella knew that Marcia's pills were in her bag. What if Marcia kept her medication at home?"

Brown had an unusually pleasant expression. "That was me and some good old-fashioned police work. We searched Dr. Deaver's house and found her supply of fen-phen, and her husband's supply of heart medication. Donnatella used Marcia's own meds to commit the first murder. So when it came time to poison Gordon and Timmy, she still had her husband's stash."

George frowned. "But if Marcia was blackmailing Mrs. Donnatella, I can't imagine they would have been friendly enough to exchange personal information about their health. How did Mrs. Donnatella even know Marcia had a heart condition?"

We were silent for a moment, and then I remembered our teacher health forms. "Every year we have to fill out these unbelievably detailed and invasive questionnaires. For God's sake, they even ask for our blood type. The disclaimer states that only the nurse has access to the information, but it wouldn't surprise me if Mrs. Donnatella were able to get into the personal files. Hell, she wouldn't even have to do that. Most people toss their health forms in the nurse's mailbox. Plenty of people hand them to Donnatella. There is more privacy in the average prison than there is at the high school."

Tom rubbed his two-day-old beard. "We should have noticed the coincidence about the names."

I remembered not to nod. "I agree. Especially since I've never heard anyone refer to Bill as Billie. I started thinking about names. Jack's given name is John. Mine is Elizabeth. Yours is Thomas. So then I started wondering, who could Billie be, other than Bill? That's when I thought Wilhelmina...Willie...Billie. While I find it disturbing to think of Mrs. Donnatella wearing a thong, I can definitely imagine her wielding handcuffs and a whip as the sadistic side of an S&M movie. Marcia probably threatened to post the video on YouTube, assuming it isn't there already."

Detective Brown grimaced. "That's a picture I'm going to try to forget."

"Me too. I can't tell you how happy I am that you guys will be the ones to confirm that little bit of evidence. But that does remind me of something else that didn't add up. The Billie of Marcia's dossier was in a gay porno movie. That didn't fit with the Bill I know. I mean the guy salivates over young, female teachers. Not that I can easily imagine Bill in any porno movie, but a straight one seems a better fit."

Tom said, "We should have given Bill more credit. He was the only one who denied Marcia's charges when we questioned him, but we suspected him anyway. Timmy cracked immediately; it took him all of about ten seconds to admit that he'd had a "fling" with Ashlee, but he swore that it hadn't started until after she'd graduated from the high school. And Caroline was completely unfazed when we interviewed her. Turns out she faked her master's degree. She claimed she completed all the coursework and that she earned her position, if not her title. She straight up told me to publish and be damned."

I couldn't help laughing. My department chairperson is not easily intimidated or impressed. "That's Caroline. But it's too soon for me to go back to disliking her, after she saved my life."

Brown scratched his head, as if still a bit bemused by having to deal with Caroline. He said, with grudging respect, "She's a pretty cool customer. Timmy, by the way, sweated like a pig throughout the entire interrogation."

I finally asked the question I'd been avoiding. "The thing that baffles me the most is why she went after Timmy and Gordon, but only threatened me."

Tom shook his head. "She probably wanted to get you out of the way. She got lucky, if you want to call it that, with Gordon. You were on her radar, but you weren't the immediate threat the other two were. She had plenty of opportunity to poison them, and not nearly enough opportunity to get at you. Your classroom is on the second floor and apparently you don't often leave it."

So true. Pathetic, but true.

Thinking back to the night I jumped out of Timmy's window, I asked, "Do you know if she was the one who stalked me on Back to School Night?"

Tom said, "I don't think there's much doubt of that. My guess is that she saw your shadow through the window and returned to investigate. I gotta hand it to the woman; that took guts. She probably had some kind of weapon with her that night, and I don't think she would have hesitated to use it. On the other hand, I still have trouble imagining that fat old woman tiptoeing around in the dark."

"She's not that old," I objected.

Tom looked doubtful.

I remembered hearing the heavy, menacing tread, as I cowered under Timmy's desk. "She wasn't exactly tiptoeing. It sounded like a flat-footed zombie was coming toward me. Hey, did she threaten Timmy with poison pen letters? Because that spooked me as much as anything else."

Tom, who'd worn a path in the carpet, finally sat down. "Interestingly, she didn't. Timmy got too close to her, and she had plenty of opportunity to get at him. You were a little harder to manage. I'm sure she was hoping the letters would at least slow you down until she got the chance to kill you."

I felt as if an age had passed since I found Marcia's dead body. "Do we know what finally pushed Mrs. Donnatella over the edge? How long had Marcia been threatening her?"

Brown took over. "Not long is my guess. Mrs. Donnatella spent years trying to adopt a kid. The adoption was close to coming through when Dr. Deaver started threatening her. Donnatella was frantic to stop Marcia, and with all the money she was spending on the adoption, she couldn't afford to keep paying her. Mrs. Donnatella is not the slightest bit sorry, by the way; she said 'the bitch had it coming to her' and that she'll be acquitted."

George frowned. "There's still stuff I don't understand. How did you figure out that Caroline was the target of the lesson plan on *The Talented Mr. Ripley?* I majored in English and I don't remember any clues that would have pointed you in Caroline's direction."

Brown answered. "More grunt work. We checked the background, family, employment history—the works. Turned out Caroline doesn't have two advanced degrees. She has one—from an online university. The other is fake."

No wonder Caroline had been so jealous—and so snarky—about Marcia's doctorate from Cornell. "Is it terrible of me to be enjoying that fact?"

Brown looked as amused as I felt. "I don't think Caroline cares very much. She said she told Marcia to, and I quote, 'bugger off.' And I believe her."

I had only one more question. "That does sound like Caroline. What about Marcia's obsession with conspiracy theories about Shakespeare? Did that have anything to do with what happened?"

Tom answered, "A little bit. Her home computer had a ton of stuff about that DeVere Society you told me about. Deaver is a variant of DeVere, and Marcia wanted to prove she was a descendent of the guy. She hired an ancestry expert to prove it, and I guess she figured Timmy and Donnatella would finance that and her trips to Europe. According to Dr. Deaver's boyfriend, she was becoming as unglued as Donnatella. We finally tracked him down. He's at a car dealership in West Palm Beach, living with a wealthy widow."

I was drained of energy, and the throbbing in my face and neck and head became too distracting to bear. I didn't want to miss out on any information, so I downed two pain pills, which a few hours earlier I was sure I wouldn't need.

George continued to tick off loose ends. He looked from one detective to the other. "And Marcia's husband?"

Tom answered that one. "Bellinger? I think he's the one who trashed Liz's classroom, and he probably would have been happy to break her knees to get his hands on the documents Marcia used to blackmail Timmy and Donnatella. But he's not a murderer."

George was still not satisfied. "Even if Bellinger got his hands on the lesson plans, what good would it do him? From what you've told me, he doesn't sound smart enough to decode them."

Brown snorted his agreement. "Yeah, you got that right. The part no one got right was those numbers on the lesson plans. We all figured those were the cash payments. But they correlated to numbered files in Dr. Deaver's apartment, where she kept the real evidence. God knows how she got it all, but she did. VHS recordings of Wilde Billie. Pictures of Timmy and Ashlee getting it on in the school library. And Caroline's transcripts. Our investigators found them right about the time Donnatella was locking you in the safe."

I didn't answer him. I wasn't thinking about the horrific experience of being locked up. I was thinking about Marcia and how she'd challenged my knowledge of literature. After her death, I had, somewhat fancifully, believed she was talking to me. And maybe she was.

Brown said, "You've been pretty brave, Ms. Hopewell. I'll give you that." He stuck his hand out, and I realized after an awkward moment that I was supposed to shake it. After that, Tom did the same and they both left.

I reached for a pile of essays. That's all I remember, though, because before I finished a single one, I fell into a deep and dreamless sleep, courtesy of Percocet and exhaustion.

CHAPTER 26

IT'S A WONDERFUL LIFE

Bit by bit, more details of the murder emerged. When the police interrogated Alberto Silva about the chair in Marcia's room, the custodian truthfully told them he knew nothing about it. Mrs. Donatella had told him to move a number of items on the first day of school, but none of them were in Marcia's classroom. Alberto had been so nervous when the police questioned him he didn't dare say anything more than was strictly necessary. Because no one told him the reason for the interrogation the poor man thought he was going to be accused of theft.

In a shockingly short period of time, life resumed its normal rhythms. I took a week off from work, partly because of the pain, partly because it was difficult to speak with two fat lips, and partly because I needed the ministrations of a seriously talented hairdresser. Susan came to the rescue and treated me to an emergency hair intervention with a famous Stylist to the Stars. I now sport a bob that is longer in front than in the back, but the asymmetrical angles look rather chic and not at all like the aftermath of an unfortunate experiment with hedge clippers. George says he likes the way it looks, but let's face it, how objective can a husband be when his wife has been kicked, sliced, and chopped?

On my first day back at work my face still had yellow and dark bruises, but the swelling had subsided, and I felt well enough to want to get out of the house. I was welcomed back to school with this love letter:

Dear Mrs. Hopewell,

    Now that all this publicity is over I think it's time for you to get back to business! It is my understanding that you have been appointed the Theater Club Advisor. I must tell you that at this point last year Dr. Deaver had already chosen the play, held auditions, and begun practicing. Of course, I know that you have been out of commission, but as soon as you're back we need to get cracking!

You need to know that Jack has had a major role for the last two years and I am looking forward to more of the same. Of course, I expect that the rehearsal schedule when it is announced, which will hopefully be very soon, will take into consideration his many commitments.

Jack attended a summer program at Columbia University before his freshman year, and all of the drama teachers said that they had never had an actor as talented as Jack.

Do not hesitate to contact me if you have any questions. Have a nice day.
Sincerely,
Mrs. Tumbleson (Jack's Mom)
President of the Board of Education

And neither last, nor least, a few pearls from Timmy:

Dear Staff,
Progress reports are due in two weeks. Those of you who have not updated your online grade book should do so immediately. Even though the parents have access to their student's progress on a daily basis you still have to submit progress reports.

We can't support you unless you support yourself with constant communication with parents.

Communication is Key. Have a nice day,
Timmy

Not to be outdone by Timmy, Caroline had the last word.

Dear Fellow English Teachers,
We have a department meeting next Monday. The agenda is:
- *Late lesson plans*
- *Failure to collect fines for lost and damaged books*
- *Delinquency at English meetings*
- *Getting rid of the Summer Reading Program once and for all*

- *How to do everything right in the era of No Child Left Behind (LOL)*

Tata,

Caroline

When we began house hunting in New Jersey, I was intimidated by the many roads and routes. Route 3. Route 78. Route 280. My favorite was the Parkway. George loathed the traffic and the tolls, but I was entranced by the initials. I thought GSP stood for the Gilbert and Sullivan Parkway, and I was impressed that the state named its choked and iconic highway after the duo that gave the world *The Pirates of Penzance*. Even after I learned that GSP stood for Garden State Parkway, I was still pleased at the happy coincidence.

But on the day Mrs. Donatella pleaded guilty to murder, George and I avoided the highways. We both took the day off, rode the train into the city, and spent the day ambling about downtown Manhattan as if we were still young and in love. We ended up tired and hungry at my favorite, very downscale East Village Indian restaurant. I ordered the sag paneer.

I always order the sag paneer.

George pointed to the enormous menu. "Why don't you try something different for once?"

I ignored his advice, since I don't like change. "When it comes to food, I might be a bit on the conservative side. But how can you imply that I lack a sense of adventure now? I'm a hero."

"You are." George took my hand. "Are you happy now?"

"No. Yes. No and yes." I wasn't ambivalent, or maybe I was, but unlike Elizabeth Bennet, I felt happy more than I knew that I was happy.

George appeared amused by my answer. "Let me know when the final vote is in."

A long time had passed since he seemed to care about how I felt. I wanted him to understand. "I'm happy enough with my life, but there are things I miss. And right now, I'm sad that Marcia, horrible though she was, and Gordon are dead. I'm sad that Mrs. Donatella's life is also over, and more than a little horrified that I didn't see earlier what sort of person she is."

George put down the menu to look at me. "No one saw that. Why should you have?"

"I don't know. I think I sometimes have an inflated opinion of my own intuition."

George smiled. "I wouldn't say that, exactly. I think it's that you've lived an important part of your life in books. You react to the books you read more intensely than other people do to real events. But books aren't people."

George was right. And he was wrong. To paraphrase, there's nothing more real or true than fiction. With few exceptions, it's a good a place as any to live one's life.

I dipped a piece of papadam into spicy green chutney. "That's depressing. Pass me the onions. I need something to cheer me up, and you have been hogging the onions. Don't think I haven't noticed."

George motioned to the waiter. "This is a restaurant, Liz. If you want more onions that can probably be arranged." We ate in comfortable silence. After the waiter cleared the table George asked, "Do you miss your old life? The one before me? Or maybe...do you miss our old life? When we weren't worrying about mortgage payments and college tuitions and we ate out every night?"

I didn't want to answer first. "Do you? Do you miss those times?"

"I got what I wanted. A large mortgage, two demanding kids, and an emotionally unstable wife. Who could ask for more?" George got up and slid into the booth with me. He put his hands on my face and kissed me. This was not typical behavior. He doesn't like public displays of affection, even if the only witness is an elderly waiter.

I kissed him back. "I never long for a time that's past. I find it unutterably depressing whenever I hear people talk about high school as being the best years of their life, or college, or whatever."

"Me too."

We ate and we drank and we kept talking, untying a few of the knots that had tangled our relationship over the past months. After dinner, I persuaded George to splurge on a taxicab. We got stuck in traffic and arrived at Penn Station in time to see the 10:44 leave the platform.

Chapter 27
The Annals of the Former World

There were no funerals on the day my sister and I visited Washington Cemetery. The peace was broken only by occasional assaults from the elevated J train that loomed over the entrance. Sunday traffic was light, and I found a parking spot close by.

Susan met me by the wrought iron gates that guard the dead from the living. Her loud greeting, "Welcome to the big city!" earned me amused looks from the owner of the adjacent newsstand. Susan wrapped me in swirls of perfume. "*Comment ça va*? How was the trip?" my sister trilled.

I hate it when Susan does this. "Aw, shucks, things is jest fine down on the farm. Pa an' me, we're almost done plowin' the fields, and we air so danged happy to be in this here Big Apple."

"*Je t'adore, ma soeur!*" Changing her tone, Susan complained, "I wish you would agree to go to Paris with me. We'd have such a great time."

I peered down identical lanes of cemetery plots, trying to orient myself. "Great to see you, Sue. Uh, maybe we should get going?"

"*Mais oui!*" Despite her enthusiastic response, she followed me rather slowly, stopping often to admire the more elaborate headstones.

I complimented (in English) Susan's Paris dress and Venetian glass earrings (so cheap if you know where to shop!), and I mostly ignored her reminiscences about our childhood.

We paused at several sites. Nana and Grandpa. Uncle Max. Henry and Sylvia. Morris and Ruth. Finally, we arrived at our mother's grave. The sun, already low in the sky, took on the peculiar and unpleasant ashy-pink color of the gravestone. Like Susan's dress and earrings, it had been on sale.

I didn't cry. Susan squeezed out a few tears.

A sudden wind whipped through my thin sweater, and I turned to go. I understand why Susan continues to search for reasons why a beautiful and intelligent woman dedicated her short life to a man more interested in betting at Aqueduct than holding down a steady job. Like other big questions, the mystery of our mother resisted easy answers. This uncertainty orphaned us in a way that death never could.

"Liz! Let's go out to eat. It will be the perfect end to the day."

I said no. The thought of sitting in a restaurant while traffic to the Brooklyn Bridge and Holland Tunnel took on epic proportions did not appeal to me.

"Why do you have to be so sensible all the time?" She wrinkled her nose and sounded aggrieved. The day had been emotional for both of us.

And so instead of going home, I agreed to eat thousands of unnecessary calories in an obscenely overpriced bistro in Brooklyn.

I called George and told him to order pizza for himself and the kids. Judging from the background noise, this change in plan was greeted with an enthusiasm that my cooking rarely provokes. As Susan likes to say, friends come and go, but you can always count on your family.

LIZ HOPEWELL WILL RETURN IN:

LINKED TO MURDER

ACKNOWLEDGEMENTS

 would like to express my gratitude to the people who have inspired and encouraged me. Many thanks go out to:

The entire staff at Barking Rain Press. I am so lucky to have had the opportunity to work with this talented group.

Editors Cindy Koepp and Lourdes Venard, who were instrumental in helping me find the book inside the manuscript. They provided the perfect ratio of advice, criticism, and encouragement.

Hank Phillippi Ryan, who so generously gave of her time and her talent.

The New York chapter of Sisters in Crime and the Guppies, where every writer has a place to call home

For inspiration, I look no further than my kids, Becky, Jesse, Gregory, Geoffrey, Jacob, and Luke. Their confidence in me made the difficult possible.

If I had my choice of sisters, I couldn't do better than the one I grew up with and the one I got through marriage: Karyn Boyar and Lisa Robbins.

I also want to thank my writing partner, Corey LaBranche, as well as Lisa Stack and Claudia Cutler, the kindest and most generous of friends.

This book, of course, is dedicated to Glenn, the best husband any insomniac ever had.

LORI ROBBINS

COMING SOON FROM LORI ROBBINS

Linked to Murder: *Master Class Mysteries,* **Book 2**

Murder in First Position

———

WWW.LORIROBBINS.COM

ABOUT LORI ROBBINS

Brooklyn-born Lori Robbins began dancing at age 16 and launched her professional career three years later. She studied modern dance at the Martha Graham School and ballet at the New York Conservatory of Dance. Robbins performed with a number of regional modern and ballet companies, including Ballet Hispanico, the Des Moines Ballet, and the St. Louis Concert Ballet. After ten very lean years as a dancer she attended Hunter College, graduating summa cum laude with a major in British Literature and a minor in Classics. She is now an English teacher in New Jersey. The mother of six, Robbins has vast experience with the homicidal tendencies that everyday life inspires. She is working on her second *Master Class Mysteries* book, as well as a new mystery series, set in the world of professional ballet. Find out more on her website.

WWW.LORIROBBINS.COM

ABOUT
BARKING RAIN PRESS

D id you know that five media conglomerates publish eighty percent of the books in the United States? As the publishing industry continues to contract, opportunities for emerging and mid-career authors are drying up. Who will write the literature of the twenty-first century if just a handful of profit-focused corporations are left to decide who—and what—is worthy of publication?

Barking Rain Press is dedicated to the creation and promotion of thoughtful and imaginative contemporary literature, which we believe is essential to a vital and diverse culture. As a nonprofit organization, Barking Rain Press is an independent publisher that seeks to cultivate relationships with new and mid-career writers over time, to be thorough in the editorial process, and to make the publishing process an experience that will add to an author's development—and ultimately enhance our literary heritage.

In selecting new titles for publication, Barking Rain Press considers authors at all points in their careers. Our goal is to support the development of emerging and mid-career authors—not just single books—as we know from experience that a writer's audience is cultivated over the course of several books.

Support for these efforts comes primarily from the sale of our publications; we also hope to attract grant funding and private donations. Whether you are a reader or a writer, we invite you to take a stand for independent publishing and become more involved with Barking Rain Press. With your support, we can make sure that talented writers thrive, and that their books reach the hands of spirited, curious readers. Find out more at our website.

Barking Rain Press

WWW.BARKINGRAINPRESS.ORG

Also from Barking Rain Press

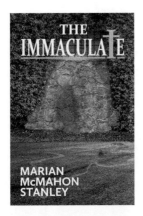

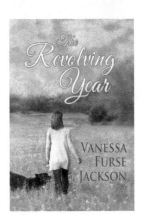

Read 4 Chapters of Any Book
at our Website

CPSIA information can be obtained
at www.ICGtesting.com
Printed in the USA
LVHW01s1658071117
555372LV00003B/656/P